LITTLE COMFORT

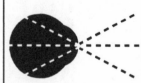

This Large Print Book carries the
Seal of Approval of N.A.V.H.

A HESTER THURSBY MYSTERY

LITTLE COMFORT

EDWIN HILL

THORNDIKE PRESS
A part of Gale, a Cengage Company

GALE
A Cengage Company

Farmington Hills, Mich • San Francisco • New York • Waterville, Maine
Meriden, Conn • Mason, Ohio • Chicago

Copyright © 2018 by Edwin Hill.
A Hester Thursby Mystery.
Thorndike Press, a part of Gale, a Cengage Company.

ALL RIGHTS RESERVED
Thorndike Press® Large Print Mystery.
The text of this Large Print edition is unabridged.
Other aspects of the book may vary from the original edition.
Set in 16 pt. Plantin.

LIBRARY OF CONGRESS CIP DATA ON FILE.
CATALOGUING IN PUBLICATION FOR THIS BOOK
IS AVAILABLE FROM THE LIBRARY OF CONGRESS

ISBN-13: 978-1-4328-5370-9 (hardcover)

Published in 2018 by arrangement with Kensington Books, an imprint of Kensington Publishing Corp.

Printed in Mexico
1 2 3 4 5 6 7 22 21 20 19 18

To Betty and Jack, always and forever

ACKNOWLEDGMENTS

Anyone who's written a novel, especially a first novel, knows that a lot of people need to give you a chance for the work to see the light of day. There have been so many people who have taken a chance on me throughout my life, too many to mention in this space, but here are a few.

To Rhonda Bollinger, Ellen Gandt, and Jonelle Calon, for seeing something special in a habitual wanderer and leading me toward a career that changed my life. To Carolyn Merrill for teaching me how to be make tough decisions. To Joan Feinberg and Denise Wydra for showing me that the quality and attention to detail trump all else. And to Simon Allen, Susan Winslow, Ken Michaels, and John Sargent for taking me places I never, ever imagined I could go.

To all my advance readers who took a

7

chance on a very unfinished work and saved me from myself: Kate Flora, Philomena Feighan, Mary Finch, Mike Harvkey, Martha Koster, Patricia Mulcahy, Stephen Parolini (The Novel Doctor), Anne Shaughnessy, and Ellen Thibault.

To Katherine Bates and her trusty assistant NBS for their expertise in social media. To the real Sam Blaine (and her partners-in-crime, Nancy and Kate), may you spend every day chasing rabbits. And to Thomas Bollinger, for his unparalleled skills with the camera.

To my parents, who took a chance on me starting on day one and never let up, and to Christine and Chester, who continue to cheer me on. To all the Rowells and the Hills, to the Starr family for welcoming me into the fold, and to Edith Ann, who continues to like my first drafts enough to eat them.

Little Comfort may never have been noticed had my fantastic agent Robert Guinsler not taken a chance on me when I struck up a conversation with him at the Muse and the Marketplace conference in Boston. Robert stuck with me long enough to find editor extraordinaire John Scognamiglio and the team at Kensington: Steve Zacharius, Lynn Cully, Vida Engstrand, Lou Malcangi, Tracy Marx, Robin Cook, and everyone else behind the scenes, and I couldn't ask for a better publishing team.

To my partner Michael, who took a big chance many years ago, and who never once scoffed when I told him I wanted to be a writer, and then shut myself away nearly every weekend for three straight years while I tried to prove it. He read through drivel, corrected hundreds of typos, and helped me focus on making this story the best it could be.

And finally to you, readers, who took a chance on a first time author. I can't tell you how much I appreciate it. Thank you.

Be in touch at edwin-hill.com.

PART ONE

PART ONE

CHAPTER 1

All Hester Thursby wanted was a single day to herself, and today was going to be that day — even if it killed her. She left the baby monitor on the nightstand next to her snoring non-husband, Morgan, and slipped out of the house with Waffles on the leash. Okay, maybe she glanced into Kate's bedroom to be sure her three-year-old niece was still alive; maybe she crept up to the queen-size bed where the tiny girl slept within a protective barricade of stuffed animals. And maybe Hester felt a wave of relief when Kate rubbed her nose with a fist and rolled over. Kate had been staying with them since September, and no matter how much Hester wanted to keep the kid from cramping her style, she still hadn't adjusted to worrying about another human being all day and every day. "We're making this up as we go along, kid," she whispered, kissing Kate's forehead.

13

Outside was quiet and dark in the way only a frigid morning in December could be. Today was Morgan's day to watch Kate — the first free time Hester had had in nearly three months. She took the dog straight to Block 11 in Somerville's Union Square, where she ordered the biggest cup of coffee available and a scone to split with the basset hound. She added cream and seven sugars to the coffee. At the park, she let Waffles off the leash to have at it with the other dogs and then planned her day. Maybe she'd hit the Brattle Theater for that George Romero series, or wander the streets of Cambridge, or drink till she was drunk. Maybe she'd do all three.

"You're off somewhere."

Hester glanced up at Prachi — O'Keefe the greyhound's "mom" — who loomed over her (though even some ten-year-olds loomed over Hester). As always, Prachi, who was a partner in a corporate law firm, looked relaxed, with her cocoa-colored skin and the well-rested eyes of the child free.

"Just daydreaming," Hester said.

"We missed you last night," Prachi said.

Prachi and her partner, Jane, threw an early-winter party each year, one where guests spilled into every room and the air smelled of curry instead of cloves. It was an event Hester looked forward to, but the party hadn't started till eight, which had meant nine, well after Kate's bedtime.

"Finding a babysitter on a Friday in December is next to impossible," Hester said. "Who knew?"

"Darling, you can still hit the town," Prachi said. "It's not like you died. We all love Kate."

"I'm learning how to do this as I go along. Turns out there's no manual on raising someone else's kid."

"Any word from Daphne?"

"Nada," Hester said.

Daphne was Kate's mother and Morgan's twin sister. She was also Hester's best friend. Hester had known her since college, long before Daphne had introduced her to Morgan. Three months earlier, in September, Daphne had skipped town while Hester and Morgan had been out to dinner with Prachi and Jane. The four of them had come home, drunk and ready for a nightcap, only to find Kate asleep with a note beside her. On it, Daphne had written in block letters: *Back in an hour. Tops.*

They hadn't heard from her since.

Hester wasn't surprised — Daphne had a history of disappearing for long stretches and then showing up unannounced as

15

though she'd gone to the gym for an hour — but Hester still worried about her friend, and the kid thing upped the stakes, to say the least. She didn't have kids of her own, and that was by choice.

She called to Waffles. As usual, the basset had found something far too fragrant to bother coming. "I should see what she got into," she said to Prachi. "I'll catch you tomorrow."

At the house, Hester heard Kate say, "No," her not-so-new favorite word, and she opened the door in time to see a plastic bowl of Cheerios skid across the kitchen floor. Morgan was on the phone, his red morning hair still sticking straight up. He was handsome in a kind way, with freckles that merged into each other and green eyes that matched his sister's. He went to the gym, but without conviction. He mouthed "please" as he handed over a piping-hot bowl of oatmeal. Ever since Kate had moved into the house, Morgan had proven himself to be hapless at childcare. He gave Kate orange soda for breakfast and let her run wild in the park while he yammered on his cell phone. And whenever Hester tried to bring up Daphne, to talk about what was happening to them, he acted like leaving a three-year-old alone in an apartment while you skip town was normal behavior for a parent. But then Morgan and Daphne always watched out for each other, no matter what the behavior. They were twins in every way.

Hester let the leash drop so that Waffles could do the majority of the cereal cleanup, and then lifted Kate from her high chair while the kid shouted, "Kate hate Cheerios!" even though some days she ate *only* Cheerios. Hester chased her through the living room, around the dining table, into Morgan's office, up the stairs, through each of their bedrooms, and down the stairs, till she finally caught Kate, lifted her up, tickled her, strapped her into the chair, and poured another bowl of cereal, which Kate ate like she hadn't been fed in a week.

"Never," Hester said, as she mussed Kate's curly hair. "I will never understand the logic of being three years old. Not in one million years."

"Not in one million years," Kate aped.

Morgan hung up the phone. "That was the emergency animal hospital in Porter Square."

Though Morgan had his own veterinary practice, once Kate had moved in with them — and her preschool bills had begun showing up — he'd started taking spare shifts

17

whenever he could.

"They need someone last-minute."

Hester smiled at Kate and then waved Morgan to the other side of the apartment. "Are you shitting me?" she whispered.

Morgan smiled in a way that usually got him what he wanted, but all Hester could see was a spot of fury that had taken the place of the day on her own.

"Sorry, Mrs.," he said

A part of her understood, the part that knew they needed the money. But most of her wanted to scream. Plus, she hated it when he called her "Mrs." "You owe me," she said. "Big time."

Morgan kissed her cheek, put his coat on, and whistled for Waffles to come with him. Soon Hester heard him back his truck out of the driveway. "You're stuck with me today, kid," she said, though now Kate was only interested in her stuffed monkey, Monkey, dancing the toy across her lap and saying, "Monkey One Hundred Forty Silly Pants eating bananas," which sounded like "Mokah anhendrd farty sesty pints tang banants." Hester couldn't believe she understood anything the kid said. It was a secret language that only she, Kate, and Monkey spoke. In truth, Hester couldn't believe any of this was happening. But it was.

She sat at the counter and tapped a finger on the granite. The long, unstructured day stretched in front of her. One of the mothers at day care had asked to schedule a play-date only yesterday, and Hester had answered evasively, still unable to commit, still wondering whether Daphne would stroll through the door at any moment expecting things to go back to normal. What was normal, anyway? She pulled up the Brattle Theater schedule on her phone and wondered momentarily if Kate could sit through *Night of the Living Dead* without getting too scared.

She really was a shit parent.

Her phone rang. She didn't recognize the number with a New Hampshire area code but picked up anyway.

"I heard that you find people," a woman said. "That you're discreet."

Hester ran a little side business finding random strangers, a business she'd begun more than fifteen years earlier when she'd been working toward a master's in library science. At the time, the library provided access to information unavailable to the average person, and Hester had managed to reunite all different types, from long-lost prom dates to birth parents with their children. Eventually the Web gave most people the tools they needed to find their own missing connections, and she'd assumed the business would go the way of the corner video store. It turned out, though, that there were always people who chose to live quiet lives off the grid, to keep to themselves, and to stay away from technology.

She dumped her uneaten oatmeal into the garbage disposal. "I can be discreet," she said. Whenever she got one of these queries, she listened to the tenor of the voice on the other end of the phone. It was surprising how many people could give off crazy in a few disembodied sentences.

"I'm in the city today," the woman said. "Can we meet?"

"What's your name?"

"Lila Blaine."

"Who are you looking for?"

"My brother Sam. He's been missing for twelve years."

"Pink poodle!" Kate said.

She and Hester were on the bus headed from Union Square toward Cambridge talking about what Santa might bring for the holiday. They'd already gone skating in the morning, and to the Boston Aquarium that afternoon, where Hester had made the rookie parenting mistake of telling Kate that sharks ate people. Kate had pressed her hand to the glass as a shark swam by and then pulled it away with a shriek. "Shark eat people!" she'd said.

"Don't tell your uncle Morgan," Hester had said. "You'll get me in trouble."

Now they were on their way to Harvard Square to meet Lila Blaine.

"Do you mean a poodle with pink clothes or a poodle with pink fur?" Hester asked. Kate kicked the seat in front of her and said, "PINK FUR" in two piercingly short notes.

"Inside voice," Hester said.

Had those words really come from her own mouth? The things she said these days in the name of friendship! She'd met Daphne nearly two decades earlier at Wellesley, where Daphne had taught self-defense for Women's Safety Week. On the first day of the course, right in front of a dozen other women, Daphne pinned Hester to the ground with her knee, shouting, "Size doesn't matter. Fight!"

Daphne was a solid field hockey player, much bigger and stronger than Hester, but Hester kicked anyway. She squirmed. She twisted. Or at least she tried to. She heard one of the women in the course giggle while most of them cheered her on.

"Survive!" Daphne shouted. "Use your strengths. Be smart. The only thing you think about is how to stay alive."

And Hester relaxed. She grew even smaller than she already was. She pulled into herself. She felt the pressure from Daphne's knee release the slightest bit. She twisted away. Her elbow shot from her side. She felt a crack and a crunch and then a thick warmth, and Daphne stumbled back with her hands covering her face as blood streamed from her broken nose.

"I'm so sorry," Hester said.

"Sorry?" Daphne said. "Fuck sorry. That's how you stay alive."

Daphne was used to fighting. For anything and everything. She and Morgan came from a family of ten children. They'd grown up in South Boston, where, by all accounts, nearly everything but other bodies had been scarce. They'd watched out for each other, though, in ways that Hester, who'd spent a lifetime watching out for herself, couldn't comprehend, and they'd both succeeded by their own wits, Daphne getting into Wellesley on a field hockey scholarship and Morgan going to UMass. By the time Hester met her in college, Daphne had morphed into a leather chick who quoted Adrienne Rich and called NPR too conservative. On most Saturday nights, she roped Hester into riding the Fuck Truck to MIT frat parties and then disappeared into the upstairs bedrooms.

After graduation, Daphne and Hester rented an apartment in Alston. That's when Hester met Morgan. Like Hester, Morgan loved his sister more than anyone, and ignored that she moved rapidly from one job to the next, always leaving on explosively bad terms. They both made excuses for Daphne's dangerous boyfriends, and when her experiments with drugs veered away from dabbling. But then Kate came along, and everything changed. And things kept changing — the dynamic in their relationships, their priorities, Hester's own outlook — and she suspected that those changes, and all the tensions that came with them, had only just begun.

The bus pulled into Harvard Square. Hester worked as a librarian at Harvard's Widener Library, though she'd taken a leave of absence in September when Kate had come to live with them. She'd be back at work come spring semester, and a part of her couldn't wait for that routine, but for now she took Kate's hand as they hurried through the cold, across Winthrop Square

23

to Grendel's Den, a bohemian pub located a few blocks from the bus stop. She grabbed a table with a clear view of the doorway, pulling out a coloring book, a My Little Pony, and a box of crayons.

"Aunt Hester is meeting a friend in a few minutes," she said to Kate. "Do you think you can be quiet while we talk?"

"Kate quiet!" Kate said in a voice that was anything but.

A very young and very tattooed waitress stopped by. "Sam Adams," Hester said as she unzipped Kate's coat.

"ID?" the waitress asked.

Hester slid her license across the table.

"Is this for real? You look about twelve."

At four feet, nine and three-quarters inches tall, Hester was a quarter inch into little person territory. She weighed eighty-nine pounds and had black hair, alabaster skin, and the voice of a two-pack-a-day smoker. More than one obnoxious stranger had told her she looked like a china doll, but Hester had learned long ago to make up for her height with confidence, even when she had to fake it. As Morgan often told her, there was nothing sexier than a woman who took charge.

"How old is Aunt Hester?" she asked Kate.

"Thirty-six."

"Good enough?"

The waitress nodded. "What does she want?"

"Orange soda," Kate said.

The waitress cocked her head for confirmation.

"How about apple juice instead?" Hester said, prepping herself for a tantrum, but Kate, miraculously, settled in with the coloring book and pink crayon. Hester took advantage of the momentary silence to open her tablet and read through what she'd learned about Lila Blaine. A quick search of Lila's Facebook page had shown that she valued her privacy settings. She didn't have a LinkedIn account, but Hester had managed to determine she was thirty-five years old and lived in Holderness, New Hampshire, an enclave of New England's WASPy elite. The only mention of her online was when she petitioned the town to change the terms of a trust on some lakefront property. Hester had spent the day imagining a woman clad in head-to-toe Patagonia, someone who skied, hiked, and entertained friends on a lovingly maintained Chris Craft, and at five o'clock on the dot, the door to the pub opened and a woman entered who nearly fit that description, minus the wealth. She wore a navy parka, had a no-nonsense auburn-colored braid that tumbled down her back, and had the healthy build and complexion of someone used to working outside. She also didn't look like someone who'd put up with much.

"Lila?" Hester said.

"You're Hester Thursby?"

"In the flesh."

Lila put her hands on a chair and surveyed the scene in front of her — a tiny woman and a three-year-old dressed in head-to-toe pink — and Hester could only imagine what was going through her head. "It must have been a long drive," she said. "Grab something to drink."

Kate put a pink rubber boot on the table. "Aunt Hester like my boots?" she asked.

"I love them," Hester said.

"You didn't mention there'd be a kid," Lila said.

"I'm new to the kid thing," Hester said. "I still forget that she goes where I go. Sometimes there's a dog too. But like I said on the phone today, there's no obligation. If you decide you'd rather hire someone else, then I'll be on my way."

Lila shrugged and then flagged down the waitress to order tea. She struggled out of the coat, and they made conversation till the waitress set the teapot on the table. Lila's hand shook as she poured and added sugar. Finally, she said, "I expected someone a bit . . ."

"Taller?" Hester said.

"And . . ."

"Tougher?"

"Yeah, that too."

Hester was used to easing clients through their reservations, and would have been wary of anyone who wasn't at least a little reluctant to hire her. "I don't carry a gun or know how to fight very well, but I do have a pretty good track record in finding people. And if it helps, I've worked with plenty of people who've lost someone. Once, a couple hired me because they'd lost one of their grown daughters. She was number seven of thirteen, and they'd simply forgotten about her for a while. Turned out she moved to the next town over. Really, I can help you find your brother. If that's what you want."

Lila scratched at her index finger like she had eczema. "What do you need to know?"

Hester opened the folder. "Let's start with the basics. What's your brother's name?"

"I haven't a clue what he goes by now."

Okay, this could be interesting. "Was he adopted? I've worked plenty of adoptions. Those can sometimes be pretty easy."

"He wasn't adopted."

"Were you?"

"No, that's not it at all." Lila sat back in her chair. "His name is Sam Blaine, like I said on the phone. I've looked before and haven't found a trace of him. He's eight years younger than I am, and we haven't seen each other since he was a teenager. We had a falling-out. A fight, really, and we haven't spoken since. It's time to make amends."

"What did you fight about?"

"For that, I'll need to know you *a lot* better." An edge slipped into Lila's voice, and Hester made a mental note to return to the subject later.

"Most people are pretty easy to track down nowadays," she said. "Why haven't you been able to find him yourself?"

"That's a long story."

"I'm not going anywhere."

Lila swung her braid from one shoulder to the other. "I may need something stronger than tea."

"I hate to drink alone."

Lila ordered a beer, and they sat in silence till Lila poured the beer into a pint glass and drank half of it in gulps.

"So?" Hester said.

"I'm not sure he wants to be found," Lila said.

"Why not?"

Lila scratched again, and this time it looked as though she might draw blood. "Because I'm pretty certain he changed his name. I think he may have changed it every time he's moved. And he's moved a lot."

CHAPTER 2

Lila dug a photo from her handbag and showed it to Hester. It was of two boys standing on a wooded lakeshore. One of them looked cocky. He glared reluctantly at the camera, his hair falling in his eyes. He had the lean body of an athlete and the fine bone structure of someone who would always seem young.

"Handsome kid," Hester said.

"That's Sam," Lila said.

"So you've looked for him yourself," Hester said. "Sorry to cut to the chase here, but are you sure he's not dead?"

"He's alive. I know that much, at least."

Lila opened her bag again and took out stacks of postcards held together with rubber bands. She tossed them onto the table.

"He sends me these. Usually one every couple of months or so. He makes them himself from photos. See, here's one from when he lived in San Francisco."

She turned over a postcard of the Golden Gate Bridge. It was taken from the Marin Headlands. The bridge, and San Francisco behind it, was shrouded in fog. On the back, printed in the handwriting of someone who'd gone to finishing school, was written, *If you were in my position, you'd do the same.*

"Before you ask," Lila said. "I have no idea what it means. You'll see, none of them make sense." She thumbed through a stack and pulled out a photo from a farmer's market. Sam had written, *The science department should be able to help us.*

"That sounds like it's from *Star Trek*," Hester said. She read it through again. On the other side of the table, Kate, who'd been remarkably quiet through the conversation, looked up from her coloring book. "Potty," she said.

"Time to move!" Hester said, taking a stack of the postcards with her in one hand and Kate's hand in the other and rushing to the bathroom before disaster struck. In the stall, she examined the cards while Kate perched on the toilet and yammered about peeing. The postcards were from cities all over the United States. In some, Sam had taken photos of famous landmarks like the Golden Gate Bridge or the Empire State Building, while on others, he'd used more obscure locations, like doorways or street signs. Most likely, he'd chosen postcards because they were harder to trace than e-mails or phone calls, but there was plenty of information on the cards that Hester could use to find him, or at least trace where he'd been. The postmarks would make it easy enough to pull together a timeline of where he'd lived, and there had to be some pattern to the messages he wrote. She had to admit the whole scenario had her intrigued.

"Do you know Sam's Social Security number?" she asked when they returned to the table and she'd managed to get Kate settled with her coloring book.

"He hasn't used it in twelve years," Lila said. "I already went down that road."

"Leave it with me anyway. How about his date of birth? I can't do much without that."

"April third, 1992."

"And his full name? Samuel?"

"Just Sam Blaine. My parents liked to keep it simple."

"And what about your parents? Where do they fit into all of this?"

"They don't," Lila said. "They're dead. Both of them. They died when I was nineteen. Sam and I lived together after that, till he left, at least."

"So you haven't seen him in twelve years. That would have made him, what, fourteen, maybe fifteen when he left. That's not moving out or leaving, that's running away. Didn't the police look for him?"

"Of course they did, and so did I. Everyone looked for him."

"Did he have friends? Was there someone else he might have been in touch with over the years?"

Lila picked up the photo of the boys by the lake. "Him," she said, pointing at the other boy, whom Hester had barely noticed. He smiled right into the camera, and yet still faded behind Sam's vitality.

"That's Gabe DiPursio," Lila said. "He was a foster kid who stayed with us that summer. They ran away together." It seemed to take some effort for Lila to look away from the photo. "Gabe was, I don't know . . . he was quiet. A cipher, almost. Sam brought him home from school one day that spring like a stray puppy, said they were having a sleepover, and Gabe basically never left. He'd been living with a woman across town who kept five, sometimes six foster kids at a time. I don't think she even knew he'd moved to our house till the social worker pointed it out."

Hester went through her notes. "And how

old would that have made you? Twenty-three?" She jerked a thumb at Kate. "I can barely handle this one, and I'm a full-fledged adult. You had two teenage boys living with you?"

"Gabe stayed with us. It was pretty unofficial. To be honest, I couldn't have gotten rid of him fast enough, but I have a bit of a conscience. I mean, who would take in a fourteen-year-old foster kid, especially one like Gabe? He'd been through the system since he was a toddler. His mother was a junkie, and his father was a drunk. The kid barely had a chance from the start."

"Are his parents still around?"

"They may be, but I'm not sure. They brought a suit against the state when Gabe left and then they moved to Reno afterwards."

"Okay, I'm trying to fit these pieces together. What's the woman's name? The foster mother. The one Gabe had been staying with before. Does she still live in town?"

"Cheryl Jenkins," Lila said. "She'll never leave. She's New Hampshire through and through. But the cops talked to her. She didn't know anything either."

"And what about family services? Didn't they want to know what happened to Gabe?"

"Not so much," Lila said. "I got the impression that his social worker was happy to focus on other things."

"And what was her name?"

"You mean his name. Robert Englewood. Bobby. He and I went to high school together, and he's definitely still around. Unfortunately."

Hester wrote the names down. "Any chance you know Gabe's birthdate?"

"He only came around for a couple of months. I can see if Bobby has it."

Hester looked down at her notes. All she had to go on were a few random names and dates. Even with the postcards, Sam might be too well hidden to find. Still, she could use a good puzzle to solve. "Where did the last card come from?" she asked. "At least I'll know which city to start with."

Lila dug a thin stack of postcards from her bag. The one on top was of a townhouse somewhere on Beacon Hill or in the Back Bay. It was taken in the fall, when the maple trees lining the streets blazed red. "He's been in Boston since March," Lila said.

Hester turned the top card over. Sam had written, *It's amazing how fast you get used to such a big place.* The rest of the stack showed other settings from around the city, like the side of a brick building, a chain-link fence, and a café. The last one was of a street sign for Louisburg Square.

"Maybe he lives there," Lila said.

"Is he rich? He'd have to be to live on Louisburg Square."

"I wouldn't put it past him," Lila said. "Sam had a taste for the finer things. Even as a kid. But, honestly, I haven't a clue who Sam is or who he may have become. I do know that he was smart and slick when he was fourteen, and that was when he'd spent his whole life in the backwoods of New Hampshire. God knows what some life experiences have brought him."

Hester flipped through the postcards once more.

"Take them," Lila said. "The photo too."

Hester put the cards and the photo in a manila folder. "I can guarantee one thing about Sam," she said. "You're right. He doesn't want to be found. Not by you. Not by anyone. And people who don't want to be found usually have a reason. Why now anyway? After all these years?"

Lila finished her beer. "To be honest, I'm not sure I want to find Sam either, though I can't help but be curious about what he's become. I owe it to him. My parents owned a little piece of lakefront property that I'm putting on the market this spring. The cabin is a ruin at this point, and I'm tired of being land poor." She paused. "You seem smart. Maybe you'll find him, maybe you won't, but my money's on yes. If Sam doesn't want to see me, tell him I'm selling Little Comfort."

Later that evening, after she'd put Kate to bed and had dinner with Morgan, Hester sat cross-legged with a tablet balanced on her lap and the postcards Sam had sent Lila spread out on the coffee table. A little online research and a quick call to Reno confirmed that Gabe DiPursio's parents hadn't heard from him in years. Nor, from their tone, did they care to.

After hanging up, Hester put the phone aside and could hear Morgan snoring through the wall. She hadn't told him about her meeting with Lila today. She had a feeling he wouldn't want her digging into strangers' lives with Kate in tow, and if she told him they'd have to *discuss* it, which would lead to her admitting he was right. But truth be told, Hester needed the distraction. So she put together a timeline of where Sam had lived over the past twelve years using the postmarks. The first card had come from San Francisco the November after Sam had left New Hampshire, more than twelve years earlier. That meant there'd been a gap of about four months between when Sam ran away and when this card arrived. That was a long time for two teenagers to be missing without anyone seeming to mind too much. What had Lila done when this first card finally came in the mail? Had she let the local police know to contact the San Francisco authorities, or had she kept quiet? Lila herself had admitted she'd been glad to be rid of Sam's friend Gabe. Had that ambivalence extended to her brother too? How had twenty-three-year-old Lila felt about the burden of raising a teenage boy?

She jotted down the question and then put the kettle on and waited for it to whistle while moving stacks of dirty dishes out of the sink. She was in her own apartment, a tiny aerie in the third-floor attic of the house she and Morgan owned together. They'd bought the house in the heart of Somerville's Union Square nearly seven years earlier, long before the square became hip. The house had three apartments. The ground floor, where Daphne and Kate used to live, was vacant awaiting Daphne's return. Morgan lived in the largest apartment on the second and third floors. That was the adult apartment, the one where they entertained and had dinner together. On most nights, Hester and Morgan slept in his bed, with his down pillows and thousand-thread-count sheets, and in the morning they made coffee and drank it at the granite kitchen island while reading the paper on their tablets. Morgan liked things neat, so keys had their place by the door, books stayed on bookshelves, and dust never settled.

To Hester, it sometimes felt like a prison.

Her apartment had a tiny red-and-green-plaid love seat and an ancient VCR attached to an even older TV set. The slanted walls were lined with stacks of VHS tapes and novels and possible treasures she'd picked up at yard sales. The bedroom had a single bed and a tiny closet filled with shoes. Hester couldn't remember the last time she'd vacuumed. Here, dust had a permanent home. In fact, anything that entered the apartment had a permanent home. It was her sanctuary, and symbolic of her independence. Morgan had given up proposing to her a couple of years ago after she'd said "no" one too many times, and she knew that he both understood and didn't understand why, maybe even more than she did. To her, they were as good as married. She couldn't understand what scared her about giving in to commitment. She supposed that a part of it was simply fear of admitting that she wanted it, or that once she admitted it, that it would somehow go away.

She went into the bedroom and crawled into the closet. At the very back, a dog door was cut into the wall that connected to Morgan's walk-in closet on the other side. She stuck her head through the hole, and could nearly, but not quite, squeeze all the way through. Even Hester wasn't that small. "Waffles," she whispered. "Come here."

She heard a whine, and then a thump as Waffles jumped off Kate's bed in the other room. The basset's nails clacked on the wooden floors, and then, through the dark, a wet tongue lapped at Hester's face. "Come," she said. "Be with me."

Waffles shimmied through the hole. "Good girl," Hester said.

In the kitchenette, she rinsed old tea leaves out of a chipped brown teapot and replaced them with new ones. When the tea was ready, she piled the dirty dishes back into the sink, and then slid the original *Friday the 13th* into the VCR for background noise while nestling with Waffles under a quilt on the love seat. The dog rested her snout on Hester's lap and sighed.

"Tough day?"

Waffles fell fast asleep and started to snore.

Hester picked up another card. It was a photo of the Castro Theatre, in the heart of San Francisco, with its Spanish-colonial baroque façade. The marquee showed a double feature of *Alien* and *Aliens* that Hester would have loved to have gone to. On it, Sam had written, *What was your special order?* Hester read the quote again. For a moment, she thought she had a connection, but it slipped away.

Other cards in the group showed scenes from around the city, including a view of San Francisco Bay with a beautiful house in the foreground that Hester thought might be in Pacific Heights, a street sign for Pacific Avenue, and the photo of the farmer's market. The last card in the group was the one of the Golden Gate Bridge.

She created a quick spreadsheet to record the date, city, zip code, image, and message from each card. Sam had lived in San Francisco for nearly eighteen months and had sent a total of nine cards. The majority of them had a 94110 zip code, which turned out to be the Mission District.

After the last card from San Francisco, there was a break of nine months before postcards began to arrive again, this time from Chicago. What had Lila thought during those long months? Had she hoped that Sam had moved on or worried that something had happened to him? Had she scratched at her fingers with anxiety like she had today? What had she felt each time one of these cards arrived in the mail? In Hester's years of finding lost people, she'd learned that families came in many different shapes, sizes, and forms — like her own odd family of Kate, Waffles, Daphne, and Morgan — and that much often lurked beneath the story a client told.

The cards from Chicago went on for more than a year, followed by another break before Sam wrote from Baltimore and then New York. In all, Sam had lived in four cities before moving to Boston, and the longest he'd stayed in any of them was two and a half years.

Finally, Hester laid out the cards he'd sent from Boston. There were five in all, with the first one coming in March of this year. Most of the cards had a 02144 zip code, which was right up the road on the other end of Somerville. She read through the messages again, but like the ones from the other cities, they made no sense without context.

She yawned. She'd lost herself in this

project and it was already two a.m. *Friday the 13th* still played on the TV, though it was coming to the end where all the counselors but the Last Girl were dead. The girl clutched an axe and was about to save herself till the beginning of Part Two, but Hester had seen this movie dozens of times and didn't need to watch to know what would happen next. She turned the light out and lay on the love seat. Waffles woke with the movement, and then settled in with a sigh. Hester closed her eyes and listened to the sounds of the movie, the music (*ch-ch-ch-hah-hah-hah-hah*) the dialogue, the screams. She could practically recite the script herself. Maybe she'd sleep right here tonight and let Morgan take care of Kate in the morning. It *was* his turn, after all. Maybe she'd stay in bed till nine.

But as she felt herself drifting off, she sat up, fully awake, and turned on the light. The thought that had flitted through her mind earlier had returned, fully formed. She flipped to the very first postcard Sam had ever sent, the one of the Castro Theatre, and then read the message again, *What was your special order?* She searched for the exact wording online. She was right. Now, what the hell did it mean?

CHAPTER 3

Three days later, listening to NPR on the radio with Waffles on the passenger's seat beside her, Hester looked out the frosty window of her truck toward the mansion on Louisburg Square. She compared it to the house on the postcard Sam had sent. It was definitely the same building. The mansion was four stories of austere beauty, with Christmas wreaths hanging in each window. It had been easy enough to find the location using Google Maps and painstakingly "walking" down the street till she recognized the image from the postcard. With the address, she'd accessed the property records and learned that it belonged to Pearly and Elise Richards, the multi-millionaire former owners of a local sneaker company. They'd sold the company a few years earlier and become well-known conservationists. They were prominent enough to employ a publicist, one who tracked their travels. One online photo showed Pearly, ruggedly hand-some, scaling a mountain. Another of Elise, blond and tight-skinned, featured her speaking about preserving local architecture. Right now, they were kayaking off the coast of Chile, near a 2.2-million-acre preserve they'd bought to protect the rain forest.

Pearly and Elise had one child, a daughter named Wendy, who called herself a philanthropist and a lifestyle guru, but who was more like a Boston-based Kardashian. Everyone knew who she was, but couldn't explain why. Wendy, who had to have been in her early thirties, was all over social media alongside stories about farmers' markets and yoga. She was tall and striking, with chestnut-colored hair that seemed to engulf anything and anyone around her. She served on various boards and committees, including ones for a charter school, a women's shelter, and the VA. A glance at her LinkedIn page showed that she'd gone to Boston College for undergraduate, and Harvard for business school, and since then had worked for her family managing their considerable wealth.

"Kate want juice!"

Hester glanced in the rearview mirror, where she saw Kate waking from her nap. She dug a juice box from her bag and speared a straw through the tiny foil hole. She really needed to come up with a Plan B for days like today, when Kate woke with the sniffles and couldn't go to day care. Bringing her on a stakeout for a guy who changed his name every time he moved definitely fell in the shitty parent column.

"Need anything else?"

Kate sucked at the straw and shook her head.

Hester looked out the window toward the house. Thanks to the photo of the Castro Theatre with the double bill of the *Alien* movies, she'd also managed to connect Sam's notes to quotes from films, a different one for each city. San Francisco was *Alien,* Chicago was *The Big Lebowski,* Baltimore was *Terms of Endearment,* New York was *The Shawshank Redemption,* and, finally, Boston was *The Shining.* A few of the quotes were famous, but most were simply lines from the movies, and if Hester hadn't seen *Alien* a half a dozen times, she might not have recognized them. She looked for connections between the movies and found a couple — Stephen King had written the source material for two of them; *Alien* and *The Shining* were both horror movies; they had themes of escape and home, which was interesting, though only Sam could say what it meant to him — but nothing else stood out. Not even the directors or actors were the same.

And now that she'd found this house, what next? Somehow she didn't think walking up to the front door and knocking would work, not with public figures like the Richards family, but she was in the middle of trying to build up the courage to do it when her phone rang. Waffles nearly raised her snout in the air to bay. "Good girl," Hester said. "But keep quiet."

She glanced at the phone's display and recognized the 608 area code from New Hampshire.

"Any news?" Lila Blaine asked.

"Maybe," Hester said. "I've made some progress, at least. Tell me, was Sam into any movies growing up?"

"We used to rent videos from the general store."

"Nothing else?"

"That's all I can really think of. The closest movie theater was in Meredith, so we didn't go that often."

"Okay," Hester said. "I haven't found him yet, so don't hold your breath."

"Do me a favor," Lila said. "If you do find him, watch him for a few days before you say anything. Tell me what you see."

Hester sat up and turned the radio down. Lila wasn't the first client who'd gotten cold feet, but it said something that she had. "I thought you were selling that property," she said.

"I am. And if I do, I'll send him a check. Right now, I want to have some time, though. I think that's fair after twelve years of these fucking postcards. Speaking of which, I have another one for you. I'll text it to you."

A message beeped on Hester's phone a moment after she hung up. Lila had taken a photo of the new postcard, this one of the Beacon Hill Tavern on a snowy night with a message that read *I just need to think things over.* At least, Hester thought, the snow matched the setting in *The Shining.* The Beacon Hill Tavern was right around the corner, and the first snow of the season had fallen a week and a half ago on a Saturday, and then melted the next day. Sam must have been at the bar that night.

Hester got out of the truck and held the door so Waffles could jump down after her, and then opened the rear cab.

"Where go?" Kate asked as Hester lifted her from the car seat.

"We're going to a bar." Hester checked her watch. "It's after noon, right?"

The Beacon Hill Tavern was one of the last old-fashioned Irish pubs left on Charles Street. The oak door was heavy, the floors sticky, and the delightfully warm air scented by rotten beer taps. It was still early afternoon, so only two customers looked up as Hester walked in holding Kate's hand. Waffles bounded in too and went straight into hound mode, sniffing around the edges of the room and chomping on something Hester hoped wouldn't stink up the truck later on.

"You usually bring your kid to a bar?" one of the patrons asked, a woman with dishwater blond hair.

"Can't start too early, right?" Hester said.

The woman raised a glass and went back to her phone.

"Jaysus, no mutts," the bartender said in an incomprehensible Irish brogue. He had white hair and a permanent flush of broken capillaries across his cheeks and nose. "You'll have to take him outside."

"Her," Hester said, lifting Kate up on a stool and unraveling her scarf and hat. Kate waved a pink-mittened hand at the bartender, who sighed.

"I'll be a minute," Hester said.

"And it takes a second for the health inspector to fine me. Away with you. I mean it."

"Be nice. Give us a sec to warm up. It must be ten degrees out there. I'm freezing my tits off."

"Freezing tits off," Kate said.

"Don't say that," Hester said.

"Nice," the bartender said, though even he smiled.

"Don't judge," Hester said. "I barely know what I'm doing, and besides, I'm sure you've heard worse."

She took the photo of Sam and Gabe from her bag. "Would you take a look at this, and then we'll go. Any chance you've seen this guy around? The one on the left? The photo's about twelve years old now."

"What do you want with him?"

"Old friend," Hester said.

"We all have old friends," the bartender said.

"How often does he come in?"

The bartender took out a rag and wiped down the counter.

"He's been here, right?" Hester asked.

"I've seen him once," the bartender finally said. "Maybe twice. He met up with one of

50

my regulars the other night. They left together."

"Did you catch his name?"

"I thought he was an old friend."

"What's it to you?"

"I can certainly tell him a midget's been asking about him the next time he comes around. How would that work out for you?"

"Hey, fill me up," the woman at the end of the bar said. She waggled an empty beer pint.

"You said you'd be a minute," the bartender said. "Get your mutt out of here."

Hester called to Waffles, who was too busy sniffing under one of the tables to come. She hopped off her stool and told Kate to stay put, and then dragged the dog away from whatever she'd found before realizing that she'd left Kate perched on a bar stool, and that she could fall and crack her head open. She let go of the dog, who ran right back under the table. "I could really use a drink," she mumbled, as she gripped Kate around the waist.

"You and me both," the bartender said.

"Could you just tell me if you got this guy's name?"

"If it'll get you out of here, then no, I didn't. He was too busy chatting with his new friend."

"And who is that? His friend."

"A woman who comes in here four or five times a week. Felicia something. Sweet but stressed out. Chubby. Good dresser. A Japanese last name. She works for a family up on the hill. Those people who own the sneaker company."

"The Richards family?" Hester asked.

"Yep. And that's about all I know."

"That wasn't so hard now, was it?" Hester said, slapping a ten on the counter. "Now we'll go."

"Thank Christ."

At the truck, Hester got on her tablet and searched on the name "Felicia" and all versions of the Richardses' family names, till finally a photo from a gala popped up showing Wendy Richards towering over a short, plump Asian woman identified as Felicia Nakazawa. A few more searches, and Hester had Felicia's address, employment history (she'd only ever worked for the Richards family), and a blurry photo from her Facebook wall that looked very much like Sam dancing at a club. Felicia had written "Fun with new friends," and 223 people had liked it, including Wendy Richards.

"Freezing tits off!"

In the rearview mirror, Hester saw Kate

playing with Monkey and talking to herself. The kid had been patient and quiet all day. "Kate, I had a nice time with you today."

Sometimes Hester had to remind herself to say nice things to Kate, but this time she was surprised not to be stretching the truth. It had been fun to hang out and to figure out a bit more about the mysterious Sam Blaine. "I'll take you to the Disney store over at the Pru, but you have to promise you won't say *tits* in front of Uncle Morgan. You'll get me in trouble."

"Freezing tits off!" Kate said.

"That's exactly what you shouldn't say. Why don't we get pizza for lunch too?"

"Kate like pizza!"

"So does Aunt Hester."

"Uncle Morgan like pizza?"

"Uncle Morgan loves pizza, especially Hawaiian. Unfortunately."

"Waffles like pizza?"

"Waffles likes everything."

"Mommy like pizza?"

Hearing Kate mention Daphne surprised Hester. Kate hadn't mentioned her mother in weeks, and Hester had actually wondered if Daphne had begun to fade from the girl's memory. Even for Hester, it took some effort to remember that her friend was more than resentment or the woman who'd left her kid behind, or that, in spite of every-thing, Hester still thought of Daphne as the very best of best friends. Why else would she be doing all of this for her? Hester's job was to find lost people. She could have figured out where Daphne had gone in a day, maybe two, tops, but she understood that her friend had left because she wanted to be lost, because she'd needed time to herself, and for now, no matter how annoy-ing, Hester planned to give Daphne what she needed.

"Mommy loves pizza," Hester said. "She likes anchovies, which may be even worse than Hawaiian."

"Kate like ankobees."

"I bet you do, sweetie."

And that's when the front door to the mansion opened. Hester recognized Wendy Richards, who stepped out onto the front stairs, the points of her stiletto heels poking from beneath her tailored suit. She looked about seven feet tall, with that mane of chestnut-colored hair following her like a taffeta prom dress. She spoke to someone inside, her breath freezing in clouds of white. Then Sam Blaine stepped out after her. He'd filled in a bit in twelve years, but there was no doubt in Hester's mind that it was him. He had the same arrogance that had taken over that photo and made the lakeside setting and the other boy nearly invisible. And it happened here too, where the mansion, and the holiday decorations, and even Wendy Richards, with her privileged confidence, faded into the background as Sam kissed her on the cheek and waved goodbye. Wendy went back into the house. Hester told Kate to stay put and got out of the truck. Sam tripped down the stairs to where a town car idled. He turned to the house and opened his arms as if to embrace everything in front of him. He seemed amazed, by the day, by his life. He looked happy and grateful and proud. And, like Hester, he looked like someone who had experienced how quickly everything could change, for the good or the bad.

CHAPTER 4

A week and a half earlier, Sam Blaine had stepped out of the Park Street T station in downtown Boston. The winter light had faded, and the air was heavy with pending snow. It was the first Saturday in December. Sam tucked his plaid scarf into his collar, buttoned up the pea coat he'd stolen from the back of a chair in a coffee shop, and headed into the Boston Common. All around him, elms and maples were lit up with long strands of looping white lights. On the Frog Pond, skaters glided in a circle. He crossed into Beacon Hill, with its gold-domed capitol building, where gas lamps bathed the narrow cobblestone streets in a warm glow.

He wandered till he found himself in Louisburg Square — again. He stood in the shadows, across the green from the Richardses' house. Sam had come to this square a few times over the past months, ever since he'd met Wendy Richards at a benefit where he'd worked an evening as a catering waiter. He'd observed her more than met her, the way she moved through the room, confident in a black cocktail dress, towering over nearly everyone else at the party. She'd slipped him a hundred-dollar bill at the end of the night for keeping the wine flowing. "I can't make it through these things without it," she whispered.

It had been easy enough to find her house, and since then, he'd come to watch how she lived, and she lived well, in a way Sam could only dream of, in a way that he *had* dreamed of. She had cars and clothes and knew people Sam wanted to know. She belonged to the University Club and golfed in Brookline and went to Nantucket for the weekend. Here, tonight, he could see her, on the second floor, looking out into the darkness, the glow of a fire lighting the room behind her. She *must* have plans. She had to! It was a Saturday in December, and people like Wendy didn't stay home with Netflix when there were parties to go to, and everywhere Sam looked another party was starting. Couples alit from taxis in Brooks Brothers and velvet, with expensive gifts from expensive stores, wrapped in expensive red-and-gold paper. He could have felt like the little match girl, wandering in the cold. He could have felt put out, but this was where Sam belonged. All he needed was a way in. All he needed was one small chance.

He wasn't sure how long he'd been standing in the shadows when the front door to the mansion opened. From across the street, he recognized Wendy's athletic frame as the butler helped her into her coat. Her dark hair was wound around in a sort of cone that threatened to topple her over. She clutched at a gift and hurried down the stairs and onto the sidewalk, her heels clacking against the brick. Sam followed, stepping lightly between shadows so as not to be heard. The street, so full of energy before, suddenly felt empty. It was cold, and Wendy pulled her coat in close. Her feet moved so quickly she practically ran. Still, Sam nearly got close enough to smell her perfume.

She came to another house, and another set of stairs, where Sam could see a holiday party in full swing through the parlor window. She climbed halfway to the door, and turned. The light from over the doorway silhouetted her pale face. "Who's there?" she said.

Sam stepped into an alley. He'd have to

be less eager in the future.

"I can hear you," Wendy said, "I can hear you breathe. So fuck off," and then she rapped on the ornate doors.

Another butler greeted her as piano music filtered from inside. Sam could almost smell the gust of pine-scented air that rushed into the night. Through the front window, he saw Wendy make her way into the parlor, her cheeks flushed from the cold, but otherwise seemingly recovered from her walk. She took a glass of champagne from a passing tray and then seemed to greet each and every person who passed her. Sam imagined standing beside her. He could almost feel his fingertips as they found the crook of her arm. When she laughed, he laughed too. He imagined the tick of clocks, the scent of linseed oil, the hum of small talk — season tickets to the Red Sox or the symphony, weekend jaunts to Nantucket, square footage, board meetings, CrossFit. Inside, in the warmth, he'd have focused on the way people spoke, on the cadence of their voices, on the clues that dropped around him like a million keys to a million locks, so that when he finally spoke, he'd feel as though he'd been part of this world for his entire life. More than anything, Sam wanted to be at the center of that world.

He stepped out from the shadows and nearly collided with a well-dressed elderly couple who tottered up the street. "Excuse me," he said, catching the woman's arm before she fell. He inhaled a wave of Chanel No. 5.

"Oh, thank you dear," the woman said. She put a hand to her silvery chignon.

"I need to watch where I'm going!" Sam said. "Off to a party?"

"To the Wigglesworths'!" the man said, as though there was nowhere else to be.

"Of course," Sam said. "The Wigglesworths'!"

He watched as they creaked up the stairs and into the party, and then he plunged down the hill to the shops and restaurants of Charles Street. A young man with the close-cropped hair and good looks of a frat boy eyed Sam as he walked by. Sam thought about a quickie — a reward for a good day at work — but he had places to be. A moment later, he burst through the oak door of the Beacon Hill Tavern and into the empty bar. "How about an IPA?" he said to the bartender, who asked for ID and then barely looked at it.

Nowadays, Sam used the identity of one Aaron Gewirtzman. It was a name he hadn't gotten used to, one that belonged to a young man buried in a cemetery outside New York whose Social Security number Sam had borrowed. Last year he'd been Casey Crawford in New York. Before that, he'd been Justin Rogers in Chicago, Gavin Kennedy in Baltimore, and Jason Hodge in San Francisco. Now he was getting to know Aaron, who was twenty-six, a year younger than Sam. Aaron was born on July 22 (a Cancer), and wore corrective lenses. He'd grown up in New York and worked a series of temp jobs where, Sam hoped, no one would remember the nerdy young man who'd died in a random car accident. Thankfully, the real Aaron Gewirtzman had barely left Manhattan in his entire short life, so the chances of bumping into anyone who'd ever met him were slim to none.

Sam downed a beer and ordered another, and had nearly finished that by the time the tavern door opened. A woman wobbled in wearing a black Lycra dress that might, possibly, have fit a few years earlier. She puckered her less-than-thick red lips as her eyes adjusted to the dark. Then she teetered toward the restrooms as though she'd recently learned to walk in heels. "Shot of vodka," she said to the bartender, and a moment later she was at the bar, texting madly.

"You're back," Sam said, moving to the

stool next to hers. He'd met her for the first time two nights ago in the same spot.

She downed the shot and swiveled toward him. "So are you," she said, signaling to the bartender for another round and pointing at Sam's beer. He nodded.

"That's it?" she asked.

"Give me a shot too," Sam said. "On a date tonight?"

"What's it to you?" She lifted her glass. "To new friends," she said, snapping her head and grimacing. Sam raised an eyebrow in a way he'd practiced in the mirror, arrogant and sure. The vodka slid down his throat. "Aaron Gewirtzman," he said, extending a hand toward the woman.

"Felicia Nakazawa," she said.

But Sam already knew that.

He'd seen Felicia leaving the Richards house for the first time two months ago. Since then, he'd dug into her background and learned as much as he could about her. She lived in the Atelier, a fancy South End building with a doorman. She'd moved to Boston from San Diego fifteen years earlier to get her undergraduate degree at Boston College, where she'd befriended Wendy Richards, her neighbor in the dorm. And she'd worked as the Richards family's personal assistant ever since she'd finished school.

"No parties tonight?" Felicia asked. " 'Tis the season."

"Could say the same for you."

"I have nothing but parties." Felicia waggled her phone as a text message popped onto the screen. She scanned it and banged in a response. "On call tonight. Tonight and every night." She hit send and put the phone down.

"A drinking doctor?" Sam said.

"I wish," Felicia said. "I'm more of a jill-of-all-trades. What about you? You seem fancy!" She scrutinized Sam all over again. "I know your type. You're like my friend Ron. Spoiled gay boy whose liberal New York daddy pays for your Back Bay apartment. You have that fresh-from-the-regatta look going."

"I wish," Sam said, toasting with another shot.

"God, I wonder what it's like not to worry about money all the time?" Felicia asked as her phone buzzed again. "I should know. I see it all day long."

From what Sam had observed, Felicia didn't worry much about money either. But he supposed when it came to the Richards family and money, all things were relative.

"What I wouldn't give to have it easy for once," Felicia said. "It's the first Saturday in December, and I'm stuck in here. Tell me my story. What do you think I'm like?"

"You mean dressed up, nowhere to go, and drunk off your ass?"

Felicia hit him in the arm. "You want to see me drunk? Order me a vodka martini. Dirty."

Sam signaled to the bartender. "How's this," he said. "You're meeting a man tonight, not exactly a date, but not *not* a date either. He's older than you. In his forties, married and divorced — he claims. He's not into kids or commitments. He might take you to a hotel for champagne and chocolate-covered strawberries. He might fly you to his villa in the south of France. You never know. He doesn't stand a chance — you're too smart and you know he's only in it for the chase — but you've asked yourself whether it's worth the ride."

Felicia drank half her martini in a single gulp. "Did you make that up?"

"Two parts *Sex and the City,* one part *Private Benjamin.*"

"You *are* gay. Not even close, but I'll take it anyway."

Sam finished his drink and fished the hundred-dollar bill Wendy had given him from his wallet. Felicia put a hand on his arm. "Stay," she said, pushing the money toward him and dropping an American Express (platinum) on the bar. "Tonight's on me. I have to wait here for a while anyway."

"Why?"

"It's my job."

"Your job is to sit in a bar and drink by yourself?"

"Not really. My job is to make things run smoothly. And I shouldn't say much more about it. Another part of my job is to keep my mouth shut. I did sign an NDA."

"Got it," Sam said, wondering how much Felicia would have to drink to lose that discretion.

They talked for another hour as Sam created more of a backstory for Aaron, keeping the details general and as close to his own as possible. Aaron liked fashion and baseball and working out, just like Sam. He was a Yankees fan, though — it only made sense — and Felicia seemed convinced he came from money. Sam let that one go. Maybe it would be useful in the end. He found out that Felicia wrote nearly all of the material Wendy Richards used on her blog — probably a secret covered by the NDA — and Felicia's father still held out hope that she'd be the first Nakazawa in space. "Not very likely," she said. "But maybe, if Pearly Richards buys a space shuttle . . ." Her phone rang. "I have to grab this," she said.

Sam heard her mumble assurances for a few moments, and when she hung up, she signaled to the bartender for the check. "Sorry, I have to go. Wendy wants me to walk her home." Felicia barely suppressed a roll of the eyes. "She thinks someone followed her to the Wigglesworths' tree-trimming party tonight."

"Does she often have people . . . following her around?"

"Not till recently," Felicia said.

"Sounds important."

"It's important to her, so it's important to me. That's how I stay employed!" Felicia put on her coat. "It's around the corner." She was halfway out the door when she said, "You're coming, right?"

"I guess I am," Sam said.

He slipped one of the empty shot glasses into his pocket while he grabbed his things. Outside, he snapped a photo of the tavern door, where snow had begun to build up. "To remember tonight!" he added.

Felicia took his arm in hers as they headed up Beacon Hill. Snow clung to her long, black hair as they came to the Wigglesworths' house. Felicia punched a message into her phone, and soon Wendy in her red dress, hair still twisted toward the ceiling, appeared in the parlor window, bending down to hug the hosts.

"She's tall," Sam said.

"Six foot four in heels!" Felicia said. "But don't mention it if you want her to like you. It's an easy way to get on her bad side . . . and you don't want to be on Wendy's bad side. But she's smart, and she works hard. I had no idea who she was when we met or how fucking rich she was, and her family has never been anything but generous. They take me on trips and pay for my apartment and have me over for dinner."

"To their house?"

"Where else?"

"What are her parents like?"

"Pearly and Elise? They're . . ." Felicia stopped and seemed to catch herself. "I've had a lot to drink," she said. "And we barely know each other."

The front door to the townhouse opened. "Thank you, thank you," Wendy said, hugging Felicia. "I know it sounds crazy, but I swear I heard someone behind me on the way here, and it freaked me the fuck out . . ." She stopped mid-sentence when Sam stepped into a circle of light cast from a streetlamp. Wendy let Felicia go.

"This is Aaron," Felicia said quickly. "He's a friend of mine. We were having drinks when you texted."

Wendy extended a gloved hand. "Nice to meet you," she said. "I didn't mean to disturb your evening. The house is a few blocks away. Then the two of you can be on with your night."

"We're happy to swing by," Sam said, mirroring her finishing-school style like it was a first language. "But you're not going home already. It's only nine o'clock!"

Wendy glanced at Felicia and then at Sam. "Do I know you?" she asked.

"I doubt it. I'd have remembered meeting you."

"Don't you two want to be alone?"

"The more, the merrier," Sam said.

"To Club Café?" Felicia said.

"Where else?" Sam said.

"Club Café!" Wendy said, turning to Sam and seeing him anew. "We haven't been there in forever!"

"If you really do have a stalker," Felicia said, taking her friend's arm in hers, "you can't get much safer than the middle of a gay bar!"

At the club, Wendy's hair unraveled into an

unsettling mass that seemed to fill the room on its own. They danced to eighties hits while videos blared on the screens around them. They also took breaks to slam down more vodka shots and post photos to Instagram, though Sam ducked out of them or obscured his face. He avoided any online presence. He could feel more than one set of eyes taking him in, and as the club grew more crowded, he stripped off his shirt and tucked it into his jeans. Maybe he'd get lucky tonight after all.

"Someone works out," Felicia said, her hands grazing his flat stomach.

"Every morning," Sam said.

"Keep it up."

A twink in a pair of hot pants came by with Day-Glo shots. Felicia bought three and stuffed two twenties in the boy's shorts.

"She's always been a fag hag," Wendy shouted in Sam's ear.

"Oh, shut up," Felicia said with a giggle as she tossed the blue liquor back.

"We came here all the time in college," Wendy said. "It's the best place to dance without getting harassed."

"Seems like both of you are fag hags," Sam said.

Wendy downed her shot too. "We like to have fun," she said.

"So do I," Sam said.

"Selfie!" Felicia shouted.

Sam managed to turn his face into Wendy's mane of hair as he heard the phone click.

Later, Felicia stormed outside in a drunken rage over something Sam didn't see, but that he thought might have involved a bull dyke and her femme girlfriend.

"What happened?" he asked Wendy, who laughed.

"She's a terrible drunk. Wait till you see her sobbing in front of the toilet. Let's go find her."

Outside in the snow, Felicia insisted she wasn't drunk. "But you two can walk me home anyway."

"Weren't you the one who was supposed to walk me home?" Wendy asked.

"We'll get you an Uber," Felicia said as she stumbled down the sidewalk. "Or stay over."

She mumbled something else and nearly fell over. Wendy and Sam each got on a side and helped Felicia navigate home, up the elevator, and into her enormous loft apartment, with its floor-to-ceiling windows looking out on the Prudential building.

"I'll get her some ginger ale," Wendy said, heading toward the kitchen.

Felicia watched her go, and then shoved all her weight into pinning Sam to the wall and trying to kiss him. "I'm so fucking horny." Her words slurred together so that he could barely understand her. "And you're so Goddamned cute."

Sam stood stiffly, hands at his sides, waiting her out. He'd played straight plenty of times, but his path to knowing Wendy better would be through having Felicia as a friend, not a lover. She gave up, and then twisted her ankle running for the toilet. Sam heard a long gag, and then a splash. "Why, why, why!" Felicia said through tears. "Oh, God, would someone hold my hair?"

Wendy hurried in from the kitchen, swept Felicia's hair into a ponytail, and tied it with a rubber band. "Make yourself at home," she whispered to Sam. "I'll take care of her."

"Isn't she supposed to be the one taking care of you?" Sam said.

"We trade off."

Sam left the two of them sitting on the bathroom floor. He listened from the hallway outside and then went into Felicia's bedroom, where he opened the closet door and slid his hands under piles of cashmere sweaters until he happened upon a tiny bag of cocaine, which he added to the shot glass in his coat pocket. A photo on the bedside table showed Wendy and Felicia with a man Sam recognized as Pearly Richards on what looked like the summit of Kilimanjaro. In the kitchen, he dug up a box of saltines and took them to the bathroom, where Felicia lay flat, her cheek pressed to the tile floor. Wendy sat with her back against the wall.

"Would these help?" he asked.

"I don't think anything will help at this point." Wendy struggled to stand without waking Felicia. She stepped out of her shoes and came a bit closer to earth. "We'll check in later to be sure she's not drowning in vomit."

She took his hand and led him out to the living area, where she opened a bottle of red and grabbed two goblets. Felicia's taste in furniture was an expensive blend of contemporary Scandinavian and mid-century modern chic. They sank into an overstuffed sofa and turned on the gas fireplace. An Alex Katz print hung over the mantle.

"Where did you come from, anyway?" Wendy said. She ran a hand down Sam's knee. "You're exquisite."

"The street," Sam said.

"My favorite place!"

Even after all these years, it still surprised Sam how trusting people could be, how willing they were to let handsome strangers into their homes and their lives. It was easy with someone needy and desperate to please like Felicia — or Ellen in San Francisco, where he and Gabe had fled after they ran away from New Hampshire, and where everything had seemed possible. Ellen had worked at that Internet startup where Sam had found a job as a receptionist named Jason Hodge. She was fleshy and smelled of damp talc, and at first, from the way the other employees talked about her, he thought she might be the office manager, not the owner of the company, along with her brother, Zach.

Ellen was lonely. Her brother, who was handsome and gregarious, could flirt with women and high-five his bros, while Ellen sat in her windowless office, seemingly bewildered by anything but the game of Mine Sweeper staring at her from her computer screen. She seemed like someone who simply wanted to be liked, and Sam started with tea. Herbal, soon learning to bring her ginger lemon. And then he moved on to cookies. Gluten free. "I'm sure you don't want any of these," he said one day, popping his head into her office with a Tupperware container of chocolate chip cookies he'd bought. "I made them with rice flour."

Ellen took one. And then another. "I get rashes if I have dairy," she said.

"Nuts give me hives," Sam said.

She took another cookie and smiled.

"I should let you get back to work," Sam said, backing away.

"You can stay," Ellen said.

After that, she took him under her wing, and when he found out how truly rich she was, he wondered why she even bothered to work. She lived in a house in Pacific Heights with four cats and views of the Golden Gate Bridge, existing in a world of solitary excess, a world where the thought of what something cost never came into play. Sam slipped right into his place in that world and came away with gifts of electronics and clothing, all for the price of a few frantic moments of slobbery grunting on Sunday mornings, cats walking over his face, and whispers at work. Sam didn't mind the whispers, and soon he didn't go to the office anymore anyway. And then "Jason Hodge" left town.

He sometimes wondered if he'd still be Jason if Ellen's brother Zach hadn't been the one who watched the family finances, but then, he reminded himself, it wasn't worth looking back.

The sound of Felicia retching again rang out from the bathroom.

"I should check on her," Wendy said.

Sam touched her hand. "Stay," he said.

As easy as it had been to win over Felicia, he relished the challenge of taking on the privileged few, those like Wendy who didn't need anything from anyone, those who knew instinctively not to trust. He leaned in and poured her a glass of wine. "Cheers," he said.

She gathered that hair into a knot. Sam took a sip of his wine. It tasted like dirt.

"You were at the Wigglesworths' party tonight, right?" he said. "How do you know them?"

"Everyone on the hill knows the Wigglesworths," Wendy said. "They're an ancient Boston family. They're the type of people to know if you want to know those types."

"Do they have kids?"

"Of course. They need to carry on the line. Brennan is almost as cute as you."

"How old is he?"

"Twenty-seven, maybe twenty-eight."

"I thought so. I think we went to college together."

75

"Would he remember you?"

"We didn't know each other that well," Sam said. *Or at all.*

"He'll be at my party next week. You can meet him there."

"What party?"

"The Crocus Party! I throw it every year. It's a benefit for the VA. We give scholarships to disabled veterans. *Bloom early! Stand out!* That's the theme. The whole house will be filled with uniforms!"

"And crocuses? In December?"

"They're forced, silly! It costs me a fortune. You're coming, right?"

Sam snorted into his glass. "Sweetheart, you may not be as bad off as that one." Sam jerked his thumb toward the bathroom as he heard Felicia dry-heaving again. "But you're still drunk off your ass. You won't remember one thing from tonight, including me. I'll come, and you'll have me thrown out."

"Shut up," Wendy said. "I'll remember you. Please come." She put a hand on his thigh and lowered her voice. "I'm not someone who usually has to beg."

"If I didn't know better, I'd think you were flirting with me, Ms. Richards."

"I'm not?" Wendy said.

"How do you know I go that way?"

"That's what I'm trying to find out. Do you?"

Sam took another sip of wine. He could suddenly see new paths opening in front of him, a bright future full of opportunity. He set his glass on a coaster. "I think I do," he said.

A few moments later, they left Felicia snoring in her bedroom and grabbed an Uber to Louisburg Square, where Wendy lived in the guesthouse behind her parents' mansion. Sam walked her through a courtyard lined with fountains and espaliered trees, and waited while she unlocked the door.

"Home safe," he said, when she pushed the door open and stood on the threshold. "You must have sobered up by now."

"Maybe."

Wendy went inside and left the door ajar. Sam followed her into a tiny living room attached to a kitchenette. The ceilings here were low, so low Wendy nearly had to duck her head. She took champagne from the refrigerator, popped the cork, and drank right from the bottle. "Do you want to help me finish?"

Sam gulped down a mouthful of wine that had to have cost fifty dollars.

"Does this mean you're not a regular at

Club Café after all?" Wendy asked.

"Haven't you heard that good things come to those who wait?"

"I don't wait for anything," Wendy said, grabbing Sam by his shirt collar.

She kissed him aggressively. Still, she was soft. Softer than Sam was used to. Upstairs, she pushed him onto the bed, and when he woke a few hours later, it took him a moment to realize where he was. Then he saw that mass of hair on the pillow beside his and felt the soft sheets that enveloped him. Wendy rolled toward him, that hair twirling above her like a tornado of curls. He felt her hand on his thigh. "Already?" she asked.

"Is this a hookup?" Sam asked.

"Do you care?"

"Do you?"

"I'm not sure."

He grinned and rolled on top of her. He moved a lock of hair and kissed her neck. She liked to face the wall. His hips found a rhythm. He could get used to this, like he had with Ellen. Yes, he could definitely get used to this.

In time.

CHAPTER 5

It amazed Sam what a difference a few days could make. He tripped up the stairs to the Richardses' mansion and rang the doorbell. When Harry the butler answered, Sam strode right in as if he owned the place. Inside, a small army of decorators hung wreaths, garlands, lights, and baubles in every room in preparation for the Crocus Party, which, it turned out, was more like a gala, and was definitely a Very Big Deal.

"Wendy's expecting me," Sam said as Harry took his coat.

Harry nodded and disappeared, leaving Sam alone. The house smelled of pine and burning wax. A twenty-foot balsam fir rose through the foyer, from the black-and-white marble floor to the ornate ceiling. To the left, a huge ballroom with a parquet floor and chandeliers had been cleared of furniture in preparation for the party. To the right, a long mahogany table set with wreaths and candles stretched through the dining room. In a few days, pots of forced crocuses would dot the house with splashes of purple, yellow, and white. The preparation was fit for a dignitary, and Sam had already begun to feel a part of it, like this world had welcomed him with open arms, and he stood there, taking it in, as though he could pull meaning from everything in front of him, as though he could work through this puzzle till he found where his own jagged piece fit.

He stepped over to the tree and pocketed a small silver ball. He looked to where that staircase swept from the foyer to the landing above. He ran his hand over the marble's ornate detailing and imagined the care and expense that had gone into building it. This was the type of home where he belonged.

"Oh, God. It's you! I was just thinking about you, and now here you are."

Sam turned to Felicia, whom he hadn't seen since he'd left her passed out in her apartment, though she spoke to him as though they'd known each other their whole lives. "I didn't know if I'd ever see you again," she said. "But the party is in less than a week and there's so much to do! I could use all the help I can get."

"Where's Wendy?" Sam asked.

"Are you meeting her?"

"I was supposed to."

"She's with Twig," Felicia said, rolling her eyes. "Her co-chair for the benefit. The three of us went to BC together, but Twig is a real See You Next Tuesday. The only thing that comes out of their meetings is long lists of things for me to do. She's the one who's supposed to be recruiting veterans to come to the party, so guess what I need to add to my list? Come. I'm putting you to work."

Felicia took Sam's arm and led him through the house, first to the kitchen, where they tasted samples from the caterers, including "Wendy's Famous Crabbies." "Work on these," Felicia said. "They taste like cat food. I found that recipe in an issue of *Good Housekeeping* from 1973. Wendy Richards has never opened a can of crab meat in her life."

She checked a liquor delivery against the invoice and then led Sam down a steep set of stairs to her damp basement office, where she found a stack of invoices and leafed through them, and then opened up her laptop to a spreadsheet. Sam walked around the tiny office. No one would have accused Felicia of being organized. Stacks of papers and files lined walls and every surface of the room. Pots of forced crocuses, samples from florists, Sam assumed, balanced precariously on various perches. A tiny, dirty window let in a stream of winter light that danced off dusty air. "Why the Crocus Party?" he asked. "Especially during the holidays. It's the wrong season."

"They've been doing it for years," Felicia said. "Wendy likes to be different."

Sam pushed some files off a wooden stool and sat.

"Why were you meeting Wendy?" Felicia asked. "Have you seen her since we went out on Saturday?"

Sam had seen Wendy nearly every night in the last week, and it surprised him that Felicia didn't know already. The two of them had seemed so close, more than employer and employee. "A couple of times," he said.

"Are you friends now?"

Sam swore he heard a catch in her voice, enough so that he answered carefully. "Maybe friends. Definitely friendly."

Felicia smiled. She chewed on her lower lip. "I shouldn't have had so much to drink that night," she said. "But forget about it. Do you want anything to eat? Are you hungry? Harry can bring us something."

Sam shook his head, but Felicia picked up the wall phone anyway and told Harry to bring them sandwiches. "And no mayonnaise," she added as she hung up. "He always forgets, and I have to send them back, and it really ruins my afternoon. Is roast beef okay?" she asked without waiting for an answer. "I'm glad you popped by. I was wondering if I'd ever see you again. I wanted to chat you up, but I couldn't find you online. You don't have a Facebook page or Instagram. Nothing. It's like you don't exist. I mean, how many Aaron Gewirtzmans could there be? It's Gewirtzman, right? I'm really good with names. You have to be when you have a job like this one. Rich people like to be remembered."

"I'm old-fashioned," Sam said. He kept a low profile, in every possible way, including online. "You can always text me. I'll leave my number."

"Apparently you've been around all along, though no one bothered to tell me."

"I'm telling you now."

Felicia returned to the spreadsheet. "You should watch yourself," she said a moment later. She said it quietly, almost as though she didn't want Sam to hear. She tabbed through cells and typed in some information. "Don't let Wendy fool you. She knows when people are using her. She sees through things like that. I mean you met her four days ago, so don't think you're best friends all of a sudden."

"Why would you think I'm using Wendy?"

"I didn't say that."

"Really? It sounded like you did."

"I'm looking out for you," Felicia said, flashing him that practiced smile. "I don't want you to get hurt."

Sam clucked his tongue. Felicia was worth keeping an eye on. "How do you find anything in here?" he asked, changing the subject. "It's a mess."

"I can find pretty much anything."

"See, I hardly know either of you," Sam said. "We only met a few days ago. Is Wendy dating anyone?"

"Are you interested?"

"Didn't we all go to a gay bar on Saturday?"

Felicia scrolled through the spreadsheet again. "Is there something about the ice sculptures over there?" she asked. "Maybe under that pot of crocuses?"

Sam lifted up the pot and found a Post-It. He read off the delivery information.

"She's not dating anyone," Felicia said. "She says she wants to, but every guy she meets doesn't have *it*. She dated this guy named Hero for about three months earlier this year. He was a filmmaker and must have had a trust fund, because God knows his movies didn't bring in any cash. We had to sit through this boring documentary he made called *Cleaning in Nonantum* about this lecherous guy who ran a Laundromat in Newton. I mean, it was bad, I'll admit that. And Hero was kind of moody and vain. He wore the tightest t-shirts. But he could not have been cuter. I'd have done anything he asked, but Wendy dumped him right after we saw the documentary. She said it showed his limitations."

"What about you?" Sam asked. "You must date."

"Oh, shut up," Felicia said, waving a hand at him dismissively. She seemed to have warmed to him again. "I spend my life riding in the sidecar, and I'm happy there. No one even notices me. Besides, I thought we went over this the other night. I'm dating an old guy. One who flies me to France, right?"

"That's right," Sam said. "And I have a rich daddy who pays for my Back Bay apartment. I guess we can both dream."

"I don't think you'd have any trouble finding a *sugar* daddy."

"Maybe I should apply myself," Sam said.

He'd had sugar daddies — and mamas — in other lives. Plenty of them. He'd learned from those experiences. He'd learned how far a pretty face could get him when he needed it to, with men and women, straight and gay. He didn't discriminate. He'd learned to read the situation and to take opportunities when they presented themselves, and that boredom could lead to greed, and that greed nearly always led to exposure. Would he still be in San Francisco right now, swatting Ellen's cats from his pillow, if he hadn't told her to make a move on the company? Surely he'd known from the start that Zach wouldn't give in without a fight?

Felicia's phone rang. She answered and then listened for a minute. "I don't see how that's my problem," she said. There was another pause, and then she said, "You did this. You made the mistake. You fix it!"

She hung up and let her head fall to her desk. "That was the photographer," she moaned. "She double booked. I need to find someone else. Oh, God, oh, God, oh, God, what am I going to do? My to-do list is as long as my arm." Felicia's phone rang again. "What?" she said, and then she listened for a moment and hung up. "Jesus, that was the delivery truck with the tables and chairs," she said. "They'll be here in five minutes, which is two days early. Go upstairs. Don't sign for them till they're set up and they haven't scratched the floors."

"I think I can handle it," Sam said. "And call the photographer. Tell her to send an assistant and to comp you or you'll write a bad Yelp! review. It works every time. And let's go out tonight. Just the two of us." Being on Felicia's good side would pay off. He had to remember that. "I'll text you."

He reached over and checked off "Tables and Chairs" from Felicia's to-do list and then headed up the narrow stairs, taking a deep breath of fresh air when he stepped from the musty basement and into the foyer, where the activity had risen to a frenzied state. He met the delivery guys and watched as they unloaded and set up the furniture. After they left, Sam glanced up the marble staircase and imagined skulking from room to room, sliding his hand into drawers, lying down on beds, sitting in windows, and being part of this life. In the ballroom, he tapped his heel on the parquet floor and ran his hand along the wainscoting. He touched the gold-and-ivory wallpaper. He dimmed the crystal chandeliers. He danced a few steps from a waltz with an imaginary partner, and then closed his eyes and pictured the room filled with people dressed to the nines. A string quartet played Mozart. He swept across the room, holding his partner at her waist, bending her toward the floor as the music swelled. He knew everyone in the room watched him. He knew they either wanted to be him or be with him and that all he needed now was to keep this act going.

"There you are."

Sam stopped his dance. Wendy Richards stood in the doorway. Sun from the French doors streamed across the floor and lit up her dark eyes and delicate features. She really was a beautiful woman; even he could appreciate that. She clapped so that the sound reverberated through the empty room. Sam blushed, and for once it wasn't practiced. "How mortifying," he said.

"Don't be embarrassed. We don't use this room often enough. Maybe you'll put it to good use."

"Only if I have a partner," Sam said.

"Grace has never been my strength."

"I don't believe that. May I?" he asked and then placed a hand at her waist. He looked into her eyes and smiled. "Follow my lead."

"You'll regret this," Wendy said. "Or at least your feet will."

He led her around the room, talking her through each of the moves.

"You're tall," Wendy said. "I hadn't noticed."

"Almost as tall as you," Sam said.

"Not many men can say that."

"I'm not like most men."

"No," Wendy said. "You're not. And this time, I think it's you who's flirting with me."

"Maybe," Sam said. "But you didn't tell Felicia about us?"

"There's not much of an 'us' yet," Wendy said. "All we've done is sleep together. I don't even know where you live." She paused. "Where do you live anyway?"

"Somerville," he said.

"Slumerville," Wendy said. "Very hip!"

Sam thought about the ground-floor apartment that he shared with Gabe, where the air smelled of boiled hot dogs and mold and the pot smoke that wafted from under Gabe's bedroom door. "Yeah, very hip," he said.

Wendy stepped on Sam's foot and winced, a look that said *Told you so.* "So," she said, "Felicia gave you the third degree?"

"It wasn't too bad."

"I bet she yammered on about Hero?"

Sam shrugged.

"We're like sisters," Wendy said. "We know how the other one thinks, and I think she wanted Hero for herself. The same may be true for you."

"She thinks I'm gay."

"Good," Wendy said. "It'll help her mind her own business, and keep my father from nosing around. I told Twig all about you over lunch. She understands. Her father's the same way, maybe worse." She assessed Sam, reaching out and mussing his hair. "I like the glasses," she said. "Boys in expensive glasses work well online. And we'll get the hair taken care of on Saturday. What are you wearing to the party?"

"I don't know," Sam said. "I'll see what I have."

"Yeah, that won't be good enough. I have a brand to watch out for. I need people to talk and tweet, and for that I need you to look great. They'll like the mystery too. They'll wonder who you are."

Sam felt a seed of alarm. Online, it was easy to connect one image to the next. But a moment later he'd forgotten the panic as he found himself careening through the streets of Boston in Wendy's Audi. She was at the wheel, and her long legs worked the pedals. "Honestly," she said, "you'd think you'd never been to a benefit in your life."

They zipped past people and streets. Wendy swerved her car into an alley, and made her way across the Charles to Drinkwater's in Cambridge. She parked and headed into the exclusive men's store. Sam trotted to keep up with her long strides. "Logan," she said to the sales clerk.

"Miss Richards," Logan said with a polite smile.

"Take care of my friend, would you? We need something festive and sexy. Something that reminds you of crocuses."

"My pleasure," Logan said.

"I'll leave you two," Wendy said. "Back in a few."

Sam waited while Logan brought pants and shirts and jackets and shoes to try on. He didn't dare look at the price tags as he breathed in the scent of leather and ran his fingertips over the soft fabric.

Logan held up a pair of pants. "These are nice and tight."

Sam changed into the new outfit and felt like he was changing his skin at the same time. In the mirror, he saw Aaron Gewirtzman and who Aaron might become, and it made him feel high, higher than he had in months.

"I should measure that inseam," Logan said as he kneeled down and unwound the tape measure. He had the efficient attractiveness of the best in retail. His salt-and-pepper hair was neatly clipped, and his skin had a moisturizer glow. "Miss Richards is a generous woman. You're not the first, you know. She likes a pretty face and to have a plaything. I'd like someone to be that generous with me."

That was bold. Rude. Cause for dismissal. But Sam hardly cared whether he was the first or not, because he was the one right now. He looked at himself in the mirror, at the way the pants hung, at the cuff links that peeked from his jacket sleeves. He worked out every morning, running through Somerville for an hour no matter how cold it got, and then lifting weights in that tiny bedroom while Gabe stunk up the house with fried bacon. The Crocus Party would be another night to remember. And when Sam looked this good, how could anything possibly go wrong? He swayed his hips into Logan's face, whose hand froze in his crotch.

"I can be generous," Sam said. He adjusted the Windsor knot on a pink tie, but decided right then to go without at the party. After all, a flash of skin never hurt. "Just don't stain the fabric."

Chapter 6

Gabe DiPursio didn't want much out of life besides to belong somewhere. Anywhere.

And to have someone love him.

And to love someone. And to have a family and kids, a house, a dog. To be ordinary, in every way.

Loving someone, at least, was easy. Too easy, at times, as Sam often told him.

Gabe was in love right now, so in love that he'd left his computer for once and braved the cold to stand outside the Somerville Theatre in Davis Square and watch the girl working the concession counter. He loved the way she moved deftly from the popcorn machine to the soda fountain, the way she wore that baby-doll dress that seemed too thin for a day like today. She ladled extra butter on popcorn for anyone, even those who didn't ask. He'd seen her for the first time two weeks ago when he'd come for a midnight showing of *Back to the Future.* "I love this movie," she'd said as she handed him a ticket.

"Me too," Gabe had said. At least he wished he had. Instead, he'd stared at her till she asked if he needed anything else.

So today he practiced what to say: *Are you going to the Girly Man show next week?* or *It sure is cold outside!* Ordinary things. Things that anyone could say and that wouldn't make him stand out. No matter what, he wouldn't tell her that he knew her name and where she lived or that her roommate left for work at 8:13 on the dot every weekday morning. He wouldn't mention the spare key he'd found hidden under their porch either. Maybe he'd ask for Sno-Caps. He definitely wouldn't tell her that he liked her tits.

Gabe pulled the theater door open. Inside, the lobby smelled of popcorn, and the air was warm and dry. He swore that she glanced down the short line and paused when she saw him, that she bit her lip to keep from smiling. Maybe he'd ask for Milk Duds and popcorn and tell her that if you shook them together you called it Popcorn Surprise. "Here, be surprised," he might say as she glanced toward a coworker in a way he was sure meant yes. He should have shaved his beard before he came. Who wanted to kiss someone with a beard? And he should have worn something besides flannel.

Her name was Penelope.

He was next. He stepped up to the ticket counter. Did her friends call her Penny? "You're always here," he said.

"I work here," Penelope said, glancing to the line behind him.

"Can I . . ." he began.

"Which movie?" she asked.

"Dinner?"

"The thing is," she said, "you're not my type."

A blast of cold air swept through the lobby as a couple came in from the outside. Penelope's blond hair lifted around her face. Her nipples, he swore, popped beneath that thin pink fabric, and even though he tried not to stare, she winced. "Do you want a ticket or not?" she asked. The smile was gone.

Gabe turned and left.

He walked quickly out into the cold, his eyes aimed squarely at the ground and his face burning with shame. Thankfully, a wave of people flooded out of the T entrance and swept him into the heart of Davis Square. He looked around the crowded sidewalks. It was a Tuesday in the afternoon, and the sidewalks were filled with people. Christmas lights lined the streets, while small groups huddled in a crowded café. Gabe could only imagine heading inside to that steamy warmth and noise. He could only imagine belonging, or being seen. He wondered where Sam was, but Sam had better things to do than sit around the house. If Gabe went home, he'd be even more alone.

He stopped in the middle of the square, a few hundred yards from the movie theater. It had begun to snow. He lifted his face toward the sky and felt the snowflakes dot his cheeks. Even here, in this crowded square, snow brought peace. He opened Tinder on his phone and scrolled through profiles till he found "Ally-Kat," who was "raring to go." She'd done the duck face in her photo and looked slutty and not too pretty.

He swept right. She'd be perfect for a day like today.

Ally-Kat was plenty slutty, though her tits were average. Average size, average nipples, but not too veiny, at least. A solid B. She liked to be on top, to sit straight and sort of bounce up and down while Gabe lay there like a dead fish on her futon mattress. She also liked to chew gum. And talk. She'd talked since the moment she'd opened the door of her Cambridgeport apartment and motioned him in as she finished a phone call. She talked as she pulled her t-shirt off and undid her belt. She talked when she straddled him and told him she wouldn't even *think* about kissing. "Because there is *no way* I am getting a cold sore," she said.

And now, she talked about her mother and her cat and an ex-boyfriend named Rooster and her job as a pediatric resident. "I hate kids, really," she said. "Wiping noses and pink eye? It's not anything like on TV and sometimes I really . . ." She squeaked. "Yup, right there. Sometimes I think I chose the wrong specialty."

Gabe had on two condoms. For protection. And to make this last. He'd have put on a third too, if that hadn't seemed too weird.

"I'm twenty-six," Ally-Kat said. She took the gum out of her mouth and stuck it behind her ear. "I never thought for one second that I'd get to twenty-six and be a doctor and *still* have roommates."

Gabe closed his eyes and pushed away Ally-Kat's high-pitched voice. He thought about the lake, about Sam, about Lila. He could see Lila, in that yellow bikini bottom and tie-dyed t-shirt. He could see the three of them, hiking through the woods past

97

granite and ferns. He could smell the mulch in the air from the forest floor. All they brought with them were cigarettes and beer as they wound their way along the well-worn path till the lake, as blue as a raspberry Slushie, opened in front of them. The cabin's roof had already caved in by then, but the wooden sign announcing Little Comfort hung over the doorway. The dock looked like it might disintegrate beneath their feet. Still, Sam took a running start and leaped off the end into the clear water. He called to them to follow and then swam into the cove.

Lila held her nose and jumped in feetfirst. When she surfaced on her back, Gabe watched as her breasts splayed out on each side and her fifty-cent-piece-sized nipples popped beneath the worn cotton of her t-shirt. *Her* tits got an A.

All Gabe wanted was to lie on the warm planks, to drink his beer, and to watch. Dappled sun shone through birch leaves while Lila sang a few notes from "Pocketful of Sunshine" and pulled herself through the water. Out in the cove, Sam dove deep and came up yards away like a loon. Gabe touched the surface of the lake. Water bugs floated over the concentric ripples that circled out. A sunfish poked at a stone on the lake floor.

Lila treaded water in front of him. She'd taken her hair from the braid, and it floated in an auburn mass behind her. She was beautiful. He handed her an icy can of Coors Light. She asked what he was thinking about, and he shook his head and said nothing. But he was thinking about Lila's legs clinging to his hips, and burying his face in her breasts, and the smell of lake water. He was thinking about fucking her brains out.

Ally-Kat stopped bouncing with one last squeak. "Done?" she asked.

He was. Gabe pulled off the condoms and searched for a place to throw them away.

She pointed to the hallway bathroom, her face suddenly sour. She didn't have much to say anymore either.

"Where are your roommates now?" Gabe asked.

"We're all *doctors*," she said, which really didn't answer the question.

She'd put on an Oxford shirt and boxer shorts. Gabe's fingers brushed her arm, and she winced. He nearly touched her neck. Somehow, somewhere, he'd lost the signs — the sweat, the tingling skin, the pit in his stomach — that distinguished good from bad, that told him he was going too far, though logic and reason could still prevail. He could have broken her neck right then and there and no one would have been the wiser, except for Ally-Kat's parents, whom he imagined as preppy and blond, like her. They'd have learned that their baby was a hookup slut. The police would have been wiser too. They'd have traced Ally-Kat's final call right to Gabe's phone, and then Gabe and Sam would be on the run. No, Gabe reminded himself, he should go. "I should go," he said.

"You think?" she said.

He *should* go.

But . . .

He didn't want to leave. "I love you," he said.

It surprised her. He could tell. It even surprised him a bit, though all he wanted now was to take her away from this house, away from those roommates. Neither of them should have roommates anymore. She let out a laugh, half shock, half — Gabe couldn't tell — delight? He ran a hand through her hair, and then leaned into her, pinning her legs to the mattress. Her heart pounded against his. It made him feel warm. She squirmed. He remembered just in time that she wouldn't kiss. "I don't have cold sores," he said.

She turned her head away, into the pillows. He focused on where her hair had stuck to the pink gum behind her ear. She had tears in her eyes now, which wasn't what he'd wanted. Not at all. "I'm sorry," he said, letting her shove him from her room. "Thanks," he added at the front door. "That was . . . fun."

He went to hug her, and she shrank away. He stood in the doorway for a moment. The falling snow dotted his shoulders and hair. It was dark now. "Is your name Allison or Katherine?" he asked.

"Neither," she said.

He smiled. Flirting. "I bet you're lying."

He stepped out onto the stoop. She slammed the door.

He felt as light as the snow falling around him, lighter than he had in days. He could feel Lila all over again, with her horsy braid and breasts. She'd stayed with him all these years, in spirit at least, and it reminded him that he wasn't alone. There'd been other women. Michelles and Lisas and Amys and Jennifers. So, so many Jennifers. But mostly there'd been Sam. Sam, who said to make a mark, to be someone, to find people who could make it happen, who said do something, anything, besides wander. Sam, who guided Gabe through a world that stretched out like a vast, colorless sea. Sam, who wouldn't let Gabe fade away. He remembered the first time they'd met, in the cafeteria, after Gabe, new again, had spent two weeks wandering the halls of the high school like a shadow. He used the green punch card to pay for his subsidized lunch and sat at the end of a long cafeteria table, where a quartet of basketball players bent over their trays and ate without seeming to breathe. Some kids who got free lunch were targets for ridicule, but not Gabe. Never Gabe. To be bullied, you had to been seen. And Gabe had spent his life observing others and making himself disappear. He'd mastered it. It was his way of surviving.

He could still taste the lunch they'd served that day: turkey and gelatinous gravy, a pile of mushy carrots, an ice-cream scoop of salty white rice. He ate quickly to be sure he got every bite. As he finished, Sam came out of the lunch line and paused to survey the room, and it seemed, to Gabe, as though the cafeteria grew quiet in a gentle wave as Sam walked through the crowd, head high, smiling, as though he knew all eyes would be on him. Gabe also remembered Sam walking straight to where he sat. Almost instinctively, Gabe piled trash onto his tray to leave. He didn't know the rules of the new school yet, and he certainly hadn't mastered where to sit in the cafeteria, but Sam said, "Stay," as he took the seat across from him without asking.

With that, the spell on the room broke. The basketball players went back to eating. The lunch line began to move. Conversation rose to a dull roar. Sam took a bite of his lunch. "This sucks," he said, then shrugged and kept eating. "How have your first two weeks been?"

Gabe hadn't known what to say.

"I'm Sam."

If Gabe could have a found a way to melt away, he would have. He wasn't used to being noticed.

"You're Gabe, right? We're in algebra together."

Gabe nodded. He couldn't find his voice, but at that moment, in that cafeteria, on a day in early March one month after his fourteenth birthday, Gabe felt a wave of joy start in his stomach and spread though his body. He felt as though the sun had shined on him for the first time in his life.

Gabe shouted Sam's name the moment he stepped into the house, even though the air hung with dank emptiness and the smell of ramen. He shuffled his boots across the worn carpet in the front hallway to clean off the ice and snow. In the spring, Gabe and Sam had moved from New York to this ground-level apartment in Davis Square when Sam's relationship with a stockbroker he'd been dating soured. These days, Gabe was supposed to call himself Barry Bellows, even though on the rare occasion that he spoke to anyone, he usually forgot.

He went into the kitchen and opened the fridge, and stood at the laminate counter eating cold pizza from the night before. He checked to see if any of his clients had Slacked him. Gabe worked as a freelance programmer — it was how he and Sam paid for everything, including the car and this apartment — and he could have used some complicated code to debug right then to keep his mind off Ally-Kat and Lila.

And Penelope.

He could have been upset about being rejected earlier. Maybe he should have been. But what, he asked himself, would he have done had Penelope taken him up on the offer to chat? After the pleasantries, he'd have been stuck with nothing to say. Still, he wondered what she'd have called him after their third date? *Sweetheart,* maybe? Or *darling* if she was pretentious, and he thought that maybe she was. She probably wanted a loft apartment with stainless-steel appliances. Really, he told himself, he'd dodged a bullet.

He paced around the kitchen. If he went by Penelope's house, her roommate wouldn't be home yet. Maybe he'd misunderstood her earlier. Maybe there'd been too many people around or her boss was watching or maybe she wanted to play hard-to-get and he hadn't known to play.

Maybe he should go on Tinder again.

He went to his room to light up. His stash was empty. He crossed over to Sam's room, even though Sam never had pot of his own. The room reeked of neatness, a dry blast of control, weights lined up for tomorrow's workout, the beginnings of a diorama of trinkets from this Somerville life spread across the dresser: a shot glass, a nip of cocaine. They'd left similar displays behind before. Gabe texted Cricket to order a half ounce, and she said she was close by.

And then the front door opened.

It was Sam.

Sam's arms were laden with fancy bags that he tossed on the floor, boxes spilling out. He ripped open the boxes and threw silky clothes in the air. He was talking about a woman and a benefit and a town car, and

Gabe didn't care. He could barely hear any of it. He was too happy not to be alone.

"Dance with me," Sam said, and Gabe shook his head but danced anyway. Like he always did. It was too hard to say no. Too easy to let Sam take the lead.

Sam put a hand on his waist and spun him around the room and then ripped open another box. "Hermès!" he said, holding up the tag on a pair of black pants.

When Cricket showed up, Gabe paid for the pot even though Sam chastised him for ordering it via text. "It leaves a trail," Sam said, but that didn't keep him from lying on Gabe's bed and taking a long hit from the bong. "I think we can make Boston work," he said. "This can be home."

All of Sam's hopes, all of his wants and needs, were on full display. Always. The desperate need to belong, to be a part of some place. But you had to look. It surprised Gabe that more people didn't see that. Gabe lit the buds and inhaled. He heard the water gurgle, and felt the smoke tickle his lungs, and held it there as long as he could.

"Things are good," Sam said. "Really good."

Things had been good before, but Gabe pushed that thought away. When Sam was here, it was all that mattered.

The doorbell rang. Sam had fallen asleep, but Gabe crept into the hall and put the chain on, a habit he'd gotten into when they'd lived in a crack den in San Francisco. He drew the deadbolt and opened the door an inch. A miniature woman with square glasses, ruddy cheeks, and long black hair poking from a jaunty beret stood on the stoop in the weak afternoon light. A little girl dressed in pink from head to toe clutched her hand. And a basset hound sat at her feet.

"Hester Thursby," the woman said. "I'm here to see the apartment."

Gabe slammed the door and took off the chain. He opened the door wide as a blast of cold air swept into the hallway. The snow had stopped. He saw the woman sniff. The whole house must stink of pot. She adjusted an expensive looking orange bag over her shoulder. "Is it still available?" she asked as she stepped inside. "Nice," she said, though the crease in her forehead said anything but.

"This apartment isn't for rent."

"Really?" Hester said. "I swore this was the address."

The girl pulled on Hester's sleeve. "Pee," she said.

"Here," Hester said, handing Gabe the dog's leash. "Do you mind? And take this too. There are dog treats in there." She gave him the orange bag. "Where's the bathroom?"

Gabe paused, and then nodded down the hallway. "Through the kitchen."

"Thanks. You can't imagine how quickly these emergencies escalate."

Then she hurried away and left Gabe standing in the hallway. The dog whined while nosing the bag. Gabe ran his hands over the orange leather. He searched the pockets, caressing a wad of receipts. He found a plastic bag filled with dog biscuits, but kept searching anyway. He snapped open a wallet. He trailed his finger through her change. He took out her license and memorized her address. She lived right here in Somerville. If Sam had been the one pawing through the bag, he'd have taken something small to add to his collection, something like a pen or a lipstick. Gabe had more discretion. He gave half a biscuit to the dog as Hester and the girl returned from the bathroom. He blushed suddenly at the thought of her seeing the kitchen, with its dirt-crusted counters and cabinets the color of an old toenail. He shouldn't live like this anymore.

"He was whining," Gabe said, handing her the open bag. Even though she'd told him about the dog biscuits, he knew he still looked guilty. He dropped the second half of the biscuit to the floor as if to make the point.

"She," Hester said. "Her name's Waffles." She took the leash and the bag. "And sorry to bother you . . ."

Gabe waited for her to finish her sentence, and then realized she was waiting for him to fill the silence. But with what? "Are you a vegetarian?" he asked.

"Not at all," she said. "Why?"

"Because I'm tired of vegetarians."

"Okay," Hester said, and then laughed in a way that made her seem complicit and kind. "I hadn't thought about it that way. So am I."

Gabe smiled. She smiled back and glanced toward the front door, and for a moment he saw himself through her eyes: a tall guy who'd forgotten to shave, who spent most waking hours alone, staring at code on a computer, who had bloodshot eyes. She, on the other hand, could have been a doll, with that porcelain skin and silken hair. She wore a fringed suede vest, gray wool leggings, and a miniature miniskirt. Her legs, in their own tiny way, went on for miles and ended in a pair of go-go boots that didn't look like they'd stand up to the snow. An American Girl for the boho chic. A part of Gabe wanted to touch her, to run his fingers through her hair, to see if she was real. He clasped his hands behind his back to be safe. "Do you like tacos?" he asked.

"Doesn't everyone like tacos? Except vegans, I guess."

"I had one for lunch. With steak."

"A vegan?" Hester asked.

"No, a taco," Gabe said.

Hester smiled. "I know," she said, and after a pause, added, "Have you lived here long?"

"A while," Gabe said.

"Me too. In Somerville, at least. I was thinking of moving to Davis Square, but rents are expensive around here."

"Even for dumps like this one," Gabe said.

"Let the woman get on with her day."

Gabe hadn't noticed Sam come out of the room to stand next to him, but with his presence Gabe instantly felt himself fade into the background. Sam's hair stood up from lying down, but Gabe could see Hester take him in. Women — even most men — paused when they saw Sam for the first time.

"This is . . ." Gabe began. What was he

110

supposed to call Sam again?

"Aaron," Sam said. "I bet Barry didn't introduce himself either. He gets tongue-tied around women."

"Not around me," Hester said, lifting the orange bag onto her shoulder. "Aaron and Barry?"

"That's right," Sam said.

"Well, thanks for the bathroom."

"Any time," Sam said.

"And sorry for the mix-up. I'll have to get the right address from my real estate agent."

Fresh air swept into the house as Sam pulled open the door. Gabe watched as Hester headed down the front steps with the little girl and the dog pulling on its leash. The scent of evergreen wafted over him from a wreath on the front door. He smelled pine and composting leaves. He tasted sweet lake water on his lips and remembered stroking forward, deeper, into the cold dark until his lungs felt like they would burst. Above him, he saw the moon, a blur of white against black. He remembered Lila, whom he'd called Ms. Blaine for way too long. She'd called him Sport or Curly or, his favorite, Big Guy.

Now, Gabe watched as Hester walked down the path to the chain-link gate and out to an enormous blue truck. She stepped onto the running board to put the girl into her car seat. Gabe wondered if she'd be tall enough to get into the truck, let alone drive it. Maybe she'd need his help.

"Don't be a fucktard," Sam said, following his stare, an edge of warning in his tone. "Come back to earth. Let's smoke some dope." When Gabe ignored him, Sam added, "Have I mentioned Felicia Nakazawa? I'm going to the Burren with her later. Come. I'll introduce the two of you. Don't you like Asian chicks? She's kind of needy, a bit chunky, is hung up on another guy, and sort of thinks the whole world is out to get her, but you can deal with that better than I can. I'll set you guys up." Sam put a hand on Gabe's arm. "And let's be honest. You could use a good screw!"

Gabe shook him off.

"Come on, Gabe. She has a kid. Women with kids usually have husbands at home."

Even if Sam was right, all Gabe wanted was for Hester to turn and wave to him, even though a part of him knew it would be better for her if she didn't, and even though girls with bags that expensive rarely looked back.

Then she did.

CHAPTER 7

Hester felt Gabe watching her from his front stoop as she drove around the corner and pulled to the side of the road. She'd felt Gabe's eyes on her the entire time she'd been in that house, from the moment he'd peeked through the crack in the door to when she'd grabbed what looked like a piece of junk mail on the kitchen counter and stuffed it in her pocket, to when she'd found him going through her bag. From what she'd been able to tell, Gabe wore his awkwardness like a sweater for anyone to see. It almost made him likable, while Sam was nothing but veneer and caution. He'd held her off from the moment he'd seen her, snapping into an upper-class politeness that seemed more home-schooled than innate. Gabe would be the easier one to get to know.

She jotted down the name *Aaron Gewirtz-man,* which poked out from beneath the cellophane window on the envelope. "All's well that ends well, right?" she said to Kate as she rooted through the bag to see if anything was missing.

"All's wheel ends wheel," Kate said to Monkey.

Hester had followed Sam from Beacon Hill and then sat outside the apartment for nearly an hour before knocking on the front door. Now, she typed a text to Lila that simply said, *Found them!* but looked at the screen, her thumb hovering over the send button, and then hit delete. Not yet, she told herself. She was curious to see what else she could find out.

At home, she put Kate down for a nap and took the baby monitor with her to her own apartment, where she sorted through the postcards again and spent some time searching online for "Aaron Gewirtzman," without much luck. She tried it with Sam's date of birth and Social Security number. Still nothing. When she narrowed the search to New York, she did get a number of Aaron Gewirtzmans, including the obituary for a twenty-five-year-old who'd died in a car crash last winter. Sam must have stolen the man's identity, but without a Social Security number it would be hard to prove. She slid *Prom Night* into the VCR and nestled into the love seat. Waffles shimmied through the dog door and jumped up beside her, and soon Hester's eyes had closed, and she'd fallen into a deep, dreamless sleep.

When she woke a while later, the movie had ended and the smells and laughs from an evening at home wafted up the stairwell. The baby monitor was silent, so Morgan must have turned it off on the other end to let her relax. It was dark out, and Hester wondered how long she'd been asleep. She stretched, making these few precious moments alone last. Waffles woke and lapped her face. Hester listened to Kate shriek with laughter and Morgan's deep voice, and felt like she actually might be missing something. "Come," she said to the dog, and the two of them pattered down the stairs.

When Hester opened Morgan's door, she let the sights and sounds envelope her: Kate's stuffed animals lined up for a party, Morgan's red hair poking out from a top hat, a pot of chili bubbling on the stove. Behind them, the Christmas tree, the first one Hester had ever put up, was alight with colorful bulbs. Waffles joined in the festivities as she howled in delight.

They made macaroni and cheese from a box to have with the chili, and then sat in Kate's bed and read four stories in a row, ending with *The Cat in the Hat.*

"Do you need the truck tomorrow?" Hester asked, as Kate drifted off to sleep.

Morgan slipped out from under Kate's comforter and tucked it in around her. "All yours," he said. "I'll take the bus in the morning, but can you take the dog with you?"

"That I can do," Hester said. "Kate has preschool tomorrow. Can you drop her off?"

"Not a problem."

"Pick up too?"

"Yep, I can do that."

This, these negotiations, was Hester's life now. She kissed Kate on the forehead and turned out the bedside light. Something about the darkness made it easier to talk. "Have you heard from Daphne?" she asked.

Morgan took a moment to answer. "Nothing. Have you looked for her?"

Hester could feel the sadness in Morgan's voice seeping into the air around them, and she wanted him to be more than sad. She wanted him to be angry or hurt or betrayed. She wanted him to react. To engage. To be part of what was going on, like she had had to be every day. When Daphne had first left, Morgan had insisted that they'd take on the challenges of raising Kate together, but since then Hester had been the one to take a leave of absence from work. She was the one who woke at night and spent her days worrying. Morgan was close to his sister in a way that Hester would never understand. He'd tried to shield Daphne from her own demons for years, and this, all of this, Hester suspected, made him feel as though he'd failed.

"You know she doesn't want us to find her," Hester said. "I'd have looked if I thought she did. But aren't you worried? What if something happened? What if she's hurt?"

Morgan wrapped his arms around her, and they stood together quietly. "We'd know if she was hurt," he said. "And I can't think about it too much."

But we need to, Hester nearly said. Eventually, at least. If we don't, this will eat away at us till there's nothing left. She thought about where Daphne might be, living in a hovel like Sam and Gabe's apartment, one that smelled of cheap weed and masturbation. She thought about the hours of pickup and drop off and play dates and soccer practices, all the things she'd never signed up for and didn't know if she wanted. But Morgan kissed her neck and ran a hand under her sweater, and she went with it. It was easier that way. She pulled his face to hers, kissing him hard, feeling the day-old scruff of his beard against her skin. She let him lift her to the bedroom, where their clothes fell to the floor. He laid her on the bed, his hands and tongue finding the right places, and then she thrust him onto his back to find the right places on his long, lithe body. Waffles jumped up beside them, her cold, wet nose jabbing at Hester's naked buttock. They laughed, the spell broken for a moment while Hester shooed the dog out of the room and closed the door.

"I'll spend the rest of my days with you, Mrs.," Morgan whispered when she returned to the warmth of the bed. He rolled on top of her and slid gently inside her.

"Me too," she said, closing her eyes and staying in the moment. They'd be fine. She believed that she and Morgan were strong enough to survive anything. For now, at least.

"You'll make her laugh," Sam said.

Gabe wondered if he'd ever made anyone laugh.

"Felicia will like you, and if it's lame, you can be home in five minutes."

Sam hadn't said one nice thing about this Felicia Nakazawa since he'd mentioned her — needy, chubby, paranoid — but he stood in Gabe's bedroom door and had that look he got when he wouldn't take no for an answer, so Gabe got ready to go. At the bar, Sam breezed past the bouncers and through the heavy red door while Gabe stopped to pay the ten-dollar cover charge for both of them. The Burren was a cavernous pub in the heart of Davis Square that served salty Irish food, and where bands played and hipsters drank and the walls were painted black. Gabe supposed that if he belonged anywhere, it could have been here. There was enough flannel, and almost all the men seemed to have beards. Tonight, a folk rock group tried their best to sound mournful over the rhythms of banjos and accordions.

Felicia showed up an hour late, wearing a slash of red lipstick and teetering on heels like they were a pair of stilts. She paused in the doorway and brushed imaginary lint from the sleeves of her cashmere coat. Gabe was pretty certain she didn't frequent bars like this one. Sam waved her over, and she kissed him on both cheeks. "Classy place," she said.

"This is Barry," Sam said.

Gabe noticed her smile falter. After they shook hands, he saw her shoot Sam a glare in between checking her phone and asking Gabe to repeat himself whenever he said anything. "The music's loud," she shouted.

Gabe asked her how old she was.

"What?" she asked.

He excused himself and went to the bathroom, and when he got back the band had taken a break and the bar was blessedly quiet, something Felicia apparently hadn't noticed. "Jesus Christ, he looks like the Goddamned Unabomber," she shouted. "Was this supposed to be a fucking setup? Are you serious? Thanks for nothing."

Gabe slid into his chair, and she had the decency to blush. "What do you do, Barry?" she said after a silence.

"Clean up other people's messes," Gabe said.

"Sounds like what I do too," Felicia said.

"You hardly clean up messes, either of you," Sam said. "Barry's a programmer. And he makes a fortune."

"Maybe you can help me with Wendy's website," Felicia said.

"Sure," Gabe said, but he couldn't have cared less about Felicia Nakazawa or what she thought of him. He already had a girl. At least he hoped he did.

Hester jolted awake. Morgan snored softly beside her. Kate yammered away on the other end of the monitor. Hester groaned and then changed into her pajamas and crossed the hallway to Kate's room, where the kid sat chatting away with Monkey. "Kate want water," she said.

"And then what?" Hester asked.

"Play game?"

"How about sleep?"

"No sleep!"

"We at least have to play quietly. Let's not wake Uncle Morgan."

"Kate want water." Kate stood and jumped on the bed. Waffles wagged her tail and joined her.

"Well, Aunt Hester wants scotch." They were at the beginning of a long, sleepless night. "Come. We'll watch *The Little Mermaid.*"

Waffles pattered after them as Hester carried Kate down the stairs, through Morgan's living room, and into her apartment, where she put a videotape of the movie into the VCR and snuggled in with Kate. By the time they sang "Under the Sea" together, Kate's eyes had begun to close. She didn't make it to the end of the song. Hester, unfortunately, was wide awake.

She took out her tablet and reviewed her notes. What she hadn't told Morgan was that she planned to drive to New Hampshire in the morning. Maybe she'd talk to Lila, but there were two other people she wanted to talk to first: Cheryl Jenkins, the woman Gabe had lived with before he moved in with Lila and Sam, and Bobby Englewood, his social worker. Maybe they'd have a different take on this story. She found their addresses and mapped out her route. Then she put the tablet aside and wondered if she'd manage to sleep before the end of the movie.

Gabe pulled up her Facebook page. Again. She was the only Hester Thursby in the entire Facebook world. She had enough privacy settings in place so that all he could see was a single photo of her, on a summer day, sitting on a beach. Her hair was loose and fell around her shoulders. She'd traded in the black-rimmed glasses for shades. She looked happy. He thought about friending her, but then thought better of it. Besides, she shouldn't know who "Gabe DiPursio" was.

He changed quietly to keep from waking Sam in the other room. They'd left the bar an hour earlier, sending Felicia off toward Boston in the back of an Uber. Now, it was well after midnight, and Sam would be angry if he knew what Gabe was doing. Outside, the night was crisp and clear, with stars blanketing the sky. Snow crunched under his feet as he hurried through the darkened streets and checked the address he'd memorized, barely feeling the cold as he descended the hill into Union Square. She lived in a blue house with a chain-link fence, a neatly shoveled front path, and a mahogany door. He snuck up the path and onto the stoop, where he took out a flashlight and read the names on the three mailboxes. There she was, on the third floor. He ran a finger over her name, THURSBY.

What would she think if she saw him here, checking to see if the doors were locked; going through junk mail she'd dumped in a blue recycling bin; stuffing a credit card offer into his pocket because it had her name on it; taking fifteen minutes to find the spare key hidden in a plastic rock in a bed in the backyard? Would she see a kindred spirit, one who wandered the streets at night and watched from the outside? Probably not. He knew in his heart that if she saw him here she wouldn't feel anything beyond rage and fear. They never did. But knowing couldn't keep him from hoping.

He slid the key into the lock and turned it quietly. No alarm system. A smile started in the pit of his stomach and exploded up his spine and onto his face. The stairs creaked the tiniest bit on his way up to the second floor. He ran his hand over the door to the third floor and found a spare key right where he thought it would be, but the apartment was unlocked anyway. He turned the knob slowly and looked up the steep, carpeted stairs. He imagined her asleep. He wondered what she wore to bed, pajamas or an oversize t-shirt?

Nothing?

He wondered what she did with the child.

As Gabe stood in the hallway, the dog padded to the top of the stairs, its long ears nearly hitting the floor. She woofed softly as though considering whether to be a friend or foe, and then waddled down, tail wagging as Gabe crouched and offered his hand. She sniffed and let Gabe scratch her neck. She probably remembered the biscuit and hoped for another. "Quite the watchdog," Gabe whispered.

He tested the first step. It was quiet, no squeaking. He took two more and could hear the low hum of a TV. The dog bounded up the stairs in front of him, and then turned to welcome him, tongue hanging from the side of her mouth. Gabe crept up the few remaining stairs quickly, to where the flashing from a faux-wood nineteen-inch TV was the only light in the tiny apartment.

The Little Mermaid was playing.

Even in the near dark, Gabe could see that the apartment was a mess, with stacks of papers and books nearly everywhere. He could also see her, lying on a threadbare love seat in a nest of blankets, sound asleep, with the little girl lying across her chest. Gabe stepped closer. He reached toward her, daring himself to stroke her cheek, to wake her, to say hello. He'd have to put a hand to her mouth to keep her from screaming.

The little girl moved. Her eyes opened, and she sat up, her mop of curls lit up by the light from the TV.

Then the dog jumped onto the sofa beside Hester and pawed at her chest, and Gabe managed to retreat into the shadows as her eyes popped open. "Waffles," she mumbled. "Go to sleep."

"Aunt Hester," the girl said. "Man here."

"Shh," Hester mumbled. "It's the TV."

She rolled over, even as the dog followed Gabe down the stairs in his retreat. Gabe scratched its neck one more time and then shut the door with a gentle click and left. He'd return another time.

Outside, he stood quietly on the sidewalk for a few moments till the corner of one of the curtains on the third floor moved aside.

It was the little girl. Gabe waved. She waved back shyly. Then he stepped away and melted into the darkness, running to Highland Street, his boots pounding on the pavement. He ran all the way home, and when he got there, he dashed into his bedroom and crawled beneath the blankets, exhausted for the first time in months.

He imagined Hester sleeping beside him, a soft snore keeping him awake in a way that he hoped would never end. He imagined her as she'd been today, that beret clinging to the side of her head, and the girl clutching her hand. He imagined a family. He wanted a wife and kids more than anything. He wanted a house with a pitched roof, a tree on one side and a driveway on the other, and a yard for the dog to play in. He wanted to bike to a boring job and take family trips to Disney World.

She had all of that, except for him.

And she looked curious and smart and crafty and fun. She looked beautiful. She looked like everything Gabe had ever wanted.

CHAPTER 8

The gray sky hemmed in the White Mountains as Hester pulled the truck off Route 93 and headed east toward New Hampshire's lake country. Waffles slobbered on the passenger's-side window beside her. It was early, maybe too early after a long night with Kate, and the drive from Somerville had taken an hour and a half. The road snaked past a series of Dunkin' Donuts and gun shops, through towns of clapboard-covered farmhouses and forests of pine, knotted maple, and white birch. The GPS led her a few miles from the highway, and then around the perimeter of Lake Winnipesaukee, and into the foothills.

Once Hester got to Holderness, she turned down a dirt road that led to a rundown motel on the opposite side of the street from the lake. The motel had a neon sign missing some letters, and tiny outbuildings. It was the kind of place where people

127

didn't stay anymore. A rusty Civic with two Bush-Cheney bumper stickers sat in the rutted driveway. This was Cheryl Jenkins's motel. Hester had thought about calling ahead before coming and then had opted for surprise instead. Now that she was here — now that she saw that it was the kind of place that showed up in the horror movies she watched — she wondered if that had been a mistake. At the very least, she was glad she'd left Kate with Morgan.

She took the keys from the ignition. Across the street, the lake had frozen over into a thick sheet of gray that stretched almost to the horizon. Snow from earlier in the week covered the shoreline, which was dotted with a mixture of sand and trees. Hester still wasn't sure what she wanted to ask this woman, but, more than anything, she hoped to get a better sense of who Sam was as a person, and why he and Gabe had run away. Even more so, Hester wondered why Sam and Gabe had stuck together all these years and through all these moves. Part of that story must lie here. She knocked on a door to a small house with a sign that read "Guest Registration" over it. She heard the patter of footsteps. A thin woman in a flowered bathrobe opened the door a crack. She must have been in her mid-fifties, and had wispy, graying hair falling to her shoulders. "Can I help you?" she said in a girlish singsong.

"Cheryl Jenkins?" Hester asked.

"Yes, but I don't have any money, whatever you're selling." She smiled like someone who'd brushed off years of Girl Scouts cookies. "And if you're looking for a room, we're closed for the season."

"I'm not selling anything," Hester said. "I have some questions, though. About a foster kid who stayed with you a while back."

"I've had dozens of kids stay with me," Cheryl said. "Some of them I remember better than others." She laughed and added, "But mostly I remember the bad ones."

"This boy's name was Gabe DiPursio. Do you remember him?"

The smile faded from the woman's eyes for an instant, then returned in full force. She glanced over her shoulder into the house and pulled her robe closed as if realizing for the first time that she wasn't dressed. "What do you want with him?"

"Could I come in?"

"I don't think so."

"I'll only take a minute of your time. I have a few questions."

"And I don't want to answer them."

Hester smiled and shrugged, making

herself look as unthreatening as possible, which wasn't much of a stretch. Daphne had always told her that was one of her strengths, but when it didn't seem to work with Cheryl, she said, "I drove all the way from Boston."

"And you can drive right back." She went to slam the door.

"I met Gabe yesterday," Hester said quickly, which seemed to catch Cheryl off guard.

"And where's that?" she asked.

"Down in Boston. In Somerville, really."

"Are you telling me he's only been in Massachusetts all these years?"

"No," Hester said. "He's lived all over the place."

"So you met him yesterday, and decided to hop in your car and drive to an abandoned motel to speak to me? He must have had good things to say about me."

"He didn't have anything to say about you."

Cheryl lifted her chin. She was quiet, her silence smoldering, but she finally gave in. "Wait here."

The door slammed shut, and from outside, Hester could hear footsteps moving away, then the one-sided hum of Cheryl's voice on the phone. When the door opened again, she'd changed into a red Christmas sweater and a pair of green sweatpants. "I'll give you five minutes," she said.

"Do you mind the dog?"

"Whatever."

They passed through the registration office and into a small kitchenette behind it. The house was clean and tidy, efficient yet surprisingly spacious. Christmas lights hung along the tops of the cabinets, and out in the living room an artificial tree was covered in gold and red balls. Fox News bellowed from a sixty-four-inch television set as, Hester suspected, it did most of the day. Cheryl filled a kettle and put it on an electric burner. She was a bird of a woman, someone whose hands always moved, from her thin hair to the bobbles on her sweater, to the appliances on the kitchen counter. Even after she'd made two mugs of instant coffee and topped Hester's off with Cremora and sugar, she could barely keep from straightening anything within reach.

"Gabe DiPursio," she finally said. "Of all the kids that stayed with me, he was not one I expected to hear about again. Not from someone like you, at least. I mean, you're not a cop, are you? You don't look like a cop, but these days you never know."

"Imagine me as a cop," Hester said. "I

don't think they'd let me fill out the application! But why would you think I was a cop?"

"Just curious. But mostly I'm curious why you're curious."

"Gabe stayed with you, right?" Hester said. "Where? Here?"

"You first," Cheryl said.

She still smiled, and her voice still skipped from word to word. She put her mug down on the coffee table, then moved a coaster under it. She straightened a pile of magazines, forcing Hester to fill the silence. "Gabe went to live with another family after you, right? He went to live with Lila Blaine and her brother."

"I wouldn't say *family*," Cheryl said. "*I* had a family. That house was more like a big-boobed tart and her faggot brother."

The rage in Cheryl's voice caught Hester off guard. She took a sip of her coffee and set the mug down. "Lila Blaine hired me," she said. "To find her brother, Sam. The boy Gabe ran away with. I found Gabe too."

"Those two are still together. What? Are they a couple?"

"I don't think so," Hester said. "At least not from what I saw, but you never know. Did you think there was something going on between them when they were kids?"

"Not between them," Cheryl said. "A lot happened that summer. And a lot of it wasn't good." Hester nearly asked her to elaborate, but now that Cheryl had started, it was as though she couldn't stop. "I didn't always live here," she said. "I used to have a house down the street too. A nice house, with a barn and animals. Cats. Dogs." She scratched Waffles behind the ears. "The house was big, with lots of room for kids and family. I sometimes had eight foster kids staying with me at the same time. And it wasn't for the money. I'm not one of those awful people you hear about on the news. It was for those kids! It was fun, and full of life, and every single day felt like a day at camp and, well, it was a good time in my life. It's a time that I miss." She looked out the window at the barren lakeshore in the distance. "And then it wasn't."

"What happened?"

"Gabe happened. He went to live with that Blaine woman without telling me."

"He went to live with her and you didn't know?"

"Now you do sound like the cops," Cheryl said. "You sound like they did that summer. I had seven other kids staying with me. I'd say where's Gabe, and one of them would say he's over at the Blaines' house. I'd call, they'd say everything is fine and dandy, and I'd say, right, come home when you like, or stay if you like. I'd ask Lila if she was fine with him staying there, if she needed anything from me, and she'd say, nope, we have it all covered. That went on for a week, then two weeks, then two months, and then he ran away and let's just say . . ." Cheryl lowered her voice. "The shit hit the fan."

"That must have been terrible for you," Hester said. "I'm sorry. I shouldn't make you rehash this."

Cheryl seemed grateful for the small kindness. "It was," she said. "It was the worst thing that ever happened to me. I lost all my kids. And then I had to hire a lawyer because Gabe's junkie parents listed me in a suit against the state, and that meant I lost my house. And all along, Lila was sitting pretty down the road. She still has her lake house too. How much do you think that place is worth now? Do you know how much this dump would be worth with a bit of shorefront?"

The smile had left Cheryl's face, and her voice had lost its spring. Hester tried to imagine how she'd have felt in Cheryl's place. She'd have been angry and resentful, maybe even vengeful, but to her, Cheryl simply seemed resigned. "Will you see him again?" Cheryl asked. "Gabe?"

"I don't know," Hester said.

"My advice would be to stay as far away from him as you can." Cheryl leaned forward. "I had a lot of kids come through my house over the years. Probably thirty or forty in all. Some of them were sweet, others were angry. Some were sad. I could deal with any of those types. Angry was even my specialty. But Gabe was something else. He wasn't anything. Having him in the house was like living with an empty shell. I could never tell if he was waiting to be filled up, or if it was even possible to find something to fill him with. If one of my cats had gone missing, Gabe was the first kid I'd'a pointed the finger at. I thought he'd be dead or in jail by now."

Note to self, Hester thought, don't bring Kate to that house in Davis Square again. "So you were glad he went to stay with Lila?"

"Not glad. *Relieved* might be a better word."

"And why didn't you go to family services and get him another placement?"

"Who says I didn't try? Finding a placement for a fourteen-year-old isn't easy, especially one who's been in and out of the system so many times. Honestly, I wish I'd listened to my instincts and insisted. None of this would have happened if I had."

Waffles lifted her head and barked. A few seconds later, a car pulled into the driveway outside. Hester glanced through the window to see an ancient teal-colored hatchback blocking in her own truck. A moment later, the kitchen door slammed open, and a wiry man wearing a sheepskin coat came in.

"Bobby," Cheryl said. "This is Hester Thursby. She knows Gabe."

Bobby Englewood. He'd been the next person on Hester's list to visit. She watched as he shut the door behind him without showing the slightest sign of surprise at the mention of Gabe's name. She knew he lived down the street from Cheryl, in Moulton-borough, and worked for a private agency placing children in foster homes. He must have been the one on the other end of the phone a few moments earlier. He was in his mid-thirties and had the look of a man who thought a lot about his hair but never quite got it right. He had a guarded confidence and seemed the antithesis of any social worker Hester had ever met. This guy, she suspected, had roamed the hallways in high school like a predator and had done any-thing but protect the weak. He also smelled like a bar. As he stepped into the living room, Cheryl's house suddenly felt crowded, and there was a palpable tension as he glanced from Cheryl to Hester, a tension so thick Waffles howled toward the ceiling. Hester put a hand on the dog's collar to quiet her.

"Cute," Bobby said. He let Waffles sniff his hand, and then scratched her neck. She left Hester's side and rubbed up against his leg.

"Very discerning," Hester said, to lighten the mood, but Cheryl's hands had begun to flutter again. She touched a magazine and her hair and picked up her empty mug and put it down.

"I don't want to take up any more of your time," Hester said.

"But I just got here," Bobby said.

"You're blocking my truck."

"Yeah, sorry about that."

Hester couldn't tell if he meant it as a threat. She felt in her pocket for her phone. How long would it take the police to get out here? Did the Holderness police department even have more than one deputy? "Could you move it?"

"Maybe."

Bobby leaned against the wall like he was practicing his James Dean moves.

"And maybe not?" Hester asked.

He raised an eyebrow and winked at her.

"Quit it, Bobby. You're being a jerk," Cheryl said, sniffing the air around him. "And have you been drinking? It's not even ten o'clock in the morning." Her voice, surprisingly strong, seemed to cow Bobby for a moment. "She's harmless, okay. Completely harmless. She knows Lila Blaine. She's been looking for that brother of hers and stumbled on Gabe. Turns out Gabe lives down in Boston."

"Good ol' Lila," Bobby said, cupping his hands at his chest.

"I got it," Hester said. "She has big tits."

"Pocket-size here has a temper."

Hester took a step toward him, and when he laughed, Cheryl stepped between them and led Bobby to the sofa. "Sit down and drink some coffee. Maybe it'll sober you up and make you human again. She barely knows Gabe. Met him yesterday. Came here today," she added in a way that made Hester feel as though she was feeding Bobby cues. "Come and sit down, sweetie. He's a jerk, but he's harmless."

Hester perched on the arm of a chair. Waffles jumped up beside her and tried to climb on her lap. "I'll stay," Hester said. "But don't call me 'pocket-size' and don't call me 'sweetie,' and you can either move your little go-cart when I'm ready to leave or I'll drive my truck right over it. Got it?"

Bobby let out a long belch.

"Honestly, Bobby, you'd think you were raised by wolves," Cheryl said.

"Wasn't I?"

"Oh, do shut up," Cheryl said. She took a sip of her coffee. "What's Lila want with that boy anyway?" she asked. "Her brother? She didn't seem very concerned when he disappeared. I figured she knew where he was all along. Didn't you, Bobby?"

Bobby shrugged and seemed to resign himself to having a civil discussion. "It sure would have helped if she'd offered up some information then. I don't know if she knew where those kids went or not, but I can guarantee she was thrilled they were gone. Lila's not exactly the nurturing type. She didn't tell anyone they'd left for weeks. She said she figured they'd turn up and only got worried when they didn't come back in time for school."

That answered Hester's question about how hard Lila had looked for her brother. After all, it had only taken Hester a couple of days to find him. "Did she ever tell anyone about these?" she asked, taking the postcards from her bag and quickly explaining where they'd come from.

"That little cunt," Bobby said under his breath as he thumbed through the cards.

"I'll take that as a no," Hester said.

"Yeah, that's a no. She knew all along where they'd gone?"

"At least since the cards started coming," Hester said. "What else can you tell me about Lila?"

Bobby let out a sigh. "Got a beer?" he asked. "I could use a drink."

"Not at this time of the day," Cheryl said.

"Cheryl here is always looking out for my best interest," Bobby said, "whether I want her to or not."

"No one else does," Cheryl said.

"It's good to have friends, right?" Hester said.

"When you want 'em," Bobby said.

"So tell me about Lila," Hester said. "Was she ever a friend?"

"Not exactly," Bobby said. "She was a year behind me in high school, and we dated for a while. Went to the prom together, but I wouldn't say we ever actually liked each other. She knew how to party, I'll tell you that much. We went to Plymouth State together too, her first year, at least. She had to drop out when her parents died."

"And how did she take that?"

"I'm not really sure," Bobby said. "We

140

weren't exactly on speaking terms by then. I fucked that one up in the way only a horny teenager can."

Hester returned the postcards to her bag. She asked a few more questions but didn't learn anything she didn't already know. Finally, she pulled a business card out. "I've taken up enough of your time. Call me if you think of anything. And thanks for your help."

"I'm not sure if we helped much," Cheryl said.

"More than you know," Hester said, putting her coat on and heading toward the door with Waffles in tow.

"I'll move my car," Bobby said, grabbing his keys, but outside he didn't seem in a rush. He leaned against the cab of Hester's truck and ran a hand through his hair, and in that move, Hester could see him as a high school student, all confidence and swagger. He'd have been a boy whose attention Hester would have yearned for, and hated herself for craving it. Even now, it annoyed her to find him attractive.

"It's cold," Hester said, her breath freezing as she spoke. "And I should get going."

"Nice ride," Bobby said. "An F-150. How do you even drive this thing? Are you big enough to reach the pedals?"

"I manage," Hester said. "I move the seat close and turn off the airbag. But thanks for pointing out my height. I love it when people do that."

"What does one of these things go for? Thirty grand? Forty?"

"I don't know. It's my boyfriend's. He uses it for work. I don't even own a car. I don't really need one in the city."

Bobby looked toward Cheryl's house, then out over the lake. "Sorry I was such an ass-hole inside," he said. "We're close-knit around here. We watch out for each other, and when Cheryl called, I guess I thought she might be in some trouble again. Hearing that DiPursio kid's name dredged up bad memories."

"Happens to the best of us," Hester said. "And apology accepted. How do you even know Cheryl?"

"We go way back. I lived with her in high school. She's always watched out for me. She made sure I went to college."

Suddenly their relationship made more sense, the subtle give-and-take, the way Cheryl could scold Bobby without eliciting any anger. "You came through the foster system?" Hester asked. "You were one of her kids."

"Yeah. And sometimes I feel like I still

am." Bobby turned his gaze from the lake to Hester. "Tell me. Why's Lila interested in those boys again after all these years? Why now?"

Hester still had that same question, no matter what Lila had claimed. "She told me she's selling her lake property. Half the money belongs to Sam."

"Is that what she told you?" Bobby said. "Are you sure this isn't about the body?"

Hester felt the cold creep into her coat as a chill ran down her spine.

"The one they found over by where Lila lives," Bobby said. "It's all they've written about in the news this week. They dug it out of a shallow grave on Saturday."

The same day Lila had called Hester.

CHAPTER 9

Hester pulled into the icy driveway and cut the engine. Lila Blaine's house was old, with a ragged stone wall that ran along the snow-encrusted property. Two outbuildings that looked like they might collapse leaned along the back of the yard, where a horse stuck its head from its stall and a brood of hens huddled together against the cold. Hester smelled smoke from a wood fire and for a moment heard only the gentle silence of winter. Then Waffles sat up, her bay joining a chorus of barks coming from inside the house. The side door opened. Five dogs ranging in size from small pony to teacup charged into the yard. The largest of the dogs leaped at the truck door as Lila followed, that braid hanging over one shoulder and a rifle cocked and ready to fire.

Hester sank into her seat. She rolled the window down an inch, as Waffles clawed across her lap. "It's me. Hester Thursby.

144

Sorry for the surprise."

Lila snapped her fingers and the dogs surrounded her. She patted the biggest one, which looked like a cross between a Saint Bernard and a bear. "This one's Samantha," she said. "Then Professor, Taco, Ace. The littlest one is Soccer Ball. He's the meanest of the bunch."

"And the gun?" Hester asked. "What's that called?"

"Clovis here? Ah, don't worry about her." Lila cracked the rifle and showed Hester the empty chamber. "She's not even loaded, though I have some slugs in my pocket if we need 'em. I know guns scare your flatlanders."

She snapped the rifle together and went inside. A moment later, she stuck her head out. "Well, come on," she said. "It's too cold to talk out here."

Hester inched the truck door open and suffered the indignities of five curious noses while she tried to keep Waffles from leaping into the fray.

"They don't bite," Lila said.

Hester let the dog jump out of the cab and scamper across the snow. She followed Lila into the kitchen, where a fire glowed from a wrought-iron stove. Built from rough pine, the kitchen was lined with bookshelves and taxidermy, both large and small.

"Do you always show up unannounced like this?" Lila asked.

"Do you always greet strangers with a rifle?"

Lila ignored her. "We do have phones, even out here in the backwoods."

"Sometime a surprise helps get straight answers," Hester said. "It forces the issue."

Lila stared at where Hester stood in the doorway. Then she filled a kettle with water and put it over a flame. "Still have that kid?"

"I do."

"And how are things going with that?"

"Doing the best I can," Hester said.

"Where's she today?"

"Morgan took her to day care. I didn't think this was a trip she should come on."

Lila spooned tea leaves into a flowery teapot that seemed too girly for the rugged woman. "Morgan? Is that a man or a woman?"

"Does it matter?"

"Not to me," Lila said. The kettle whistled, and she poured boiling water into the pot. "Sit," she said, waving to the bench at a long farmer's table. "I don't get many visitors this time of year. I'd offer you something stronger, but I put all that away once the time changes. If I take a sip in November, the next thing I know it's May, and I have a pounding headache."

Hester stepped out of the doorway, sat, and sipped the tea, then fished dog fur from her mouth. "Are the deer heads yours?"

"Most of 'em. I'm a pretty good shot," Lila said.

"Killing things doesn't make you feel bad?"

"They eat my roses," Lila said pointedly. She put the teacup down so that it clattered against the saucer. "But it's a long drive from Boston to here, so let's quit the small talk. This is a tiny community. Even when we loathe each other, we still gossip. I heard you were over to Cheryl's place asking questions."

"And I heard someone found a body along the lake. I pulled over and read all about it on my way over here. Fascinating reading. They found the body down the road from your house on Saturday morning — the same morning you called me."

"I have no idea what Cheryl or that stupid Bobby Englewood told you," Lila said, "but that body has absolutely nothing to do with Sam or Gabe or me, or anything that happened that summer. And no, the body was not found on my property. It was in the next cove over, on conservation land."

147

Lila stopped. Hester let silence fill the room for a moment before speaking. "Cheryl and Bobby said you didn't report the boys missing till school started. Didn't you tell me they left at the beginning of August? That's a whole month they were out in the world, and you didn't think to say anything?"

"Why is that any of your business?"

"You made it my business when you hired me."

"That's right. I hired you. I can fire you too. Cheryl told me that you talked to Gabe DiPursio yesterday down in Boston. Were you planning on telling me? Did you find Sam too?"

"Yes," Hester said, and for the first time since she'd arrived, she saw Lila's face soften as the news sank in. "He's fine," Hester added quickly. "Healthy. Handsome as ever. I haven't told him yet that you hired me."

"I can't believe it," Lila said. "After all these years, it didn't even take you a week to find him."

Hester reminded herself that stories had many sides, and that she hadn't heard all of the sides of this one yet. "You were right about the name change," she said. "He goes by Aaron Gewirtzman now."

"Gewirtzman? What, does he celebrate Hanukkah? And why does he change his name anyway?"

"I wouldn't know. We barely spoke to each other. Gabe goes by Barry something."

"And they're still friends?"

"As far as I can tell. They live together, at least." Hester sat back and listened to the dogs barking in the yard. "Do you have coyotes around here?" she asked, suddenly worried about Waffles.

"Yeah," Lila said, her mind obviously still on Sam. "They get the chickens sometimes, but Samantha can take care of them. Soccer Ball too."

"Waffles is a city dog."

"And you're a city girl."

"I am. A Masshole too." Hester leaned forward. "So tell me about the body. What does it have to do with all of this?"

Lila shrugged. "I know what you know," she said. "Remember when we had the nor'easter in November? A bunch of trees fell down around here. A guy over in Sandwich was walking his dog and found a tree that had lifted right out of the ground. The remains were under some roots. I knew they weren't Sam's because of the postcards, but . . ." Lila sighed. "A small part of me thought the body might be Gabe's. I'd always worried that something . . . had happened to him. And yes, that's why I called you. That's why I got you involved, and that's probably why we're sitting here right now. But today the police released more information about the victim. They still haven't identified who it was, but it's the body of a middle-aged man, not a teenager. He was murdered with an axe."

"I read that too . . ." Hester waited for Lila to fill in the rest of the story. When she didn't, she added, "And they think it was sometime between ten and fifteen years ago, right when Sam and Gabe left town."

"I get it," Lila said, her voice softening as if she was giving in. "But if the body isn't Gabe's, then I don't know whose it is. I'll leave that to the state police to figure out. All I need to worry about is what to do with Sam. What was he like when you met him?"

"Like I said, I only talked to him for a few minutes," Hester said. "I had Kate with me and . . ."

"And what?" Lila asked.

"When we first met, you said that you and Sam got into a fight right before he left. What was the fight about?"

"We're not going there," Lila said with a quick shake of her head. "I don't know you well enough to get into the gory details."

"How about a few of them, then? If you want answers, then you have to work with me."

Lila stared into her tea. "Wait here," she finally said. A moment later, she returned with two helmets in one arm and Clovis the rifle in the other. She stuck her head outside and called the dogs. Waffles, in full pack mode, trotted inside.

"Ever ridden a snowmobile?"

Hester shook her head.

"Figures. Clovis here has a pal named Cynthia. You want to bring a rifle?"

"I don't think so," Hester said. "I don't know how to use one."

"You'll need to borrow some orange tack. It's the last week of deer season, and hunters are shooting whatever they can."

A few moments later, Hester had left any misgivings she had about heading into the woods behind, and straddled the back of the snowmobile, clinging to Lila's waist as they flew through the forest. They careened around trees. Blue sky peeked through bare branches, and all around, the world was soft and white. Lila drove them off the trail, over a road, straight down a hill and up the other side to where the lake, gray with ice, opened in front of them. "The surface froze a couple of days ago," Lila shouted over her shoulder.

Hester squinted against the wind, trying to imagine the lake in summer, blue beneath the sky, with the sun dappling the shore in golden light. She'd have traded a day of her life right about then for a few degrees of warmth. Lila revved the engine. They sped around an outcropping of granite and into a clearing on the edge of the lake. A cabin, overgrown and iced in, was tucked into the trees. Lila pulled to a stop, swung off the snowmobile, and grabbed the rifle from where she'd strapped it to the back. Hester trudged after her through the eight inches of snow to the edge of the lake, where water had frozen right around the remains of an old dock. "Gabe and Sam and I used to come here that summer," Lila said. "We drank beer and smoked cigarettes. We spent practically every day here."

"It's beautiful," Hester said.

"It is," Lila said. "I'll be sad to see it go."

"Why sell, then? Couldn't you fix up the house and rent it out?"

"Sure, if I had the money. But this place takes every cent I have in taxes. They cost me forty grand last year. That doesn't leave much for fixing a roof or putting in a septic system."

"Forty thousand dollars?"

152

"Welcome to New Hampshire."

"What do you do anyway? How do you pay for this?"

"Whatever I can find," Lila said. "Turnover work in the summer, cleaning lake houses and making sure they're ready for the next renters. The rest of the year, I pick up what I can. I'm pretty handy, though you wouldn't know it looking at this house. I can fix a stone wall or build a deck. This is a place where the rich move and the poor are stuck and anyone in between leaves."

"And that's why Sam wanted out?" Hester asked.

"I haven't a clue why he left. That's what I hired you to figure out."

"You must have some idea," Hester said.

Lila looked out over the ice. "Gabe and Sam used to sneak out at night. They thought I didn't know, but I did. We had a canoe down here, and they'd take it onto the lake and go to houses that Sam knew were empty for the week. We did turnover work then too, so it was easy enough to know who was here and who wasn't. Sam liked to pretend that he was rich. He'd sip their gin and practice a Brahmin drawl. He'd take little tokens that I'd find in his room. He'd go through their things and try to figure out how they'd become the people they were."

"And that's why he ran away? Because he couldn't become who he wanted to be if he stayed here."

"Maybe," Lila said. "That was at least part of it."

Hester kicked at an outcrop of icy granite. "Gabe was still Cheryl's responsibility, not yours. So what happened? He showed up one day and never left?"

"That's about right. But he would have left after the summer. Sam wasn't happy about that either."

"Why not let him stay?"

Lila paused. "Things got weird."

"Weird how?"

"Just weird, okay?" Lila walked away, up the front steps of the cabin, and through a screenless screen door that looked like it was about to fall off its hinges. Hester gave her a moment and then followed. The cabin was built from brown-stained pine. It had a pitched roof, windows covered in thick-gauge screens, and a brick chimney that ran up one side. Hester stepped carefully up the rotting stairs, to where Lila stood in the cabin's single room. The air here was raw. Remnants of many teenage gatherings — beer bottles, cigarette butts, condom wrappers — littered the floor. Someone had spray-painted *Tina N Tyson 4eva* on a wall. There were twigs and branches piled up in the corner and ashes in the fireplace.

"Kids find this place every summer no matter what I do to keep them away," Lila said. "And they all think they're the first to discover it. It leads to no good. We were no different."

"You got in trouble?"

"Sometimes."

"How?"

When Lila didn't answer, Hester took a tentative step forward. The wide planks bowed beneath her weight. In part, she felt as though she'd spent the day climbing a mountain and now, here at the top, didn't know what to do besides head back down. "Why did you hire me?" she asked. "It wasn't about selling this property. And it wasn't really about the body either, was it? Why now?"

"Because I needed to know," Lila said.

"What?"

"That none of it mattered."

"None of what?"

Lila laid the rifle on the floor and sat beside it. "I told you things got weird and that Sam and I had an argument. It was over Gabe."

"In what way?"

"In a sexual way."

"Did he have a crush on you?"

"It was a little more than that," Lila said without looking Hester in the eye.

And to Hester the whole story suddenly snapped together. She could have lived it herself. She remembered being that age, being young and vulnerable and alone and having no one to look out for her. She remembered wanting to be wanted. "You slept with Gabe," she said.

Lila exhaled. "Yep," she said. "But it didn't mean anything."

"You were an adult. You were *the* adult."

"I wasn't that much older than he was," Lila said.

"Twenty-three is a lot older than fourteen." Hester was surprised by the anger that seeped into her voice, and watched as Lila's face blanched, from shame or rage, Hester couldn't tell.

"What does it matter now?" Lila asked.

"It clearly matters to you. I bet it matters to Gabe too. Do you have any idea what it's like to grow up alone?"

"Gabe was a mistake," Lila said. "I can't believe what a colossal mistake I made, one I've regretted ever since. I wanted to see . . . I wanted to see if I could undo anything or apologize or make it better."

156

"Even Sam knew what you were doing was wrong. That's what the fight was about, wasn't it? He wanted to get Gabe away from you. He wanted to get him as far away from you as possible."

Lila seemed stunned at first and then laughed without smiling. "You're a real fucking bitch. Don't try to make Sam into a hero. That's about as wrong as you can get. Sam doesn't do anything for anyone but himself."

"He looks out for Gabe, from what I can see," Hester said. "They've managed to stick together. That couldn't have been easy."

"Yeah, I don't think you heard me before," Lila said. "I told you we had an argument, and the argument was over Gabe."

"Did they sleep together too?"

"Not that I know of, but they might as well have. They were as tight as can be, and Sam didn't like that Gabe turned to me. He didn't want to lose control."

"I watch out for my best friend. I have since I've known her. That's what friends do. They were two kids stuck living with a pedophile."

"I am not a pedophile! Jesus. What is wrong with you?" A strand of spittle flew from Lila's mouth. Hester glanced at the rifle, and Lila followed her gaze. "I have half a mind to shoot you in the fucking head," she said, and Hester felt herself back into the wall and raise her arms in the air.

"Oh, don't worry, you Goddamned moron. Tell anyone you want about this. No one will believe you. And if they do, what the fuck can they do about it anyway? Here's something you should know about Sam. Before he came to live with me, he lived with our grandmother over in Tamworth till he was twelve. She died, and it was a week before anyone found her. She was at the dinner table, facedown in a plateful of spaghetti. It was July and the house stank."

"So?" Hester said.

"He was old enough to use the phone," Lila said. "He knew the neighbors and could have told any one of them. But he came and went all week long, taking money from her wallet, visiting friends down the street, acting like nothing had happened. Think about that the next time you see him. He took what he needed from the situation. Sam will look right through you. He'll look right into your soul. He'll uncover your dreams, your demons, and your very core. And he'll use all of it to get whatever he wants."

"What did he know about you?" Hester asked.

"That I wanted to go! I wanted to leave this place so much." Lila looked around the cabin. "It didn't work out that well, did it?"

All Hester wanted at this point was to drive away from this town without looking back. She wished she'd never met Lila or any of these people. She had to get out of these woods, and back to the truck to pick up Waffles, but as she watched, Lila stopped and cocked her head to the side.

"What?" Hester snapped.

Lila stood and picked up the rifle. She stepped toward the door.

A blast of wood splintered into the cabin. A pinprick of light streamed through the wall. Hester felt a splatter of warmth across her face, and Lila gripped her shoulder where a rosette of red burst from her coat. "Get down," she shouted.

CHAPTER 10

Wood splintered into the cabin again. Lila tackled Hester, and then groaned as her wounded shoulder hit the floor. This time Hester heard the crack of a rifle shot. "Who the hell is that?" she said. "They're shooting at us!"

"We're here!" Lila shouted. She rolled onto her back and tried to open her rifle's chamber, but her right arm didn't seem to be working. "Hunters," she said. "They don't know we're in here." She fumbled with a box of bullets. They scattered across the floor.

"You're bleeding," Hester said, having her doubts whether it was a hunter.

"Thanks for the memo." Lila winced. "Jesus, that hurts. Help me. But stay down."

Hester wriggled across the floor. She gathered up a fistful of bullets and jammed them into her pocket.

"Open the chamber," Lila said as another

bullet cracked through the cabin.

Hester snapped the rifle open and slid a bullet in.

"The other way," Lila said, and Hester took the bullet out and flipped it around.

"Shoot it!" Lila said. "Into the roof."

The closest Hester had ever come to a rifle was a water gun, but she aimed the barrel toward the sky. It felt terrifying and empowering and exhilarating. She squeezed the trigger. Nothing happened.

"You fucking flatlander," Lila mumbled.

She slid the safety, and this time when Hester squeezed the trigger she felt the blast all the way down the side of her body. A hole in the roof opened up and debris rained down around them. Then she slid a second bullet into the chamber and pulled the trigger again.

Lila touched her arm. "Listen," she said.

Hester closed her eyes and lay there for a moment. She heard herself breathe. She heard Lila breathe. Then she heard the sound of footsteps in the snow as whoever had shot at them retreated through the woods. "Are you okay?" she asked Lila.

"It's a flesh wound," Lila said. Hester heard her sit up. She opened her eyes to see the other woman tightening a belt around her shoulder.

"It'll stop the bleeding till we can get out of here," Lila said, as though she was putting a Band-Aid on a cut finger.

"Who was that?" Hester asked.

"Probably some kids, by the way they took off." Lila held the tourniquet in her teeth and tied it off. "I told you it was the last week of deer season."

"Do hunters usually shoot at houses with people in them?"

"Sure," Lila said. "If the house is a wreck, and it has deer standing in front of it."

"I didn't see any deer," Hester said. Her rational side told her to stay put, but the pissed-off side was too angry to listen. That hadn't been a hunter or a teenager shooting at them. She grabbed a fistful of bullets from the floor and barely heard Lila shout after her as she ran from the cabin. She stood in the clearing. She listened, but all she heard was the cracking of ice as the lake froze. She loaded another bullet and swung the barrel toward where the shots had come from. She ran into the trees. The sound of her feet crunching into the hard snow rang through the forest. She swept branches from in front of her. She stopped. She spun around. She ran farther into the trees till she found a patch of trampled snow and three spent shell casings. A single set of footprints led in from a copse of evergreens and then straight out toward the road. She took a few steps toward the trees, and then finally paid attention to the voice telling her to get away from here. To stay safe. To remember that the first time she'd ever shot a rifle had been about two minutes earlier, and whoever had shot at her probably had years of practice.

Somewhere, off in the distance, she heard the slamming of a car door and the screech of tires on an icy dirt road.

She put the rifle down and picked up one of the casings. The heat from the blast had melted the snow, which had refrozen in a slick of ice. Lila struggled down the cabin stairs and limped across the snow toward her. "It was a hunter," Lila said. "I know you're not used to it, but this kind of thing happens all the time around here."

"We should call the police."

"And tell them what? They'll say we shouldn't have been out here in the first place."

"Don't be stupid," Hester said. "I'm calling them even if you don't. And we should get you to the hospital anyway. Don't hospitals have to report gunshot wounds?"

"I'm not going to the hospital," Lila said. "The bullet barely grazed me. The bleeding already stopped, and I don't have the money for an emergency room visit anyway."

Hester closed her eyes and leaned her head against the trunk of a tree. New Hampshire suddenly felt like a very different world from the one she was used to. She was cold and tired and ready to get home. But whatever Lila claimed, that hadn't been a deer hunter shooting at them. "Cheryl Jenkins called you this morning and told you I'd come around. What else did she say?"

"Not much," Lila said. "That you were asking about Gabe and that you'd talked to him in Boston. She wanted to know why I'd hired you."

"What did you tell her?"

"I didn't tell her anything except that it was none of her business," Lila said. "We're not exactly on the best of terms. She hates my guts."

Five minutes earlier, all Hester had wanted was to walk away from this whole mess and pretend she'd never met any of these people. Now she wanted to find a way to tie this whole story together and figure out who'd shot at her and why. She suspected that if she'd been out on that road a few moments earlier, she'd have seen a teal-colored

hatchback skidding away, and Bobby Englewood at the wheel.

CHAPTER 11

"Wendy wants the house filled with uni-forms for the photographer," Felicia said to Sam as he sped into the parking lot at the VA in West Roxbury. "Remember I told you who was supposed to take care of this? Wendy's co-chair, Twig. She never does a fucking thing. So now it's up to us. We need to make sure they know to come."

They hurried through the cold and into the building, where they stopped by the front desk, and Felicia told the receptionist that Wendy Richards had sent them. It amazed Sam to see the change in attitude as soon as Wendy's name was dropped. The receptionist called him "sir," and soon the hospital administrator appeared, a slender black woman in her mid-forties named Dymond, who seemed to know Felicia well. Sam listened as the two of them caught up. Dymond told Felicia that she'd posted fly-ers around the hospital about the benefit and had mentioned it to most of the staff.

"You're coming, right?" Felicia asked.

"I wouldn't miss it!" Dymond said. "And I'll gather up as many of the guys as I can. Let's see who we can get to commit today. We can head to the library. Then maybe we can stop by some of the group sessions."

She led them down the wide, tiled hallway, through a doorway, and up a set of stairs into a large, open space lined with bookshelves. A group of mostly men sat at tables around the room, and a librarian staffed the circulation desk. Dymond introduced them, and Felicia spoke about the Crocus Party and the importance of education, and encouraged as many of the veterans as possible to attend, but Sam could tell that the party would be a hard sell to this group. "They don't seem too interested," he mumbled.

"Let's try talking to them one on one," Dymond said.

She led them around the room and introduced them to some of the soldiers. Finally, she stopped by a computer terminal where an enormous black man had squeezed himself into a chair. He had to have been six foot eight and weighed three hundred pounds. "This is Jamie Williams," Dymond said. "He goes to UMass Boston. He's studying video game programming."

Jamie seemed to have trouble focusing, and when Sam asked him what he was doing, it took a moment for him to answer. "I have a math test," he said.

"Jamie has a head injury," Dymond said, as though she was saying he had curly hair. "He was serving with the Marines last year in Afghanistan and was shot. We're lucky to have him."

Sam held up a fist. "Semper fi!" he said.

"Hoorah," Jamie said, loud enough that the librarian shushed him. "You in the Marines?"

Sam shook his head. "But I know lots of guys who were."

He glanced around Jamie's terminal and saw a video game before Jamie managed to minimize the screen. "I'm pretty good at math," Sam said with a smile. "Why don't the two of you head off and I'll stay here."

"Are you sure?" Felicia asked.

"Absolutely," Sam said, and then waited till the two women had left the library before taking a seat. *"Arab Assault?"* he asked.

Jamie nodded.

"Move over," Sam said, and for the next half hour they two of them sat side-by-side blowing away turban-wearing men with machine guns while ignoring the glares from the librarian. After Jamie won the third game, Sam nodded toward a poster on the wall for the Crocus Party. "You're coming, right?" he asked.

"No, man. Not with this." Jamie touched a scar on the side of his head that stood out against the dark skin beneath his buzz cut.

"Come. I'll look out for you."

"Maybe," Jamie said.

"I'll pick you up. Where do you live?" But when Jamie fidgeted and glanced toward the exit, Sam apologized. "Too much, right? I do that sometimes. Come on too strong. But see, I'm trying to impress the woman who's throwing the party, and if I bring you, well, she'll be impressed!" Jamie really was the type of soldier Wendy wanted to see at the party. "Help a guy out, would you? Plus, there'll be free booze. Great food. All that stuff."

"Okay," Jamie said.

"You mean, okay, you'll come?"

"I mean, okay, I'm gonna think about it."

"And bring some friends?" Sam asked. "And wear your uniform and all off your medals?"

Jamie started up the game again. "Don't press your luck," he said, pausing between each word. But he smiled in a way that told

Sam he'd won.

Gabe glanced at the time on his laptop. It was five p.m. and he had a meeting at five-thirty with some marketing folks who lived in California and who couldn't tell a line of JavaScript from Groovy, which was good for him. It kept him employed and allowed him to call some of the shots. His clients didn't care whether he'd graduated from high school, what he looked like, or how he dressed. Most of the time, as long as he got the job done, they didn't even want to talk to him, which was exactly how Gabe preferred it. Clients paid him via a bank account he'd set up long ago in San Francisco, and all correspondence was done electronically. According to the IRS, Gabe (and they did know him by his real name) was a resident of California, and the little mail he received went to a PO box there and was forwarded on a monthly basis. That was how Gabe had managed to stay invisible all these years. That and not talking to people.

Since there was still plenty of time to make the call, he opened Hester's Facebook page again. He downloaded the photo of her on the beach and saved it in a folder called "2014 TAX RETURN," in case Sam went snooping. And then he scrutinized every bit of the photo — her gingham bathing suit, the straw hat that sat on the back of her head, the way her nails were painted gold — for any clue to who she might be, till a Slack message popped up on his screen. *WHERE ARE YOU???* one of the marketing people had written. It was almost six o'clock.

Gabe's clients were always ready to criticize and not understand, and these ones were among the worst. They never bothered to remember that Gabe lived on the East Coast and that five-thirty was technically after the close of business. Today, he didn't want to deal with the swagger (besides, good luck replacing him). He slammed his laptop shut and left the house. He thought he might grab a burrito for dinner, or at least that's what he told himself he was doing. He headed toward the taqueria in Porter Square even though the one in Davis was closer, and then kept on walking till he came to her house. It was already dark. The truck was parked in the driveway, but lights on the third floor of the house weren't on, and he wondered if she was even home. Multifamily homes lined the quiet street. He imagined heading off to work in the morning and seeing her standing on the stoop, wearing an apron, waving. Would she want to stay here in Somerville or move out to the suburbs? The Somerville schools weren't all that great. Or at least that's what he'd heard, and they'd both want more for the girl. They'd want more for their children too.

Then the front door opened, and she stepped out with the dog. He crouched behind an SUV and watched her pull her coat closed and adjust her earmuffs. She hurried down the sidewalk as quickly as the basset hound would allow, and turned the corner. Gabe followed, dashing from car to car, till she headed into a dog park. She took the leash off the dog, who immediately ran to join the pack. An elegant Indian woman crossed the frozen mud to stand with Hester, and Gabe couldn't help it, he opened the gate and headed into the park too. And he stood by the fence and stared at her till the Indian woman glanced over Hester's head and pointed to where Gabe stood by a trash can overflowing with shit-stained plastic bags. Gabe tried to stay still and look right at them as though every microbe in his entire body didn't quiver as Hester handed her leash to the other woman and said something with a shrug, and then crossed the park toward him. He could feel himself sweat. He pretended that he couldn't place her. He snapped his fingers. "I remember now," he said. "I was passing by and saw you in the park. You came by the house. Any luck with the apartment search?"

"Barry, right?" she said.

He'd nearly forgotten. Again. "Barry Bellows," he said to emphasize the name.

"And your roommate? What was his name? Aaron?"

"Good memory," Gabe said.

"How'd you two meet anyway? You and Aaron?"

Shit. She wanted him to set her up with Sam. This always happened to Gabe. Women — and men — were desperate to meet Sam. "When I moved into the apartment last spring." Always be general, Sam had coached. Spring, not June. It helped keep the stories straight. It kept you from being caught in a lie. Plus, if Gabe barely knew Sam, then he couldn't facilitate a meeting. "We run in different circles."

"That's smart," Hester said. "Keep home and life separate. Roommates can get too intimate if you're not careful. Any idea where he comes from?"

"I haven't a clue," Gabe said. "Why so many questions?"

"Making conversation," Hester said. "And

I decided to stay put in my apartment. Thanks for asking."

"Where's your little girl?"

"Kate? She's at day care."

"Do you have other kids?"

"I don't have any kids," Hester said. "Kate's on loan."

"You aren't married?"

She took a moment to answer. "Nope," she said.

He noticed now how she looked him over, taking in specifics — haircut long past due, shoes he'd picked up at the Goodwill. She stepped back when he moved toward her, keeping her hands out of her pockets. Wary. Careful. She checked to be sure her friend kept watch.

"How about you?" she asked. "Where are you from?"

"New Hampshire," Gabe said, without really thinking through where Barry Bellows might have grown up.

"I love New Hampshire," Hester said. "Ever been to Polly's Pancakes in the White Mountains? I could eat there every day."

Gabe's life in New Hampshire hadn't really been about pancakes or scenery. What he remembered from that time — what he tried to forget — was clinging to cookies offered, to old women who briefly invited him to call them grandma, to sheets on beds, and to brand-new tubes of Aqua Fresh. Some houses had kids stacked up like logs, whole rooms lined with bunk beds, troughs of American chop suey, fights over yellow-stained briefs. Gabe had almost liked those houses best, where he felt safe knowing he was worth $750 a month in state support. That's what Cheryl Jenkins's place had been like, at least at first. The day he met her, he'd been called to the office, where the principal had had that sad look people got when they had bad news to deliver. She stood next to a wiry man, and Gabe went numb.

"Hey, kiddo," the man said. "I'm Mr. Englewood. But call me Bobby, okay?"

Gabe listened while Bobby and the principal talked at him, something about new towns, new schools, new chances. The principal even knew his name and managed to use it more than once without glancing at his file. And then Bobby grinned. "Car's packed. Should we head out?"

The principal hugged him and ruffled his hair. "We'll miss you," she said, even though she'd probably never see him again, probably never think about him either.

Gabe's suitcase, everything he owned, sat in the backseat of Bobby's car. He'd been staying with a couple in Woodstock, but had already known his days were numbered when the woman's waist began to swell. As they drove away, Bobby told him that he'd love the next spot with his friend and mentor. "She can handle anything," Bobby said.

Did that mean him?

Down the road, they pulled into a gas station, where Bobby told Gabe to follow him and do what he did. Inside, a teenager read a magazine at the register, and Gabe trailed behind Bobby through the aisles of soda and junk food, till Bobby slipped a Slim Jim into his pocket, and followed it with a roll of powdered doughnuts, and Gabe thought that maybe he didn't mean to, till he caught the twinkle in Bobby's eye. Was he supposed to do the same? Or was this a trap? His fingers brushed the cellophane wrapper of a Whatchamacallit. He could practically taste the chocolate and caramel, feel the crunch, but his stomach nearly came out of his throat at the thought of taking it, the thought of handcuffs and juvy. Bobby shrugged with disappointment and paid the teenager for the gas.

"You always pay for the gas," Bobby said, as he pulled out of the station and tossed Gabe a bag of Combos. "Otherwise they get you."

Gabe stared at his lap. "Are you really a social worker?"

" 'Course I am," Bobby said. "And that's for you. You'll have to tell me what you like` next time. You were a chicken shit back there."

Gabe tore into the package and ate the pretzels three and four at a time, barely chewing or tasting the saltiness. Ravenous. Impossible to satiate.

They drove for a half hour or so. It was the depths of winter, and snow blanketed the White Mountains. Soon, they were speeding along the shore of a frozen lake and then Bobby pulled into the driveway of an old house with a red barn. Gabe had long ago stopped feeling anything when he came to a new house. He was used to moving, and used to being discarded. A woman wearing a parka over her nightgown stood in the doorway and barely moved when Bobby got out and took Gabe's suitcase from the back of the car. "I found you one," Bobby said.

As Gabe stepped into the cold, an orange cat slunk from behind the barn and ran across the yard. The woman held the door open and let it inside. "That's Pumpkin," she said. "Who are you?"

When Gabe didn't answer, Bobby said,

"This is Gabe. He's been staying in Wood-stock for the past month."

"How come they kicked you out?" the woman asked.

Gabe shrugged.

"Deadbeats," Bobby said, winking at Gabe again. He tossed him a Snickers bar, which Gabe gripped in his fist till he felt the chocolate melting.

"You'll do," the woman said, standing aside to let him into the house. "Well, come on," she said. "Before all the heat gets out."

Bobby carried the bag inside, and Gabe followed. The woman held out her hand. "I'm Cheryl Jenkins," she said.

Gabe hated it when they hugged him. Hated it when they told him to call them "Mom."

"You can call me Cheryl or Ms. Jenkins. Whatever you prefer. You're in the bunk room. Top of the stairs, on the right. There's one empty bed. Should be obvious which one."

Three other boys also lived in the house right then, all about Gabe's age. When they got off the school bus that afternoon, Gabe could hear them as they wrestled from the street to the front door, through the kitchen, up the stairs, and into the room. They didn't seem to realize how big they were, or how long their limbs had grown. Eyebrows was the leader. He shoved a skinny kid covered in pimples, and called him a fag. Pimples shoved back, but the third boy, one with a gut, made it two against one. They barely noticed Gabe. Eyebrows may have said hello, but Gabe had perfected disappearing.

That first night, Cheryl made the biggest vat of macaroni and cheese that Gabe had ever seen. Eyebrows went first, and in any other house, he'd have taken much more than he deserved, and the rest of them would have been left to fight over the remains. Here, though, there was too much to go around. By the time Gabe's turn came, he could fill his plate to overflowing and still go back for seconds. Cheryl sat with them. She asked about school. Eyebrows said that his English teacher was gay, and his math teacher was a slut. Beer Belly laughed at everything he said, and when Pimples said something about a girl named Allison, Eyebrows cupped his hands on his chest and flicked his tongue. None of this was new to Gabe, who was used to houses of wall-to-wall testosterone, energy that couldn't be contained. What was new was that Cheryl refused to let him disappear. She coaxed information out of him, getting him to tell her small things like his favorite subject in school — math — and whether he knew how to swim — yes. After dinner, while the other boys worked on their homework, she let Gabe sit at the kitchen table and have thirds on dessert. And then she let him sneak away to the bunk room, which was exactly where he wanted to be.

The boys came and went over the next few weeks. Pimples was replaced by Glasses, who gave way to Farty. Eyebrows disappeared one afternoon, leaving a vacuum of energy in the house that Mohawk eventually filled. All the while, Gabe kept to himself, eating last, but always eating well, and going to his room to work on homework. The times he saw Bobby, they headed to convenience stores and practiced shoplifting, till Gabe could line his coat with chips and leave paying for nothing but a pack of gum. When Cheryl asked him one day if he liked living with her, he managed to say, "Yes," and believe it. He believed it more than anything he'd ever believed in his whole life.

"You're special, you know," Cheryl said. "I don't think you even know it. But you wouldn't want this to end, would you?"

Gabe piled chili onto his plate and added a mountain of cheese. "No," he said between bites.

And he'd hoped it never would. But that was before. Before the motel. Before the men. Before Sam.

The pack of dogs ran a loop around the park. A greyhound led the way, and Hester's dog, the basset hound, held strong at the back. Gabe wondered what it would be like to have sex with a woman as tiny as Hester, someone he could probably lift with one hand. He felt himself getting hard and pulled his coat closed. He wanted to touch her hair.

"What are you doing?" She jerked her head away from his hand, which had somehow reached out on its own and stroked one of her pigtails.

"Sorry." He let his hand fall.

She stepped away and waved to her friend to say she was okay. "Honestly," she said. "Don't do that again." She softened her tone. "I mean, you're hardly the first. I'm like a pregnant belly. People touch without asking. They seem to think I'm a doll." She looked out toward the dogs. "Waffles took a dump," she said. "I should go."

She went to leave, but turned back. "I know this sounds strange, especially from someone who barely knows you, especially when you just did . . . *that,* but I think you

181

think you're weirder than you actually are. You're dopey, but you're better looking than you let yourself be. And we have more in common than you know. I bet you're not half bad. You should remember that."

Gabe felt a smile start in his chest, a smile he couldn't push down even if he'd wanted to.

She took a deep breath. "And I should tell you I was in New Hampshire today. Right there in Holderness. I know Lila Blaine. I know your real name too, Gabe. And Sam's."

The smile dried up.

She came close. He could almost feel the warmth from her body. He wondered if she was pleased with herself, whether she was happy to see him squirm. She lowered her voice, and in that moment, her expression changed. She seemed kind. Concerned, even.

"And someone shot at me," Hester said. "With a rifle. And I bet I'm only telling you this because I'm still upset about it. I'll probably always be upset about it, and I can't tell anyone that it happened because they'll freak out, and I just . . . I don't need that right now. But I know what it's like to be you. I know what it's like to not be wanted, and then to find someone who sees you. I know what it means. They found a body last week," she added. "By Lila's cabin. In the next cove."

She touched his arm. Like with Sam, it felt like the sun, spreading through him, filling him with life.

"I saw Cheryl and Bobby today too."

The names hit him squarely in the gut, enough to want her to stop, but not enough for him to ask. He stumbled and then turned and ran, out of the dog park and onto the street toward home. He tried to run from the past, but it caught him, like it always did.

"Come," Cheryl had whispered that first time, shaking Gabe awake and leading him past the other sleeping boys and through the silent house. They drove her car down the road to the abandoned motel, and then sat in the driveway, heat blasting at their feet.

"You're special," Cheryl said. "Everything about you. You know that, right? I tell you that enough, don't I?"

Gabe nodded.

"You'll have to be special tonight. For me."

She climbed out of the car. Bobby's hatchback sat in the driveway too, and Gabe could see the glow of a cigarette behind the steering wheel. Cheryl waved for Gabe to follow, leading him to one of the small, overheated cabins. It was cold and raw, the last gasps of winter in mid-March. A tiny man wearing a baseball cap sat on the bed, his gut hanging over the waistband of his gray cotton sweatpants.

"This is . . ." Cheryl said. "What's your name again?"

The man looked annoyed by the question, and then grinned. "Oh, yeah," he said. "I'm Mr. Rogers. This your neighborhood?"

"Nice one," Cheryl said, barely hiding her disgust, and as she stepped into the cold night Gabe went to follow her. "No, sweetie," she said, her breath freezing in clouds. "You stay with . . . Mr. Rogers. I'll be back in a bit." She touched his hair and smiled down at him with sad eyes, and then closed the door as she left.

Gabe faced the room. It was small, with a single bed, a sink, and a shuttered window that opened toward the lake. Mr. Rogers stood. He wasn't much taller than Gabe. He took a pack of cigarettes from his pocket and held it out, but Gabe said no.

"Suit yourself," the man said, lighting up and inhaling deeply. "You should come on in," he added.

Gabe didn't move.

"Sit. On the bed. Right here."

Gabe's feet felt heavy. He sat on the edge of the bed as told, and watched the man fiddle with the waistband on his sweatpants.

"What do you like?" the man asked.

"I don't know," Gabe said.

"You got to know something," Mr. Rogers said, stepping closer. He stomped the cigarette out on the floor. "I want to hear you tell me what you like. Okay? Do you like baseball?"

"Yes."

"Ice cream?"

Gabe nodded.

"And girls with big tits?"

Gabe nodded again, but Mr. Rogers clucked his tongue in disapproval. "I want to hear you."

"Okay."

"Say it."

Gabe inhaled. "I like girls with big tits." It was true. Even saying it gave him a boner.

"And wet pussies?"

"And wet pussies." That too.

"What else do you like? You'll say it, okay? And you'll mean it. Even if I have to tell you the words."

Mr. Rogers tore the top off a yellow vial and inhaled sharply. The room suddenly smelled of old socks. He stroked Gabe's hair, gently at first, but when Gabe recoiled, his grip tightened. He tore the top off a second vial with his teeth and held it to Gabe's nose. "Inhale," Mr. Rogers had said. "You'll want it. It helps."

Despite the December cold, sweat poured down Gabe's face as his feet pounded the pavement. He should have been stronger. He should have fought or run, though in reality, until it started, until he was chanting whatever Mr. Rogers told him to, hoping it would make it stop sooner, he hadn't really known what was happening, and there had been no place to run or hide. Besides, Bobby had been waiting for him in the parking lot. Afterward, Bobby had even taken him to a 7-Eleven in Plymouth where they'd stolen a dozen candy bars.

Gabe stumbled into the apartment and went straight to his room and shut the door, where he opened his laptop and closed all the angry Slack messages. He searched on "Holderness" and "murder," and the first thing that came up was a newspaper story about the body on the lake, which he read through ten times before erasing his browser history.

He erased the photo of Hester at tthe beach, though every pixel of it was seared on his memory. Sam couldn't find any of this.

Not half bad, he reminded himself to help him forget the motel. To forget Mr. Rogers and the men who'd followed. That's what Hester had said about him. And if that was true, none of the rest of this mattered.

Not half bad!

That was good enough!

CHAPTER 12

Hester hadn't planned to tell Gabe about meeting Lila, or knowing his name, or the visit to New Hampshire, or being shot at. It had all spilled out on its own as she'd watched him watch her. Hester's own childhood had been hard. Lonely. Not a subject she liked to dwell on. She'd grown up in a small town on the South Shore of Massachusetts with a mother who could barely get out of bed, and she'd often wondered if she had been brave enough to leave whether things could have been better. Or at least different. She'd never known her father and had often come home to find her mother lying in a dark room, somewhere between sleep and wakefulness. Hester subsisted on the food she could scavenge and went to school in torn, dirty clothes that had other kids calling her Dirty Thursby. She saw no bright lights in that childhood, no friendly neighbors or caring teachers. Her only

188

escape had been the local library, where she'd stayed most nights till closing, huddled beneath a carrel, reading whatever she could find and hoping to stay instead of going home. Those were years of persisting, of working hard, of focusing on only those things she could control, like making good grades and having a plan to escape.

She managed to get herself to Wellesley on a scholarship. She remembered climbing onto a bus with a duffel bag, riding into Boston, and realizing in the time between what was and what would be, that she was completely alone in the world. It made her giddy. On campus, the other first-year students' fathers helped them unload their SUVs. Later that day, the new students sat in a circle with the residence advisor and shared where they were from and what they planned to major in. As her turn approached, Hester saw that she had a once-in-a-lifetime opportunity to become whoever and whatever she wanted to be. Unlike the women whose parents called on the dorm phone and visited during parents' weekend and paid their tuition, Hester owed nothing to anyone. No one needed to know her past or her truth. "I'm an army brat," she told the circle. "I grew up all over. My parents are in Greece." It felt immediately like the truth. "I doubt we'll see them this year."

"Will you visit?" the RA asked.

"Hope so!" Hester said, crossing her fingers for everyone to see.

She'd held onto that truth with everyone but Daphne, reinventing herself like Sam and Gabe had. And like them, she understood how important it could be to guard a secret.

"Who was that?" Prachi asked.

Prachi wore a Prada suit and Louboutins to the park and somehow managed to escape any of the mud and gunk that covered Hester's boots.

"A guy I know," Hester said.

"Darling, if he's someone you know, you should watch yourself. I saw him staring at you for nearly five minutes before I pointed him out. That man has a crush on you a mile wide."

"Yeah, right. We met yesterday."

"It hardly takes more than that for a man to start thinking with his penis. And what was that with your hair? It looked like he was stroking it."

"It was nothing," Hester said. She suspected what Prachi had seen in Gabe had been more confusion than desire, though

190

what did she know? Maybe he liked that she was tiny. She'd dealt with plenty of men with size fetishes.

"Well, don't let Morgan see him looking at you," Prachi said. "Or touching your hair. Jane and I would be in therapy for months if a man looked at me like that."

"You and Jane have been in therapy practically since the first day you met, so that doesn't say much," Hester said. What she didn't say was that she had plenty of faith in Morgan, as she believed he had in her. It would take much more than an admiring eye to get either of them to question their commitment.

"Oh, shut up," Prachi said as she called to O'Keefe. The greyhound bounded over, with Waffles right on her heels. "In the meantime, darling, you and Morgan should let us see your perfect relationship in action. Come to the Independent with Jane and me tonight for dinner. It's been ages since we went out. Bring Kate. I'm not taking no for an answer!"

Hester attached the leash to the dog's collar. Waffles put her muddy front paws right on Hester's coat and lapped her face, and suddenly she wanted company that night more than anything. "Come to our house instead," she said. "I'm not quite ready to be the mom who brings her kid to a pub. I'll get there. But not yet."

"We'd love to," Prachi said.

"And don't mention the hair thing."

"See, I told you so."

Hester didn't really care that Gabe had touched her hair, but she didn't want to tell Morgan about Gabe, or what she'd learned, or about getting shot at. Not yet, at least. What she'd said to Gabe was true. The gunshot had freaked her out, but she could deal with that in her own way. If she told Morgan (or Prachi, for that matter) what had happened earlier, she'd lose control. They'd have to discuss it, and Morgan would want to take charge in some way he couldn't, and she knew in the end she'd have to listen to reason, which was the last thing she wanted.

In New Hampshire, she'd gone straight to the police station after leaving Lila's, where the deputy on duty had taken her statement about the shooting and then asked her if she knew it was deer season.

Hester put the casing on the counter between them. "Does that mean it's okay to shoot at people?"

"Looks like a .22 to me," the deputy said. "That's what most people hunt with."

Hester nearly mentioned Bobby Englewood and Cheryl Jenkins, but held back. This town was small, and she didn't want word to get to them yet. She also didn't have any evidence to support her suspicions. Besides, if she did tell the police why she'd come, she risked exposing Gabe and Sam.

"My best advice is to wait till next week to go walking in those woods," the deputy said.

"I heard you dug up a body."

The deputy glanced over his shoulder to see if there was anyone else around. "And you think there's a connection?"

"Whose body is it?" Hester asked. "How long has it been there?"

"I could put you in touch with the state police if you like. They'll want you to stick around to make a statement."

"That's fine," Hester had said, and as she'd left the station, she'd sworn she'd heard the deputy mumble "flatlander" under his breath.

At the house, Hester opened the door to Morgan's apartment and let Waffles off the leash. She plugged in the lights on the Christmas tree and then lit a fire in the fireplace. Waffles curled up on her bed by the hearth. Hester turned on NPR, and then turned it off, preferring to enjoy the momentary silence while she pulled together chicken and kale enchiladas for dinner. She popped open a beer. By the time she heard the door downstairs open and the patter of Kate's boots on the stairs, the house was warm from the fire and smelled of garlic and tomatoes and chili peppers. The door to the hallway opened, and Kate burst into the apartment, a drawing on construction paper clutched in one hand. Hester lifted the girl into the air and spun her around, and then guessed correctly that the drawing was of Santa Claus and a pile of presents.

"Kittens!" Kate said.

"Is that what Santa's bringing this year?" Hester asked.

"Kittens, kittens, kittens!" Kate shouted, and Hester smiled and gave the little girl a raspberry. This was the longest they'd been apart in three months, and Hester had looked forward to this moment all day, which came as a surprise. She'd been fighting since Daphne had left — to stay removed, to keep her distance, to avoid *wanting* this — but she knew the instant she gave in to these feelings of joy skipping over her heart that she'd finally and definitively set herself up for despair.

"Sorry, Mrs.," Morgan said from the doorway. He held a box in one arm that pulsed, and the moment he put it on the floor, kittens spilled from the top of it.

"How many?" Hester asked.

"Six," Morgan said.

One of the kittens had already launched itself into the tree, ornaments showering to the floor, but Hester hardly cared. She gave thanks that the most annoying and inconsiderate thing Morgan ever did was save unwanted animals without asking. She gave him a kiss. "How long?" she asked.

"Till next week," he said, as the drapes on one of his windows cascaded to the floor and two kittens leaped from the pile of fabric.

"You're on litter duty," Hester said.

"I figured as much. What smells so good?"

"Enchiladas. Go get ready. We're having company tonight."

When he asked how her day had gone, she really did consider telling him everything, but in the end the moment seemed too precious to spoil. At least that's what she told herself.

Prachi and Jane showed up right on time (a rarity). Hester and Prachi shooed away kittens while they set the long farmer's table with placemats and mismatched Fiestaware while Morgan mixed drinks and Jane wrestled with Kate and Waffles. Jane, who taught yoga for a living, had a blond ponytail and a long, solid body.

At dinner, there was plenty of food. Kate gobbled up her enchiladas, even the kale, without a note of complaint, and when they'd finished everything, Prachi scraped the crisped cheesy remnants out of the casserole dish and ate them right off the serving spoon. Jane checked her phone. "It's below zero out," she said. "It's been ten years since I moved here from Santa Barbara, and I'm still not used to the cold. I'm not looking forward to the walk home!"

"Then don't leave," Hester said, giving her friend a gentle hug.

Sitting there in the snug warmth, Hester could almost feel the cold surrounding the house. She smiled. Tonight, here, at this dining room table, nothing was wrong. She was well fed and loved, and her trip to New Hampshire felt like a long-ago dream. She wished the evening, every second of it, could go on forever.

The shriek pierced the night.

Hester barely knew where it had come from, whether it was real or imagined, but she was on her feet, out of bed, running across the hall and into Kate's bedroom with Waffles at her heels. Her heart pounded. She fumbled for the light, and when she couldn't find it, she plunged forward, tripping over landmines of toys and dolls. She stubbed her toe on the edge of Kate's bed as the little girl let out another cry. Hester found the bedside lamp and flicked it on to find Kate sleeping peacefully, a thumb in her mouth.

It was after midnight, and now Hester was wide awake while Morgan hadn't even stirred. Two of the kittens had found their way into the room and had curled into each other on one of Kate's pillows. It seemed that the only souls on earth awake at this time were Hester and Waffles. Hester slid into bed beside Kate and patted the blankets so that the dog jumped up too, jostling the mattress enough to pull Kate out of a deep sleep. If Hester couldn't sleep, why should she?

"You scared me, kid," Hester whispered. "Why were you screaming like that?"

"Kate dream."

"Aunt Hester was dreaming too, but now she's wide awake. What were you dreaming about?"

"The man," Kate mumbled.

"What man?"

"The man in the window."

Hester glanced to where the glow from

the streetlamps shone through the frosty panes. She thought of *Salem's Lot* and couldn't help but imagine a vampire hovering outside the second-story window, ready to fly in and snatch the girl away. The idea terrified her enough to swing out of bed and cross the icy floor. No one was out there, either on the street or suspended in midair. Still, she checked the locks before getting into bed again.

"Do you want me to read a story?" Hester asked.

Kate nodded, even though her eyes had already begun to close. Hester took the copy of *Olivia* from the bedside table and made it through two pages before Kate had fallen fast asleep.

"Thanks, kiddo," Hester said, ruffling the girl's curly hair.

Hester was too wired to fall asleep, so she headed downstairs with Waffles at her heels, where she poured two fingers of scotch and found an old episode of *The Vampire Diaries* to veg out to while curled up on the sofa. But even as the familiar story unfolded, she found herself drifting to thoughts about her conversations that day, to meeting Cheryl Jenkins and Bobby Englewood, to the sound of gunshots in the woods. Today, everything that had happened made her think about

Kate and Daphne. It worried her in a way she'd never worried before, not about Gabe or Sam or Lila, but about her own odd family, about Kate and the terrible predicament of being caught between belonging. Kate would always be welcome here, in this house, with her, but when would she truly belong somewhere? When would the temporary become real?

Hester opened her tablet and found the website for the *Lakes Region Dispatch,* a local paper that usually covered town meetings and petty thefts, but now had running updates on the body in the woods. The state police were treating the case as a homicide, and confirmed that the injuries sustained were consistent with those of an axe wound, but they were still trying to determine a timeline for the death. "That's all we have now," a detective was quoted as saying.

Hester closed the newspaper and noticed a new e-mail in her in box, and was surprised to see that it was from Daphne, as though, wherever she was, she knew Hester was thinking about her. It was the first Hester had heard from Daphne in three months, and it took a moment to steel herself to read the note. She wondered where her friend was right now, and what had caused her to think of Kate on this of all days. She opened the e-mail. Daphne wrote that she was okay, that she needed some time to sort things out. She didn't mention where she'd gone or how long she planned to stay there. *I had to go,* she wrote in her last lines. *It wasn't an option anymore, and I can't explain it any better than that. I hope you understand.*

Hester read the e-mail again. *I do understand,* she wrote back, her cursor hovering over the send button. She did try to understand. Daphne had spent years trying to hold herself in, to be normal, to conform, and Hester knew how much effort it had taken. She'd seen her own mother fail at it so spectacularly. Daphne wanted to be alone. And Hester would give her that at the very least. She lay down on the sofa and turned off the TV. In the silence, she listened to the house. To her house. To her life. She listened to the wind outside, to the creaks, to Morgan's snoring. She imagined Kate, upstairs, fast asleep. What Hester had learned today on her trip to New Hampshire, what she hadn't really ever known, was how important it was to be wanted, in a way that Sam and Gabe had never been wanted. In a way *she* herself hadn't been wanted until Daphne had changed that. She wanted Kate to be loved completely. She wanted to love her without condition, and what she couldn't tell Morgan — what she could barely admit to herself — was that in her heart she hoped that Daphne would stay away for good. She hoped that she could shape a world for Kate unlike her own lonely childhood, one where love was at the very core.

She deleted her response and typed in a new one. *I do understand. You know that I do. You know how much I love you. And do what you need to do, but don't come back. Not unless you plan to stay. I mean it, Daphne. Kate's doing well. She's finally adjusted to you being gone. Don't fuck this up too.*

She read through the e-mail one more time and hit send. Even though she knew Morgan wouldn't agree with her, even though she knew this message would come with a cost, she'd suffer those consequences when they came.

Up in Kate's room, she slid into bed beside the little girl. "There's no man in the window," she whispered.

Kate rubbed her nose, somewhere in between awake and that deep childhood sleep that could only come without worry.

PART TWO

Part Two

Today was all about lists. To-dos, checklists, deadlines. Felicia Nakazawa had to make sure everything, every single last thing, went flawlessly, because today was the Crocus Party. First she had to get out of bed. Then she had to get on the elliptical machine for at least twenty minutes. Then she had to call the caterers and make sure they'd reworked that crabby recipe so that it didn't taste like cat food.

She looked at the clock. It was 3:43 in the morning. How about sleeping in? Could she add that to her to-do list? How about having enough time in the day to binge-watch some mindless TV show? How about waking up with someone other than another pillow to spoon? How about waking up next to Aaron, even if he was probably either A) in some one-night-stand's bed, or B) with Wendy. Felicia, no matter what Aaron and Wendy claimed, guessed it was probably

B. She'd seen the way Wendy looked at Aaron, the way they laughed with each other, the way they secretly conferred whenever she tried to dig into their plans. Wendy did that. She lied about the boys she dated, and they were all boys. Felicia had found Aaron. She'd found Hero too. She'd even slept with Hero — Jesus, they'd gone to Ikea together! — before Wendy swept in and started calling him brilliant. An artist. A filmmaker. Once that started, Hero couldn't even see Felicia anymore. He talked to her like the help. And frankly, Hero was a videographer at best, and even that was a stretch. Felicia hoped he was back to weddings and bar mitzvahs.

And why had Aaron taken them to Club Café? Why hadn't he corrected her when she'd said he was a spoiled gay boy? And why couldn't she find him on Instagram?

It was fine.

Not worth dwelling on. None of it.

Back to the list.

Call the caterer; confirm the photographer; make sure the ice sculptures were delivered to the courtyard; confirm that Pearly and Elise had a helicopter available to take them to Lima; set up silent auction; check in with Dymond at the VA. There needed to be plenty of men and women in uniform tonight or else Wendy would *lose her shit.* That fucking bitch Twig hadn't done a thing, and she was supposed to be the co-chair for the benefit. Maybe Aaron could help again. He'd been useful the other day when they'd driven to the hospital.

Felicia grabbed her phone and texted him, forgetting how early it was. *Where are you?* she wrote.

He didn't write back.

Was he porking Wendy right now? Had he seen Felicia's text pop up and ignored it?

Felicia was suddenly on the balcony outside her apartment, snow falling around her, wearing nothing but her underwear. She climbed the icy bannister with the dark street four stories below. She saw an empty shot glass on the edge of the roof, next to a tree ornament and that little plastic bag of cocaine she'd lost, and she stretched across the gaping space for them. Her fingertips barely grazed the shot glass when she slipped. Right off the banister, into the night air, her heart surging to her throat, head over feet, plummeting toward the asphalt.

She woke with a start. Her phone had beeped. It was a text from Wendy *See you for brunch! Twig's coming. Right after yoga.*

Brunch? With awful Twig? On the day of the Crocus Party? The last thing Felicia needed was to have three hours of her day eaten up. It was 6:11, and time to get going.

Wendy sat in the back corner of the restaurant, tucked into a booth. As Felicia watched, two women at a nearby table whispered till one of them walked up to Wendy, and the next thing Felicia knew, Wendy had pressed her cheeks between the women's faces as a waiter took a snapshot. That would wind up on Instagram in a matter of seconds. Felicia didn't get the appeal Wendy held — she didn't do much beyond post photos and opine on healthy living and take credit for other people's recipes — but the society pages loved her, the Internet loved her, and so did these two women, apparently.

Felicia waited till the fuss was over before joining. "Your fifteen minutes keep ticking away," she said. "Going national soon?"

Wendy ignored her, tapping away on her phone while Felicia ordered a Bloody Mary from the first waiter who rushed past, and then made sure he'd heard by repeating the order to the next waiter she saw. "Extra spicy," she shouted after him.

"They know what you like," Wendy said.

"I want it to be right."

"They know that too." Wendy checked her

phone one more time. "Twig's running late. She'll meet us in a bit."

Twig was always running late.

When the Bloody Mary arrived, Felicia felt the vodka flow into her bloodstream. She ordered another one, along with a mushroom omelet and a side of sausage. Wendy ordered a Cobb salad, no cheese, no bacon, dressing on the side.

"Virtuous," Felicia said.

"I try," Wendy said. "You look like you could use a Xanax," she added, in a way that made Felicia wonder if Wendy had any idea what went into planning events like the one tonight.

"Or about two years on vacation."

"My parents are taking you with them to South Africa in January."

Keeping Pearly and Elise on schedule and entertained was hardly much of a vacation.

Their food arrived. Unlike Felicia, Wendy barely noticed food. She picked at a tomato from her salad, checking to be sure it was free of bleu cheese. "Why not take a real vacation?" she asked. "You've earned it."

"And do what?"

"Go to Yosemite. Isn't that on one of your lists?"

"It's December," Felicia said. "Maybe this summer."

"That's what you always say."

Felicia had already managed to inhale most of her omelet. "What did you do last night?" she asked.

Wendy glanced off across the dining room, looking anywhere but at Felicia. "Not much."

"Did you hang out with Aaron?"

"Why do you ask?"

"Just curious," Felicia said, signaling the waiter for the check.

After breakfast, Wendy managed to cajole Felicia onto the narrow streets of the South End and over to the open market, even though it was so cold out it hurt to breathe. "We're meeting Twig there," Wendy said when Felicia tried to bow out.

At the market, vendors and antique dealers and food trucks had taken up residence outside an abandoned factory. Crowds of people streamed through the winter farmer's market, where Wendy dropped fifteen dollars on a bunch of organic beets and had Felicia take a photo, where Wendy looked charming and effortless. Like usual. Wendy sniffed a sample of clover blossom honey, and Felicia took a photo of that too. Later, she'd have to dig up some recipe that used both ingredients and write an essay to post. Wendy seemed to know everyone they saw.

Half of them were coming to the party tonight. Inside the brick factory, they visited a booth filled with overpriced vintage furniture. Behind a mid-century modern sofa sat a vase covered in purple flowers. Crocuses. It sent Felicia straight to her to-do list.

"What's wrong?" Wendy asked.

"Nothing," Felicia said.

"Oh, stop," Wendy said. "I know that look. The edges of your mouth have nearly hit the floor."

It was the party. It was. And for a moment, Felicia contemplated running through every item on her list so that Wendy might finally understand. Instead, she said, "What's going on with Aaron?"

"Aaron?" Wendy said. "Nothing."

She said it emphatically. Too emphatically.

"Who is he?" Felicia asked.

"I don't really know," Wendy said. "You're the one who found him."

"Doesn't it bother you that you don't know anything about him? That he doesn't have friends or family? I didn't find anything about him online. Nothing. And here he is in your life."

"Now you sound like my father," Wendy said. She glanced over her shoulder to see if anyone could hear, and then whispered. "Why don't you hire a detective? Have him dig up dirt. Honestly, I like the mystery. At least for now. We've known the guy for two weeks. He told me he knows Brennan Wigglesworth. They rowed crew together at Columbia. If you're really curious, see what Brennan can tell you."

Wendy looked up. Her face changed as she took on her public persona, a broad, welcoming smile, while a gaggle of women, all wearing nearly identical yoga outfits and carrying bouquets of sunflowers that couldn't possibly be local, surrounded her and kissed her and exclaimed about her beets. The women filtered away till only one of them was left, Twig. Felicia hadn't even noticed her there. Twig had an outdoorsy charm topped by a carefully colored blond ponytail.

"You know Felicia," Wendy said.

"Of course," Twig said, holding out a hand. Her fingers were cold and her hand bony. "I've heard so much about you."

Twig had lived two halls over from Felicia and Wendy at Boston College, and had gone to prep school with Wendy. By now, she'd met Felicia for the first time at least a hundred times.

"Felicia's helping with the party tonight!" Wendy said. "You'll be there, right?"

"I wouldn't miss it!" Twig said. "I helped

plan it."

Twig had a way of making Felicia feel invisible, which usually enraged her. But today, she took advantage of it. She left Wendy and Twig to their own "plans" and hurried off toward Beacon Hill. The list called!

Sam stomped his feet free of ice. He passed by Gabe's room, where he heard the clack of a keyboard behind the closed door and smelled pot smoke. He didn't belong here. He belonged somewhere beautiful, somewhere special. He envisioned the party later on, filled with girls in cocktail dresses and boys with square jaws. He imagined Wendy standing by his side, all eyes turned to them as they raised their glasses to toast their guests. He saw himself truly belonging.

In his own room, he took a new postcard from his bag. It was a photo of a pot of crocuses. On it, he wrote, *I just want to go back to my room,* a quote from *The Shining,* and addressed the card to Lila. Later, he'd drop it in the mail on his way to the benefit. He wished he'd chosen a movie with more hope to represent Boston, but then he suspected that the notes to Lila would end soon. He'd told himself that when he finally finished his journey, that he'd fade out of

Lila's life for good, and away from everything that had come before. Besides, with Wendy at his side, New Hampshire and Little Comfort wouldn't matter anymore.

He'd started sending the cards when he'd first moved to San Francisco. He'd felt out of place in that city and in his new life there, and then he saw *Alien* at the Castro Theatre, and he met Ellen, who he thought might take him places, so he'd sent off the first card with a quote from the movie. A part of him had wanted to remind his sister that he was still out there, that in a way everything that had happened on the lake had been her fault. Gabe had told Lila about the motel, but she didn't want to believe him. Sam had tried to picture the look on her face when the card arrived, and had wondered if she'd shown it to anyone. No one had ever come looking for Sam in San Francisco, and in the end, Lila, he suspected, had been as glad to be rid of him as he'd been to escape New Hampshire.

Sam's phone beeped. Felicia Nakazawa's round face popped up on the screen beneath a message asking when he planned to arrive at the benefit tonight. She'd been texting all day. *See you there!* he texted back.

But WHEN??? Felicia texted an instant later. *I don't want to be alone.*

Sam turned the phone off. The last thing he wanted was to have Felicia hanging on him all night long. He needed to meet the right people and prove to Wendy that he could hold his own. He slipped into the silk shirt and slim-cut pants Wendy had bought for him at Drinkwater's. He put on cuff links and made sure they peeked out from his jacket sleeves. He slicked his freshly cut hair into a classic part and donned a pair of thick-rimmed glasses that showed off his cheekbones.

Out in the hallway, Gabe stood in his bedroom doorway wearing a t-shirt and jeans. Sam could have landed a helicopter on his pupils.

"The party's tonight," Sam said.

"You look like a movie star."

Even after all these years of living together, it still surprised Sam that Gabe found him so attractive. They'd never hooked up, not once, but Sam often wondered what would have happened if he'd initiated it. Sex was powerful, especially with someone impressionable like Gabe, and it could have shifted Sam's sense of control, the idea that he could count on Gabe for anything at any time.

He remembered watching Gabe at school that first year, before that easy summer, before Gabe had begun spending more and more nights with him and Lila. He heard other kids whispering, calling Gabe a freak. But he always felt Gabe's presence, felt his eyes boring into him from across the room, and it made Sam want to know what Gabe wanted.

Once spring came, Sam noticed that Gabe disappeared into the hills around the school after classes ended, so one day in early June he followed him up one of the hiking paths. The day was unseasonably hot, and he hadn't gone a hundred yards when a trickle of sweat ran down his back and gnats swarmed his head. He turned a bend and came to a halt when he found Gabe splayed on a discarded blue-and-white-striped mattress.

"Gabe DiPursio," Sam said, as if they'd met there a hundred times before.

Gabe seemed so surprised that Sam had remembered his name that he checked over each shoulder as though another Gabe DiPursio might be there.

"Yeah, you," Sam said, taking out a joint and lighting it up, and then handing it to Gabe, who looked as though he'd never seen anything like it before. "This is where you come to get high, right?" Sam asked. Why else would someone have an old mattress behind the school?

"Where'd you get that?" Gabe asked.

"Old Man Twombly. The janitor. Hands 'em out like candy if you know how to ask."

"How do you ask?"

"You don't. He just sort of knows."

Sam jumped onto the mattress next to Gabe. Sam had always been the type who didn't have to ask. He had a girlfriend when he wanted one (which was almost never) and enraged teachers by getting A's without studying. He ran a finger along a yellow stain on the mattress. "These yours?" he asked, licking his fingers, which made Gabe blush.

"Playing with you, Gabby," Sam said, passing him the joint again. "Take a chill pill."

Gabe inhaled ineptly, but Sam could see the mellow go through him in a wave.

Sam closed his eyes and lifted his freckled face to the sun. "Word is you're a serial killer. That's what they say about you at school, at least. True?"

And when he looked at Gabe again, he could see that he'd replaced mellow with paranoia.

"Don't worry about it, Gabby," Sam said, with a wave of his hand. "Secret's safe with me. I've got one too. Want to know what it is?

"Why would I?" Gabe managed to ask.

"I don't know," Sam said. "You tell me."

And he waited. He suspected that Gabe had plenty of secrets. Plenty of dreams. He suspected that more than anything in the world, Gabe wanted someone to remember his name.

"Tell me," Gabe finally said.

"Patience," Sam said, pulling himself up from the mattress and ambling toward the path. "Meet me tonight. On the lake. Midnight. I'll show you then."

Later, the two of them crept down to Little Comfort, where they took the canoe and paddled to a camp Sam knew would be empty. "My sister and I clean these houses," Sam said. It felt dirty to even admit that. "I always know when they'll be empty."

The camp was enormous. Hardly a camp at all, and inside, Sam raided the pantry and found two boxes of Chips Ahoy. In the great room, he mixed a concoction of gin, vodka, peach Schnapps, white crème de menthe, Kahlúa, cognac, Bailey's, Frangelico, port, sherry, vermouth, and, finally, Chartreuse. A bit off the top of each bottle. He poured some for Gabe, who gagged on the first sip.

"Scrabble?" Sam asked as he dug through a stack of damp board games.

Six moves in, Sam slid AQUILINE onto a triple word score. "If you want to be one of these people," he said, leaning back on the wicker settee, "you have to understand how they live. They drive beat-up Volvos and crow over ambrosia salad and know inherently that Exeter trumps Groton. Do you even know what Exeter is?"

It was obvious that Gabe didn't have a clue. But he said, "Please," with a roll of the eyes, and then laid CAT on the board, for a total of four points.

That whole first night together, Gabe never once said he wanted to leave, or protested at breaking the law. Sam didn't learn about the motel till later in the summer, but deep down he sensed that Gabe hid a secret, and he suspected that for Gabe, finding a way to matter, a place to belong, trumped all reason. Gabe began staying for dinner, and when it was obvious he didn't want to go home, staying the night as well. Lila didn't seem to mind. After school ended for the summer, during the day the three of them would clean houses, and at night, the two boys would sneak onto the lake, where'd they'd live like the other half, for a few hours at least.

But when Sam was truly being honest with himself, he admitted that the real reason he'd kept Gabe around all these years was simple. Gabe came the closest he'd ever felt to having a friend, to genuinely believing that he liked someone.

Now, outside the house, Sam listened to the clack of his new heels on the pavement as the sound echoed through the crisp evening air. What he'd give to be at one of those camps right now, to be at the beginning all over again. At the corner, he turned toward the house. He could see Gabe's silhouette in the first-floor window, lit up against the light from the hallway. He raised a hand to wave. Gabe waved back, his stare, even in the dark, so intense that it stopped Sam in his tracks.

At the stroke of eight p.m., Wendy stood on the marble staircase and toasted everyone at the benefit. She looked resplendent (a word Sam had long wanted the opportunity to use) in a violet-colored dress, velvet for the season. Her hair was perched on top of her head in a terrifying ball that threatened to explode. Sam stood in the crowd below, while Wendy kept to the speech she'd prepared about providing educational opportunities to returning vets. He looked over to the corner where Jamie Williams stood by himself drinking a beer from a bottle. The former soldier had worn his uniform like Sam had asked, along with his purple heart. Sam promised himself to make his way over there eventually.

At the end of the speech, Wendy raised a glass and encouraged guests to bid "often and generously" in the silent auction. Around them, the guests applauded and dispersed into the ballroom, where the string quartet began to play, and an army of waiters swooped in. Sam had to remind himself not to stare at the Sargent hanging in the foyer, or the butler, or the clothing, or the people. Already this felt like a night where anything that could go right would. The guests were as he'd imagined, the strapping young men and tarty women that Wendy collected. Sam piled a half dozen crabbies onto a cocktail napkin as the din of conversation rose around him. He said hello to Dymond. Across the crowded room, Wendy glanced at him over a bare shoulder. Her earrings sparkled in the lights. She'd seen him earlier, right when he'd arrived, and had whispered, "Find me if you're feeling lonely," as she'd squeezed his hand.

He raised his glass to her. She tilted her

champagne flute in his direction and smiled, and then returned to her conversation.

"How long have you been here?"

Felicia appeared at Sam's side. She wore a silver blouse and matching heels that she could barely stand in.

"Only a moment," he said, kissing her chubby cheek. "You look like you're about to topple over. Have you ever considered flats?"

Felicia shot him a glare. "Didn't you get my texts?"

Sam imagined her texts piled up, each one angrier than the last. "Now you've found me," he said.

She snatched a glass of champagne from a waiter passing by. "Welcome to society," she said. "These people all talk to me like the hired help."

Which, Sam nearly reminded her, she was. "Have you bid on anything?"

"I can't afford anything."

"That's why they treat you like the help," Sam said, taking her hand and leading her through the crowd. He'd made it, into this house and into this life, and even Felicia's mood couldn't dampen his spirit. People spilled from the foyer to the ballroom to the dining room. They sipped champagne and whiskey. Sam sampled caviar and mini lamb chops and steak tartare.

"Brennan!" Felicia said a moment later. Already blushing, she tottered up to a tall, bland-looking man in a navy blazer whom Sam recognized from a LinkedIn photo as Brennan Wigglesworth. Sam had used the site to learn that Brennan had gone to Columbia undergrad and Harvard Business School, and now, like Wendy, managed his family finances. Sam had also pulled up the Columbia web site and memorized dorms and professor's names and curricula. He'd learned as many rowing terms as he could. He stuck out his hand and let "Brennan Wigglesworth," trip off his tongue. "Good to see you again," and when Brennan seemed confused, added, "Aaron Gewirtzman. No reason you'd remember me. Columbia. You were a senior when I was a first year. You captained the eight-man, and I barely made the four."

A waiter swung by with a tray of hors d'oeuvres. "Wendy's famous crabbies!" Sam said.

"Delicious," Brennan said.

They talked about Columbia, about dorms and the core curriculum.

"Wendy mentioned you might know each other," Felicia said.

"Of course," Brennan said. "I couldn't

forget Aaron!"

Eventually one of the caterers whispered something in Felicia's ear, and she said she'd be back in a moment.

"Felicia's a great girl," Brennan said, in a way that meant anything but.

"Sure is," Sam said.

"Were you in Geller's Frontiers of Science?" Brennan asked.

"I was," Sam said.

"Maybe that's where I remember you from. Man, do you get to New York much? Harlem's changed since we graduated. It used to be rough."

"I got held up my first week there," Sam said. "Right on Riverside Drive!"

Later, Sam wandered into the ballroom, where he bid eight hundred dollars for a round of golf at the Country Club in Brookline.

"Do you even own golf clubs?" Felicia asked, as she materialized out of nowhere again.

"Nope," Sam said. "It's early in the evening, though. I doubt my bid will last, but it'll help bring in more money."

"What if you win?"

"We'll figure it out if it happens. Come on. What are you going to bid on?"

Sam led her to the next item, box seats for a Patriots game.

"There is no way in hell I'm freezing my ass off at Gillette Stadium," Felicia said.

"How about this then," Sam said, showing her a photo of a pair of sapphire earrings donated by a local artist that no one had bid on yet. "Those would go with your eyes."

"Fine," Felicia said. "But I'm not going over two hundred bucks." She jotted her name in the first slot on the list and starting the bidding at fifty dollars.

"Let's keep going," Sam said. "It's fun to pretend, isn't it?"

Wendy had donated the top-billed item, a trip on the Richards family's yacht for a week-long stay in their Nantucket "cottage." The minimum bid was ten thousand dollars. There were a photo and profile of Wendy and all the work she'd done to raise money for veterans, as well as an electronic picture frame with a slideshow of sun-dappled photos. The house sat right up on the cliffs in Siasconset. Its weather-worn shingles were covered in pink roses. It had a private beach, access to the yacht, and a helicopter pad.

"Twelve bedrooms, sixteen bathrooms," Sam read from the description. "A restaurant-quality kitchen. And a chef!"

He touched the frame. The photo reminded him of the "camps" on the lake. "Have you been there?" he asked.

"Of course," Felicia said. "And you should stop counting your doubloons before Wendy catches on."

She stepped over to the next item, and Sam followed her. He stopped himself right before grabbing her arm. "What do you mean?" he whispered.

"Oh, please. You're practically drooling," Felicia said, surprising Sam with a sudden burst of anger. "I thought you wanted to be *my* friend."

He glanced around the crowded room to see if anyone had heard, but the noise in the party had absorbed Felicia's outburst. He touched her arm, gently, very gently, and led her to the side of the room. "I do," he said.

"Then you should act like you do. How about returning one of my texts?"

"My phone was off."

"Okay, how about telling me when you're getting here like I asked? Is that too much?"

Sam paused for a moment. "We got off to a good start, don't you think? But we're still getting to know each other. Why don't you tell me what has you so upset?"

"Are you serious? It's happening all over again." Felicia bit her lip and seemed on the verge of tears. "I don't want to lose to Wendy. I always lose to her! Hero was *my* boyfriend, or at least he almost was. She has the money and the looks and the personality. I'm the sidekick, and no matter what I said earlier, I'm sick of it."

"Honey," Sam said, "I'm not that interesting, and I'm certainly not worth getting this upset over."

Sam's phone rang. He looked at the display and saw Wendy's name. So did Felicia. "Go ahead," she said.

"Are you sure?"

"You're on call. Like me."

Sam clicked the phone on. He glanced around till he found Wendy across the room. She smiled and waved. "I thought you might need rescuing," she said. "Felicia's on the warpath."

Sam held a finger up to Felicia and mouthed that he'd be back in a minute.

"Whatever," Felicia said.

Through the French doors and in the courtyard, ice sculptures of flowers glimmered beneath a canopy of tiny white lights. Music from the string quartet filtered into the night. "It was loud in there," Sam said. "I'm outside now."

"Don't go too far," Wendy said. "There are some people I want you to meet. My friend Twig is here. Or at least she texted that she was here."

"I'll come find you."

He clicked off and stood at the French doors looking through the glass into the ballroom at the crowd. He wanted a moment alone to cherish all of this. In front of him, a well-dressed couple stumbled off, his hand trailing down her ass. A pair of middle-aged men lit up cigars. Felicia stuck her fists into her ample hips. What could he do about her? His breath froze, and he wondered whether she could see him watching her. Sam wanted to stop time and fast forward all at once, to hold on to every second of every moment of this evening and still get to where he wanted to be. Tonight, he'd stand at Wendy's side and when the moment was right, he'd make her wait that awkward second, make her believe that maybe it wouldn't happen, before he pulled her in for a long kiss. He wanted to wake up beside her tomorrow and know that she wanted him to stay. He wanted to be Aaron.

Someone touched his arm.

"Excuse me," a woman said. "Are you going inside?"

He turned to see a young woman wearing

an emerald green cocktail dress beneath a long overcoat. She'd pulled her blond hair into a ponytail and wore a string of pearls around her neck.

"Oh, hello!" she said.

"Hi," Sam said.

"Oh, my God," the woman said. "I can't believe it!"

"Can't believe what?" Sam asked, though a seed of anxiety had begun to take root in his stomach.

"Laura Ambrose," the woman said. "Some people call me Twig. From the lake. You used to clean our house. I'd recognize you anywhere. You're Sam, right?"

Sam caught himself before he nodded. "My name's Aaron," he said.

It took longer than he'd have suspected for the panic to set in.

Chapter 14

The sound from the laugh track filled Gabe's room, where he lay on his bed staring at the ceiling. He'd turned on the TV and smoked two pipes to drown out his thoughts, but he barely heard a single joke as the images flashed across the screen. He stood and went to the window, staring out into the night. Another visit to Hester's apartment would be too risky, even as he imagined leaning in, waking her from a peaceful sleep, smelling her skin. He fumbled with his phone, punching in numbers, and then deleting them. He knew Lila's number by heart. He typed it in all over again and listened as the phone rang. Did she have a land line, even now?

"Hello?"

He'd have recognized that voice anywhere. He remembered showing up at Lila's door, night after night, the way she'd welcomed him inside for dinner, and he remembered

walking into the kitchen one night, moonlight streaming in through a window, to find
Lila with her robe pooled around her ankles,
her breasts two glowing white orbs. He went
to leave, but she pulled him in to her and
put a finger to his lips. "Don't tell," she
whispered, and he couldn't believe it was
real.

But mostly, he remembered the way Lila
had talked to Cheryl on that yellow phone,
the receiver tucked under her chin. "Yeah,
he's here," she said, while Sam and Gabe
sat, joints lit, beer bottles strewn across the
dining room table. "Can stay as long as he
likes. Don't worry about him."

Back then, she used to talk about taking
him hunting in the fall, about the thrill of
hitting a deer and seeing its knees buckle.
She straddled him and took him inside her.

Now, he waited for her to speak into the
phone again.

"I can hear the TV," she said. "I know
someone's there. Is that you, Sam?"

Did she live alone? Was the house falling
in around her? Had she cut her braid? He'd
looked her up plenty of times online to
know she hadn't married anyone yet.

"Fuck you," she said and hung up. A moment later, the phone rang, and her number
flashed again. He picked it up before it went

to voice mail, even though his voice mail message was a computer reciting his number.

"Who is this?" she said and waited, and when he didn't answer she added, "Stop calling me!" and hung up again. Was she worried someone was outside looking in? Did she hear noises in the winter night and wonder what was lurking beyond the dark?

For the first time that day, he relaxed. He lay in the pillows and turned the sound up on the TV. He closed his eyes, all thoughts of Lila or Bobby Englewood or Cheryl Jenkins, or those hands groping at him, long gone. As his eyes grew heavy, he imagined her again. Not Lila. Hester. An August night. Crickets chirping. A game of Wiffle ball. Air that hung with honeysuckle. Lightning bugs flashing. The dog racing across grass. Shrieks of joy. Peace.

Gabe jolted awake. His phone rang. He nearly let the call go to voice mail, but he peeked at the display only to see that it was Sam this time, not Lila.

"I don't know what to do," Sam said.

Gabe was in a pair of jeans and a sweater without even having remembered getting out of bed. "Where are you?" he said, and Sam gasped into the phone about the lake and someone named Twig and having to get away.

"It's bad," Sam said. "Really, really bad. It's all over. It's all coming to an end."

"Don't move," Gabe said. "Don't do anything. Stay exactly where you are. I'll get there as soon as I can."

He hung up, took a few moments to gather supplies, and then left the apartment. Outside, the cold took his breath away. He stepped over a snowbank and yanked open the creaky door on their ancient navy blue Nissan. He drove toward Boston, at the speed limit, stopping for yellow lights. He let pedestrians pass on crosswalks and there seemed to be mobs of pedestrians out on a cold night in December. He came to the Mass Ave Bridge, which passed over the Charles River and led right into the heart of the city. The whole Boston skyline was lit up in front of him.

Gabe never felt more alive than he did on nights like this one.

Sam clicked his phone off. He looked around the Public Garden. There was a full moon tonight, and the sky was clear and filled with stars. Over in Copley Square, the bells on Trinity Church rang eleven times. He crossed the path to where Laura Ambrose — Twig — sat on a park bench.

"I talked to Wendy," he said, his breath freezing in thick, white clouds. "Told her we bumped into each other. Thanks for waiting!"

"Happy to," Twig said with a smile. "I can't believe it's you!"

Back at Wendy's house, even after Sam had told her that his name was Aaron, Twig had insisted that she'd known him from the lake. "I wouldn't forget your face," she said. "Not in a million years. And you haven't changed a bit."

"I was going for a walk to get some air," Sam said quickly. Too quickly. He stopped himself. He stepped toward Twig. He took control.

Twig caught his eye. "I should go in," she said. "Wendy's waiting. Find me!"

"It's hot in there. And someone's smoking a cigar."

Twig glanced over her shoulder through the French doors. Beyond the glass, Felicia still glared toward them with fists on her hips. "Wendy's helper must be pissed at me," Twig said. "I was supposed to be here two hours ago."

"Come," Sam said. "I'm just going around the corner." He grinned. The grin he practiced in the mirror. Confident and sure. He grinned to cover his panic. "It'll be good to catch up. And let Felicia stew in her own misery!"

And then he walked away, convinced that Twig would follow. And she did. Down the side of the house, onto the sidewalk, and away from the party. Don't look at her, he told himself. Walk like strangers. Pretend that you have someplace to go. Get away. From Wendy. From Felicia. From everything and everyone. He moved to a narrow side street. Why hadn't he thought this through? He should have known he'd bump into someone from the lake eventually, especially here in Boston. He should have known that Wendy, in her circle of rich friends, would know the rich fuckheads who owned the houses on the lake. But why had it happened on a night that meant so much?

They walked in silence till they got to the Public Garden a few blocks away. Here behind the gates, in the cold and dark, surrounded by shrubs and ancient trees, it felt like they were the only two people in the city. They walked to the edge of the pond, where in the summer, tourists rode the swan boats in a circle.

"Wendy told me you were coming," Sam had said to Twig. "But I didn't know it was you. Let me give her a quick call. Tell her we'll be back in a minute."

He'd stepped away and made the hurried call to Gabe. Now, despite what Gabe had said, Sam had to get Twig away from here. As far away as he could.

She pulled her overcoat in close but still shivered. "I almost didn't come tonight. I broke up with my boyfriend a few weeks ago and haven't been in the holiday spirit, but then I told myself to buck up and get out and meet someone, and here you are. It's such luck."

What luck, Sam thought. "What luck!" he said. "When did you get to the party?"

"A few moments ago. I was about to drop my things in Wendy's house and saw you standing there."

"Did you come with anyone?"

"No," Twig said with a shrug. "You were the first person I saw."

"How do you know Wendy?"

"We went to high school together! College too. I'm on the board for her foundation."

"Wendy and I are dating," Sam said, and when Twig's face fell, he added, "But it's casual," to give her some hope. She wanted him. She had to want him.

Twig dug in her bag. "I have to take a photo!" she said. "Susannah won't believe I ran into you! You remember my sister, right?

We both had such a crush on you! Do you remember that day we took you out on the boat? We talked about that for the rest of the summer."

Sam did remember. It had been a perfect day, with clear skies and blue water and endless hope. But he put a gloved hand out to stop her. "Let's take a photo later. Inside. Where the light's better. Do you still have the lake house?"

"Of course! I'd die if we ever sold it. It's the most special place in the world."

"It is, isn't it?" Sam said. "It would be good to catch up. I'd love to hear what Susannah is doing as well. We could grab a drink around the corner, then head to the party."

"It's freezing out," Twig said.

"Don't worry," Sam said, draping his coat over her shoulders. "It's not far. Besides, I'll keep you warm."

Twig glanced down, and then up, her eyes shining in the light from the moon. "I'd like that."

Sam's phone beeped. It was a text from Felicia. *Whered you go?* she asked. He clicked the phone off and stuffed it in his pocket. He'd deal with Felicia later. He smiled at Twig. His high from the past few days was gone. Everything with Wendy had been too easy, too simple, and he should have known it would unravel, that it could disappear as quickly as it had come. He should have known that this time would turn out like all the others. He offered his arm and led Twig farther into the garden, to a dimly lit path. She looked over her shoulder, back toward the street, but he put a reassuring hand over hers. He remembered her and her sister, in their bikinis, lounging on the deck of their Chris Craft. He remembered them watching him lug the cleaning supplies into their camp, and how they'd whispered and called him onto the deck. Twig asked him to come out with them on the boat to go water skiing, and her sister giggled and suggested skinny dipping before slapping a hand over her mouth to squelch a laugh. Now he imagined being on that boat again, back in New Hampshire, the roar of the engine beneath them. The boat hurtled forward, across the lake, as water sprayed over them and cooled the summer air. But you couldn't ignore connections to the past. You remembered how much you had to lose, and that not losing meant no one here could ever meet Sam Blaine. And you knew, as unfortunate and distasteful as it was, and no matter what you'd promised yourself, that this was inevitable.

"Where are we going?" Twig asked, glancing over her shoulder once more.

"To the Taj," Sam said. "It's over there. On the other side of the park."

They crossed beneath a lamp, the slivers of ice crunching under their feet. And then they tripped forward. Into the dark. She leaned into him, flirting, letting her head fall to his shoulder. "You're what I needed tonight," she said without a hint of doubt to what would happen next. "It's been a rough month."

"We're alone," Sam said. The path was lined with trees.

"We are," she said.

He felt her. Pressed into his body. The kiss surprised her, but she snaked a hand inside his coat and pulled his waist toward her. "I could tell you worked out," she said.

She was aggressive too, her other hand reaching into his crotch and stroking. "We can do better than that," she said. "You said it's casual with Wendy, right? She's one of my best friends. So we'll keep this between us."

"Between us," Sam said.

"You don't even have to let her know we met. I don't want any drama."

"No, definitely no drama."

"And I'll keep your secret." She smirked. *"Aaron."*

She would.

"I should tell them I'll be late."

"I already told them."

"But I'm on the board. They're expecting me. I already missed most of the evening."

He kissed her again.

"Hold on," she said with a giggle. "This'll take two seconds."

She dug in her purse for her phone, and he put a hand over hers.

"What are you doing?" Fear hadn't yet reached her voice.

"Put your phone away."

"No."

Sam held her hand down and squeezed till she dropped the phone.

"Stop," she said.

What did she think as he touched her neck? He swore he caught a glint of welcoming mischief in her eyes even then. His wrist pressed into her windpipe. What hope did she cling to as the blood stopped flowing and her eyes, so shiny moments ago, blurred? She grabbed at his coat, and clawed at his wrist, and tried to cry out. He held steady, though.

"Relax," he said. "This'll only take a moment."

CHAPTER 15

Gabe drove into the Back Bay and parked
the car on Beacon Street, a broad avenue
lined with brownstones. The streets were
empty. In his mind, he reeled through what
the steps might be, one by one, though the
only step he really had to remember was
don't get caught.

And he wanted this rush to last as long as
it could. He turned off the engine and
stepped into the night.

A moment later, that warmth of the car
already a memory, he found Sam huddled
in a doorway.

"Where?" Gabe asked.

"Over here," Sam whispered.

"Did anyone see you?"

"How the fuck do I know?" Sam said.
"She wouldn't stop yammering. She wanted
to go out with Wendy. To talk about the old
days. She thought it was funny that I used
to clean houses."

He led Gabe through the iron gates of the Public Garden, where he'd shoved the body beneath a rhododendron. Gabe didn't remember the woman from the lake, nor, he suspected, would she have remembered him. Her blond hair was fanned around her waxy face, and a splash of green fabric poked out from beneath her dark overcoat. Her eyes were open, milky and staring at nothing. It made Gabe feel for her, seeing her on that frozen ground. He wasn't a monster, even if he did have to take care of this. Even if he had to protect Sam.

"It takes one mistake," Sam said. "And she wouldn't stop. She wouldn't be quiet. And then she kept fighting and kicking, and . . ." Sam slid to the ground. "The bitch scratched me."

"Where?" Gabe asked.

"Here. On my wrists." He held up his cuffs, where bloodstains looked black in the night.

"Okay," Gabe said. "You'll need to keep those covered till they heal."

Gabe had known from the moment Sam called that it was too late. He lifted Sam's chin. "We'll find a way out of this," he said. "We always do."

Sam buried his face in his hands and sobbed. "I'm so sorry," he said.

"I know. And now you need to be quiet. Very, very quiet."

Gabe watched Sam stifle a sniffle and then look around the garden, as though he was aware for the first time that they were still in a city, that buildings surrounded them, and that people saw and heard things that they didn't always understand at first. With any luck, no one was out on a cold night like this. Somehow, Gabe reminded himself, Sam always got lucky.

"We'll have to get her to the car," Gabe said.

He slung a backpack from his shoulder and took out the pair of garden shears. Her hands were small and delicate. After a split second of hesitation, he cut off her bluish fingers, feeling the bone snap between the blades. He laid the fingers like hot dogs in a sealable, quart-sized plastic bag. Later, he'd sort through the ones with skin under the painted nails and put those in a separate bag and soak them in bleach. He struggled to get her coat off till he finally motioned to Sam, who stumbled over to help. They wrapped her head in the coat and smashed in as many teeth as they could with a brick. Gabe added the teeth to the fingers. "Did anyone know she was with you?" he asked.

"No one," Sam said. "Or no one that matters."

"What does that mean?"

"Nothing," Sam said.

"Can anyone connect you to her?"

Sam sighed. "There were people all over the party. I talked to her for maybe fifteen seconds, and that fat fuck Felicia might have seen me with her, and now she keeps texting. How long can I tell her I'm in the bathroom?"

Gabe took the phone from Sam and turned it off. The police could track the signals on those things and triangulate them. Anyone who'd ever watched TV knew that, but Sam was panicking. "Help me get her coat on," he said.

She hung between them, her head lolling forward, rigor mortis still a couple of hours off. At least, if they held her up between them, she'd look like a drunk. Gabe lifted her fur-lined hood and tied her scarf around her sunken mouth. "Did she have a bag?" he asked.

Sam nodded and tossed a black leather bag to Gabe, who hung it over her shoulder. "Let's go," Gabe said, but Sam, staring out toward the street, gasped.

In the light from the streetlamps, a group of people stumbled down the sidewalk.

245

Gabe heard a wail start in the back of Sam's throat, which grew louder. He put a hand across Sam's chest and pressed him into the shadows, drawing a finger to his lips in warning even as his own stomach rose in his chest. A man stopped at the iron gates. The flame from a lighter glowed on his bearded face. He took a step forward. He squinted and held the lighter up. Gabe clutched at the brick and closed his eyes to keep the streetlight from reflecting off his pupils. He counted to ten, and imagined doing what he'd have to do, what he'd had to do before. But when he opened his eyes, the man was gone.

"I think I might throw up," Sam said.

"Well, don't," Gabe said. "At least not here. That's the last thing we need the police to find. Let's leave before someone else comes along."

They lifted her between them, struggling beneath the weight of her body. Her feet dragged across the uneven pavement. One of her shoes fell off. "Pumps," Sam said as he squatted to retrieve it.

Outside the garden gate, Gabe glanced each way before they stepped onto the fully lit avenue. He'd managed to find a spot three cars down, but those fifteen yards were among the longest he'd ever walked in his life as windows with who knew what behind them peered down from all directions. Halfway to the car, a door across the street to one of the brownstones opened. Music spilled into the night as a couple hurried down the cement stairs and walked away, too engrossed in each other to notice two men walking a drunken woman wearing one shoe to a car. Gabe clicked the keys and opened the back door, and between the two of them, they slid the body into the backseat and then covered it with a blanket. Sam slammed the door and then stared, as if he'd only now realized what he'd done. That feeling of excitement had begun to spread through Gabe's body. Somehow it felt like they'd escaped the worst, even though they had plenty more to do. And he'd still have to rely on Sam. "You have to go to that party," he said. "You have to make sure you're seen."

"I can't." Sam clutched Gabe's arm so hard that Gabe could feel fingernails breaking his skin. He brushed hair from Sam's face and cupped his cheek in his hand. "Listen to me," he said. "You can do this."

Sam looked at the ground. He closed his eyes and squared off his shoulders, seeming to steel himself right then for what was to come.

"I'll wait here for you," Gabe said. "Use your phone. Create a phone record that shows you were there. But don't call me again."

After Sam left, Gabe slouched down in the front seat of the car. He swore he smelled Twig's body beginning to rot. No matter how hard you tried, you couldn't run away from what was. For Gabe, it always came back to New Hampshire. To the lake. To that body that had spent twelve years decomposing on the shore, the body Hester knew all about.

That last night in New Hampshire, they'd snuck down to the lake after dark like usual, he and Sam, where they'd taken the canoe from Little Comfort and paddled it to the house they'd cleaned that day. The house would be empty for the week, but still, Sam said to be quiet as they glided into the dock. Gabe nodded and swung himself out of the boat. He secured his end with two half hitches, and then followed Sam as he crept from the wooden planks to the cool, lichen-covered granite shore. All about them, crickets chirped to mark midsummer. Out on the lake, a loon cried. Gabe looked through the trees toward the camp. It was enormous, hardly a *camp* really. It was set back from the lake and surrounded by birches that glowed under the full moon. Gabe had a knot of anxiety in his stomach. "We should go," he said.

"Don't be a chicken shit," Sam said. "And chill out. This'll be easy. You want the money, don't you?"

Gabe needed the money. And he trusted Sam. And this, tonight, the ad on Craigslist, the photos, the promises, and the e-mails, were part of that trust. Inside, he followed Sam up the narrow staircase to one of the many bedrooms, where they found a Victrola and stacks of 78s, and old photos hanging on the walls of men holding oars and wearing what looked like black underwear. "*They* all went to Exeter," Sam said, as he put one of the records onto the turntable and cranked the player till tinny jazz filled the room. "All those guys rowed crew. That's another thing they do. Head of the Charles!"

Then Sam opened a dresser drawer and slid a hand beneath a pile of mismatched sheets. "Bingo," he said as he shoved a dog-eared copy of *Flowers in the Attic* into his waistband. Whenever they came to these lake houses, Sam took something easily misplaced but not forgotten — a matchbook from a long-ago wedding, a seashell, a postcard. Sam cranked the Victrola one more time. "Will we be friends after you leave?" Sam asked.

"We'll always be friends," Gabe said. At least he hoped they would be.

They sat quietly till the record slowed, and Sam turned the crank again. "Do you want to dance?"

Gabe sat still. Was Sam joking?

"Come on."

Even though Gabe said no, even though he really didn't want to dance, soon he was swinging around the room and laughing, with Sam in the lead, doing something Sam called the foxtrot, even though he seemed to be making it up as he went along. When the record slowed again, Gabe wished Sam would turn the crank one more time. Instead, they listened to the sounds of the lake: water lapping at the shore, insects pinging against screens, a coyote crying in the distance.

"What time is it?" Gabe asked.

"Nearly midnight."

They were almost there. Gabe could almost smell the money. It would keep him from going back to Cheryl's house. It could save him.

"When I leave town," he asked, "would you come with me?"

Sam didn't even pause. "Yes," he said.

Sam sat up and put a hand on Gabe's arm as headlights cut across the room. A moment later, the screen door downstairs clacked open.

"Hello?" A syrupy voice that took Gabe straight to the motel oozed through the night.

Footsteps pattered up the stairs and down the hallway until a man stood silhouetted against the door. He felt along the wall and flicked on the overhead light. A mass of chest hair spilled from his open collar. His shorts strained against his belly. It was Mr. Rogers.

"This was a mistake," Gabe said.

Sam touched his arm. "It's okay. Trust me."

And Mr. Rogers actually gasped. Sam was almost beautiful.

"Where's the money?" Sam asked.

The man pulled a wad of twenties from his pocket and dropped it on a dresser. There were fifty of them there, more money than Gabe had ever seen in his life.

Double the pleasure, double the fun.

Plenty of cash to get him far from New Hampshire.

Sam touched the man's arm. It was as if

he'd pushed the fast-forward button. Mr. Rogers came at him, lips parted, hands everywhere. Feral in his desire.

Afterward, Gabe told Sam to follow him, to tread lightly, to keep from touching anything. They passed the first smear of blood on the wall, and then they were in that great room, and Gabe felt the thick warmth beneath his bare feet before he slid across the floor in a pool that looked like crude oil. He could still hear the *thwack* of the hatchet into flesh and the word "Stop!" catching in his throat at the flash of the blade. He heard Mr. Rogers crying out in surprise, and then terror, as he fled down the hallway. He saw Sam's eyes, alight with joy, the hatchet springing in his wrist. But another sound filled the night. Gabe hadn't heard a sound like that ever. He realized that it was coming from Sam, and Sam was saying what happened and why and what can they do, and Gabe gripped him by the shoulders. "Listen to me," he said. "You can do this."

Then Gabe heard footsteps. A tap and a thunk. Across the pine needles. Across the lichen-covered granite and onto the deck. The hollow sound of the canoe bobbing against pilings. The slap of a wet rope echoing across the lake.

And Gabe was running too. Sam's voice in his head, the hatchet in hand. His feet pounding on the forest floor. Moonlight on water. Bats overhead. Gabe saw the man's face. Panicked. White under the moon. Blood matting his hair. Paddling with one arm. And Sam's voice ran through Gabe's head. *You're at the stern. You're in control. You can finish this.*

And he did.

Then they spent the night scrubbing the floor. They wiped away fingerprints, and paddled to the middle of the lake to drop the hatchet into the water, and then they dragged the body deep into the woods. They dug around roots and granite till they had a shallow grave. Gabe finally started to feel like it might actually be okay. As the sun rose over the lake, they'd taken the money and the man's car. They'd driven out of town and out of state without a word to anyone. And they'd disappeared. Together.

Gabe glanced at the body in the backseat of the car and tried to push away thoughts of that night on the lake, of the power that had surged through him with each stroke of that hatchet, of Cheryl and Bobby, of waiting in one of those motel rooms for the door to open, of seeing Lila's eyes glaze with terror as the truth spilled out and he sobbed into her breasts. Not till years later did he understand that he'd signed up to be Sam's cleanup guy for life. Gabe thought of driving to Newburyport with Sam, where they'd taken the train to a bus to another train, all the while watching the stack of twenties dwindle away. He thought about that first-floor apartment in San Francisco's Mission District where they'd wound up, of being crammed into a single room, of the smell of crack smoke that seeped through the walls, of that feeling of finally being free and happy. This Mission, the one where they'd lived, wasn't about cocktails or restaurants that showed film noir. It was the world of the 24th Street Gang and overripe mangoes, of markets that smelled of meat, and children posing as adults. Sam went out at night, and when he came home, he had cash, and Gabe didn't ask where it had come from, because he'd already seen enough of that for a lifetime. He spent his days wandering, his stomach rumbling, searching for food wherever he could find it in a city where everyone talked about eating. He trolled the farmer's markets. He hiked to Golden Gate Park, to Haight-Ashbury, to the Sunset. He used the shoplifting skills he'd picked up from Bobby. When he tried to talk about the camp, about the blood, Sam said it wasn't worth dwelling on, that sometimes you had to go through something and go through it together to get to the other side.

San Francisco had been when everything had still seemed possible, when Sam had told Gabe to start calling him Jason. Jason Hodge was twenty-two, not fifteen, which opened up the world to them. He had a work history and a license and a Social Security number, and Sam even started carrying himself in a way that made bouncers stop questioning his age. He got a job at a temp agency, and they moved to a new apartment, still in the Mission, but in the other Mission, the one that showed up in food magazines, the one with window boxes and baby carriages and brunch. They still shared a room, but this one smelled of jasmine and roses, and the young men who lived there too fawned over Sam and talked about eating and not eating and working out and how to be skinnier, and Gabe couldn't imagine now what it had ever felt like to be hungry without choosing it himself. He went to the library and taught himself programming languages. One of the boys got him a gig that payed $150 for two

255

days of work, and Gabe blew the whole wad of cash on a new pair of jeans.

And then Sam stopped coming home for a few days, and when he did, he said, "We have a ticket!"

"Where?" Gabe asked.

Sam lay back on their futon and took a long drag from a joint. When he finally exhaled, the smoke swirled up toward the ceiling, then out the window. "To a new life," Sam said.

What about this life? Gabe nearly asked. This one, where things might not be perfect, but at least they were good. It was a feeling Gabe had never felt, and now, he wondered again what would have happened if he'd simply stayed behind after Sam told him about Ellen's brother Zach's fall from the Marin Headlands. What would have happened if he'd told Sam he was on his own? Would he have found new friends, a wife, maybe, a family? Maybe tonight he'd be living with them in the East Bay. Maybe he'd bike to work, and they'd all be vegans.

But then, he owed Sam for what he'd done on the lake, for taking him away, for leading him to *this* life. And this life was far better than what he'd left behind at that motel.

A swatch of green fabric poked out from

beneath the blanket in the backseat. Gabe tucked it in and accidently touched Twig's skin, which had already begun to cool.

The party didn't feel wondrous anymore. To Sam, it felt as though everyone in the house stared as he slipped through those French doors, as though the music and the chatter and the clink of glasses all stopped. Wendy still held court across the room, but even she seemed to pause as a gust of frigid air swept in, lifting skirts and hair, sending cocktail napkins flitting across the parquet floor.

They all had to know. Right? They'd seen him talking to Twig. They'd watched as he'd led her off. The police were on their way and had probably already found Gabe with the body.

It was over.

"Where the hell have you been?"

It was Felicia. And with that, the spell broke, and the party seemed to recharge. Felicia closed the door behind him. The string quartet began to play (had they ever stopped?), and conversation around them rose to a dull roar. Sam hadn't had a chance to fade into the remnants of the crowd, or to add his name to any of the auction items. He hadn't had a chance to be seen and remembered. But he smiled at Felicia anyway. He'd never been more relieved to see someone in his life. "I got your texts," he said.

"Yeah? You could have answered them."

"Didn't I tell you I was in the bathroom?"

"For an hour? It looks to me like you were outside."

"Well, in the bathroom, outside, talking to people, and here. This is a party, right?"

"I haven't seen you."

"There are a lot of people here. And you're seeing me now."

"Don't ditch me again."

"Deal," Sam said. "But I don't think I was gone for an hour. More like twenty minutes."

"Okay. Maybe it was twenty minutes. Christ if I know. Every minute at these things is interminable, and I still have to close it down after the rest of you leave. Where's Wendy anyway?"

"I was just with her," Sam said. "She's over there."

He glanced to where Wendy towered over a small cluster of women. Behind her, he saw Jamie Williams from the VA, standing by himself against a wall, uncomfortable and out of place.

"Have you seen that guy Jamie Williams?"

Sam asked. "One of the soldiers we met the other day?"

"Which one?"

"Black guy. Big."

"The one who looks like a retard?"

"Shut up," Sam said. "You can really be unpleasant."

Felicia raised her hands in surrender. "Okay, okay," she said. "I'm sorry. Yeah, I saw him lurking by himself. He's around here somewhere. He gives me the creeps."

"Racist much?"

"Shut up yourself. What happened to your cuff, anyway?"

Sam put his hand in his pocket. Was there anything Felicia didn't notice? "Wine," he said. "Speaking of which, let's get a drink before last call."

"Now you're speaking my language," Felicia said, taking his arm in the same way Twig had as they'd strolled into the Public Garden.

"What's wrong with you?" Felicia asked. "You should see your face."

Sam caught himself. He focused on relaxing into a smile. "Sorry," he said. "I was off somewhere."

"Don't take me there anytime soon."

"Have you ever thought about calling that guy Hero? The one that you liked."

"Hero? Why would I do that? He was an asshole to me."

"You still like him," Sam said, his voice skipping over the words.

"I do not."

"Give him a chance to make it up to you. People will surprise you."

"Not in the way you want them to," Felicia said.

"Hey, you two winos." Wendy stepped between Sam and Felicia and draped an arm over each of them. She looked as though she'd had plenty to drink herself. "They're closing up shop. And I'm heading across the courtyard to my place."

"I've been ready to leave since I got here," Felicia said.

Wendy waved to a group on their way out, tossed back the last of her wine, and then tapped a text into her phone. "You never saw Twig, did you?" she asked Felicia.

Felicia shook her head. "I thought I did," she said. "But maybe it wasn't her."

"She texted a while ago and said she was here." Wendy shrugged. "She's a flake. As soon as she volunteered for this, I knew I'd be on my own."

"Who's Twig?" Sam asked.

"I told you about her," Wendy said. "She's a friend from high school. Laura Ambrose.

260

Her father is Donald Ambrose, the investment guy. She's loaded."

"You should talk," Felicia said.

"Even I think Twig is loaded," Wendy said.

"Do you have a picture of her?" Sam asked.

"Sure." Wendy scrolled through the images on her phone and pulled one up of her and Twig in the bleachers at a football game.

"I definitely saw her tonight," Sam said. "She was talking to Jamie Williams. One of the guys we brought over from the VA."

"I guess I'll find out where she went in the morning." Wendy turned to Felicia. "Get our coats, would you?" she said, with a touch of the imperious in her voice.

Felicia stomped off toward the coat check. As soon as she was out of earshot, Wendy whispered in Sam's ear. "You're staying tonight, right?"

Sam glanced to where Felicia waited for their coats. She scowled. A part of him was tempted to leave Gabe to solve their problems himself. It would be better if Sam spent the night with Wendy, wouldn't it? It would strengthen his alibi, and there was no way anyone could ever connect Gabe to Twig. Still, Gabe needed him. "I have to help out a friend first," Sam said. "Can I come by in an hour or so?"

"I'll leave the door unlocked," Wendy said.

Sam grabbed a beer from the bar. Instead of leaving, he headed across the room. "Having fun tonight?"

Jamie squinted at him. "Loud," he said in bursts. "Hard for me to talk."

"You know what?" Sam said. "Thanks for coming, but I hate this party. How'd you get here anyway?"

"Bus," Jamie said.

"Let's get out of here. I'll give you a lift home."

Gabe jumped at the sound of someone tapping on glass, and then rolled down the window. "What took you so long?" he said to Sam. "Get in."

"This is my friend Jamie," Sam said, stepping aside. "We're giving him a ride home."

Gabe nearly swore when he saw the enormous man standing behind Sam. "What?" he said.

"He lives in Everett. Practically in our backyard. Take the front seat," Sam said to Jamie. "Your legs are longer."

Jamie got into the passenger's side of the car, and Sam climbed in the back and sat on Twig's body. Gabe gripped the steering wheel with both hands, hardly knowing what to do next. All it would take was a glance into the backseat for this man to start putting some pieces together.

"We bought a new carpet," Sam said. "I doubt you'd fit back here."

Gabe shot him a glare and then pulled the car onto Beacon Street and headed toward Cambridge. Again, he kept to the speed limit and stopped at yellow lights. Sam's friend breathed through his mouth and stared straight ahead. He was tall enough so that his head brushed the top of the car. At the intersection with Massachusetts Avenue, the last of the evening's bar hoppers surrounded them and tapped on the windows. Gabe could see Sam in the rearview mirror, the confidence he'd brought with him evaporating as he closed his eyes and waited for the crowd to pass. "Get us over the river," Sam said.

Jamie rolled the window down a crack. "Get the fuck out of our way," he said to the college kids, who scattered on command. He smiled. "Big and black," he said. "Nothing wrong with a little power."

Gabe pulled through the intersection. What would they do once they got out of Boston anyway? And what would they do now that this guy was with them? The rivers and ponds had frozen over. Even the ground was frozen now. Dumpsters were too exposed. They could bring the body deep into one of the state parks close by, cover it with leaves, and hope. That had worked in New Hampshire, till recently, at least.

Gabe pulled through the last light in Boston and onto the Mass Ave Bridge. It wasn't till he was halfway over the Charles River that he noticed the flashing blue lights ahead of them. Two cruisers blocked one of the lanes, and cars filtered into the other. An officer in a long parka shined a flashlight through the windows of passing cars and selected certain ones to pull over.

"Everyone's seat belt on?" Gabe could hear the tremor in his own voice.

"Don't do anything stupid," Sam said. "We're all in this now, right, Gabe?"

"Why would I do anything stupid?" Gabe asked, with a glance toward Jamie. "I haven't had anything to drink tonight."

For good or for bad, Gabe and Sam had been in this together for years. Besides, Sam was the one who'd invited a black guy into the car, which increased the odds of being pulled over by about a million percent. Yet Gabe wondered what it would be like to be caught. Would confessing bring relief? At least if he confessed, he'd know this couldn't happen again. He'd probably make these cops' nights, and give them something to talk about into retirement. Maybe one of them would wind up on the fast track to detective.

They were next.

"Be cool," Sam said.

Gabe was always the cool one. When it mattered.

He pulled to a stop and rolled the window down halfway. The cop was black. He shone the flashlight in the window, blinding Gabe and then moving on to Jamie. "You're good," he said, waving them along.

Gabe glanced in the rearview mirror and saw the cop wave the car behind them to the side of the road. He let out a quiet sigh of relief and hoped that Sam's luck never ran out. He followed Jamie's directions and drove the car to a sleepy side street outside of downtown Everett, careful to take roads without any tolls. There, Jamie thanked them for the ride and headed into the ground-floor apartment in a triple-decker. Sam moved into the front seat. They sat quietly till the lights in the apartment went out. "Do you have her bag?" Sam asked.

Gabe reached into the backseat and tossed the bag onto Sam's lap. Sam took out her phone. "No password," he said as the phone lit up. "Wendy wants to know what happened to her. Let's tell her. *'Couldn't bring myself to stay tonight,'* " he read off the screen as he typed into the phone.

Not thirty seconds later, a text came in from Wendy asking if everything was all right.

" '*Met someone*'," Sam read out loud. " '*Like my coffee, black and strong. I'm slumming it in Everett!*' "

He hit the send button and tucked the phone into Twig's bag, then Gabe and Sam struggled to lift the body between them, carry it down an icy path along the side of one of the houses to a shed in the backyard. The world here seemed to be asleep, but that didn't keep a tiny dog from yipping as they passed the ground-floor window. Gabe nearly dropped his end of the body. And then he laughed nervously.

"Steady there," Sam said, and Gabe could already feel their dynamic shifting again. He did what he was told as they pulled the door to the shed open. Her body slumped facedown on the frozen ground.

"Where are the garden shears?" Sam asked.

Gabe tossed the shears and brick onto the floor too. Sam added the handbag and phone.

In the car, they drove toward Somerville in silence. Tomorrow, Gabe would take the car in to have it detailed, which might look suspicious, but not as suspicious as having one of her blond hairs turn up. And then he'd lay low. He'd been home all night, not the best of alibis, but his phone records at least would support that.

"It was an awesome party tonight," Sam said, as though none of what had happened actually had. "Anyone you'd want to know was there. Wendy wanted to go to her place, but . . . well, I had other things to do. Should I go over there now?"

"Do whatever you want," Gabe said, and later, after Sam had dropped Gabe off and driven back toward Boston with the car, Gabe took two fingers from the plastic bags, one with skin under the nail and one without, and hid them behind the asbestos-covered boiler in the basement of the apartment. In the basement light, he could see she'd painted her nails royal blue. Then he took the rest with him as he hurried through the night to the dog park where he'd seen Hester the other day. He buried the fingers deep among the plastic grocery bags filled with frozen dog shit, where no one would ever look for them.

On his way home, he passed by Hester's house again and thought about letting himself in, but opted against it. There'd be other times. Besides, he'd pressed his luck enough for one night.

The party had closed down, but the door to the guesthouse was unlocked as Wendy had promised. Sam slipped inside, and then up the narrow stairs to Wendy's bedroom, where he stood in the doorway watching her sleep. She looked peaceful, breathing steadily and softly. Her hair was fanned across her pillow, and for a moment he imagined what it would be like to wake up next to that hair every morning. To find long strands of it in his mouth, in the drain, on his clothes. What was it like to realize someone was never, ever going away?

He undressed and slid into bed beside her, where she woke momentarily and smiled. "You made it," she mumbled. "I'm glad."

"I'm glad too," Sam said.

Felicia finally got to her apartment at three a.m. It had taken her that long to close down the party, to send off the last guests, to pay the bartenders, to check off the final items on her list. She stepped out of her heels and slid off her Spanx in favor of flannel pajamas. She found some pad Thai in the refrigerator, which she ate cold, right out of the Styrofoam container, and then poured herself a glass of pinot grigio straight from the box and lined up ten mini cheesecakes on the concrete counter to defrost. In her pink slippers, the radio tuned to Magic 106.7 where Fleetwood Mac played, she spun like Stevie in front of the windows, wine in one hand, noodles dangling from a fork in the other.

The party had been a success! Twig had bailed. The crabbies hadn't tasted like cat food. Aaron had probably crawled into bed with Wendy by now, but for some reason Felicia didn't care anymore. She didn't care about where he'd come from or who he was. Wendy could have him. She thought about crocuses. In a few months, the snow and cold would be gone, and it would be nearly impossible to imagine the wind against skin or these claustrophobic days. She punched Hero's number into her phone, and when he answered and said her name (he hadn't deleted her from his contacts list!) she told him that she loved him. That he was brilliant. A filmmaker extraordinaire. He told her to call in the morning, when she'd sobered up.

Yes, spring would be here soon.

■ ■ ■ ■

Part Three

■ ■ ■ ■

PART THREE

CHAPTER 16

The only investigating Detective Angela White planned to do today was into how long it took to microwave a bag of popcorn. She'd already sent Isaiah off to school, and Cary off to work, and had even made them lunch, a rarity. She hadn't showered or changed out of her sweatpants, and the chances of either happening weren't great. The sofa called, the TV called, a mid-morning nap beckoned. So when her phone rang, every bit of her shouted to ignore it.

But it *could* be Isaiah calling from school. Worse, it could be the principal calling about an accident. Maybe the bus had run off the road, or the school had caught on fire, or . . .

She snuck a peek at the display, only to see Stan's number pop up.

Sergeant Stanislaus Pawlikowski. Her friend. Her mentor. Her boss.

"Ain't nothing gonna get me out of this

house today," she said.

"The chances of this being anything are somewhere between nil and nothing . . ." he began.

"Dammit, Stan. You know this my day off."

"I need your help. This could go sideways if the press gets hold of it. I need someone who can handle themselves."

Angela groaned, but in spite herself, she couldn't help but be curious. "Spill it."

"Do you know who Donald Ambrose is?"

She turned the TV off. Now she really was interested. "The venture capital guy?"

"That's him. He's loaded, and he's friends with the mayor. And he thinks his daughter's missing."

Which was how, two hours later, after visiting Donald Ambrose at his office in the Hancock Tower and listening to his concerns, Angela found herself on Louisburg Square, ringing the bell at number thirty-one and flashing her badge to a butler wearing a full-on uniform. "I'm here to see Wendy Richards," she said.

He stepped aside and let her in. Was she the first black person ever to have crossed this threshold? The house dripped with blue blood, from the dour portraits on the walls to the threadbare carpets that covered the marble floor in the foyer, the kind of blue blood that attended NAACP benefits and kept her kind in Dorchester and Mattapan. But she shoved that thought aside. She shoved all preconceived judgment aside, especially about Wendy Richards. She needed a clear head and a clean slate to talk to these people. She unwound a scarf from her neck. The butler offered to take her coat, and she declined. She also declined coffee. Finally, the butler nodded and led her up a set of marble stairs to an overheated second-floor study, wood-paneled and lined with leather-bound books, a fire roaring in the hearth, a garland of holly hanging from the mantle. "Ms. Richards will be with you in a moment," the butler said, leaving her on her own.

She repeated the butler's words under her breath in an English accent, while standing by the doorway and doing her best to keep still. She held her hands behind her back and leaned forward on the toes of her boots. But the room beckoned. She found herself roaming along the perimeter, reading the spines of the books, running a hand over a bear's head mounted on the wall, looking out the window over the Boston skyline. The windows were old, with the wavy blue panes of glass that dotted the houses on Beacon

Hill. Frost had formed on the inside of the glass, and Angela could see her breath when she got too close. The room, like the house, was grim and foreboding, except for the pots of crocuses that covered a mahogany desk. Angela picked up one of the pots and breathed in the fresh scent.

"Remnants of Saturday night."

Angela recognized Wendy Richards from seeing her on the local news. Like Donald Ambrose, she was one of those people you knew about, even if you didn't pay attention or care. She wore a neatly tailored gray suit and had her hair tied back in a voluminous ponytail. She strode forward, hand outstretched with an innate confidence. "You caught me between appointments," she said. "But I'm happy to help with whatever you need."

Angela shook Wendy's hand and introduced herself. "What was Saturday night?" she asked. While she might drop an "is" or say "ain't" with Stan, that wouldn't fly here, not in this house.

"A party," Wendy said with a laugh. "I get so caught up with myself. Sometimes I forget that I'm not the center of everyone's world. Sit. Did Harry offer you coffee?"

"He did."

The butler brought in a silver coffee

service as if on cue and set it down on a side table.

"Cream or sugar?" Wendy asked.

"Really, Ms. Richards, I shouldn't take up too much of your time."

Wendy nodded to the butler, who retreated without a word.

"Have you spoken to Laura Ambrose recently?" Angela asked.

"Twig? Of course. I saw her on Saturday. She came to the party."

"Her father's worried about her. She didn't go to work today."

"That's hardly new," Wendy said. "Mr. Ambrose worries all the time. And Twig is a flake. On everything. She shows up late, or on the wrong day, or simply forgets. She has as long as I've known her."

"Does she like working for her father?"

"As far as I know. I don't think he asks much of her. She's the VP of strategy, or something ridiculous like that."

"Did you notice anything when you saw her on Saturday? What time did she leave the party, anyway?"

Wendy poured herself a cup of coffee. "Are you sure I can't get you any?"

Angela nodded. "All set."

The cup rattled against the saucer, coffee sloshing over the lip. Wendy placed it down without drinking. "I saw her earlier in the day," she said. "After her yoga class. We were supposed to meet for breakfast, but she was running late, so we caught up afterwards. She was excited to come to the party. She said it was one of her favorite events of the season. But the party was big. We had over three hundred people here. I never actually talked to her that night."

"But you saw her."

Wendy shook her head.

"How do you know she came, then?"

"She texted to say she was here. But then I don't think she stayed all that long."

"And you weren't worried when she disappeared?"

"It's not like she disappeared. She left. And no, not at all. Honestly, it would have surprised me more if she had stayed. Especially . . ." Wendy stopped herself.

Angela took a moment to jot something down on her pad. "Especially what?" she asked.

"Nothing," Wendy said in a way that, Angela suspected, was meant to get her to stop asking, but Angela rarely let anyone like Wendy Richards intimidate her.

"Let me decide if it's nothing."

"I don't want to make trouble," Wendy said. "But Twig was dating someone we

278

both know."

"David Winslow?" Angela said, and Wendy nodded. "Laura's father mentioned David when we spoke earlier today. He's in Beijing on business. He's been there since last week. Did anyone actually see Laura at the party? Or anyone that you know of?"

Wendy thought about it for a moment. "I think Aaron did. Aaron Gewirtzman. He's . . . I guess he's my boyfriend. He was with me all night."

"I'll need to talk to him. Do you have his number?"

"Really? I hardly think you need to worry. Twig sent me a text that same night. She said she'd met someone."

"Show me," Angela said.

"All it said was that she met someone."

Angela waited till Wendy took out her phone and scrolled till she found the last text from Twig. "Sorry," she said.

The message said something about Twig liking her men black and strong. "Slumming it in Everett, huh?" Angela said, forwarding the whole thing to her own phone. "Were there actual black people at the party?" she added, barely keeping the snark from her tone.

Wendy shrugged. "A few."

"Does Laura hook up a lot?"

"She's not like that," Wendy said. "She's been upset about David, and, I don't know. People do odd things when they're upset."

"So she *has* been hooking up lately."

Wendy nodded. "Don't tell her father."

Angela put her pad away. "I'll try not to, but I'll need a list of everyone who came on Saturday. And photos. I assume you had a photographer."

"Are you serious?" Wendy said. "Do you have any idea who came to this party? They won't want the cops showing up at their doors. And if the press finds out about this, they won't let it go."

"Do you have any idea where your friend is?"

"Fine," Wendy said. "My assistant will have to get the list to you. Felicia Naka-zawa. She's not here right now."

"Was she at the party?"

Wendy nodded.

"Good," Angela said. "Tell her to bring the list with her when she comes by the station today. Here's my card. She can call to make an appointment."

It was freezing out, and, according to the radio, a storm was on its way up the coast headed straight for Boston, with over a foot of snow expected after midnight. Hester turned on the ignition in the truck to warm up the raw air as she sat outside Gabe and Sam's apartment and watched their front door. It had been nearly a week since she'd spoken to Gabe in the park, and in those few days she'd contacted a handful of foster placement agencies in New Hampshire to see what more she could learn about Gabe and the other children who'd lived with Cheryl Jenkins. The kind but firmly uncooperative social workers had refused to offer up even the tiniest scrap of information, till finally one of them asked how long it had been since Gabe had left the system.

"Twelve years," Hester said.

"Then there's nothing we can do anyway," the social worker said. "Those records are destroyed after seven years."

"Why?"

"Beats me. It's the law."

Hester also called the local high school in Holderness to see if anyone there would talk to her. One of the secretaries told her they didn't give out information about students, ever, and then threatened to call the police. Hester's last-ditch attempt was a search on LinkedIn and Facebook for kids who'd graduated from the high school the years around when Sam and Gabe should have graduated. She'd come up with a list of about twenty students, and had written them all to see if anyone would return her message. So far, no one had.

Now, after an hour of sitting in the truck and listening to NPR, Hester was nearly ready to pack it in. She wanted to find a way to speak with Sam, though, to learn more about him. She wanted to ask what those postcards meant. She wondered, too, what he'd thought when Gabe told him that the little woman who'd stopped by to look at their apartment knew Lila. What memories had it brought up for him? Hester rarely revisited her own past, and she suspected Sam was the same. She'd seen a part of herself in Gabe's loneliness. She wondered if she'd see another part of herself in Sam.

The front door to the apartment opened. Hester turned the radio down and peered over the dashboard. Sam strode down the flagstone path, seemingly unaware that anyone was watching him — and yet fully aware that anyone would watch. He moved with every bit of confidence Gabe lacked, tucking a green-and-blue scarf into his pea coat, and climbing into an old Nissan before speeding away. With her feet stretched toward the pedals, Hester made a quick U-turn and followed through Somerville, into Cambridge, and finally along the frozen

Charles River on Memorial Drive where a few brave souls ran in the subfreezing air. She continued to follow him across the river, zipping past Fenway Park and zigzagging along the Emerald Necklace through Roslindale and into West Roxbury, where Sam pulled into the parking lot of the VA hospital, a huge institutional building on the outskirts of town. He hurried across the lot and into the building. Hester grabbed an interlibrary loan bag from the backseat. Inside, she walked with conviction past the registration desk, and then down wide, tiled hallways littered with abandoned wheelchairs, posters for support groups, and signs for terrifying wards like Prosthetics and Respiratory Therapy. An orderly stopped her. "Are you lost, miss?" he asked.

"Not at all," Hester said, patting the interlibrary loan bag.

"Keep going this way," the orderly said. "You'll see the library on your left."

At the next corner, she stopped when she saw Sam sitting in the waiting area outside the mental health ward with his back to her. He perused a magazine and periodically glanced up at the three others in the waiting area: an older couple who held hands and stared at the ever-blasting television set, and a woman in her late twenties or early thirties who wore a Celtics sweatshirt and had tied her messy hair into a ponytail. As Hester eased out into the corridor to get closer, the woman stood, pacing the hallway and peering through the windows of a swinging door.

"Need anything?" Hester heard Sam ask the woman. "Coffee, maybe?"

"No," the woman said. "Thanks, though."

Sam showed her a page in the magazine. "Who are you waiting for?" he asked.

"My husband," she said. "He has PTSD, like all of them. These group therapy sessions are good, but I sometimes think they dredge up more than we can handle." She shook her head. "We'll get through this. My mother is with the kids. Honestly, it's good to have a moment to veg out."

"I bet," Sam said. "There's only so much TV, right?"

"Right!" the woman said. "If I watch another episode of *The Young and the Restless* I might shoot myself. Who are you waiting for?"

"A friend," Sam said. "I help out when I can."

The door to the ward swung open. A young man with cropped blond hair shuffled out, and the older couple flanked him as they left. Two more men and one woman left the ward on their own, followed by a huge man wearing a down parka.

"Jamie!" Sam said.

"You came," the man said.

"What did you expect? I told you I'd be here."

Another man came out of the ward, and the woman gave him a hug and then they headed off together.

"How was the session today?"

Jamie took a moment to answer, and then simply said, "Good."

"Well, good is great, right? Should we get you home to the pooch?"

Sam turned too quickly for Hester to duck away. His eyes caught hers. "I remember you," he said. "You came by the apartment."

She smiled. She'd expected him to say something about Lila or to mention her conversation with Gabe in the dog park. At the very least, she'd expected him to ask why she was following him around. "I thought I recognized you," she said.

"Aaron," Sam said. "And this is my friend Jamie."

Jamie looked away when she said hello to him and introduced herself. Up close, she could see the shadow of a scar beneath his buzz cut, and she felt his size as he shifted from one foot to the other. He filled the

285

entire room and seemed uncomfortable with it.

Hester patted the library bag. "Making a delivery. I work at Harvard."

"Jamie here is studying video game programming at the community college." Sam paused and looked at Hester. He took a step forward and studied her face. "Actually, he's working on a design program and is supposed to sketch some new characters." Sam turned to Jamie. "She has an interesting look, don't you think?"

Jamie nodded.

"Could we snap your photo?"

"Do I get a superpower?" Hester asked.

"This is more of a thinking person's game. You'll be one of the thinkers."

"So you're looking for nerds?"

Sam grinned. "More like sexy librarians. Do you mind?"

"Maybe another time, if we get to know each other. We live in the same neighborhood. You'll have to buy me a drink one of these days."

"Maybe I will," Sam said. "I'd better get you home, Jamie. You have homework."

"Where's home?" Hester asked

"Everett," Jamie said.

"I saw your roommate the other day. He

came by the dog park. He didn't mention it?"

Sam shook his head.

"He probably didn't think anything of it. We barely said two words to each other."

"I bet," Sam said. "He's not one for small talk."

A few moments later, Hester hurried across the parking lot. She put the truck in gear and pulled away from the hospital. On the radio, the newscaster talked about the coming snow storm, but Hester barely listened. Sam seemed nice enough. More than nice, really. How many people would drive all the way out to West Roxbury to tote an injured vet home from his therapy sessions? But why hadn't Gabe mentioned seeing her? More important, why hadn't Gabe told him that Hester knew Lila? And their real names.

At the next red light, she heard her phone beep. An e-mail had come in from one of the people she'd contacted through LinkedIn, a man named Paul who'd gone to school with Sam and Gabe. *I knew Cheryl Jenkins,* he wrote. *I can meet with you. But come alone.*

Hester managed to wedge the truck into a parking spot on the outskirts of Harvard

Square and cut across the Yard, along the shadowy paths lined with snowdrifts, past clusters of students on their way to finishing papers and exams. And even though she was in a hurry, in the middle of the Yard she stopped at the serious, marbled entrance to Widener Library and thought about going in to say hello to her coworkers. If she went inside, if she smelled the close air heavy with old paper, if she asked about research or students or who was working on what project, she'd never want to leave.

She heard a familiar voice calling her name. It was Kevin, the head reference librarian. He tripped down the steps toward her, tossing one end of a blue-striped scarf over his shoulder before pulling her in for a bear hug. "The undergrads are relentless," he said. "Relentless and anxious and rude and ill-prepared for the end of the semester. They're nightmares. Every one of them."

Kevin and the library and the other librarians and the whole world that they existed in was Hester's and Hester's alone, a world that she didn't have to share with Morgan or Kate. It was good to be reminded, even momentarily, that that world was still there. They talked for a few minutes. He told her about one earnestly impatient sophomore who needed articles on Laotian immigration and language acquisition, and didn't understand why she couldn't have them in a half hour. "The best of the day," Kevin said, "maybe the best of the year, was this pair of giggling girls who wanted to research the history of the dildo."

Hester laughed. "I hope you told them you'd work on that one together," she said.

"Do you think I'm a fool?" Kevin asked. "I made an appointment with them on Monday!"

Hester glanced at her watch. "I should get going," she said.

"No," Kevin said, clutching both of her hands. "Come to lunch with me instead."

"I wish I could, but I'm meeting someone."

"Where have you been?" Kevin asked. "It's like you dropped off the face of the earth."

There were a lot of people whom Hester hadn't reached out to since Kate had come to live with her. She didn't know if they'd understand how hard it had been or, frankly, whether they'd want to hear about it. She'd hated listening to people talk about their kids. "It's intense. The kid thing."

"A lot of us have been through it."

"Sometimes it feels like I've lost control of my own life, even if I probably shouldn't say that out loud."

"You can always say it out loud to me — and anyone else who's ever had a kid. We've all felt that way. And we miss having you around. Come to the holiday party. It's on Wednesday, the day after the students leave."

"I'll try."

"Don't try," Kevin said. "Just do. And if you have to bring the kid, so be it. You won't be the only one."

"I will," Hester said, giving the man a hug and then dashing away through a wrought iron gate and onto Mass Ave.

She headed down a side street and into the subterranean John Harvard Pub, with its brick walls and warm lighting. There, she took a stool at the bar and waited, checking her phone periodically for any updates from "Paul." She'd tried to find out what he wanted to tell her, to no avail. Now, she wondered whether he'd even show up, but ten minutes after she'd arrived, and two beers in, a man stopped at the hostess stand and looked quizzically toward her. He was about the same age as Sam and Gabe, though reedy and unformed, as though he hadn't quite graduated from adolescence. He had greasy hair that poked from beneath a knit cap and a wispy beard that clung to his chin. Hester nodded, and he came over.

"Thanks for coming," she said. "Paul, right?"

"That's right."

When Hester pointed to the stool beside hers, he perched on the edge of it, as though he wanted to be able to flee at a second's notice. She tried to chat him up, but he glanced warily toward the door and barely seemed to hear her questions. He worked at Verizon as a sales rep. He lived in Alston with five roommates and a cat, and he'd left New Hampshire "as soon as he possibly could," which seemed to be a theme. Beyond that, Paul didn't share much.

"Are you expecting someone?" Hester finally asked.

His eyes shifted from the doorway to her. "Are they coming too?"

"Who?" she asked.

Paul pursed his entire face together and nodded. "You know."

"But I don't."

He picked up the menu and leafed through it. "Are you buying?"

"Sure," Hester said. "As long as you start talking a bit more. Time is money, you know?"

Paul ordered a shot of whiskey with a beer chaser, which got him carded.

"I get carded all the time too," Hester said. "You look old enough to me."

"Thanks. I guess. I'm getting lunch too."

Paul ordered a lobster roll, the most expensive item on the menu. Hester ordered a Reuben. "Extra fries," she said. "And bring me another beer."

After the bartender moved away, she swiveled toward Paul. "You're the one who wrote me. You didn't have to do that. So if I had to bet, I'd bet that you have something to tell me. And that it has something to do with Gabe DiPursio or Sam Blaine. They disappeared, right? And it seems like no one cared about it. I'm trying to figure out why. I put all that in my e-mails, though. Tell me what you remember about them. Were you in any classes with them or the band? Did you play sports? Anything."

Paul slammed down the shot and followed it with half of his beer. He coughed, and then drank down the rest of the beer and ordered another.

"You're not driving, are you?" Hester asked.

"I'll take the T."

"So, Sam and Gabe?"

"Gabe came to town in the middle of freshman year," Paul said. "And no one really noticed him. Not till he started hanging out with Sam. Sam was one of those guys that you did notice. Girls liked him. Guys liked him. He was good at soccer and singing and playing the clarinet. He was comfortable. But you never really knew him. The two of them hung out at school, like, all the time. They were fags. Or at least that's what everyone thought, especially when we found out they ran off to San Francisco."

"You knew they went to San Francisco?"

"Sure."

"How? Who told you?"

"I don't really remember," Paul said. "It's a small place. Once one person knows something, pretty much everyone does."

"Did Sam's sister tell you? Lila?"

Paul smirked into his beer in a way that made Hester cringe. "Yeah, maybe that's who it was. Lila. She was the town slut."

"I've figured that much out."

Paul lowered his voice. "She was my slut for a while. At least till I moved on to something better."

"When you were in high school?"

Paul nodded. "Tenth grade. Used to go by her house after school and watch pornos."

Strike two for Lila Blaine.

The bartender delivered their plates. Paul

squeezed a mound of ketchup over his fries and then went at the lobster roll as though he hadn't eaten in a month.

"How come you even remember Gabe?" Hester asked. "Most people I talk to say he was invisible. Not someone you even noticed, let alone remembered."

"Well, I knew Gabe better than most of the other kids. We lived together."

"You were a foster kid?"

"For a bit," Paul said with a shrug. "My mom went through a tough time."

"Was this with Cheryl Jenkins, or before?"

Paul paused. "Yeah, it was with Cheryl."

"What was it like at her house? I met her earlier this week. She made it sound like Shangri-La."

"Shangri-what?"

"Like heaven."

Paul drank down his second shot and followed it with a bit less beer this time. "Are you friends with her?"

"Not at all," Hester said.

"Do you know Bobby?"

"Bobby Englewood? Yeah, we've met."

"It was okay there at first," Paul said. "There were six of us, all boys, but more like a revolving door because some kids would come in for a couple of weeks and then move on. We slept three or four to a room, and it was like summer camp. We'd play baseball on the front lawn. She had dogs. Made good food that kids like. Mac and cheese and that type of thing. We'd all kind of sit around and work on our homework together at night, so my grades even went up. My mom's a great person now, but not so much then. She got hooked on drugs and went into rehab and then we lived out of the car for a while. Cheryl's place seemed perfect at first. And I wasn't there all that long. Only a few months."

Paul dragged a wad of fries through ketchup and stuffed them into his mouth. "You don't look much like a private investigator," he said.

"So I've heard," Hester said.

"Who're you working for? Is this some kind of lawsuit? How much money is involved?"

"There's no money or lawsuit. Why would there be?"

"Don't try that. I'm not giving it up for nothing, so tell whoever you're working for to cut me in."

"There's nothing beyond this lunch. I'm trying to find out what happened that summer. Why Gabe and Sam ran away and why no one bothered to look for them. And it seems like you might have some information. I'll tell you who hired me. It was Lila Blaine. Sam's sister. The town slut. There's no money coming from Lila."

"I heard Gabe was doing her for a while. Cheryl couldn't stand that. She wanted him home, back at the house, not over there."

"Why?"

Paul checked over each shoulder to see if anyone was listening. "I'm not admitting to anything," he said. "Especially if there isn't any cash. I was barely there long enough for anything to happen anyway."

"Tell me," Hester said. "Off the record. Lila doesn't even know I'm meeting you. No one does."

"Cheryl liked to have the boys indoctrinated, really dependent and grateful, before it started. She wanted to be sure they knew to keep their mouths shut, and they did, for the most part. I mean, what boy in rural New Hampshire would want to admit to sucking cock all night long?"

Hester put her sandwich down and gulped at her beer. Her mouth still felt dry.

"So you *can* put two and two together," Paul said. "I can see it on your face. It was the early days of the Internet. Well, not that early. But it was when you still thought things were anonymous. They pimped those boys out. You knew your turn was up when

Bobby showed up to drive you over to the motel. And they had a roster of clients willing to travel and pay top dollar. Alone. In groups. They'd have parties some Saturday nights, a thousand bucks a head. And when Gabe disappeared, it all ended fast. There were too many cops around, and Cheryl had to take cover. In a way, Gabe saved all those kids." Paul put on his coat and swung his knapsack over one shoulder. "Thanks for lunch," he said. "And for the memories."

Hester watched him leave and then paid the bill. She hurried outside onto the street to catch him, to say something, to apologize for pulling him into this, for making him remember. But he'd disappeared.

CHAPTER 17

Sam was unnerved in a way he wasn't used to being. Who was that woman? Why had he seen her twice now? And why hadn't Gabe mentioned bumping into her at a dog park? He unlocked his car and slid into the driver's seat. Jamie got in on the other side. Sam scanned the VA parking lot and found her monster truck, which he remembered from when she'd come by the apartment. He waited till she left the hospital a moment later and snapped a photo of her. The image was blurry and distant, but it was clearly her. Later, he'd show it to Gabe to be sure that Gabe understood that any slip-up, however small, could mean the end for both of them. He started up the car and headed toward Route 128. "Type 'Hester Thursby' into your phone," he said to Jamie. "See what you can find out about her. There can't be too many people with that name in the world."

"Her Facebook page's blocked," Jamie said.

"What else do you see?"

Jamie scrolled through the search results. "Nothing but hits from Ancestry.com."

"Hester isn't really a twenty-first-century name, is it?"

"This is a blog about finding old friends," Jamie said a moment later. "This woman found everyone in her second grade class. She in touch with a few, and found most of the others online. But there were two she needed help with. Hester helped her."

"At the library?" Sam said. "She helped the woman because she's a librarian, right?"

Jamie read a few more lines. "More like as an amateur investigator. She finds people who go missing."

Sam drove onto the highway and edged into midday traffic. He could feel his blood pressure rising. Someone — someone from the past or present — had hired Hester to find him or Gabe or both of them. And now there were connections between her and this mysterious person, connections he didn't know about. There were e-mail trails and phone calls and exchanges of money, and any one of them could lead right to him.

Jamie lived with a little white dog named

Butch, who yapped as they came in from the cold with a pizza. Sam wanted to kick her. He could barely concentrate as they ate lunch. He'd nearly forgotten that Twig's body was frozen in the shed out back. This was a connection, wasn't it? Being here. Working with Jamie. Knowing him. He shouldn't have come here. He touched the scratches on his wrists, which had nearly healed over. In twenty-four hours, they'd be all but invisible. He felt terrible about what had happened to Twig. Really, he did. He'd tried to explain that to Gabe, who'd barely gotten out of bed yesterday, and when he did, Sam had had to talk him down, to convince him that they didn't need to flee Boston. "What could possibly connect us to her?" Sam had asked.

"How about the party?" Gabe said. "Or that anyone who digs too deep will figure out that you grew up in the same town where she has a summer house. Or that your new girlfriend is her BFF?"

"Nobody saw her," Sam said.

"In a crowded party right in the middle of the holiday season?" Gabe said. "I guarantee you someone saw her. You just don't know who yet."

Gabe was pissing Sam off. "Drink something or look at porn or smoke a joint or do

300

whatever it is you do to calm down," he said. "No one even knows she's missing yet."

"They'll know soon enough," Gabe had said. "Rich people don't disappear without someone taking note."

He'd been right. Sam knew Gabe was right, and that he should have listened, and that the entire Boston police force would come down on this case, but Sam hadn't wanted to listen. He wanted to be in Wendy's house, in Wendy's life.

He wanted to become who he was becoming.

He finished up a slice of pizza and proposed a game of Warcraft to Jamie. After they'd played three times, he asked Jamie to pull up a web browser. "Do me a favor. Search on Laura Ambrose."

"Laura Ambrose?" Jamie said as he typed the name in.

"Someone I used to know," Sam said, as Twig's photo popped up on screen. It was a professional photo, taken at a studio, and meant to make her look businesslike and sexy at the same time. She wore glasses, her yellow hair framing her long face.

"Nothing in the news?"

"No," Jamie said.

The news would come soon enough. "Search on Wendy Richards now. See if

301

there's anything about her."

Wendy's name brought up plenty of hits, including her website. There was a link to a society page that covered the Crocus Party, complete with photos. Sam had carefully avoided any photographers that night, but now, a quick scan showed that no one had picked up Twig either. Not even in the background. "Bookmark that page, would you?" Sam said, as his phone rang. Wendy's name popped up on the screen. "I need to grab this," he said.

Butch followed him down the hallway, yipping as he slid into his coat and stepped onto the front porch.

"A police detective came by the house," Wendy said when he answered. "They think Twig is missing. They want to talk to you."

A tingle of dread slid down his spine. "Why me?" he asked.

"You, Felicia. She wants to talk to anyone who was at the party. She wants you to call her."

"Okay. Text me her number, would you? Have you spoken to her already?"

"It's not like I had much of a choice."

"What did you tell her?"

"Not much. That Twig was on the board of the foundation, but she barely showed up at the party."

Sam nearly asked her if she'd told the detective that he was with her the whole night, but stopped himself. He wouldn't want her to remember the question.

"Where are you?" Wendy asked.

"You remember Jamie, right?" Sam said. There was no use in lying. His phone records would show he'd been here. "I'm with him. He's being . . . I don't know. He has PTSD. Some rage issues. But it's nothing. I'll take care of it."

"Tell me."

Sam let the silence between them grow. And when he did speak, he made sure Wendy understood that he did so reluctantly. "It's almost like he's possessive of me. Like he doesn't want me to have any other friends. I told him about how happy I am with you, and I thought he might put a fist through the wall."

Wendy laughed. "Maybe he has a crush on you."

"Yeah, maybe. I don't know. It seemed like more than that."

"Call that detective," Wendy said. "But be careful what you say. And if anyone from the press contacts you, don't say anything. This'll be a mess if we don't contain it."

"Letcha know how it goes," Sam said with a breeziness he hardly felt. He went to hang up, but stopped himself. "Are you okay? Are you worried?"

"About Twig?" Wendy asked. "Not at all. This is just like her."

Sam clicked off. The thermometer hadn't risen above freezing since Saturday, but the winter air — if you knew to sniff for it — had the slightest trace of a meat locker. He reminded himself why he'd come and stole along the side of the house to the backyard, where he swung open the shed door. Here, the air smacked of rot. Twig lay facedown on the frozen ground. He left the body the way it was but grabbed the garden shears. Back on the front porch, he rang the doorbell. Butch's shrill yap cut through the air, and the house actually shook as Jamie lumbered down the hallway. Sam liked Jamie. He'd meant to do good when he'd asked him to the party. But sometimes things worked out differently than expected. He needed the police to focus.

"How about another game?" Sam asked as he crouched down to pet Butch. He gave the garden shears to Jamie. "I found these out here. Hang on to them, would you? You wouldn't want some kid to hurt himself."

Jamie took the shears in his enormous hand. No questions asked.

Gabe woke with a start to a banging at the front door. A part of him was glad to be awake, away from his dreams, where Twig's blank eyes stared at him from the dark, and a part of him yearned to be asleep again, to be as far from this life as he could get. He glanced at the clock. It was well into the afternoon. He lay in bed and hoped whoever had come to the house would leave, but the pounding continued till he trudged to the front door. A black woman stood on the stoop. It took all of Gabe's resolve not to run when she flashed a detective's badge and introduced herself as Detective White.

"Are you Aaron Gewirtzman?" she asked.

Gabe shook his head. His mouth felt dry. He didn't dare speak.

"Is he home?" she asked.

Gabe shook his head again, and the detective waited. She had a kind face, with dark, almond-shaped eyes and whorls of hair that puffed out from beneath a knit cap. She wiped her nose with the back of her hand and smiled impatiently. He was acting guilty. He knew that. He was giving her every reason to notice him when, really, she should barely remember having ever met him. He swallowed. "Aaron's out," he said. "I think he's at work."

"We have a few questions for him," the detective said.

We? Who was "we"? "Do you need his phone number?" Gabe asked.

"It'd be helpful," the detective said. Behind her, water dripped from icicles hanging off the eaves. She raised an eyebrow, and Gabe told her the number.

"You seem nervous," she said. "To me, at least. But then I just met you. Maybe you're always like this. Could I ask *you* a few questions?"

Gabe felt a jolt of anxiety, a spider running up his spine. But he stepped aside for her to come into the house.

"Let's stay out here. Stand in the sun. It's cold today, but sunny. We can cure our rickets. There's a snowstorm coming. Did you hear? A blizzard."

Gabe hadn't heard, but he said he had. He hadn't dared listen to the news since Saturday. He eyed the lump under her coat. It had to be a gun. She'd have handcuffs too. She was forty or so, sturdy, and, Gabe imagined, played "good" way more often than "bad." She had nice teeth, white teeth, so Detective White was easy to remember. And she was black, and Gabe knew the teeth thing was a stereotype, but there was truth in stereotypes sometimes. At least he thought there was. He also remembered that he had a stash in the batik box, a box that screamed "stash." Pot, he reminded himself, wasn't a big deal anymore. Unlike murder. Maybe he should worry about those two fingers he'd hidden under the boiler.

"Saturday?" Detective White seemed to be waiting for something. "Can you tell us where you were on Saturday night?"

Us? Who was *us?* But Sam had coached Gabe well. "You stayed here that night to work on a project," Sam had said. "You went to bed right after I called to tell you I wasn't coming home."

"Do you spend most nights alone?" Detective White asked.

Gabe felt himself blush, but managed a shrug anyway.

"So you stayed home and worked. And Aaron called to tell you he wasn't coming home. Can you tell me why?"

"He hooked up with someone," Gabe said.

"Who?"

"You should ask him."

"But I'm asking you, so you should tell me if you know."

"It was Wendy Richards."

The detective opened her notebook and

jotted something down. Gabe tried to read her note and she flipped the notebook closed. "Okay," she said, taking a photo from her pocket. "Do you recognize this woman?"

The photo was of Twig. Gabe had resisted searching her name online. It was too easy to trace. So this was the first image he'd seen of her alive. "I don't know her," he managed to say. "Who is she?"

"You'll find out soon enough," Detective White said.

"Is she dead?"

"Why do you ask that?"

"Because of what you said."

"You've never seen her?"

"No. Never."

"Even if you saw her on the Red Line or wandering around Davis Square, it would be helpful. You never know where something might lead."

Gabe took the photo. He touched Twig's face, her rosy cheeks. Her smile. She looked kind. Did she have a boyfriend or a cat? Did she belong to a book club or keep a Snickers hidden in the depths of her purse? He wondered what she regretted most in life, what she'd do over or undo or try her whole life to make up for.

"She's a good woman," the detective said.

"She's on the board of charities. She likes sailing and dogs. And she's missing. We don't know anything beyond that, but people are worried. Her parents are despondent. Who knows, maybe she's in Acapulco and we'll all go to bed happy, but right now I'm worried too."

She stopped talking and waited for Gabe to fill the silence. He knew enough to know that she wanted to bond with him, that she'd come on her own and had to be good and bad, and now she was good. But knowing her tricks didn't mean he wasn't susceptible. "That's terrible," he said. "But I don't know anything. I wish I could help."

"She was supposed to go to a party. The same one your roommate attended."

Gabe handed Twig's photo to the detective. "I'm sorry," he said. "I don't even know her name."

"It's Laura. Laura Ambrose."

"Well, I hope Laura is in Acapulco," Gabe said. "I could stand to be there myself."

Detective White smiled. "I guess I could too," she said, and as she turned to leave, she stopped herself, as though a thought had just come to her. "If we asked," she said, "would you let us check your computer? See what we can find? What you've erased. You know you can't erase anything these days? Once you hit the keys, it's out there forever."

Back to bad. Gabe almost liked bad better. The thing was, he didn't even have a porn account, though maybe he should register for one. It would make him less suspicious. He had looked up that article about the body in Holderness, though. And he'd downloaded the photo of Hester. Those were connections he wished weren't there. "I can get it for you," he said. "Look for whatever you want."

"Thanks, but not today. We'll be in touch if we have more questions." She handed him a card. Her name was Angela White. Did her friends call her Angie? "If you see your roommate, have him call."

"I will," Gabe said, and then watched as she headed down the front path. She climbed into an unmarked car and drove away, all the while watching him in the rearview mirror as she sped through the stop sign at the end of the street.

Gabe stood in the sun for a moment. He imagined what she was like away from work, and who she had waiting for her at home. He wondered what she looked like when she wasn't bundled up in winter clothes, when she wasn't protecting the world from people like him. He bet she was soft. That she was a good cook. That she watched reruns of *Rizzoli and Isles* and saw herself in those TV detectives.

His phone vibrated in his pocket. It was Sam.

"Why?" Sam said, as soon as Gabe answered. "Why didn't you tell me?"

Gabe swallowed. "I was about to call you," he said. "She just left."

"She came to find you there again?"

"She was asking about the party. She had a picture of Twig."

"How the hell does she know about Twig?" Sam asked.

"She's a police officer," Gabe said.

Sam sighed. "The cop was there too? Fuck! What did you tell her?"

"Exactly what we practiced."

"And what did you tell Hester Thursby?" Sam asked.

"Who?"

"Shut up," Sam said. "I know you saw her again. She's a private investigator. Someone hired her to find us."

"I barely spoke to her," Gabe said.

"Well, fuck me," Sam said. "Don't talk to her again. If she comes by, don't open the door. In fact, don't talk to anyone till I get there."

Then the phone clicked off.

Sam was panicked. And when Sam panicked, there was no telling what could happen. It had happened with Ellen, that call in the early morning, Sam sobbing about the Marin Headlands, and the Golden Gate Bridge, and the way Zach had clung to loose soil and grass. "Please," Sam had said. "She knows. I know she knows. I need you."

Gabe put his coat on and headed out. He needed to undo this. He needed to make it right. Somehow, he needed to warn Hester away.

CHAPTER 18

Sam's phone rang almost as soon as he hung up on Gabe. It was Detective White, who asked him to come by the police station. "Of course," he said, his voice smooth and controlled. "I'm happy to help in any way I can."

An hour later, he sat in the waiting room and checked his phone. Again. Felicia had promised to meet him so they could talk to the detective together, but here Sam was by himself, surrounded by the miscreants of society in this god-awful building. Felicia was always, always late, especially when she really needed to be on time. Who the hell kept the police waiting?

He dialed her number and listened to the phone ring, and when it clicked to voice mail he stabbed at the cancel button. Felicia was the type who ignored calls, and then sent text messages to follow up. He'd told her how much he appreciated promptness, and she'd actually laughed and said that he probably wouldn't like her all that much, and right about now he wanted to punch her in the face and break her nose and knock out every tooth in her mouth and listen to her beg as he watched her bleed. Then he'd kick her in the ribs. She bugged the shit out of him.

He sent her a text and asked for her ETA. He stood and paced the waxed floors and then realized that pacing was a bad idea. The cops were watching. That's why they'd kept him waiting. They wanted to see how he handled the stress and whether he showed signs of guilt. But why would he? This was all Twig's fault. Sam turned the pacing into a purposeful visit to the bathroom, where he splashed cold water on his face. In the mirror, his face was red and dripping wet. He was sweating. Could they turn down the fucking heat in this building? Save the taxpayers some money? He closed his eyes again and counted to ten. Calm. He couldn't show them anything but mild annoyance. Innocent people were annoyed when they waited more than an hour for an appointment, but not so annoyed that they said anything stupid. They answered quickly and to the point and glanced at the time. They might tap a finger silently against a thigh, or mention that they were missing an important meeting. Innocent people had never met Twig — Laura — so they could only sympathize on a theoretical level, but they couldn't truly imagine the feeling of having a sister or a daughter or a friend disappear until it actually happened. They couldn't empathize.

Sam had been lucky, he reminded himself. Always. And there was no reason for that luck to run out today. He was lucky that no one remembered seeing him with Twig at the party. He was lucky that Jamie had those garden clippers. He was lucky that everyone on earth had heard of PTSD and knew what it made soldiers do. And he'd always felt lucky to have found Gabe, to have taken him away from that Jenkins woman. He'd saved Gabe all those years ago, he'd helped him exact revenge, and Gabe owed him. He always would.

Sam stepped away from the mirror. Good. He was ready. He went to his seat. He checked the time impatiently. He did have places to be.

"Oh, my God, oh, my God, oh, my God."

Felicia slumped in the seat beside him, twisting her hands together nervously.

"Where have you been?" he asked.

"Where do you think I've been?" she

315

whispered. "Talking to that detective. They whisked me in there the second I got here. I've been in there for a half hour." Felicia glanced over each shoulder. She couldn't have looked guiltier. "They were relentless."

"In what way?"

"Questions," Felicia said. "The same questions over and over, trying to trip me up, trying to get me to contradict myself. Oh, my God, it was like on TV. I can't believe Wendy even told them I was at that party. This whole thing was a nightmare."

"What did they ask?"

Felicia gave an almost imperceptible shake to her head. "I'm not supposed to say," she said.

"But you can tell me," Sam said.

Felicia shook her head again. Her eyes widened, and she glanced up over his should as Sam felt someone behind him. A middle-aged black woman wearing sensible shoes stood in the doorway to an office.

"Detective White?" he asked.

"Thanks for making the time," she said with a smile. "And sorry to keep you waiting. Ms. Nakazawa had plenty of information for us."

Sam gathered his coat and bag and smiled at Felicia as he stood. "I'm sure," he said. "Wait for me, okay?" he added.

"It's okay," Detective White said to her. "You can still be friends. And breathe. It's all over."

Sam followed her into a windowless interview room.

"Your friend's nervous," the detective said. "Any idea why?"

"I think she's watched too much *Law & Order,*" Sam said.

"Most people have watched too much *Law & Order.* Can I get you something to drink?"

"I'll be fine," Sam said.

"We shouldn't be too long."

Sam tapped his finger on his thigh while the detective asked him basic questions about his background and connection to Wendy Richards. He answered quickly and casually. Aaron Gewirtzman grew up in New York. He'd been paying Social Security taxes for eight years. He moved to Boston in the spring.

The detective slid a photo of Twig across the table. Sam picked it up. "I'd have called if I recognized her," he said, and almost before the words were out, he realized they were too snarky. "It's awful, isn't it?"

"Awful," Detective White said.

"Yes," Sam said. "Terrible. Wendy was close to her."

"She mentioned that. She thought you'd

mentioned seeing Laura."

"I don't think so," Sam said. "And even if I had, I'd never met her. I don't know if I'd remember it."

The detective made a note. "And when did you leave the party?"

"Right after midnight."

"I spoke to your roommate. Interesting guy. He didn't go to the party with you?"

Sam shook his head. He felt his pulse quicken. He'd almost forgotten that Gabe had spoken to the detective, and any interview with Gabe was a bad idea. Gabe stood out, though he didn't know it. He thought he was invisible. And he could make Sam stand out among a guest list of three hundred.

Be patient, Sam reminded himself. Be innocent.

"Do you usually go to parties without your boyfriend?" the detective asked, which surprised Sam, though he supposed she was trying to unsettle him. To get him to react. To trip him up. Should Aaron be angry that she thought he was gay? Probably not. That happened to all attractive men. "He's not my boyfriend. Just a roommate. I went to the party as Wendy's date. We're a couple."

Detective White jotted something down. "That's right," she said, flipping through

318

her notebook. "She mentioned that. How long?"

"How long, what?"

"How long have you been a couple?"

"I don't even know if we are," Sam said.

"But you said you are." The detective read from her notebook. " 'We're a couple.' "

"Then I guess we are. Just a few days now."

"If it's just a few days, then you must know since when, right? People remember those things."

"Sure," Sam said. "But I try to be a gentleman."

Detective White tapped the photo of Twig. "We don't deal in gentlemen here. Just the truth. Tell me."

"Two weeks," Sam said.

"That's what Ms. Richards said too. See, it's easy to be straight with me. Now be straight with me again. Have you ever seen this woman?"

Sam turned up the corner of the photo. "Sorry I can't be more help. I know Wendy is close with her."

"Would you look one more time?"

"Of course," Sam said. Innocent people looked, but not for too long. "Poor thing," he said. "She doesn't seem very happy."

"Why do you say that?"

"I don't know. It's a feeling I get."

"Do you know anything about her relationship with Wendy? Ms. Richards indicates they were best friends. Best friends, especially women, tend to spend a lot of time together. But you've never met Laura?"

"Things are new between us. Between Wendy and me. We haven't known each other that long."

"So you don't know much about your girlfriend."

The detective was making Sam squirm more than he was used to. He glanced at his phone and tapped an impatient finger on the table. It was time to go. It was also time to be a bit annoyed. "You know, girlfriend sounds a bit too much right now. We're dating."

"Just dating then." The detective chuckled to herself. "Sounds like you want to play the field. Don't tell her that, but that's none of my business."

"I haven't met Laura and didn't see her on Saturday," Sam said, letting impatience creep into his voice. "I can't be much help."

"Tell me about the party. Tell me what you remember."

Sam folded his arms as though he was thinking about what details to pull out. He told her about the people, the fantastic people, and the hors d'oeuvres and the silent auction for the foundation. He made sure to sound suitably impressed. "I bid on a round of golf," he said. "But got outbid in about five seconds."

"You don't usually run in these circles."

"You could say that, but I fit in anywhere. It was a fun night. Full of possibility. The veterans were the only ones who looked uncomfortable. They stood in a cluster and drank Bud Light, you know what I mean? They didn't want to mingle. We invited them and then showed them off like circus freaks. I'm sure they couldn't get out of there fast enough."

Detective White dug through a folder and slid a list of names across the table. "Who are they?" she asked.

Sam read through the list and checked off the names that he knew. He paused when he got to Jamie's name under "W." "I was at Jamie's house this afternoon," he said. "He's a good guy."

"Is there a 'but' there?" the detective asked.

"No," he said. "Why would you say that?"

"Because it sounded like there might be."

"Not at all," Sam said. "Jamie's struggled. He got shot in the head, so it's amazing he's even alive. But, no. I don't mean to imply anything at all. He's a great guy. He lives over in Everett."

Even Detective White couldn't hide her tell on that one. She ended the meeting almost immediately, thanking Sam for coming in. Out in the waiting room, Felicia stood as soon as she saw Sam and followed him out of the station. "That was a disaster," she said as soon as they were on the street.

"A disaster? How?" Sam asked.

"Where do I start? Maybe with the fact that I'm even here? Don't you watch TV? These types of things always lead somewhere bad. They dig up information that has nothing to do with the case."

"It's sad, though, isn't it? Don't you wonder what happened to her? Wasn't she your friend?"

"I guess," Felicia said.

Sam exhaled for what seemed the first time that day. He stepped down the sidewalk and felt the rays of winter sun shining on his face. He looked around at the people hurrying by, at the police officers in their heavy blue parkas, at the cars speeding down the street. He watched as his frozen breath drifted away on a breeze. How long would it be till the police searched that shed behind Jamie's house? How long would it be till they found the bloodstained clippers with Jamie's fingerprints on them? Maybe sooner would be better than later, after all. He needed them to find the body before they ran a background check on *Aaron Gewirtzman.*

When they stepped into the next intersection, Sam noticed a man walking toward them as Felicia prattled on about calling Hero and going on a coffee date. The man wore a gray coat over a shirt opened to a tanned chest, despite the cold. A handsome stranger. Sam hadn't gotten lucky in days. Their eyes met as they passed each other, and the man stopped on the corner to wait.

"I have to be somewhere," Sam said to Felicia.

"I thought we were going for a drink?" she said.

"Were we?"

"Yeah."

"Well, I can't now. Tomorrow maybe?"

Felicia glared at him. "You're that type, aren't you," she said. "You only want what you want."

"Meaning?"

"Never mind. Sure. Call me tomorrow. If that's what you want."

Felicia lifted the strap of her bag onto her shoulder and headed off down the street. Sam waited for her to turn toward him, to smile and wave, to let him know they were still okay, but she didn't. She waddled around the corner and disappeared, and then Sam leaned against a streetlamp and waited. The man in the gray coat tossed a cigarette into the street. "Oliver," he said in a smooth English accent.

"Victor," Sam said.

It would be good to have a distraction. To forget about Twig and Wendy and Felicia and Jamie. And Hester.

"I'm at the Back Bay Hotel," Oliver said.

Sam grinned. "And I'm feeling lucky."

CHAPTER 19

It was easy enough for Gabe to find Hester at her house, and then to follow her in his Zipcar when she drove to a bookstore in Porter Square. He took an old copy of *Moby Dick* from his bag. *Moby Dick* was the kind of book he imagined college students spent their semesters reading and rereading, and it was a book he suspected Hester would know about, being a librarian and all. Inside the bookstore, he found a seat by the café counter that gave him a clear view of the whole store. His heart pounded when she stepped out from around a shelf in the fiction section. Today, she wore a chartreuse cardigan over her shoulders and had tied her hair into a spinsterish bun. She'd taken her coat off and hung it over her arm. The dog waddled at her feet, and more than one customer crouched to scratch her ears. Gabe imagined strolling up and taking those square glasses from Hester's nose and seeing her hair tumble around her shoulders. He imagined offering her a bouquet of purple irises, and that she wanted him as much as he wanted her.

She turned the corner into the next row and disappeared. He left the novel on the table and followed. He edged up the aisle that ran parallel, and then peeked around the books to where she leafed through a graphic novel with zombies on the cover. He sighed. He glanced over the colorful spines between them to where he could see her hands, tiny hands with well-chewed nails. Her index finger paused. She leaned her shoulder against a shelf to read. The dog, who lay at her feet, lifted her head up, sniffed, then let her head fall to the floor with a sigh.

Gabe had to tell her to stay as far away from him and Sam as she could, but what would she say if he told her that? What would she ask, and what would she think of him if she knew all of his secrets? Would she still tell him he wasn't as odd as he thought he was? Would she let him take her dog out for long walks? He couldn't be invisible anymore with a dog, especially a basset hound like this one, with its long ears and dopey waddle. People would stop him on the street and ask the dog's name. *Waffles,* he'd say, and he'd be Waffles's dad or Hester's husband. People would remember that about him, at the very least.

A book popped off the shelf and landed at his feet. Then another followed. And another.

"Gabe?"

He'd recognize that croaky voice anywhere. He crouched and peered through the gap in the books. He should say something charming, like in those movies, where bantering through bookshelves was code for meet cute, not stalking. Instead, he smiled.

"If you want to spy on me," she said, "you could at least put on a hat and sunglasses. I saw you out in the café. And if you just want to stare at me, then I'll get going. But if you want to be friends, ask. Maybe we could grab coffee."

"Coffee?" he said. He could practically see the word hovering over him in a speech bubble surrounded by pulsing hearts.

"Yeah, coffee," she said, taking a step backward. "Meet me over there. But first reshelve those books."

He did what she said and then met her in line. "We'll have to be fast," she said. "I'm on kid duty. You never appreciate time, do you, till you don't have it anymore? I don't even know what I did with myself BK.

327

That's Before Kate. And the money! I guess I used to sleep in piles of money, because God knows what I spent it on. She's my niece. Likes princesses, won't eat her peas. Typical. Cute, but annoying. Honestly, I hate peas too."

"Why's she your problem?" Gabe asked.

Hester waved a dismissive hand. "I wouldn't say she's a problem. But I'm earning my good Samaritan badge." They stepped up to the counter. "My treat," she said. "What do you want?"

"Coffee," Gabe said.

"Miss, you can't really bring your dog in here," the young woman working the counter said.

"We'll go outside," Hester said.

At the coffee station, she ripped the tops off of a wad of sugar packets. "I take mine with a lot of sugar," she said. "And I mean a lot. So, when you make it for me, put in as much as you think possible and then add one more. Morgan says it'll give me diabetes."

"Who's Morgan?" Gabe asked.

She started to say something and then lifted up the creamer.

He nodded. "And sugar," he added.

"It's important to know how you take your coffee," Hester said. "Especially if we're going to be friends."

"Are we?" Gabe asked.

"We'll see, right?"

A silence fell between them that Hester finally broke by jerking her head toward the door. "It's cold, and I can feel the snow in the air, but that woman keeps giving Waffles the stink-eye."

She led them outside, to a set of black café tables. The heavy sky enclosed them like a fort of gray blankets, and when Gabe inhaled, he felt as though he was sharing her air.

"I've always liked sipping coffee in the cold like this," Hester said, buttoning her coat up and enticing Waffles to lie on her feet. "There's something peaceful about it. Private too. You have the world to yourself in a way."

Gabe felt the cold metal of the chair through the seat of his pants. In front of them, the parking lot was packed, but she was right. The table felt oddly private. Like their own place.

"Do you have everything for French toast?" Hester asked. "Bread, milk, eggs. That's what everyone buys before a storm. Me? I make sure I have enough scotch in the house. Honestly, though, I love a good storm. Especially right before the holiday like this. It'll be nice to have a white Christmas. I'll take Kate sledding tomorrow and then worry the whole time she'll crack her head open, but let her do it anyway. I'm learning."

"Learning what?"

"Oh, not to be an asshole, I guess."

She could never be an asshole, not to him.

"I wasn't too thrilled when Kate came to live with me. Now . . . let's say I'm getting used to it." She took another long sip from her coffee, gripping the cup in both of her mittened hands. "Listen," she said. "I'm sorry. I've been nosing around in your business this week, and I bet it's brought up some bad memories."

She had brought up bad memories, but those were always there, weren't they? Below the surface, a wound barely masked by a scab. There were good ones there too, if you dug deep enough.

"I saw Sam today," she said. "I followed him to the VA Hospital in West Roxbury. He's working with one of the patients there, and when he saw me, I thought he'd know that I mentioned Lila to you the other day, but he didn't. You didn't tell him anything that I told you, did you?"

Gabe shook his head.

"Sam said we should grab drinks one of

these days. Should I? Should I tell him that his sister hired me, or is it not worth going there?"

It wasn't worth it. Not at all. "He wants to leave that life behind. And so do I."

"Got it," Hester said, standing suddenly. "Understood. None of my business. I should have dropped this a couple of days ago. And I have to pick up Kate. So here's the thing." She dug in her pocket and pulled out a business card. "No more stalking me in bookstores for you, and no more pretending I want to rent an apartment for me. Let's be friends, okay. Or not, that's okay too. Call me if you want, though, and maybe we'll make plans."

Gabe stood too. He wanted to run as far as he possibly could from her, to leave her to her life, but he wasn't strong enough, because he also wanted to come up with a story, the right story, a story that would get her to stop asking questions about what was and keep asking questions about what could be. He wanted to be like Sam, someone who could reinvent himself so thoroughly. Someone who could leave the past behind. "Can I walk with you?" he asked.

"I guess," Hester said.

They walked for a block. What would she say if he asked her to dinner? He looked at her hand, clutching the dog's leash, at those tiny fingers. What would happen if he slid his hand over hers? What would it be like to be wanted?

"Do you know Jamie Williams?" Hester asked. "Sam's friend. Big, black guy. Nice smile, but a bit like Lennie, if you know what I mean. He's crushed out on Sam, but most people are. I mean you are, right?"

Gabe stopped midstep.

"Oh, calm down," Hester said. "I know you're not crushed out in a gay way. You probably like the attention. Who wouldn't?"

She pulled open the door to a day care center. Inside, a half dozen other parents waited in the hallway. Not ten seconds later, the door to a classroom opened, and a wave of children ran screaming into the hallway, including Kate, with her honey-colored hair. Hester lifted her from the ground and spun her around and kissed her on the nose and cheeks in a way that said anything but that she found the kid annoying. The girl held out some Popsicle sticks that had been glued together.

"Beautiful," Hester said, holding the craft up to the light where the pink glitter sparkled. "Kate, this is Mr. DiPursio."

The girl buried her head in Hester's shoulder.

"You can say hello, can't you? You met him the other day at his house. Remember?"

Kate mumbled hello.

"Can I give this to him? I bet he'd like it." She nodded.

"All yours," Hester said.

Gabe took the Popsicle sticks from her and felt like his heart might melt right there. He wanted to lift the little girl in his arms and swing her over his head and cover her face with raspberries.

"So call me," Hester said. "Any time."

Gabe looked at the card that was still clutched in his glove.

"And one more thing. Barry or Gabe? Your choice."

"I never liked Barry," Gabe said.

He touched her hand, and they stood for what seemed like hours in silence, children running around them. He should tell her to leave, to never speak to him again. He should tear the card up into tiny pieces and forget that they'd ever met. But she looked directly at him. Kate squirmed in her arms. Her glasses had slipped down her nose, but she didn't bother to push them up. "Good to know," she said.

He reached out to keep the glasses from falling. Before he could stop himself, he kissed her, and she, he swore, kissed back.

Or at least she did till she shook her head and wiped her mouth with the back of a fist. She left without another word. He watched through the window as the two of them hurried toward the parking lot with the dog. He ran his fingers along the Popsicle sticks till glitter wore off. He imagined picking Kate up from day care. Like with Waffles, the preschool teachers would remember him. They'd be required to, since it was part of their job, but even more so because they'd see how lucky Hester was to have a man around who cared so deeply.

"Can I help you, sir?"

One of the preschool teachers eyed Gabe warily. A few parentless children milled around behind her. He couldn't help but think he'd done something wrong by being there. He headed out into the cold, trying not to think about Sam or Lila or any of it, but he could see that braid again. He could taste the tobacco on Lila's lips. He could feel her under him. He'd told Lila about the motel, lying there, in her bed while Sam slept in the other room, his head resting on her breasts. He'd told her what those men did, sobbing, wanting her to say that she'd protect him, wanting her to say she loved him the way he loved her. But he felt her tense, and then push him away. He reached for her, and she brushed him off, slipping into a robe with her back to him.

"Those men have diseases," she said.

"Help me," he said.

Lila stood and held the robe closed. "I don't want to see you again."

In the end, Gabe had only had Sam.

Ahead, a streetlamp shone like the fullest of moons, and like that, Gabe was in New Hampshire again, loping through the trees toward the dock on a night that was anything but cold.

Sam is beside him. They run in tandem, without any effort, and then guide the canoe into the water, away from the shore, with Sam at the stern. Gabe leans into his paddle, his fingers brushing along the still surface with each stroke. He doesn't know why Sam even talks to him, let alone meets him out on the lake for these late-night jaunts.

Sam is beautiful — though that's not a word for other boys, is it? — with his fine features and slender hands and eyes that find your very core. For Gabe, these nights aren't about sex. They're about escape. And they're about something else he can't name, something to do with being wanted, being seen. Feeling solid.

Sam steers the boat alongside one of

about fifteen docks that jut from the shore of a small island. He jumps lightly to the boards, wraps a rope around a piling and, before Gabe can even put his paddle up or crawl onto the dock or even ask where they are, disappears into the trees. Gabe secures the boat and hurries after him. It takes a moment for his eyes to adjust to the dark, but he soon finds a well-worn path. Intermittent moonlight filters through the foliage to help guide him to a small clearing, where church pews glow white under the moon and a pulpit stands beneath a bell tower. Gabe walks up the aisle of the tiny outdoor chapel to where Sam sits in the front row.

"Haven't you seen them on Sundays?" Sam asks. "In their bonnets and seersucker, rowing their rickety boats. This is one way in, this lake, and this island, but not when you spend Saturdays cleaning shit from their toilets."

He clears a thick layer of sodden leaves from the forest floor and uncovers the lid of a rubber trash pail that's been buried up to its rim and filled with magazines. "I like to think of the devoted worshiping at the altar of Larry Flynt," he says, tossing Gabe the flashlight with a damp copy of *Penthouse*.

"Who else knows about this place?" Gabe asks.

"Only you, my friend. No one matters but you and me."

Gabe rolls on his side. The leaves rustle beneath him. It means something to be one of two who matter. This is before, but after. Before the ad on Craigslist, and after Gabe lived with Cheryl, when he'd come to stay at Sam's house. Till this very moment, Gabe still felt hopeless and alone and like no one on earth had ever heard him cry. He still closed his eyes at night and pretended what happened hadn't.

"I'll always watch out for you," Sam says. "Always. No matter what. We'll watch out for each other."

Back then, Sam's words sent a wave of something through Gabe. He felt as though he was standing on center stage, lit up for the whole world to see. It took years — maybe till this very moment, on the side-walk, watching Hester retreat — for him to put a word to the feeling or to learn how fleeting happiness could be and how vulner-able it left him. A ravenous chasm of loneli-ness, desperate to be filled.

He closes the *Penthouse* and lays it on the leaves. "I have a plan," he says. "Will you help me?"

"Anything," Sam says.

"I need to tell you something. Promise

you'll believe me."

Gabe traced the letters on Hester's business card. He already had her number and e-mail memorized. He really should forget her, but what if he sent a text tonight to say hello, to tell Kate thanks for the Popsicle sticks? A small touch. A reminder. He'd save the dinner invitation for another time. He headed down the street toward home, barely able to keep the skip from his step. His phone rang, and even though he somehow knew that he should ignore it, that it would bring this perfect moment to an end, he believed it might be her. He dug the phone from his pocket. It was Sam.

"Where are you?" Gabe asked.

"Never mind that," Sam said, in a voice barely above a whisper. "There's someone in the other room, but I wanted to tell you that I'm sorry I lost my temper earlier. You know we have to deal with this though, right?" And when Gabe didn't respond, Sam clucked his tongue. "You've always had my back," he said. "Since day one. And I've always had yours."

Gabe touched Hester's name on the card. A wave of unbearable sadness swept through him. He found a bench and sat. He thought about that house he'd dreamed of.

"Who hired her?" Sam asked "Do you know?"

Lila's name slipped off Gabe's tongue before he could catch it.

"Lila," Sam said. "That's not good for her either."

Gabe felt the inevitable descend in heavy clouds of gray. He listened for a few more minutes, but when he hung up, he was sweating. Anxiety chewed at his stomach. He tore at his coat, ripping it off and hurrying the few remaining blocks to their house. In the basement, he checked the plastic bag where the two remaining fingers had already begun to desiccate. Under one blue nail was the faintest smear of blood. Gabe flushed that finger down the toilet. The other finger he ran along his scalp and then placed in the batik box on his dresser, right next to his stash. It would be easy enough to find there. The police would call it a trophy.

It was time to go. It was the only way.

He packed a duffel bag, filling it with fleece jackets and gloves and hats, anything for warmth. He added a pair of boots, a box of granola bars, and some fruit. He'd drive over to Burlington to buy snow shoes from L.L. Bean. They'd need them tonight.

Then, he left the house and went into the square, where he found one of the few remaining pay phones. He gripped the receiver for a full minute before he took a deep breath and dialed. No matter how much he owned Sam, no matter what Sam had done for him, there had to be another way out of this. There had to be a way forward. And besides, he could still feel her lips on his.

CHAPTER 20

No one who knew Twig Ambrose besides her father seemed worried about her, but Angela White was convinced that something terrible had happened to the woman. Nearly twenty-four hours had gone by since Donald Ambrose had called the mayor, and Angela hadn't found a single person who'd seen Twig since Saturday, not a friend, neighbor, or colleague. She'd interviewed more than two dozen people from the party. Some remembered seeing Twig, others didn't. That Felicia Nakazawa had, among other things, sworn she'd seen Twig standing outside the French doors at the Richards mansion wearing an emerald-green dress, but then Felicia Nakazawa was the type of witness who told you whatever you wanted to hear. She was the type who fingered the wrong person during a line up and sent them to jail.

By midafternoon, Angela had called her

boss, Stan, and told him that she thought this was serious and that she needed backup, and he'd put together a taskforce to wade through the remaining interviews and pull together a data trail. They'd subpoenaed Twig's phone and credit card records, and even those worried Angela. The last text Twig had sent was the one to Wendy early on Sunday morning. She hadn't used her credit cards since Saturday afternoon either.

Thankfully, Stan had fielded all of the calls from Donald Ambrose with demands for updates. If Stan was good for anything besides ruining Angela's days off, it was running interference and giving her the space she needed to do her job. Now, she drove toward Everett to interview one of the veterans who'd attended the benefit, Jamie Williams. The sun had set for the day, and she punched in Cary's number, who sighed audibly when Angela asked her to pick Isaiah up at swim practice. She wondered if Cary cared more about having to pick up the boy or that Angela had lost her day off. "I'm gonna be home right after I finish with this interview. I'll even bring Thai, okay."

Cary laughed. "You're good for a bribe, I'll give you that."

Angela clicked off, but her phone rang

almost immediately, just as she pulled into downtown Everett. It was Stan.

"Where are you?" he asked.

"Following up on a lead," Angela said, giving him a brief update on where she was with the case.

"Hold up," he said. "I think we may have something new."

We need to talk.

That's what the text from Morgan said, and it made Hester stop in the middle of clicking Kate into her car seat. She read the message again. Morgan rarely texted, period, and when he did, he was usually short and to the point.

She wiped at her lips. Gabe's kiss had stunned her, even if she'd known that he had a crush on her. It had been obvious from the moment they met. It was why she hadn't told Gabe that she lived with Morgan, that they were raising a child and a dog together, that she insisted on keeping her own apartment and her own mailbox and her own mess, even though — in truth — she rarely went to the third floor anymore. It had also made her feel good. Wanted. Like she was her own person again. But even now, after all these years of being with Morgan, of being loved, reading this text made her feel that she was on the very edge of being alone, and as much as Hester fought for independence, nothing frightened her more than the thought of being abandoned.

Can you give me a preview? she texted back.

Morgan responded a moment later. *Meet me at home. I'll be done here by 6:30.*

See you then! Hester wrote, but hardly felt the exclamation point.

She lifted Waffles into the truck and pulled out of the parking lot. It wasn't even five o'clock, but the sun had already disappeared over the horizon. The holiday lights lining the Somerville streets did nothing to cheer her up either. However irrational, she somehow felt complicit in the kiss, even though, in truth, all she'd done was to pull away and leave.

"Kate," she said, "don't tell Uncle Morgan about the Popsicle sticks."

"Kate want Popsicle sticks!"

"You gave them to my friend. Remember?" Hester said, even though that was exactly what she didn't want Kate to remember. It hardly mattered, though, because Kate had already begun to melt into a tantrum, and when Hester got to her street, she kept driving. The thought of sitting in the house, with the Christmas lights on and the kittens running over everything and this noise, was too much to bear. She turned left onto Route 24, barely listening to Kate or the newscaster on the local public radio station who talked about the ongoing search for that woman who'd gone missing over the weekend.

"Where Aunt Hester go?" Kate finally said from the backseat. She sniffled again, but the worst of the crisis seemed to have passed.

"We're visiting a friend," Hester said, and twenty minutes later she pulled up in front of an old triple-decker on a quiet street in Everett. She double-checked the address on her phone, and then lifted Kate from her car seat and knocked on the door to the first floor. She waited, sniffing the winter air, already heavy with the feel of pending snow. "Don't tell Uncle Morgan we came here," she said.

Inside, a dog scampered to the door and yipped, which got Waffles to howl too. Through lacy curtains hanging over the door's window, Hester saw Jamie's silhouette as he lumbered down the hallway and opened the door a crack.

"We met earlier today at the hospital," Hester said over the barking. "Do you remember?"

Jamie nodded and took a moment to respond. "But what are you doing here?" he asked in one long breath.

"Could I come in for a moment? I'm sorry. I brought the whole gang with me. This is my niece, Kate. And the loudmouth is Waffles."

Jamie's gaze shifted down to where Waffles howled. "I like waffles," he said.

"So do I," Hester said. "That's where she got her name."

Jamie swung the door open a bit. The small white dog he introduced as Butch scampered around his feet. Waffles dashed into the house and the two dogs sniffed each other and then ran down the long hallway and disappeared into one of the rooms. Hester held Kate's hand and stepped over the threshold. "I don't normally pop in unannounced like this," she said. "But I didn't have your phone number."

"You had my address, though," Jamie said. His voice was flat, but he smiled the tiniest bit, like he was on to her game.

"Addresses are easier to find these days. No one has a listed number anymore," Hester said.

Jamie lived in a long, railroad apartment, with dirty white walls and steaming radiators. Not a single holiday decoration hung from the walls. In fact, nothing hung from the walls. He led Hester to the back of the apartment, to a kitchen with dated, almond-colored appliances and a chipped tile floor. A pot of water boiled on the electric stove.

"Making dinner," he said.

An open can of chili sat on the counter next to a box of macaroni and cheese. He motioned to a set of stools, and Hester lifted Kate onto one and perched on the other.

"Chili mac," Hester said. "That's one of my favorites."

"Me too. You can have some."

"I'd love to. But I need to go home in a minute." She paused. "I think I'm in trouble," she added, almost to herself.

"Why?" Jamie watched the water boil, and stirred the pasta.

"I don't know," Hester said.

"I bet you do."

Hester sighed. "I've been keeping things from my boyfriend. Things I should have told him."

"That's not good." Jamie drained the pasta into a colander. He added milk and a dollop of butter, and then stirred in dried cheese till the whole pot was filled with orangey pasta.

"Kate want macaroni and cheese!" Kate said, and Hester prepared for another

347

meltdown, but Jamie filled a small bowl for her. Kate gobbled the pasta up while he dumped the can of chili into the pot and heated it on the stove.

"Do you mind if I eat?" he asked a moment later.

"Please," Hester said. "I shouldn't be bothering you."

"Why'd you come?"

"I don't really know."

"Stay," Jamie said. "It's not so bad to eat with someone."

He stood at the counter across from her and ate with a wooden spoon.

"I used to do that," Hester said. "Eat whatever I wanted, right at the counter. I'd come home from school when I was a kid and I'd have cereal for dinner. Or toast, maybe. Sometimes I'd pull every vegetable in the refrigerator out, the ones that were about to rot, and I'd mix them with pasta and ketchup and call it Bachelorette Surprise. I'd stand at the counter and watch *Jeopardy!* Sometimes, when my mother had left a bottle out, I'd drink a glass of wine on my own. I started drinking by myself when I was eight. Do you ever drink by yourself?"

"Every night," Jamie said. He closed his eyes. When he spoke, it was all Hester could do to be patient and not fill in words for him, as he told her that he did nearly everything by himself, that he'd talked about that very topic earlier that day in his therapy session. He told her that sometimes he stared off at nothing and didn't know that hours had gone by, and then would realize that someone was talking to him, and he'd see how frightened they were. "Big, black, and stupid," he said, choosing the words carefully. "At least that's what they believe."

Hester nearly told him not to say that, but she knew before the words came out that he was right. That was the way some people perceived him. Listening to him stumble through his thoughts, waiting for him to find the right words, was painful. And yet she didn't want to leave.

"Do you want a beer?" he asked.

"Sure," she said.

He popped open two cans of Bud Light.

"How long have you known Sam?" Hester asked.

"Sam?"

"Aaron," she said, correcting herself. "I meant Aaron Gewirtzman."

"Not long," Jamie said. "He asked me to a party. I'm the type you want at a cocktail party. Quite the conversationalist."

"Was it at the Richardses' house?"

Jamie nodded, and Hester thought about the postcard with the photo of the mansion on Louisburg Square. It seemed like weeks ago that she'd sat outside that house in her truck and seen Sam for the first time. What had Sam's note read? She couldn't remember, but it was a quote from *The Shining.* She hadn't given the postcards much thought for a couple of days now.

"What was the benefit like?"

Jamie shrugged. "Like being a fly in milk. Aaron barely talked to me. And that woman went missing. The one who's been in the news."

"I haven't paid much attention."

Jamie told her that he was supposed to talk to a detective about it who'd called earlier.

"What else do you know about Sam?"

"Aaron," Jamie said. "You keep calling him Sam."

"He looks like someone I used to know."

"Not a lot, but he's nice to me for some reason. I have seizures because of the bullet wound, so I can't drive. It don't take less than three hours to get to the VA on public transportation. Sometimes I can't remember simple things." He paused. "And it makes me angry."

"I bet everything that happened to you

makes you angry," Hester said.

Jamie thought about it for a moment. "Sometimes," he said.

Hester glanced at her phone. It was nearly six-thirty already, right when Morgan had said he'd be leaving work. "I don't want to go home," she said, realizing, suddenly, that it was true, realizing that this whole case, every part of it, had been about finding herself in a world that was feeling smaller and more constricted and less in her control by the day. It wasn't that she wanted to leave Morgan or Kate or Waffles, but tonight, this night, she wanted her life to be about herself again, if only for a moment. So they sat and talked for longer than Hester ever would have expected. Once she got used to the way Jamie spoke, the stops and starts, the long searches for words, he came alive. He talked about growing up in Everett, where he'd played football and scored with girls and got into a tussle with the law over selling pot. He told her about driving along a dusty road in Afghanistan and coming under a hail of bullets, and then waking in a hospital a few months later. "It been a struggle ever since," he said.

"I hope it's getting better," Hester said.

"Sometimes."

Jamie opened the freezer and took out a

cheesecake. "When you lived alone," he asked, "did you buy things like this and tell yourself you wouldn't eat all of it?"

"I'm a *Golden Girl* at heart. I've never met a frozen cheesecake I couldn't eat in a single sitting."

It was seven-thirty now, and Hester's phone had already rung three times. She turned off the ringer and let it sit silently in her pocket. She lifted Kate onto the floor so the girl could crawl around with the dogs, even if the floor did look dirty. "Kate can have a little piece, but cut the rest of it in half!"

Jamie slid the cheesecake from the box. It was covered with strawberries, their thick, red glaze bleeding down the sides. He took out a stainless-steel chef's knife that gleamed under the kitchen lights. When he sliced the cheesecake into two neat halves, he swept the knife out so that it was streaked with bright red strawberry syrup. Hester felt her stomach rumble as both dogs barked.

"Quiet, you two," she said.

But Waffles was on her feet, running down the hallway, with Butch at her heels.

Then Hester heard a noise, followed by a loud crash. "What the . . . ?"

She glanced at Jamie, confused. His eyes

had grown wide. He held the knife in front of him.

Someone shouted from the hallway.

Hester leaped from the stool. Where was Kate? Down the hallway, the front door had been smashed open. Police in SWAT uniforms swarmed in, visors down, guns raised, and Hester actually thought there must be something going on outside, something that the police needed to protect them from. And then an officer shouted at her. His words were garbled beneath his visor. He waved the gun, and she saw Kate on the floor by the refrigerator. She fought to grab the girl, and she was on her knees, the officer still shouting, and she realized he was shouting at her and telling her to get down and not to move. Another officer swept Kate up and retreated from the apartment. Kate shrieked and reached toward her. Hester struggled to follow, but the officer pushed her down again. Waffles ran after them, howling, till another officer caught her around the neck with a noose.

"What are you doing?" Hester shouted. "Give her to me!"

"Hands up!" the officer shouted.

Hester put her hands on the back of her head as a black woman walked through the lines of officers. She held up a detective's badge. "Jamie Williams?" she said. "I'll need you to put that knife down."

The entire apartment was filled with cops wearing helmets and bulletproof vests, and every single one of them had a gun drawn. Outside, through the open doorway, a sea of neighbors had already filled the sidewalk. Hester could see their phones raised, recording the moment.

"Get back!" Jamie said, slashing the knife in front of him, his eyes wide with fear.

"Jamie, give her the knife," Hester said, trying to keep her voice calm. She wanted to get to him, to tell him that this, whatever this was, would all work out.

"Please, Mr. Williams," the detective said, holding her hands in front of herself. "Give me the knife. Nobody needs to get hurt."

"I ain't done nothing," Jamie said.

The detective took another step into the kitchen. "We can talk this through." Her voice was soft. Calm. "We can leave here without anything else happening. Please, Mr. Williams. Put the knife down." She paused. "We're here to keep you safe."

Jamie lunged forward, and then Hester's face felt warm and wet long before she heard the shot. It sounded like a tiny firecracker. Jamie slumped to the floor. A red stain spread across his chest, and his eyes fluttered. The police charged forward, and in the chaos, Hester scrambled through them and fought her way to his side. She fumbled with a fistful of dish towels that hung from the stove. "Stay awake," she said, pressing at his chest. Blood pooled onto the chipped tile floor and welled up around her fingers.

"Ma'am, you need to leave," the detective said.

"He was just standing there!"

"He had a knife," the detective said. And then she shouted into the radio on her shoulder. "We need a bus!" she said. "We need a fucking bus!"

CHAPTER 21

It was nearly nine o'clock by the time Hester pulled into her driveway. She still felt numb to what had happened, and yet played it over again in her head. She could see the EMTs working on Jamie as they lifted him onto a gurney, handcuffed him to it, and rushed him to the hospital. She could also see the crime scene investigators cordoning off the backyard and pulling a mutilated body from a shed. The body was Laura "Twig" Ambrose, who'd been missing since Saturday, so soon the street outside had filled with reporters, cameras, and vans. A bit later, Hester gave her statement to Detective White. She felt exhausted as she held Kate on her lap and told the detective all about Sam and Gabe, about being hired by Lila Blaine, and what she'd found out earlier about Cheryl Jenkins and Bobby Englewood. "I don't know if there's any connection to this," Hester said. "But the two of them ran a pedophile ring. You should let the New Hampshire State Police know."

"We'll look into that," Detective White said. "What town did you say they lived in?"

"Holderness."

The detective flipped through a few pages in her notebook, and jotted something next to Hester's name. "Thank you. That was helpful. You should go home now," she said. "You okay to drive?"

"I think so," Hester said.

The whole time this had been happening, Hester hadn't turned her phone on, and only now, sitting in the driveway, did she think to check it. Morgan had left twelve voice mails and twenty-three texts. She'd forgotten that feeling of dread that had come over her with the first text he'd sent, and now all she wanted was to be with him. She lifted a sleeping Kate over her shoulder, put Waffles on the leash, and leapt out of the truck. She glanced up the street, which was quieter than normal as people hunkered down for the pending storm. Cars lined half of the street; the other half was cleared for the snow emergency. As she headed up the front pathway to the house, the very first flakes fell around her, and she turned her face up toward the sky to let the splotches of cold melt on her cheeks.

At the front door, she listened. The whole house was silent. She let the dog's leash go and followed her up the staircase, where Hester contemplated heading to the third floor and dealing with the consequences in the morning. Instead, she let herself into Morgan's apartment.

At first, she wasn't sure whether he was home. The house was dark, except for a single light over the stove in the kitchen. Kate stirred in her arms. One of the kittens launched itself from the kitchen counter and made Hester jump. Waffles scampered across the wooden floor and into the living area. It was only then that she saw Morgan sitting alone in the dark and knew that she'd been right all along. He was angry.

"There you are," she said. "Why are you sitting in the dark?"

Morgan didn't move.

"Kate potty," Kate said.

"All right, sweetie," Hester said.

She took Kate to the bathroom, and a moment later sat with the girl on her lap beside Morgan. "I'm sorry," she said. "I lost track of time. It was a . . . I don't even know how to describe tonight. It was awful."

She paused and felt like she might start to sob, but she pushed the feeling down. Still, it took her a moment to speak, and when she did, she told Morgan everything, about Sam and Gabe, about the trip to New Hampshire, about seeing Jamie get shot. Morgan listened. And then he stood and lifted Kate onto his hip. "How about I take you upstairs," he said. "And I'll read you a story in a bit."

Kate nodded. Morgan took her to her room, and a moment later he was back on the sofa with Hester. "Did you bring Kate with you?" he asked.

"To New Hampshire? No. I had no idea who I'd meet there."

"But you brought her to meet this client, right? And tonight? You brought her into a strange man's house with nothing but a basset hound to protect you? And she saw him get shot?"

"I didn't know that would happen," Hester said.

"But you didn't know *what* would happen. You didn't know anything about this guy, and you went into his house, and now it turns out he's probably a serial killer."

Hester sat up and pushed away from him. She'd expected him to comfort her, not come at her with this anger. "I'll tell you one thing I wasn't expecting," she said, sitting as far from him as she could, her back pressed into the corner of the sofa. "I wasn't expecting that there would be a body in the backyard. Should I tell Kate not to go anywhere because there might be a dead body waiting for her? I also wasn't expecting that when I got home and told you about it that you'd scream your fucking head off at me. You're an asshole. Do you know that? You're a real fucking asshole."

Two kittens chased each other across the living room, and then leaped onto the sofa.

"And you know what else?" she said, shoving them onto the floor. "I'm sick of these cats."

Morgan stood. He tossed a pillow across the room. "Do you know what I wasn't expecting? I wasn't expecting to get a call from my sister this afternoon telling me that you'd told her to stay the fuck away. Last I checked you couldn't stand Kate and couldn't get rid of her fast enough."

Hester had forgotten the e-mail she'd sent to Daphne. "I have never said that about Kate. Not one time."

"You make it so obvious! I've been worried out of my mind for three months about my sister, and you've been telling her that we don't want anything to do with her? There's no *we* in that. There's just *you.*"

Hester closed her eyes and sighed, wondering why this had to happen tonight of all nights. She put a hand on Morgan's arm, but he shrugged her off.

"That's not what I told her," Hester said.

"She read me the e-mail," Morgan said.

"Okay. You're right. You're right about everything. Some days the situation with Kate annoys me to no end. I'm a shit parent. Guilty. I'm the shittiest parent in the world. And I shouldn't have sent that e-mail without talking to you, but I knew you wouldn't let me. But let's be real here. Do you really want Daphne to come back? Do you want to spend every day of your life worrying that she'll take off again? And maybe take Kate with her? How would you feel about that, worrying about where *both* of them are? And I should have told you what was going on with these people. And I should never, ever have put Kate in danger like I did tonight. You have to know that I didn't mean to do that, but to be honest, I don't know what I'm doing half the time, and I feel like I do most of it by myself. Where have you been?"

"I took her to day care."

"One time! You took her to day care *one time,* and I'm supposed to thank you? And I keep making these mistakes and I've been . . . ." Hester lowered her voice and

whispered fiercely. "I feel like all of this happened without anyone asking me."

Morgan stared at her. He leaned forward,
hands on his knees like he was about to
spring forward. In the kitchen, a kitten
knocked something off the counter. "You're
crazy sometimes. And you should get your
story straight," he said, and Hester wanted
to hit him. "You tell my sister to stay away,
and now you're telling me that you don't
want Kate here anymore? If we don't take
care of her, who will?"

"You know this is more complicated than
that," Hester said. "You know I like Kate.
You know I love Kate and would do anything for her. That's the very reason I wrote
to Daphne. And you know I don't mind
babysitting. I never mind babysitting."

"It's not *babysitting* when it's your own
kid!" Morgan shouted.

His face was red, the freckles popping
from his cheeks. He was angry in a way that
Hester had never seen. She tried to let what
he'd said wash over her, but suddenly felt
as though she couldn't breathe. She stood
and left the apartment. Out on the landing,
she glanced down the stairs to the front
door and actually contemplated leaving.
Those were her choices, right? Stay or leave.
This life with Morgan and the kid and the

princess dresses and the bouncing horse and the never-ending threat of vomit (or worse) and the play dates, or a life by herself. None of this was what Hester had asked for. And, she realized now, what she wanted more than anything was to be *asked*.

She trudged up the attic steps to her apartment, where she stood in the middle of the piles of crap and wished this night was a night when she could still draw the bolt and put on *Jaws 2* and curl up under her ratty quilt and drink. Behind her, she heard Morgan on the stairs. They stood silently without looking at each other for five minutes. "Kate's up," Morgan finally said. "I told her she could watch *Cars.* She wants to know why we're shouting."

"So do I," Hester said.

"Can you find anything in here?"

Even though Hester knew he was offering her an olive branch, she wasn't ready to take it. Part of her wanted to be nice and let the tension dissipate, but she was right, wasn't she? It was okay to be pissed off and whiny sometimes because most days — today included — she showed up. Most days, she was right here. And most days, she didn't ask for much. "I need you to leave," she said.

Morgan looked at her for a moment, and then started taking dishes from the sink to wash them.

"Stop that," Hester said. "Don't clean. This is my apartment."

"I'm not going anywhere," Morgan said.

"Get out."

"I'm not leaving."

She pulled him from the sink and threw the soapy dishes on the floor. She shoved him away and then clasped her hands together and fought back tears. "Please," she whispered.

He took a step back. "What's wrong with you?" he asked.

"It *is* babysitting!" Hester said. "Don't you get that? It's always babysitting, and it always will be, even if we wind up putting her through college. Every single minute of this is a favor, not an obligation, and someday someone had better thank me for it."

"Thank you."

"That's not what I meant. You need to do it without it being a fight. Without solicitation. It needs to mean something."

Morgan looked at her for a moment and then cupped her cheek in his hand. He turned without another word and left. Hester sat on the top of the attic stairs and listened to him put on his coat and head out into the night by himself. She wondered how long he'd be gone. Maybe she'd be asleep by the time he came home. If he came home. Maybe, in the morning, they could pretend none of this had happened.

Downstairs, Kate sang a song to herself. The kid was still here, and Hester still had to be good. She still had to show up and care, but it would be impossible to get the kid to sleep now. A kitten crept up the attic stairs, exploring, and Hester let it rub her leg. Waffles shimmied through the dog door at the back of her closet and trotted over the mess to Hester's side. "You always get things right," she said, scratching the dog on the neck. Waffles rolled on her back for a belly rub.

"Aunt Hester," Kate shouted a moment later. "When Kate watch *Cars*?"

"In a minute," Hester called down the stairs.

"How many?"

"Five."

Hester stood slowly and poured herself a tumbler full of scotch from the bottle on her counter, added an ice cube as a mixer, and then changed into her Little Mermaid pajamas and Lion King slippers. She washed her face, took her hair down, and tied it into a ponytail. Back in the apartment, she parked Kate in front of the TV and sucked down her scotch. Even now, even after tonight, Hester knew that no matter what she said, no matter how much she complained, she'd fight to keep Kate safe. Even if it meant babysitting for the rest of her life. She ruffled Kate's hair. "You know Aunt Hester loves you more than anyone in the world, right?"

"More than Monkey?" Kate asked.

"More than Monkey."

"More than Waffles?"

"Even more than Waffles."

"Kate thirsty," Kate said.

Hester poured some apple juice into a sippy cup. "You have to brush your teeth again if I give you this."

Kate nodded. She took a long sip of the juice and burped. "Aunt Hester like *Cars*?"

"Sure," Hester said.

She settled into the sofa, watching the animation flash in front of her, hoping to feel her brain shut off. Instead, she thought back to the postcards, to the one of Wendy's mansion on Beacon Hill, with the quotes written in neat, precise handwriting. When Kate fell asleep, she lifted the girl under one arm and the scotch under the other and headed up the stairs to her own apartment, where she slid a videotape into the VCR and flipped on the TV. She glanced out the window, where the first flakes from the storm had begun to pelt the glass, and then she curled up under the quilt as the opening credits to *The Shining* began to roll, a car driving through the mountains, the score swelling. She finished her scotch and poured another two fingers. And as usual, the quiet intensity of the movie calmed Hester and reminded her that they were all — herself included — doing the best they could. At least she wasn't trapped in a hotel with a homicidal husband.

A half hour into the movie, a sea of blood poured from the elevator into the ornate hallways of the Overlook Hotel. Bodies were strewn across the floor. One of them had an axe in its back. Hester leaned her head against the sofa as a sudden wave of exhaustion swept through her. She had to be sure not to let Morgan find them asleep in front of a horror movie, especially not with a half-empty bottle of scotch. She'd really be in trouble then.

Kate stirred and woke. She looked at the screen, transfixed by the flashing images.

"You shouldn't watch this," Hester said. "It's scary."

Kate stroked Hester's arm. "Like pajamas," she said.

"Maybe you'll get a pair from Santa," Hester said. "We can be twins. Like the girls in the movie. Do you like mermaids or cars better?"

"Mermaids."

"I thought so."

Hester muted the sound and let Kate rest her mop of curls on her lap. Daphne hated the Little Mermaid pajamas, and had since Hester first wore them at Wellesley. Daphne hated anything girly, anything that made her or Kate vulnerable to the world, but Daphne wasn't here, was she? Only Hester was.

Kate's breathing grew steady. Waffles woofed in her sleep, her legs twitching as she chased rabbits in her dreams. Hester's eyes began to close.

On the TV, Shelley Duvall ran through the hotel with her son in her arms, snot streaming down her face, long black hair falling from a ponytail, terrified by a woman hiding somewhere in one of the rooms. Hester took another sip of scotch. Don't sleep, she reminded herself. Morgan couldn't find them here.

A woman hiding in a hotel.

A phantom.

One that could kill.

A husband trying his best to keep his sanity, trying to be someone he wasn't. The imagined becoming very, very real.

Hester's leg jolted, and she sat up. She looked at the screen again, at Wendy Torrance fighting for her life, and it made sense to her. Or at least a small part of it did.

CHAPTER 22

Gabe sat in his car on that nondescript street in Everett. He'd been there for hours. He'd ducked down in his seat and watched the police arrive with their battering ram, along with Detective White.

Angie.

She looked confident leading them into the house. And she'd seemed broken when she'd come out moments later, blood staining her hands and knees. He wondered if she'd recognize his voice when she listened to the 911 tapes, where he'd told the dispatcher that the air around Jamie's house smelled like rotting flesh, or whether she'd even remember speaking with him earlier that day. He hadn't meant for anyone to get hurt, but he watched as the ambulance appeared and the EMTs wheeled out a gurney. It was all he could do not to get out of the car and join the neighbors standing behind the line of yellow tape. Of course, there was no doubt that Twig was dead. When they wheeled her out in a black body bag, the camera flashes started to go off.

As the news vans began to arrive, Gabe turned the radio to the local station, where the story had taken on a life of its own. Somehow the media had learned about Jamie's military record, that he had PTSD and, before that, that he'd played football in high school and sustained numerous concussions. "Like Aaron Hernandez," one commentator said, before going on to say that Jamie had been arrested for selling pot when he was sixteen, as part of a local Everett gang.

"A long history of violent behavior," another reporter said.

Gabe should have been happier to see things go this way.

He hadn't expected to see Hester there, or the little girl. He'd called the police to keep the two of them safe, and yet here they were in the middle of it all. He watched Hester walk out the front door of the house, clutching the girl over her shoulder, gripping the dog's leash, startled by the line of camera flashes that went off. A reporter shouted a question at her, and Angie held up a hand and escorted the three of them to the truck.

Now, two hours later, Gabe still watched from the street. Some of the reporters had packed it in for the evening, and most of the neighbors had lost interest. As he sat there, Angie came out of the house and stood on the front porch. She leaned on both hands and seemed to be shaking off tears. She lit a cigarette and answered her phone, speaking to whoever was on the other end for a few moments before hanging up, checking her notebook, and dialing. Even if Gabe hadn't been watching, he'd have recognized her number when it popped up. He'd memorized it, like he'd memorized Hester's.

"Mr. Bellows?" Angela said.

"Yes," Gabe said.

"I was hoping to talk to you. Tonight, if I could. I sent another detective over to your apartment, and it doesn't look like anyone's home. Could I meet you somewhere? It's important."

"Why?"

"It would be good to talk in person. Tell me where you are."

Gabe watched as she snapped her fingers and whispered something to a uniformed police officer, who nodded and ran inside. Was she trying to trace his call?

"Ask me now," Gabe said. "Ask anything

you like. I'll tell you the truth."

"Do you know Laura Ambrose? Twig?"

"I've never met her. Not that I remember, at least. You found her, didn't you? It's all over the news. You have a suspect too, right?"

"I can't really comment. You know that. It's an ongoing investigation. Which is why I want to talk to you. And your roommate too. Do you know where he is?"

"No," Gabe said. He listened to the radio. "The reporters want Jamie to be guilty," he said.

"Is he?"

"What do you think?"

"I'm more curious to hear what you think. Why don't you tell me where you are? I'll come pick you up. You can tell me more."

"What do you want to know?"

"Anything you want to tell me. I'll come alone if that would help. Let me . . ."

Gabe clicked off. She knew. Or at least she knew enough. If they didn't leave soon, it would be too late.

Angela hit redial. She listened again as the call went to Gabe's voice mail and a computer read off a number. She'd held off from asking him if he'd ever been to Holderness, where Twig's family had a summer house.

She'd also kept herself from telling him about the search warrant or the finger they'd found in the batik box. She fumbled with her notebook and dropped it to the porch floor, papers scattering in the wind and snow. "Give me a hand here," she said to a deputy, trying to keep the panic from her voice. "Find Felicia Nakazawa's phone number," she said.

"Here it is," the deputy said.

Angela ripped her glove off and dialed, praying that the woman answered. The phone rang. She stepped into the narrow hallway where Jamie's dog whined from her crate. Animal control would be here soon, but even from here, Angela could see the bloodstains on the dog's white coat. There was blood everywhere. In the kitchen. On the floors. On Angela's shoes and clothes. Blood, and it was all her fault. They'd found Twig's body in the shed, and then used a periscope and seen that knife and thought the strawberry syrup was blood. They'd moved in too quickly, that was all there was to it. She'd made a judgment call, and it was the wrong one. But she wouldn't have any more blood on her hands, not tonight, not if she could help it.

But she could see Felicia Nakazawa hurrying out of the police station earlier that day. And she could see Sam Blaine at her side.

Sam left the naked man sleeping in the king-size bed and slipped out of the hotel room. He considered calling Gabe one last time but thought better of it. The more distance he put between them tonight, the better. Earlier, Gabe had told Sam that he knew where the key to Hester's house was hidden. He'd told him much more, too, that he'd already been in her apartment, that he'd watched her sleep, that he'd imagined a life with her, and Sam had listened. He was a good friend that way. And he'd made sure Gabe knew, as much as he wanted it, that it couldn't be. Not this time.

He texted Wendy. *Finished with cops. We still on?*

Meet me at the house, Wendy wrote back, *I have a surprise for you,* and a half hour later, Sam was naked again, this time lying on a massage table in one of the bedrooms on the second floor of the mansion. A therapist worked at his shoulders, and he was able to push the images of Hester and Gabe and Twig from his mind. Still, Wendy, who lay on the table beside his, wanted to know about his trip to the station. She wanted to know if they were any closer to finding Twig.

"Are you that worried?" Sam asked. "Don't you think she went off somewhere with a friend and forgot to tell anyone?"

Wendy groaned. "Yup, right there," she said to the therapist. "Harder. As hard as you can."

Sam turned to see her arching back, that hair cascading from her neck as the therapist dug his elbow into her bony shoulder. The therapist winked, and Sam couldn't help but think about the happy ending he'd get if they'd been alone. His own therapist continued to work at the knots in his shoulders. A CD of pan flute favorites played on repeat, and the air smelled of sandalwood. It was so peaceful, Sam almost laughed.

"Of course I'm worried," Wendy said. "Or getting there, at least."

Sam ran her through the basics of the police interview, looking at the photo, answering Detective White's questions about his personal life. He had to remind himself that Aaron Gewirtzman had never laid his eyes on Twig. "She's pretty," he said. "At least in the photos."

"She's even prettier in real life. She's healthy and outdoorsy. Her family is into roughing it. They have a house up in New Hampshire where they spend nearly every weekend in the summer."

"Have you been?"

"Of course, but probably not again." Wendy paused as what she'd said sank in. "God, I don't mean it like that," she added. "I mean that the house is . . . rustic. They have spiders all over the place, and the shower is outdoors, and Twig's family is really into being naked. It's too much, for me at least. So what else did you tell them?"

"I couldn't really tell them anything besides the truth," Sam said.

Wendy laughed. "Whatever that might be," she said.

Sam's shoulders tightened. The therapist's hands paused and then went back to work. "Meaning?" he asked.

"Oh, come on," Wendy said. "You're so obvious, the way you watch and listen and morph into whatever you need to be. You were such a queen with Felicia, I actually thought you might be gay, even *after* we started sleeping together. I mean, what do I know about you? You grew up in New York and went to Columbia and rowed crew with Brennan Wigglesworth. That's about it. But most people have mothers, fathers, sisters, brothers. They have exes who screwed them over. They have shitty jobs. Most people have a story. You dropped right into my life without friends or family or attachments."

Sam let his shoulders relax. He willed his heart rate to slow and his breathing to steady. This was when he was at his best. "What do I know about you?" he asked.

"I'm an open book! Anyone who has an Internet connection knows about me. You know about my parents. You know that I live in their guesthouse. You know what food I eat, where I go on vacation, how I dress. You know that I'm thirty-one and the maternal thing has started to kick in. And if you want to know more, read my blog."

She rolled halfway toward him, her boyish breasts flashing the therapists shamelessly. She reached across the space between them and took Sam's hand. Her delicate bones and soft skin still unnerved him. "All I mean," she said, "is that I want to learn more. You don't have to be so mysterious. I don't really care where you're from or how sophisticated you are, or whether your father was a doctor or a lawyer or a bank robber. People sometimes don't realize that they can be real with me, that I like that. You don't have to pretend."

Wendy, Sam realized, was as lucky as he was. She was too much of a public figure to make go away, except in the most convenient of accidents. That marble staircase, out in the foyer, arms twirling like windmills, a final grasp at hope. The cliffs at Scionsett. An accident at sea. "I'll try," he said. "You'll have to let me know what you want to learn."

The therapist massaged Sam's cranium, signaling the end of their sessions. And a few moments later, Sam was across the courtyard in Wendy's shower working shampoo into her scalp. "You want to take this to the next level, don't you?" he said.

Wendy kissed him as warm water streamed over them. "I don't know how to make it any more obvious," she said. "Are you game?"

"What do you think?" Sam asked, kissing her again.

Later, they lay in bed. "There's champagne in the fridge," Wendy said. "Go grab it."

"What are we celebrating?" Sam asked.

"Everything," Wendy said. "Or at least . . . well, not everything, but let's stay in the moment for a while."

Sam left her and walked naked down the narrow stairs to her tiny kitchen, where he found the bottle of Moët in the refrigerator. He hunted down two flutes and had turned to go upstairs when he heard his phone ring. It was Gabe, and for a moment Sam considered letting the call go to voice mail but answered anyway.

"I can't do this," Gabe said.

"Of course you can," Sam said. "Where are you now?"

"Outside her house. She's there with the kid and the dog."

"That'll be easy enough."

"No it won't!" Gabe said. "None of this is easy. Ever."

Sam glanced toward the staircase and spoke as softly as he could. "Should I come over?"

"No." Gabe's voice was steadier this time. "Stay where you are."

"Maybe I should."

"I'm fine. Really."

"Be quick about it. Don't linger."

"I know," Gabe said, pausing for a moment. "Have you seen the news?"

"I've been busy."

"If Detective White calls, don't answer."

The call cut off.

Sam looked at the blank screen. He nearly pulled up the local news on his phone, but he heard the TV on upstairs, and when he returned to Wendy's bedroom, she'd sat up, her back pressed into the headboard, her face blanched. On the screen, a reporter was talking into the camera. Below her, a caption read, *Army veteran shot. Suspected in society killing.*

Sam stared at the screen as a photo of Twig popped up, and Wendy began to sob. He watched, almost fascinated, reminding himself before it was too late that his job here was to comfort Wendy, to stroke her hair and let her cling to him till the emotions had played out. He did what he should, reciting lines like he was playing a character on TV.

"Give me a glass of that," Wendy said when the sobbing stopped. "I need a drink."

Sam popped the cork from the bottle. Wendy drank the wine down. "I guess I knew all along that something terrible had happened," she said. "I was hoping it would be different."

Sam sat on the edge of the bed. He looked at Wendy for a long moment.

"What?" Wendy said. "You look like you're about to cry."

Sam imagined life with Wendy Richards and her family — the houses in Nantucket and Stowe, the yacht. He imagined Christmas, with everyone scrambling to find gifts for those who thought nothing of buying anything they wanted. His presents would be wrapped in Hanukkah paper. He imagined staying here.

On the TV, a photo of Jamie appeared, and Wendy gasped. "He was at the party! Holy shit! I thought he was creepy."

"He's not," Sam said.

"Yes, he is. He stood against the wall the whole night. He didn't have a thing to say, not a word to anyone. Why would Twig have gone home with him?"

Sam put his flute on the bedside table and sighed. "The police will be all over me," he said. "I know Jamie. I was at his house earlier today."

"They won't suspect you over him," Wendy said, nodding toward the TV. The photo must have been a few years old, and in it, Jamie was drinking a forty and wore a do rag. "Not over that guy. I mean, look at him. I can't believe I let him into my house."

"He seemed so normal," Sam said.

"They always say that. But you never know people, do you?"

"I guess not."

Wendy slid deeper into the bed and patted the space beside her. "Be with me," she said. "I need you close."

Sam filled her glass again and then folded into her body. He snaked a hand over her chest and kissed her behind the ear, but she pushed him away. "No," she said. "Not now."

He let her rest her head against his chest. Wendy smiled, and touched his cheek. "Thanks for being here," she said, as her phone beeped. "Oh, God, it's Felicia."

"Don't," Sam said. "She's pissed off at me."

"I have to. She must be devastated. Besides, Felicia wouldn't be Felicia if she didn't have someone to be angry at."

Wendy answered and muted the TV. Sam heard Felicia's voice, though he couldn't quite make out the words. He watched the screen. In the background, through the snow, Detective White paced on Jamie's front porch. An officer held Butch, Jamie's little dog.

"I should go over there," Sam said. "Make sure the dog is okay." That's what a friend would do, right?

"Sure," Wendy said, glancing at him.

She sat up. Her face had blanched again. "Okay," she said, but her voice shook.

"What's wrong?" Sam asked.

He touched her, and she flinched.

It was different, each time. The change. The realization. The dawning. He hadn't expected it, not tonight. He never did, but he should have. He'd allowed himself too much hope. He put his hand over the phone and took it away, and could still hear Felicia

383

yammering on the other end as he clicked it off. Wendy had pushed herself as far from him as she could and folded her arms over her bare chest.

"What's she saying about me now?" Sam asked.

"Nothing," Wendy said. "She wanted to talk about Twig. We were close. We all went to college together."

"Felicia hates Twig," Sam said. "She hates her guts. Twig treats her like the help, which she is."

"Felicia's not the help. She's my friend."

Sam stood and pulled his clothes on, watching Wendy the whole time. He put her phone in his pocket.

"Who are you?" she asked.

"I'm whoever you want me to be," Sam said. "Right?"

He took a step toward her.

"Don't come near me," Wendy said.

"I won't hurt you," Sam said.

He took another step toward her, and she lunged out of the sheets and across the mattress and fumbled for the champagne bottle. It slipped from her fingers and spun across the floor. He clutched the hair at the back of her neck in a fist, and she twisted around and kicked his legs out from beneath him, and then scrambled across the carpet for the bottle. He grabbed at her naked legs. She kicked again, but he yanked her toward him. Then he felt himself fly through the air and land on the mattress.

"Get off her!"

Felicia stood in the doorway, gasping for breath, black hair swirling around her face. She held a butter knife in front of her. Off in the distance, Sam heard police sirens.

He crouched. Felicia jabbed the butter knife at him in a way that made him want to laugh, but the sirens were getting closer, and Wendy had the champagne bottle clutched in her fist. He edged along the wall. Felicia stood between him and Wendy, till he managed to get in the doorway and run, down the stairs, through the courtyard, out the front gate. Snow had begun to fall. It pelted his face as his feet pounded the pavement. The sirens were getting louder. He shoved his way past a man walking a dog as he turned the corner, out of Louisburg Square and down the hill to Charles Street. He could see the train coming, pulling into the elevated station. He dashed through traffic, jumped the turnstile, and fought against the wave of people disgorging from the train, only to see the doors slide closed in front of him. He glanced down the platform. The conductor leaned through the window, and Sam ran toward him, his hands clasped. Begging.

The doors opened again.

"Happy holidays," the conductor shouted as Sam squeezed into the crowded car.

A moment later, they pulled into Kendall Square in Cambridge, across the Charles River. Sam hurried out of the train and upstairs. He could hear the police sirens on the Longfellow Bridge. He ran through the lobby of a hotel and onto Broadway. Then he put his hood up, and his head down, and let the snow envelop him.

CHAPTER 23

Wendy.

It was as simple as that. Sam had chosen the movie quotes based on character names, Wendy Torrance in *The Shining,* Wendy Richards in Boston. At the very least, Hester had a connection and a theory she could test out. She turned the movie off and left Kate sleeping on the sofa. In her bedroom, she powered on her tablet and loaded up the spreadsheets she'd put together. She'd already found the addresses of all of the houses Sam had sent photos of and had looked up the property records to see who had owned what, and now, as she scanned through the names, she saw more connections. Aurora Wright had owned the house on Hadley Square, East, in Baltimore. All the quotes Sam had used in Baltimore had come from *Terms of Endearment* a movie with a character named Aurora Greenway. The same held true for Chicago (*The Big*

Lebowski, owner named Maude Hines), and New York (*The Shawshank Redemption,* owner named Andrew Meyer). Only San Francisco gave Hester pause, because that house, on Pacific Avenue, had been owned by a woman named Ellen Gonzalez. It wasn't till Hester looked the movie up on IMDB that she remembered Sigourney Weaver's character's first name was Ellen. Ellen Ripley.

Next she found the current property records to see who owned the houses today. Only Maude Hines still owned hers.

Hester's phone rang. She answered quickly to keep from waking Kate in the next room. It was Morgan, who sounded drunk and happy. He called her "Mrs.," which she made her feel warm, grateful even. "I found Prachi," he said. "We're at the Independent. We're closing the place down!"

"I'm sorry about tonight," Hester said.

"What?"

"I love you," she said.

"I can't hear you," Morgan said. "But I'm sorry. And I love you."

Hester smiled and raised her voice as much as she dared. "I'll talk to you in the morning," she said and clicked off. A few seconds later, the phone rang again.

"You have to stop," she said. "You'll wake Kate."

No one answered. She glanced at the number on the screen and didn't recognize it. "Who's there?" she asked.

"Hi."

It took a moment to recognize Gabe's voice.

"I know I told you to call," Hester said. "But it's late."

"I'm sorry."

"It's okay." She put the tablet aside. "I was up anyway. I'm working on a project."

"Me too."

"Listen, Gabe, I wasn't honest with you today, and I guess I want to be up front. Remember when I mentioned Morgan? He's my boyfriend. He's actually a little more than that. We're like one step away from being married."

Gabe laughed, but Hester could hear disappointment when he spoke. "You can't really have a kid without a husband. I should have figured."

"Well, you can, really," Hester said. "Lots of people do. But I have a kid without having given birth. Go figure."

"Yeah, go figure. Lucky you."

"Well, I'm off the market. Do you know what I'm saying?"

She'd led Gabe on to get what she wanted, but she couldn't manage feeling guilty about that tonight on top of everything else. It was too much. "I figured out the code on the postcards, or part of it," she said to change the subject. "Wendy, Wendy. Aurora, Aurora. Ellen, Ellen. Tell Sam it was pretty clever. It took me long enough to break it."

"Research when the houses sold," Gabe said. "That should help too."

And then he hung up.

Hester pulled up the property records for the house in Baltimore. It had sold about three months after Sam's last postcard from that city. The houses in Chicago and San Francisco had sold on a similar timeline, and when she searched on Ellen Gonzalez's name, she found a series of news articles from ten years earlier. Ellen was an heiress who'd been killed during a home invasion. Her brother, Zach, had disappeared as well, and the murder had made headlines in San Francisco as the police had tried to tie Zach to the killing, showing that Ellen had made a play to take over their jointly owned company. Glancing through the articles, Hester could see that the police hadn't been able to locate Zach or to find any leads worth following, and that the case had grown cold.

She put the tablet aside and checked on Kate, who was fast asleep. She ran down the stairs, into the other apartment, took the folder with the postcards from her bag, and headed up to Morgan's bedroom, where she spread the cards across the bed. She flipped on the TV to the local news, where a reporter stood in the swirling snow. Waffles shimmed through the dog door and jumped up beside her. She looked through the messages one more time to see if anything else made sense, if other pieces fit into the puzzle. And then she glanced at the TV, where a reporter was interviewing Twig Ambrose's father, Donald, who stood in the doorway to his house. "It's such a tragedy," the man said. "I'm devastated. Everyone who knew Twig is devastated. I'll always think of her, hiking or boating or swimming in Squam Lake, doing something outdoors where she was always happiest."

Squam Lake.

Where Sam and Gabe had grown up.

Where Little Comfort was.

Where they'd found a body in the woods.

Hester turned the TV off. She felt a chill run down her back. She needed to call Detective White, but she'd left the phone in the other apartment. Wind outside gusted as the storm grew in intensity, shaking the walls, seeming to strain the very foundation of the house. Waffles lifted her nose in the air and woofed softly. Hester put a hand to her collar and shushed. There was a lull in the storm, a moment of intense silence, and in that silence she heard a key slide into the lock on Morgan's front door and the bolt turn.

Waffles woofed again.

There was someone in the house.

Hester jumped lightly from the bed and lifted the dog after her. She knew she was in danger, and yet she felt nothing but calm. She needed to get to her phone, call for help, and get Kate to safety. Everything she'd said, everything she'd done, all the anger and resentment, all the complaining, meant nothing. She lifted out of herself, retreating to simple, primal words like *run, protect, hide.* She flipped off the bedroom light, took the dog by the collar, and padded into Morgan's closet. She forced the dog through the dog door to the apartment on the other side. She tried to follow, but even she wasn't small enough to fit. "Kate," she whispered as loudly as she dared. "Wake up!"

When Kate didn't come, Hester slid a box in front of the dog door to keep Waffles on the other side. She edged to the top of the staircase. Someone had turned on the lights in the living room. She heard the refrigerator open and the lid to a beer pop off, and she nearly convinced herself it was Morgan, but not enough time had passed for him to make it home from the bar. She receded into Kate's bedroom and huddled behind the door till she heard footsteps on the stairs. Whoever was in the house continued into Morgan's room, where, after a minute, metal hangers in the walk-in closet clanked together.

Hester edged around the door and clung to the railing. Down the stairs. Across the living room. Open the latch. Turn the knob. She heard footsteps again, and this time they were pounding, and she could feel something powerful and unknown closing in on her. She fled across the landing and into her apartment, where she slammed the door shut and drew the deadbolt.

Upstairs, Kate rubbed her eyes, Monkey clutched in one hand. Hester picked up the girl and stumbled to the bedroom. She heard another deadbolt turn. She threw open a window to a blast of frigid air and snow. They were three stories up. Too far to jump. She shrieked for help, but no one was on the street. "We're all right," she said to Kate.

She heaved her shoulder into a dresser and toppled it in front of the bedroom door.

"Who that?" Kate asked.

Waffles howled.

"Inside voice," Hester said. "We're playing a game. You have to be very quiet."

Hester grabbed her phone from where it lay on the bed. She punched in Morgan's number. Kate would listen to him. While it rang, she dragged Waffles and Kate into the closet and closed them in. Kate slid easily through the dog door. Hester forced Waffles to follow, and then tried again to contort her way through, squeezing her shoulders together, wriggling, pawing at the floor.

"Be home soon," Morgan said when he finally answered. She could hear the crowded bar behind him.

"There's someone in the house," Hester said, and when Morgan tried to break in she cut him off. "Don't say anything. Listen and do what I tell you. I'm trapped. Kate's in your closet. I'm giving her the phone. You keep talking to her till you get her out of the house. Understand? And I'm sorry about tonight. I love you."

"I love you too," Morgan said.

"Get the police here."

Hester handed the phone to Kate and smiled. "Remember," she said in her gentlest voice, "we're playing a game. Do what your uncle Morgan says. Okay? Now run."

Kate smiled and nodded. She put the phone to her ear. "Hello, Uncle Morgan," she said, and then paused. "Okay," she added.

She waved to Hester, ran out of the closet, and down the stairs. Hester heard the back door slam open as Kate, in her pink pajamas and bunny slippers, ran into the storm. Waffles whined as if beckoning Hester to follow, and for the first time in Hester's life she wished she was the tiniest bit smaller.

"Quiet," she said to the dog, and then jammed the box in front of the opening again.

She heard a knock at the bedroom door. It banged against the dresser.

She turned to face the slats. She lay on her hip, with memories of that self-defense course taken long ago during Safety Week, a course that made her imagine being brave. *Use your elbows, knees, and fingers,* Daphne had said. *Aim for the eyes, the throat, the groin. Pivot, kick. Pivot, kick. Stay balanced. Gouge. Don't give up.*

Breathe.

Women unite! Take back the night!

The door slammed into the dresser again.

Fight! And Daphne's knee was suddenly

digging into Hester's back again. *Survive!*
Use your strengths. Be smart. The only thing
you think about is how to stay alive.

Hester kicked open the closet door.

CHAPTER 24

It had been easy enough for Gabe to let himself into the house using the key hidden in that plastic rock. Once he'd stepped into the dark second-floor apartment and saw the toys and sorted through the mail and batted away a few kittens, he knew that she'd told him the truth, she did have a husband, and it made him feel empty and angry and betrayed, as though he'd lost something he'd never really had.

Yet he still opened the fridge and popped the lid off a beer. He drank down half of it in a single swig and then left the bottle on the counter for the police to find. He listened and thought that maybe he heard someone upstairs, and then he found himself in their bedroom, his hands on the mattress, sorting through the piles of Sam's postcards that he found lying there. The sheets on the bed were pristine white. He lay down and ran his hand over a pillow, where he found a long, black hair that he wound around his finger. There was a photo of the two of them sitting on the bedside table, and Morgan, Gabe had to admit, was handsome. Not handsome the way Sam was. But better, with red hair and a kind face. Morgan had an arm around Hester, and she leaned into him in a way that said *don't ever let go.*

Gabe heard the dog whine. He gathered up the postcards and the rest of the file to take with him — it wouldn't do for the police to find those — and went into the walk-in closet that was lined with clothes, more shirts than even Sam owned. Gabe couldn't help but take one from its hanger and feel the soft gray cloth against his face and slide it over his own shirt and imagine what it might feel like to come down those stairs in the morning wearing this shirt. The dog whined again, and when Gabe moved a box aside, she stuck her snout through a hole in the wall and licked his hand. He looked through the hole to the back of another darkened closet, this one small and narrow and littered with shoes.

Then he heard the patter of feet behind him.

He moved the box in front of the dog door and followed. He ran, actually. Down the stairs and across the living room and he caught a glimpse of her face, ashen with fear.

Unfortunately, Sam was right. He couldn't let her go.

He heard her slam the door to the attic apartment and slide the bolt in place, but he ran his hand over the doorway till he found the spare key. Inside, he climbed the carpeted stairs. The apartment was as messy and tiny as he remembered it being. An aerie high over Somerville filled with newspapers and videotapes and secondhand furniture. On a threadbare love seat, a nest of blankets lay abandoned and still warm. A bottle of scotch had tipped over and soaked into the matted beige carpet. Gabe used a wad of paper towels to soak up the scotch, and then drank what remained straight from the bottle.

He crossed to the bedroom door. It opened an inch before slamming into something on the other side. He said her name. He pushed harder, shoving his broad shoulder into the flimsy wood till whatever blocked the door toppled over. He squeezed into the room and could see his breath as snow filtered through an open window. He could understand her panic, even when the closet door burst open and she lay balanced on her hip in a pile of shoes with one of those tiny legs jabbing toward him with a slippered foot. Her hair had begun to fall out of its ponytail. She pushed those glasses up her nose with a fist. He told her not to be afraid, which, justifiably, she seemed not to believe. The dog let out a deep, mournful howl from the other side of the wall. He tried not to laugh, and then he did. "We need to go," he said. "Before the snow. Before it's too hard to drive."

He stepped toward her.

"No!"

Jesus, that hurt. He fell backward, and she scrambled around him, still balancing on that hip, still jabbing at him with those slippers. He wanted to tell her that he would never hurt her, not for a million dollars, and not in a billion years, but he wondered if that was even true. He needed her to stop moving. He grabbed at her legs, and she kicked again, and he pinned her to the ground, but she yanked a clump of hair from his head and smashed her knee into his chin.

"Get the fuck out of my house," she yelled.

God, he loved that voice and that she dared to face him down. He would miss wishing this could be his. But outside, a police siren wailed closer. So when she grabbed a lamp, he knocked it out of her hand and jammed his knee into her back and twisted her arms behind her and wrapped her in a blanket, lugging her in a shrieking, struggling bundle down three flights of stairs, where he stuffed her into his trunk.

Now he steered the car toward Route 93 and headed north. Soon, he passed Route 128 and 495 and crossed the state line into New Hampshire. Surely crossing state lines made everything worse, though it hardly seemed fair in these tiny New England states. But then kidnapping was pretty bad no matter how you did it. His stomach growled, and he realized that he'd gone the whole day without eating. She hadn't stopped banging on the trunk yet, so McDonald's was out of the question. Even the drive-through. He hoped he had enough gas to get where they were going. He hoped she'd understand in the end.

Right before the first toll in New Hampshire, he pulled off the highway and down a dark, narrow road. He cut the engine and sat still for a moment, the only sound being that endless thumping. He couldn't leave her in the trunk all night. She must be cold, and he imagined holding her close till the shivering stopped. He imagined holding her longer than that. He swung the door open to the storm and popped the trunk with his key remote, and it clicked and then slammed open as she sat up. "You fucking, fucking fuck face," she said.

He stepped toward her. She smashed a tire iron into the side of his head. He fell backward and felt blood oozing down his face and dotting the snow, and she was on the ground where she hit him again and then she was running through the drifts, toward the trees, into the dark, those Lion King slippers popping from the snow like rabbits.

Gabe tried to sit up. He thought about going after her. But he lay in the snow instead. It was twenty degrees out and two a.m. and not another soul lived within a mile of where they were. She'd figure out that there was no place to go soon enough.

It was cold. Colder than Hester had ever imagined it could be. She huddled behind a line of trees as the snow built up around her and the headlights from Gabe's car cut through the night. She had no idea how long she'd been out here, though it seemed like hours. Her toes had gone numb in her snow-filled slippers, and the thin fabric of her pajamas provided almost no protection from the elements. She clutched the tire iron and imagined Kate out in the storm too, wandering the streets. She imagined the phone dying or dropping into a drain or simply losing its connection. Surely one of the neighbors had opened the door to Kate's pounding, but what if they hadn't?

She peered around a tree trunk. Gabe still lay where he'd fallen on the snow, and she wondered if he was dead, whether she could creep from her hiding spot and pry the keys from his hand. But Gabe sat up as she found her courage. He rubbed his head and moved to the front of the car. Hester held her hands between her thighs and tried to ward off the shivering that had begun in her shoulders, and then spread to her chest, her legs, her very core. She imagined a steaming radiator, a mug of tea, the sun. Lying on a beach, warm sand beneath her blanket, water lapping at the shore, a dog-eared book waiting to be read. The smells of salt and sand and fried clams and charcoal and lighter fluid and behind her, the docks and a restaurant.

A breeze blows through Daphne's hair. It's shockingly red, like when they were in college, when Daphne snuck into Hester's room late at night and took her away, when they'd run onto the green and around the pond and their legs moved without effort and they flew through the night into a world of their very own, and Hester, who'd never been wanted, who'd never been asked, pinched herself because she couldn't believe any of this could be real.

A wave crashes. Water spills around them. Sand melts way like caramel.

"If I swam beyond the horizon," Daphne asks, "would you let me go?"

"If that's what you want," Hester says.

"What if I don't?"

"Then stay. We'll get clams. They're whole bellies."

"I've never liked clams."

"We'll find you something else. We'll keep looking."

And now Hester is back in the trunk, and she's banging at the door and shouting and warding off claustrophobia and cold and fear, and the car bumps over a pothole and the spare tire jumps beneath her and the tire iron hits her in the head and she has it in her fists when the car stops. This time when the trunk pops open, it isn't Gabe. It's Sam. And Cheryl Jenkins. And Bobby Englewood. And they're all laughing. Hester swings the iron. Sam steps out of the way and the trunk slams shut again and Hester can't breathe. There's water all around her. It's cold. She gasps and she's clawing forward, through the dark, and there may be a light and there may not be, but she had no idea which way is up. Her lungs are about to burst. She knows that all she has to do is open her mouth and let the cold flow in. But then she feels the fingertips. She feels the hand, and she thinks it might be Daphne's, and even in the dark she knows enough to hold on and not let go. But when she opens her eyes she sees that it's her own hand, and that she only had herself to rely on.

Hester looked out to where Gabe sat on the car's hood, and then she stepped out of the trees toward the headlights. She let the tire iron fall into the snow and lifted her hands in surrender. Gabe opened the passenger-side door for her.

"No trunk?" she asked.

He shook his head. "Sorry," he said. "Can I do anything for you?"

"Seriously? How about this? Take me home and then shoot yourself in the fucking head."

"I can't do that," he said.

She got into the car, if only to escape the

cold. When he slid into the driver's side and turned the key, heat poured from the vents. The warmth enveloped Hester, and yet she still shivered. She took her feet from the sodden slippers and tried to rub feeling into her toes. She put her face right up to the vent and cranked the seat warmer as high as it would go.

"I could use some tea," she said.

Gabe pulled onto the road and drove carefully through the drifts. "We can't really stop," he said.

"I'll keep my mouth shut," she said, and he turned on the radio as if to tell her neither of them believed her. "They'll be looking for me," she added, but she also knew that the world was big with plenty of places to hide. Now that she was out of the trunk, she paid attention to highway signs. They'd headed north and had already crossed the state line into New Hampshire. She fought panic. Her toes tingled to life. They burned from the heat.

The news cut into the radio broadcast, and the top story was about Jamie Williams. He was in the hospital in critical condition. "In other news," the announcer said, "a home invasion in Somerville has resulted in a missing persons' case. The local woman is described as white, thirty-six years old, with black hair and glasses. She was wearing pajamas and is four foot nine."

"Nine and three quarters," Hester whispered.

"An Amber Alert has been issued for the woman's three-year-old niece, who is also missing."

Hester forgot about the trunk and the cold. She forgot to be frightened. She forgot that somehow, no matter what it took, that she'd survive this. The announcer's words flowed through her. They grabbed at her heart and twisted it. And she was on top of Gabe, pounding her fists into his chest. The car swerved. He managed to pull it to the side of the road and stop.

"What did you do?" she screamed. "What the fuck did you do with her?"

Gabe twisted her arms behind her back and pinned her to the passenger's seat so that the fabric ground into her cheek. "Sit still and be quiet," he said into her ear. "Or I'll put you in the trunk. Understand?"

His glove covered Hester's mouth, and nearly sealed off her nose. She could barely get any oxygen. Gabe let up a bit and then stared out the window.

"Where is she?" Hester asked.

"I don't know," Gabe said.

And in that moment of fear, of panic, of rage, Hester knew he was telling the truth.

CHAPTER 25

"Do you remember anything else?" Angela White asked Wendy Richards. "Did he say anything or do anything that might tell you where he went?"

Wendy had changed into a t-shirt and yoga pants. She sat at the foot of her bed with her head resting in her hands. Felicia nestled in beside her, a protective arm draped around her shoulders.

"He changed," Wendy said. "He morphed into a different person right in front of my eyes. How could I have been such an idiot?"

"You didn't do anything," Felicia said.

"She's right," Angela said. "You can't blame yourself for this. And you were lucky Felicia was in her office when I called. We might not have gotten here on time."

Wendy sat up and rubbed her temples. Her hair spilled over her shoulders. "All I knew was that he went to Columbia and rowed crew."

"Anything else? Did he have a job? Any friends?"

Wendy shook her head. "It was like he was a blank space that I could fill with whatever I wanted him to be."

"Do you have any idea where he might have gone?"

"He lived in Somerville," Wendy said. "That's about all I know."

"It was in Davis Square, I think," Felicia said. "I met him at a bar there one night. Him and his creeptastic, Unabomber friend. Barry something."

Angela couldn't have described Gabe DiPursio better herself. "Did Twig paint her nails blue?" Angela asked. They'd sent the finger with blue polish that they'd found to the lab.

"I don't know . . ." Wendy said. "That's something she'd have done. Why?"

"It's not important," Angela said as her phone rang. She excused herself and stepped to the other side of the room. It was Stan, who got right to the point. "IAB is looking into the shooting tonight. Honestly, Angela? A black veteran, holding a knife with strawberry syrup on it? This couldn't get much worse."

"It didn't look like syrup to me."

"Don't say anything," Stan said, and

Angela could see him in his tiny Hyde Park condo, his round face flushed from high blood pressure and stress. He'd be sitting in front of the TV in his robe and wondering whether he should head into the station. "Not a word. If you say it to me, then I'll have to say it to them."

Angela let her guard down. "There ain't nothing to say, Stan." She tried to whisper, but she could see Felicia Nakazawa eyeing her from across the room.

"The press is going to have a field day with this one," Stan said. "And I know you didn't pull the trigger, but you were the officer in charge. That's what I'm calling about. You're on administrative leave pending the investigation. You and Dwayne both."

Angela nearly protested. She nearly tried to defend herself, defend Dwayne, the rookie who'd actually pulled the trigger, but it *had* been strawberry syrup on the knife and Angela had been the one to say "Go!" And now a man was in the hospital fighting for his life, a man she suspected was innocent. "What do I do?" she asked.

"Go home," Stan said. "Not in an hour. Not in five minutes. Now. Ben's on his way to take the case."

But Angela barely heard what he said. She let the phone fall to her side. Over Felicia's shoulder, the television was on with the sound muted. Angela fumbled with the remote as images of Hester Thursby and that little girl flashed across the screen.

The names and faces from the past had begun to fade. To Sam, even the name "Sam Blaine" sounded like an old telephone number, shadowy and vaguely familiar. As he turned off 93 and onto the back roads of New Hampshire to avoid the tolls, he looked in the rearview mirror, into his own eyes, new and oddly unfamiliar. He touched a cheek and ran a hand through his hair. Could it all really be him? In the mirror, he saw only the future.

Outside, the snow had picked up. Sam drove the Nissan around the village green in a tiny New Hampshire town. He passed a man walking a golden retriever through the drifts and imagined being that man, tossing a ball and waiting for the dog to fetch it, all the while having nothing in the world to worry about but taking deep breaths of exhilarating winter air. He wondered if the man had children. Gabe had always wanted kids, and Sam realized now that he wanted them too. That would be his next life. Three kids, two girls and a boy. Kids who'd climb on him like he was a jungle gym, whom he'd throw into piles of leaves, and whom he'd read to late at night.

Wendy had wanted kids. But then, things were over with Wendy. With Aaron Gewirtzman, too. It always felt strange once he began to shed the skin of whom he'd become. He remembered the first time, in San Francisco, when he knew it had ended. Ellen's family owned a ranch in Marin, where she went to ride horses and be alone, so they'd both been surprised when her brother Zach showed up late one Saturday night. He barely said hello, or looked at Sam, and Sam knew, almost at once, that someone had told Zach about Ellen's play at the company, her plan (his plan) to oust Zach from the board. Later that night, he came downstairs to find Zach sitting in front of the fireplace drinking a glass of scotch. "First thing in the morning," Zach said, "get the fuck out of my house."

Sam could still see those hills that rose around the ranch the next morning, the way fog rolled in over them, the way Zach had dashed around the bend in the trail and seen Sam standing in his way. Had it surprised him? Had Zach known he'd run straight into his own ending?

Zach stopped, bending over his knees to catch his breath. Sam went to say something, and Zach raised a hand. "I'm hiring a private investigator," he said. "Or I will, unless you leave today."

Sam hadn't had a choice. He body-checked Zach off the trail, and then watched as the man clawed at grass and stone and sand. Zach had never had a single bad thing happen to him in his entire short life. Sam wondered, as he fell into the fog, whether he believed his shouts would somehow save him.

At least that one had been clean.

Back at the ranch, Ellen had stared out the window into the hills as though she knew something had happened. In the afternoon, she asked where Zach had gone.

"I think he went for a run," Sam said.

"That was hours ago," Ellen said. She turned from the window. Soft afternoon light filtered in through curtains onto her plump face. "Where *did* you come from anyway?" she'd asked.

Sam pulled into a 7-Eleven parking lot as his phone buzzed again. He'd turned the ringer off to keep from waking the little girl, who lay on a blanket in the backseat, fast asleep. He glanced at her in the rearview mirror, lying there in her pink pajamas, those curls fanning her face. She looked so peaceful. So innocent. So pure.

His phone buzzed again. Even though he didn't recognize the number on the display, he was sure it had to be that detective. Who else would call after midnight?

Earlier, Sam had walked through the snow to his car and driven to Union Square, where he'd watched while Gabe struggled with the squirming blanket that he shoved into his trunk. Sam rolled the window down and almost called out, but there were too many houses around, despite the empty streets. When Gabe sped away, Sam nearly followed, when he saw the girl poke her head from around the corner of the house, the phone to her ear and a stuffed monkey clutched in her hand. She only had on the pajamas and slippers, and it hadn't taken much to lure her into the car. He took the phone from her and listened as the man on the other end, huffing as he ran, shouted, "Stay exactly where you are! I'm coming! I'm almost there!"

Sam clicked the phone off, threw it into the snow, and drove away while the girl screamed. Just a little bit at first. He told her not to worry, that he was a friend of her aunt Hester's, and then he'd managed to dig out a pack Lifesavers that really did save the day. Kate gobbled down the entire roll and fell asleep a few moments later.

Now, Sam turned to where she lay in the back of the car. If she made it through all of this, he'd call her Lydia. He'd get her papers and make up a backstory for her. He brushed a curl from Kate's face. "Sorry, sweetie," he whispered. "Tough break."

He left her and went inside the store, where he picked up coffee, a bag of Doritos, and five candy bars to use as bribes with Kate as needed. The store was empty except for the clerk, who could barely tear himself from the TV long enough to take Sam's money. "Big storm out there," Sam said.

"Yep," the man said, "the plow drivers'll be in all night."

As he turned to leave, Sam noticed a photo of Kate flash across the TV screen with "Amber Alert" running beneath it.

"Those things break my heart," Sam said. "My little girl's conked out in the backseat. It'd kill me if something ever happened to her."

"I know what you mean," the clerk said. "Be sure to drive safe."

Outside, Kate woke and sat up as Sam shut the door. Her eyes were wide with shyness and curiosity and, he had to admit it, fear.

"Go to sleep," he said.

"Where Aunt Hester?" Kate asked.

"We'll meet up with her later," Sam said. "She's with her friend Gabe. Do you know him?"

Kate said something that sounded like "Popsicle sticks."

"We need to find them, but luckily I know where they're headed. We need to find some other friends too. They all know secrets about me." Sam backed the car out of the parking lot. "Have you ever had a secret? One that you didn't want anyone else to know?"

Kate nodded.

"I bet it was a big one!"

She smiled.

"I have lots of secrets," Sam said. "And I have to be sure they stay secret. Do you think you can help me?"

"Yes," Kate said.

"That's my girl!"

The windshield wipers fought a losing battle against the building snow. Gabe hadn't bothered with back roads. He drove slowly through the tolls on 93 till he finally exited and headed east toward Holderness. He dared to sneak a glance toward the passenger's side seat. She sat beside him, tiny in her pajamas, her face blank as she stared out the window into the early morning darkness.

He hadn't returned to Holderness since that summer and was surprised by how little had changed. As he sped through the small center and passed the snowy lake, he could remember going to the general store with Lila. He remembered strolling down the docks to the marina, and feeling her breath in his ear and her hand on his ass.

He followed the lakeshore till he turned into the hills. It was easy enough to find the old road into Little Comfort. The road down to the lake had grown in, but Gabe was able to pull the car in behind some trees and let the snow build up to camouflage them while they waited for morning. It couldn't be more than a quarter of a mile from the road to the lake. He left the engine running to mask the quiet. He dug one of the fleeces from his bag and held it toward her. She wasn't too proud to say yes, even if it did hang almost to her knees.

"Do you shop in the petite section?" he asked.

She glared at him.

He tried again. "I bet your dog is okay."

"I don't give a shit about the dog."

So much for small talk. He turned the radio on again, and they listened to crazy old men on late-night call-in shows.

"What did you do with her?" Hester said.

The truth was that Gabe had no idea. He'd thought the little girl would be able to get to a neighbor's house. He'd believed that she'd escaped. Amber Alert. He'd hate to be Amber's parents, to be reminded of that terrible time every time something awful happened to a child.

"You killed that woman they found in Jamie's backyard," Hester said. "You and Sam. You did it together. Just like you killed the man they found in the woods here. Who else? Ellen Gonzalez in San Francisco?"

She stared out the window, her breath freezing on the glass.

"Yes," he said, and he saw her inhale sharply. He almost surprised himself with the confession, but now that it was out, he felt years of burden lift from his shoulders. Hester swallowed and pushed away, if only a fraction of an inch. Her hand went to the door handle, and he reached over and took it away. Gently. "There's nowhere for you to go," he whispered.

He meant to be kind. He meant to keep her from the cold, to keep her from leaving. It wasn't safe. Not yet, at least. "The first person we killed was a man on this lake," he said. "He was a pedophile who no one cared about. Sam started it, and I finished it. We used a hatchet and buried him in the woods, and then took his car and drove to Massachusetts. Then there was Ellen. She was rich and homely, and Sam thought he could make her love him. After that, there was an old woman named Maude in Chicago. I took care of her cats, and we got access to her bank accounts."

Maude had been a retired emergency room nurse who'd lived alone and told Gabe to brush iodine on the back of his throat when he got strep and couldn't afford to go to the doctor. She had heavy laugh lines around her eyes, a central-European accent, and called him "honey" when they played gin rummy. One of the last times he spoke to her, she made him pancakes. "Honey, I think you have no friends, yes?" she said. "Get some. They matter. How are pancakes?"

Then her son had shown up from out of nowhere, wondering where her money had gone even though he hadn't visited in more than a decade. "Who cares?" Maude had said, and Gabe had understood, right then, that she'd known all along, that she, like him, needed friends no matter the cost. But that hadn't swayed Sam, and Gabe could still see the look in Maude's eyes when she'd woken a split second before he'd put the pillow over her face.

He watched now as the snow dotted the windshield, and he listened to Hester breathing. "Robbed her blind," he said. "She was meaner than you could possibly imagine, with no one to miss her."

That last part wasn't true. But it made him feel better to say it.

There was also the crack dealer in Baltimore and the stockbroker in Manhattan, who'd lived in an apartment with wood floors so shiny, it had been easy to mop up blood. Gabe remembered all of them, but the one that stayed with him, the one where he'd still had a chance to be someone else was Ellen.

"She knows. I know she knows," Sam had said. "I need you."

It was all Gabe had to hear. Sam needed him the way Gabe had needed Sam. It meant something. He took a bus, to another bus, across the Golden Gate Bridge, where he got off on the side of a highway and hiked into the hills. The ranch was nestled in a valley, and Gabe could still smell the scent of fennel and coastal sage, could still see the fading evening light as he crept across a dry lawn and in through the open French doors. Sam had already left. They'd agreed on that.

Ellen sat in the kitchen, facing out toward the hills, a cell phone inches from her hand. Gabe hadn't seen her before. She must have been in her late twenties and wore her dark hair in a simple bob. Big, owlish glasses covered her eyes, but she wasn't the way Sam had described. She was soft and kind looking. He imagined her voice, gentle and pure, and when he said hello and grabbed the phone away from her, he wanted to know whether he was right. Whether she sounded like someone he could love.

"Tell me what you like," he said.

She sobbed, her eyes trained on the knife. A long wad of yellow snot stretched from her nose to the floor.

"Just say it," Gabe pleaded. "Say that you like horses. I know that you do."

She shook her head and tried to run for the door. Maybe she thought she could get away on one of those horses.

But then it was done. And there was no going back. He made it look like a robbery gone wrong, and left her lying in a dark pool of her own blood.

"I'm not a good person," Gabe said.

He'd told Hester everything. Confessed it all.

She opened her mouth, and nothing came out but a terrified croak. All the bravado and kindness that Gabe yearned for, that he'd earned, was gone. He remembered believing things could be different. But even if she did know how he took his coffee, even if she told him he wasn't half bad, she had her own life. Her own story. And it had nothing to do with him.

Off in the distance, he heard rumbling, and then headlights lit up the trees around them. He put a warning hand on Hester's shoulder and eased her down in her seat as a plow turned the corner.

"Not so rough," she said.

He saw her fingers inch toward the door handle again, but he switched off the interior light, reached over her, and held the door shut. He covered her mouth and shoved her down onto the floor of the car, and it wasn't till after the plow had turned the corner that he took his weight off her. Her lip bled.

"Get off me," she said.

"I'm sorry," he said.

"Stop apologizing," she said. "You did this."

He'd have been lying if he'd said touching her hadn't turned him on, that it hadn't reminded him of what he'd seen in her all along, or the way she made him feel. But

Sam wanted Hester dead like the others. Sam had listened to him on the lake that night, as they lay in the leaves surrounded by *Penthouse*s. He listened all the way through. And when Gabe finished, Sam said, "I can get you out of this. But you have to do what I tell you. No questions asked."

And ever since, no matter what Gabe told himself, no matter what *he* wanted, no matter how he envisioned the rest of his life, he'd nearly always done what Sam wanted.

A handful of cars passed their hiding spot in the waning hours of the early morning. Each time, Hester prayed that one of them might stop, but Gabe shoved her down and smothered her with his body till the grind of tires against snow faded. Then, at the first light of day, he took the keys and stepped into the storm. "Get out," he said.

For a moment, she considered refusing. But her tongue found her bloody lip. She felt Gabe's body on top of her all over again. And she had to survive, no matter what the choices. Gabe was dangerous. Dangerous people were impulsive. She, on the other hand, could be patient. That patience might be Kate's only hope.

She pushed the door open to a blast of winter air. Her slippers filled with snow. The drifts rose nearly to her waist. Gabe handed her a pair of sneakers and a set of snow shoes. "We have to go through the woods."

The sneakers were dry and warm, a bit too big, but they were a relief nonetheless. She managed to work them into the snow shoes, and then Gabe gave her a duffel bag to carry as they set out. She searched through the trees for a weapon, a stone, maybe, or a tree branch, but here the world was solid white. She broke twigs off any branch she brushed past, a trick she'd learned from years of reading adventure stories. Soon, her heart rate had risen enough to warm even her fingers and toes. Snow still fell and, as they hiked around trees, over icy rock faces, and down a hill, she wondered how long their footprints would last, and whether she'd be able to find her way out of these woods when the time came.

The snow-covered lake opened in front of them, where the remains of Little Comfort hovered on the shoreline. On the horizon sat a small village of ice fishing huts, at least a half a mile away through waist-deep snow. Gabe followed Hester's gaze and shook his head to tell her not to bother. Then he stopped to look at the cabin.

"I was here the other day," she said. "With

Lila. She told me you used to come here that summer. You used to swim off that dock. It must have been wonderful."

"It was," Gabe said.

"She still lives in the same house. It's not far from here. We could walk there, I bet. She'd be glad to see you."

"Does she still have the braid?" he asked.

"Still there."

"She had the biggest tits I've ever seen."

"Those are still there too," Hester said. "I don't think much has changed for her since you left. Let's go see her. Let's ask."

Gabe smiled. "We're not going to see Lila," he said. "It wouldn't be safe."

"How about Cheryl or Bobby?"

Gabe's face went blank, a flash of anger in his eyes. He dug in his bag. He tossed her a granola bar, and she tore at the wrapper. Her fingers were too numb to rip the plastic. Gabe opened it for her, and she ate it in two bites. "I have water too," he said. "Don't eat snow. It'll give you hypothermia."

"You know what else gives you hypothermia?" Hester said. "Being stuck in the woods in the middle of the winter in your pajamas."

Gabe laughed, and then Hester did too. But she also hung on to that anger she'd seen. She could use that. She could use every bit of sadness and rage and confusion Gabe had bottled up.

He led her into the cabin. They took their snowshoes off and leaned them up by the door, and then broke apart a few wooden chairs and pulled some pine panels from the walls to add to the sticks piled by the fireplace. Once the fire blazed, Gabe handed her blankets from one of the duffel bags. He also balanced a small tin kettle on the fire and made tea, and by the time Hester had wrapped her hands around a matching tin mug, she felt cared for, almost warm. "I wish we could be friends," she said. It didn't hurt to play the game.

"I guess I messed that up," Gabe said.

"A bit," Hester said.

Gabe crouched by the fire and rubbed his hands together. "Are you scared?" he asked.

"I'm scared shitless."

He added another piece of wood to the fire. "I'm sorry," he said.

"What are we doing here?" Hester asked.

"I'm ending it."

"What?"

"Everything."

"You're not giving me a lot of confidence here, Gabe," Hester said, with a force she hardly felt. "I don't want to end everything."

"Sam says . . ."

"Sam can go to hell. Let me go. We'll walk up to the road, and you can take the car and disappear. You can become someone new all over again. Go to Manchester or Portland or Miami. I don't care. But go, and do it on your own this time. Be your own person."

What would happen if she stood and walked away? What if she headed up to the road without looking back? But Gabe seemed to read her mind. "Don't," he said.

"I have to find my kid!" Hester shouted, and then she was horrified to feel sobs welling up.

She pushed them away, but tears fell down her cheeks anyway. A stream of snot flowed from her nose. And then Gabe was next to her, pulling her head to his chest, and what horrified her even more than the sobs was that she took comfort in his touch. She wanted to pull him even closer and for him to assure her that things would be okay. She'd believe it if she let herself.

"You must be exhausted," Gabe said softly. "Go to sleep."

"Not in a million years." She had to push away from him. She had to get these tears to stop.

"You'll need your strength. I'll watch over you."

She wiped her face with her fists, and then closed one nostril and blew snot from the other onto Gabe's thigh. He didn't flinch. She'd give him that. He looked at her as she retreated, and she imagined what he saw: a tiny woman huddled in the corner of a decrepit cabin surrounded by blankets and scared out of her mind. How could he possibly believe he wouldn't win this in the end? How could she believe that she would?

"Tell me something," he said. "A story. Tell me something I don't already know about you."

"There's nothing worth knowing," she said. "At least nothing you don't already know."

"Everyone has a story," Gabe said.

"Not me," Hester said. "I'm like you. I recreated myself."

"Where did you grow up?"

Hester shook her head.

"Tell me."

"In a little town near the Cape," she said. "It had a beach and a yacht club and cranberry bogs and lots of rich people."

"It must have been nice."

"It wasn't. Not for me, at least."

"Why?"

Hester shrugged. "Because nobody wanted me. Just like you. And maybe we do all have a story, but I like to forget mine. I got myself out of there, and I got out of there all by myself. I live in the present. And every choice I make is about now, not then. I have Waffles and Kate and Morgan and Daphne. And I don't care about anything or anyone but them."

Gabe walked to the cabin's doorway, where he sat on the steps with his back to her. It was still snowing, and a weak sun had reached its highest point for the day yet still struggled to light up the steely sky. "I wish I could do that," he said. "Forget."

"Forget what?"

"Have you ever been invisible?"

"Most of my life," Hester said. "Until I met Daphne. That's Morgan's sister. She saved me. Sometimes I don't even know if she knows that. It's why I'm saving her now, and she doesn't know that either."

"Sam was the first person to see me," Gabe said. "And he chose me, even after Lila wanted to send me away. I told her what had happened. I told her what they were doing, and she couldn't even look at me. I won't ever feel helpless like that again."

"Gabe," Hester said. "Sam tells you that

430

he's smart and that he creates these new and exciting worlds and invites you to live in them with him, but where does it get you? He hasn't succeeded once, has he? Despite everything he promises. Even now he thinks he'll somehow be part of that world on Beacon Hill. Do you know how long it took me to find you? Two days, and that was using the Internet and common sense. Wendy's father will hire a much better private investigator than me to find out everything he can about 'Aaron Gewirtzman,' and when he does the whole game will be up."

"I think the game may already be up," Gabe said.

"Sam's a serial killer. Can't you see that? And he controls you."

"No, he doesn't," Gabe said, but without conviction.

"He chose you because he can manipulate you. He can make you do things most people wouldn't. He can trust you to be quiet."

The fire crackled as embers fell in on one another. Gabe turned toward the lake. Hester could smell him, even from across the room, even over the smoke from the fire. He reeked of sweat and desperation and regret. And fear. Even more, she realized, than she did.

CHAPTER 26

Sam closed the door to the motel behind him. Nothing had changed here in twelve years. The motel sign was still missing a "T," and the roof still looked as though it might cave in at any second. The vacancy sign hung askew from a single hook, and the "No" had probably been lost years ago due to lack of use. He wiped his freshly scrubbed hands on his jeans. He glanced to where Bobby's hatchback and Cheryl's little Civic were parked. He nearly got into Cheryl's car and turned off the ignition but thought better of it. The dead couldn't undo their mistakes.

He'd been lucky to find them both here together, and it had been fun to make Bobby tie Cheryl to the chair, to watch him stuff the socks in her mouth, to listen to the gasps as he'd tied the gag at the nape of her neck. They both searched for an escape, and Bobby didn't go down without a fight. He tried to be macho, or not so much macho, but to make his own escape, shoving Sam aside and trying to run to his car. Sam drove the screwdriver into his thigh before he was even out the door.

"Try that again," Sam said as the man writhed at his feet, "and I'll slit your throat." He turned to Cheryl. "I'd threaten you, but I doubt he'd care. He was going to leave you behind and take care of himself."

Cheryl looked to Bobby for help, those birdlike eyes beseeching him to do something, anything, to get them out of this. Sam walked over to her and tested the bindings. He ran the bloody end of the screwdriver across her cheek. It would be good to have some blood on her in the end.

"Are they tight?" Sam asked. "Try to move."

"I should have shot that woman in the head when I had the chance," Bobby said, in a voice that Sam was sure had terrified plenty of boys over the years. "Why are you doing this?"

"For Gabe," Sam said. "Why else would I do it? I'd do anything for Gabe. How much money did you make off those kids anyway? A couple of grand? A hundred grand? Was it worth it? It's not like it changed your life. You still live in this dump."

434

He thrust the screwdriver into Bobby's side and gave it a twist. Bobby gasped. He tried to stand, and then fell to one knee and collapsed. Cheryl struggled to free herself till she toppled over and lay on her side, looking at Bobby while the life drained from his eyes. A pool of blood spread across the floor till eventually it reached the side of her face, lapping at her cheek like water at the lakeshore.

"A murder-suicide always needs a suicide," Sam said. "And I'm afraid it'll have to be you. It's not a great way to be remembered."

He wondered how long it had taken her to figure out what was happening while he fitted the garden hose to the Civic's exhaust pipe and snaked it through the window. He was lucky the room was small and that it only took a few moments to fill it with carbon monoxide. When it was done, when he untied Cheryl from the chair, and put the screwdriver in her hand, and took the socks from her mouth, he hoped the state police would be too dumb to notice the bruises around her wrists. He took the sock with him in case they found fibers in her windpipe.

Now, he climbed into his own car, which he'd left parked out of sight behind the motel. "Two more stops," he said to Kate, who sat in the backseat chatting with Monkey. "Then we can go home."

"Aunt Hester miss Kate?"

"Aunt Hester?" Sam said. "Who's that? Is she from one of your stories?"

Kate's face twisted into what Sam guessed was the verge of a tantrum. "I'm only joking," he said.

How long it would be before Hester became a shadowy memory? He wondered if he could erase her completely in the end.

His phone rang. It was Wendy. He clicked the phone off, took the battery out, and tossed it through the window. He almost immediately felt lighter, freer. Things were over with Wendy, and a call from her was most likely a call from the police. Besides, it was time to be someone new. It was time to look forward.

A few miles from the motel, right where the road to Little Comfort used to be, he pulled up along the curb and looked into the trees. It took a moment for him to find the car parked there, hidden beneath snow. Gabe was here after all.

"Climb over. Come with me," he said to Kate, who scrambled over the backseat. "I'll carry you, okay? I don't want you to walk in the snow. Not with those slippers."

He lifted the girl with him and then walked to the tree line and stood with Kate balanced on his hip. He saw the remnants of snowshoe prints leading through the trees.

"It's nice here," he said.

Kate nodded and said, "Kate like trees."

"I bet Monkey likes trees too," he said.

"Monkey like trees!" Kate said with a giggle.

"Are you cold, sweetie?" he asked.

She shook her head and buried it in his shoulder, and he felt a warmth spread through him that he'd never felt in his life. He wondered if it was love.

"What should we do?" he asked. "Where should we go?"

"The aquarium!" Kate said.

"I like that idea."

Maybe they'd head to the Caribbean — the Virgin Islands or Puerto Rico. The whole world was an aquarium when you lived on an island. It was time to go. It was time to explore new possibilities. All he had to do was clean up the loose ends.

The sun had begun to set on the winter afternoon. Gabe paced the cabin floor, glancing toward where Hester watched him from the corner. Outside, he heard a noise.

Or at least he thought he did. He poked his head out and searched the trees. The dimming light had turned the entire world to shades of gray. "Sam?" he said, his voice barely above a whisper. "Sam?" he said again, but this time he shouted. "Is that you?"

"Is he here?" Hester asked.

"No," he said. "He'll be here soon."

"What happens then?"

"I don't know."

Gabe had returned to this place so many times in his mind, and it had stayed intact and dappled in summer sun in his memory, so that he'd been surprised when they arrived by how much the cabin had changed, and how different the landscape was in winter. And yet he still felt a certain comfort being here. It was important to him to know that Sam felt the same way. It would make the last twelve years mean something.

"Gabe," Hester said, "I'm hungry. We'll need something to eat soon."

Gabe had doled out the last of the granola bars for lunch. Now, they were running out of wood too. They'd have to go out together soon and see what they could dig from under the snow. Gabe pulled the last of the paneling from the wall and added it to the embers, watching as the dry wood caught the flame. He opened his bag and took out the stacks of postcards that he'd taken from Hester's bed. He fed one of them into the fire. It was a photo of Ellen's house in Pacific Heights. He watched as the flame caught the edge of the card and then engulfed the entire image. He added another card to the fire, and then another. He clicked through the weeks and months and years since he'd left the lake. He thought about what Hester had said, about why Sam had chosen him. She was wrong, wasn't she?

Sam should have been here by now.

"Gabe?" Hester said.

He looked away from the fire.

"Remember when you asked for a story," she said. "I do have one. You're right. We all do. And you get what you get, right? And you can make it into whatever you want it to be. I grew up in a house with a mentally ill mother who drank. Her parents were dead. She didn't have any siblings or friends. I have no idea who my father is or was. We got a disability check in the mail once a month and had to make it last. I read a lot to escape. I watched *General Hospital* every afternoon. I dreamed of being in the CIA. I didn't have a single friend. I didn't know that I was lonely — or that I was alone — till after I knew people, till after someone cared about me. The only person who pulled me through that was me, and the thing I carry with me through life is that I'm resilient. I never give up."

Gabe sat in the doorway and felt the wind from the storm blow around him and flakes of snow stinging his cheeks. "Before I came to the lake," Gabe said, "I moved around."

"I know," Hester said.

"I remember little things," he said. "In flashes. I remember a woman with hair parted in the middle, and a house with a rosebush deep in the woods. I remember a necklace made of candy, a jungle gym in someone's backyard, a pool party. But before here, before I came to the lake, it's all shadows, no firm details."

"What happened on the lake?" Hester asked. "What happened with the man who was killed?"

"Lila wanted to send me to Cheryl's house. I begged her not to, but she didn't want anything to do with me anymore. I told her about Cheryl, about what happened there, and she said that it was my own fault. She said I had to leave. I told Sam about the house, about the motel. He kept asking me how much they paid, if we could get a grand out of one of them. He told me we'd take photos and use them for blackmail. But then everything went wrong. The guy showed up. And we killed him. I killed him."

"How many people have you killed?" Hester asked.

"Six," Gabe said, surprised by how easily that number slipped off his tongue. "It never gets easier, even though I guess it should. I'm not like Sam." Hester was right. Sam *was* a serial killer, but if Sam was a serial killer, what did that make him? "I'm supposed to kill you too."

"Okay," Hester said slowly. Deliberately. And when she spoke again, he could hear her choosing her words. "Why didn't you? Why haven't you?"

Gabe had tried to do what Sam asked. He'd even wanted to, in a way — it would be easier, wouldn't it? He could run away again. He could be with Sam. But he couldn't because he loved her. And he loved Kate, whom he should have protected. And he loved their home and their dog and their unborn son. He loved the whole dream. Images of running through these woods flashed through his mind. Images of the man, of retreating through that house. Of losing control. Couldn't he be better than he was?

He wanted to turn to Hester, but he didn't dare. He couldn't see the way she looked at him anymore because, despite everything, despite what had happened to Kate, he'd saved Hester. She had to know that he'd saved her. He'd protected her from everything bad and evil that could happen. Or at the very least, he'd tried. "I can't tell you," he said. "You'd think I was crazy."

"Try," she said.

He dared himself. He counted to five. "Because I love you."

"I love you too."

He heard her stand, and he imagined her coming up behind him and wrapping her arms around him. He imagined the warm touch of her skin. Kissing her was the very best thing that had ever happened in his whole life, a feeling he'd treasure for as long as he lived. Did she know what that kiss meant? Did she know that it had saved her? He imagined believing she'd still be here later. He closed his eyes, and he could smell her, not now, with the scent of smoke clinging to everything, but later, when she smelled of cinnamon and vanilla and joy. When dog hair clung to her sweater, and he brought her a glass of wine because he knew she'd had a long day.

"You're a good person," Hester said. "And I don't think you know it. Sam saw you, but for the wrong reasons. He saw how he could use you."

He gripped the doorway as a wave of regret swept through him. "Shut up," he said, punching at the doorframe. "Shut up." He punched again and felt the skin on his knuckles tear. "Shut up, shut up!"

He'd done this, all of it. He understood that for the first time in a long time, maybe the first time ever. He'd made that life he dreamed of impossible. He fought the tears that welled up, covering his face with his hands and wishing so much to be undone. He heard her move. And he felt her. She was still near.

"You can leave," she said. "Really. You have time. Head to Montreal. Sneak over the border. Learn French. Become someone new."

"I can't," Gabe said. He couldn't listen anymore. All he wanted was to close his eyes and sleep, to disappear, to forget. "Not all alone." Not without you.

"You can."

"No."

"Listen to me. Do you remember when I told you that you weren't half bad? Do you remember that? In the park? I meant it. I don't mean it now, but I meant it then. Promise me you'll remember that."

"I'm sorry," Gabe said. He was, and he

only hoped that she could hear him and know that what he said was true, that he believed it more than anything he'd believed in his entire life. "For everything. I'm so, so sorry."

"I know you are. And I'm sorry for everything that happened to you. I am so sorry for what Cheryl and Bobby did you to you. I can't even imagine what it must have been like. And I understand that you had to do anything you could to escape. Really, I do."

Gabe covered his face again.

"Gabe?"

She was closer. He wanted her so badly. "Yes?" he said.

"I'm sorry for this too."

He turned in time to see the edge of the snowshoe before it smashed into his temple. Then the world went black.

CHAPTER 27

Angela rang the bell and then pounded on Hester Thursby's front door in Somerville. She had Butch's leash looped around one hand and a lasagna balanced on the other. She'd been going crazy sitting around the house, waiting. Isaiah had gone off to school, and Cary, after much prodding, had headed to work, yet somehow a bag of microwave popcorn and a day in front of the TV hadn't held the same appeal as it had yesterday. So she'd stopped by animal control and picked up the dog. Then she swung over to the hospital to visit Jamie. She watched him through a window, a tube down his throat, bandages covering his chest, till a nurse came along and told her dogs weren't allowed in the ICU. Here's where she'd have normally flashed her badge so that she could stay, but Stan had the badge. Stan had her gun, her job, her very identity sitting in a drawer in his desk.

Outside the hospital, in the parking lot, she was assaulted by a horde of reporters on her way to her car, yelling questions at her with phrases like "unprovoked" and "excessive force." A crowd of civilians followed her too, their phones out, recording the commotion, as she tried to retreat to the car, tripping over the dog's leash. Why had she gone to the hospital in a pair of fuchsia-colored sweatpants? She nearly ran into a fire hydrant as she sped out of the lot.

Stan called a few moments later. "You need to be careful," he said. "I saw what happened just now. It's already on YouTube. You're the face of this shooting. You're all over the Web."

"Tell me something I don't know," Angela said.

"This'll blow over. If we play everything right. They won't latch on to you the way they would someone else. We don't need a Freddie Gray situation here."

Angela pulled to the side of the road. Stan was nothing if not consistent. He'd do anything to keep the department free of scandal, and this time he wanted her to be the black cop, to take the fall, because for her the fall wouldn't be that steep. He wanted her to keep the department's nose

446

clean. No "Black Lives Matter" in Boston. "Hey, Stan?" she said.

"Yeah."

"I sho' 'nough didn't mean to shoot no nigga," she said. "Is that black enough for you?"

"You know that's not what I mean."

"Go fuck yourself."

Now, standing on the front porch of the blue house, she saw a pair of legs coming down the stairs, and then a gray Tufts Veterinary School t-shirt as a man with red hair that stuck out in every direction appeared. It was Morgan Maguire, Hester Thursby's partner. He looked tired, so very tired and drawn, and she wondered whether she'd actually woken him or whether, like her, he hadn't slept. She could only imagine what his night had been like. Hester's basset hound trotted behind him. Butch tugged on her leash and woofed. The man looked at her warily through the window, and, again, this was where Angela would normally have flashed her badge and seen his expression change.

Some people grew more suspicious when cops showed up, and Angela understood that. She expected it. Others grew wary or frightened or apprehensive. Some burst out crying. It surprised Angela when someone welcomed her. It made her suspicious.

"Dr. Maguire, can I speak to you for five minutes?" she said through the glass.

"Are you a reporter?" Morgan asked.

Angela shook her head, and he opened the door a crack. "Then who are you?"

"I heard you were a vet," she said. "I have this dog. I wanted to be sure she was okay."

"You should make an appointment at my office," Morgan said. He went to shut the door, but Angela stopped him. "I made a lasagna," she said, holding the aluminum tray toward him. "Actually I bought it. From Whole Foods. It's vegetarian. They said to heat it at three fifty for forty-five minutes."

Morgan looked at the tray and didn't seem to know what to do. He had green eyes and that translucent skin that so many redheads had. He looked like he hadn't eaten in days.

"I should have called," Angela said. "I'm a cop. Or at least I was. And I will be again. Right now, I wanted to ask about your wife."

"I've been talking to the cops all night," Morgan said. "And they don't really let up. And I'm tired. Who are you?"

"Sorry," Angela said. "Let me start again." She took a moment to explain who she was and that she'd been involved with the case till the night before. "So right now," she said, "I guess I'm a concerned citizen. Have they made progress? Do they know what happened?"

"Not that they're telling me," Morgan said. He took a deep breath and seemed to fight something off, tears or rage or defeat. "It's been sixteen hours," he finally said.

"Well . . ." Angela leaned forward on the tips of her snow boots and held out the lasagna again. Morgan took the aluminum pan. "I'll take a look at your dog. But you should really bring her to the office. You aren't allergic to cats, are you?"

"Not at all," Angela said, as she followed him into the house and up the stairs to a cozy apartment on the second floor where a darkened Christmas tree stood by the window and drapes lay pooled on the floor. At least a half dozen kittens ran through the house. The air smelled of old kitty litter, and the counters were covered with dishes. "Do your thing," Angela said. "I'll keep myself busy."

She preheated the oven and put the lasagna in to heat up, and then plugged in the lights on the Christmas tree. She filled the sink and washed as many dishes as should could find, and then she cleaned out the kitty litter. When she'd finished, she joined

Morgan in the living room.

"She's fine," Morgan said, putting Butch on the floor and letting her scamper off with the basset hound. "At least from what I can tell here."

"Can you answer a few questions for me?" Angela asked.

"I've been answering questions all night, and my lawyer left to get some sleep. I'd get some sleep too, if I could."

"This'll be for me. Off the record. No lawyers necessary."

Morgan nodded, and Angela asked him to tell her what he remembered from the night before. He told her about Hester coming home from Jamie's house, how she'd confessed that she'd found Sam and Gabe and gone to New Hampshire.

"Did you tell the cops that?" Angela asked. "That she went to New Hampshire."

"Yes," Morgan said. "And I know that wherever she went, there was a lake. But that's it. There must be a hundred lakes in New Hampshire."

"What else?" Angela asked.

Morgan told her about getting into a fight and that he'd gone to a bar. He met up with a friend — his lawyer — and they agreed to stay till closing. "I was pretty drunk when she called," Morgan said. "But I sobered right up. Prachi called the cops, and I ran. I ran as fast as I could, and I told Kate to get out of the house and to hide in the backyard and that I was coming. I was a block away when the phone went dead. When I got here she was gone."

He stared off for a moment. "Do you have kids?" he asked.

"Sort of," Angela said. "I had a husband and no kids. Now I have a wife and her kid. He calls me Angie, which I normally hate, but I like it when he does it."

Morgan smiled for the first time since she'd arrived. "That's like us," he said. "Kate's my sister's kid. She's been staying with us. Neither of us are parents, but Hester's good with her. I'm not. I give her soda and candy to keep her from complaining. I lost her at the park the other day for five full minutes. I was supposed to take her for the whole day a few Saturdays ago, and she went crazy and threw her Cheerios across the floor, and I panicked and lied and told Hester that I'd picked up a shift at the hospital and then went to the movies all day. Hester would kill me if she knew."

"I use the TV as a babysitter," Angela said. "And now that I'm on leave, I worry that Cary will think I can babysit all the time. We all do things we shouldn't. It's how you survive."

Butch leaped up on the sofa and snuggled onto Angela's lap. She ran her fingers through the dog's fur. "You don't mind her on the furniture, do you?" she asked.

"Look at this place," Morgan said.

"The lasagna will be ready in twenty minutes. Can you take care of it?"

"I'll be fine. Thank you, though."

Angela stood and put her coat on. "Hang in there," she said. "Don't give up hope, no matter what."

She went to shake Morgan's hand, and then surprised herself by embracing him, something she could never do as a cop. He clung to her, and she resisted letting go till she felt him pull away. "You have friends, right?" she said. "Family? People you can rely on? You'll need them."

He nodded. "A few," he said.

"Let them help. Even if it annoys you."

At the door, she checked her phone for messages and stopped. "Do you know where Kate was when she had the phone?" she asked.

"Outside," Morgan said.

"But outside where?"

"I told her to hide on the side of the house."

"Did the Somerville police find the phone?

452

Have they requested the phone records?"

"They don't really tell me much."

"Come." Angela led him out of the apartment and down the stairs. "Is this where Kate was hiding?" she asked, trudging through the snow to a clump of rhododendrons. Morgan nodded. "Call the phone," Angela said.

Morgan hit dial.

Angela closed her eyes and listened till she heard a faint, muffled ringing. When it ended, she told Morgan to dial again. Finally, she got on her hands and knees and dug till she found the phone buried in the snow. She went straight to the call history and scanned for 603 area codes. Then she called Stan. "Don't argue," she said. "I need you to find an address for me."

Sam drove the car into the hills over the lake as the final light from the day faded. He parked in a copse of snowy evergreens and pulled out the last postcard. It was black, a photo of nothing. He sat in the car as the cold began to creep in and then ruffled Kate's hair. "Are you hungry, kiddo?" he asked. "I have one more errand to run, and then we can grab something. What do want?"

"Waffles like pizza," Kate said.

"Does Monkey like pizza?"

Kate nodded.

"I like pizza too," Sam said. "But you'll have to eat some carrot sticks too, is that a deal?"

"Yes," Kate said.

Up the street, Lila's house looked comfortable nestled in the trees, much more comfortable than when Sam had lived there. All those years ago, meeting Gabe had awoken something inside Sam, something similar to what he felt with Kate right now, a need to protect. It had been exhilarating to feel that man's hands in his pants, and then the hatchet in hand. The blade had cut right through the man's skin, and blood had spilled across the floor in long, glorious splatters. More than the actual kill, more than seeing the man's life fade away, what Sam had enjoyed most was the feel of shifting power, the way the man's eyes had moved from desire, to confusion, to terror. In a way, Sam hoped that tonight's visit — the return to where it had all begun — might waken something new in him, something kind and generous that he'd never known.

As he watched, Lila's kitchen door opened, and a pack of mongrels ran into the yard, running beneath the outside lights.

454

They scampered in circles, each one prancing out in turn to yellow the snow. Lila joined them, stepping through the drifts in black rubber boots. Sam could see the braid falling down her back.

"Doggies," Kate said.

"I'll be careful with them," Sam said. "You watch Monkey, okay? Make sure nothing bad happens to him."

Lila played with the dogs for a few moments before lifting a blue tarp from a pile of wood and sweeping the snow away. A hatchet rose from one of the logs. She gathered an armload of wood, and then stopped, her head cocked to the side, her shoulders suddenly stiff beneath her jacket. She stared into the darkness, and Sam saw her face at last, even though she couldn't possibly see him through the dark. She took a step toward the street, and seemed to change her mind. She whistled, and the dogs filed in behind her in a line of wagging tails.

Sam flipped the postcard over and wrote *GOODBYE* in block letters. It wasn't a quote, but people said goodbye in movies all the time, and this would be the last of the postcards anyway. He wondered if she'd recognize him when he knocked, or whether he'd see the terror dawn the same way he had with Cheryl Jenkins earlier.

"I'll be back in five," he said to Kate.

"Daddy back in five," Kate said to Monkey.

At the door to the house, he pried the hatchet free. Inside, a chorus of barks began.

Hester raised the snowshoe over her head to smash it down one more time, but she couldn't bring herself to do it. Gabe lay sprawled on the floor. A trail of blood ran down his temple. She grabbed a blanket from by the fire and draped it over her shoulders. She struggled to fit the snowshoes over her sneakers. And she imagined. She imagined Gabe tackling her. She imagined him binding her arms and legs. She imagined Sam appearing out of the trees. She remembered being trapped in her closet at home, trying to birth her way through that dog door. She heard the slam of the trunk, and the crunch of snow beneath her slippers. She remembered believing she would die.

The shoes were on.

She could see the outline of the car keys in Gabe's front pocket. She tried to slip a hand in to retrieve them, but he groaned and grabbed her wrist. She shook him off and sidestepped down the stairs. He crawled after her into the doorway. His fingers grasped the edge of the blanket. She yanked it away.

And she ran.

She lifted the snowshoes through the drifts, running in what seemed like slow motion, ignoring the snow that fell down her back and filled her sneakers and the branches that reached out and grabbed at her. Head up. Hands out. Find an opening through the trees. Look for footprints.

Make plans.

Think about home.

Find Kate.

How would they spend the rest of their lives? She'd start by telling Morgan that she understood who they were now, that they took in strays because they could, because they had the gift of capacity in a way that others didn't, that they could open their lives to whatever came, whether dogs or cats or rabbits or rats. Or children. She imagined Waffles lapping her face. She'd take the dog to the park and throw the ball even if the damn thing refused to fetch. She saw Morgan's hair turning white and the crow's feet deepening around her own eyes.

But most of all, she saw Kate growing, getting her ears pierced, blushing over her first date, driving. She saw Kate with her, always and forever.

The blanket caught on a branch, and she left it behind. She pitched headfirst over a boulder, and then scrambled on all fours across the snow. And then she could see the road through the line of trees and the car buried in snow. She tried the doors. They were locked. She swept snow from the windshield and wrote her name on it in case anyone found the car. Then she kicked off the snowshoes and was on the road, running, looking for a house, any house where someone seemed to be home.

She'd have pizza for breakfast and watch *Cars* for the seventy-seventh time. She'd find Daphne, if only to say do what you need to do, be whoever you need to be, take whatever time you need even if it's the rest of your life, and you'll always be my friend, and I'll always love you no matter what, and I know that you trusted me. Kate can be mine, or she can be ours, but she'll be wonderful no matter what. Hester would be sure of it.

She had to pee, and she did. The warm wetness spread down her legs and soaked into her pajamas, and she was grateful for the momentary warmth.

She'd change out of these pajamas. She'd hold her feet and hands right over an open flame to defrost them. She'd say hello to her neighbors and make new friends. And she'd meet them for drinks.

She'd visit her mother.

Maybe.

She turned into the hills toward Lila's house. She passed someone else's unplowed driveway, which led to a house with no lights or cars or smoke coming from the chimney. Her lungs burned. Her arms flailed. Her legs stretched longer than she'd ever imagined they could. The tiny house appeared around the corner, lit up under a moon that poked out from behind clouds. Smoke poured from the chimney. Her stomach made a noise that was more moan than growl, the kind of pathetic, sad noise a starving dog might make. She wanted the biggest fucking pastrami sandwich she'd ever seen in her entire life. Slathered with mustard. And a mountain of French fries.

And then she stopped and dove into the trees. She crawled forward. Right in front of her was Sam's Nissan.

She listened.

All she heard coming from Lila's house was the whining of a dog. Wind lifted freshly fallen snow and blew it across the landscape in a gentle whir. She heard her own heavy breathing and felt the cold begin to creep under her skin.

She edged onto the street behind the car and peered in the windows.

It was empty.

She tried one of the doors. It opened, and the interior light flashed like a beacon across the dark night. She crawled into the back-seat and shut the door to get out of the wind. Then she searched for keys, first in the glove box, and then on the dash and, back outside the car, over each of the tires. Finally, she felt under the seats. She reached around in the dark, till her hand landed on something soft. She pulled it out.

It was Monkey. Kate's Monkey.

Hester felt every bit of the panic she'd held down since yesterday well up in one terrified, silent scream.

Kate was here. Inside that house.

With Sam.

CHAPTER 28

It was still snowing, a light, gentle snow to mark the end of the storm. Gabe had already listened to the rhythmic crunch as Hester had retreated through the trees, and now he still listened, though he wasn't sure for what. He knew she wouldn't return, though he still hoped. He hoped that she might choose him. He hoped Sam might come too. That they'd get into the car and drive away, that they'd head off toward some new horizon, toward an unrealized dream. He'd had to choose between the two of them in the end.

He stood, walked down the steps to the lake, and waded out through the drifts to a spot on the ice where he'd watched Sam and Lila swimming all those years ago. In a way, it felt like yesterday. He wondered what had happened to Lila. She was so close, after all. Gabe wondered if he could have saved her even though she hadn't been will-

461

ing to save him.

He turned to the shore, to where the darkened trees loomed over the lake, to where the cabin glowed from the last embers of the fire. He hoped when the police finally showed up that Detective White would be with them. Angela White. Angie. Maybe she'd strut across the ice with her white teeth and handcuffs, and she'd play good and bad as she read him his Miranda rights. Surely she'd have found the finger in the batik box by now, or at least the beer bottle with his fingerprints on it. Angie must be angry about shooting the disabled vet, maybe even in trouble. But finding a serial killer would make up for some of that.

He'd done what he'd come here to do. He'd left a trail of clues that led directly to him for the police to find. He'd tried his best to give Sam one last chance, a chance that was Sam's to take, whatever he chose to do with it. And he'd shown Hester mercy.

He lay in the snow to make an angel, his red parka a blackened dot in a sea of white. Up in the sky, clouds parted, and the moon began to shine through. He imagined a perfect night, with a moon like this one, and water eddying around his ankles and children on a rope swing, and someone to love. He imagined feeling lucky.

He remembered listening to the sounds of the lake, to the gentle breeze through the leaves, to insects pinging against screens, to a coyote crying in the distance. Yet here on the frozen lake, he was struck by the lack of noise — no cars or phones or people or talking — by the silence of the snow, by the peace of the falling flakes. All he heard was his own breathing. Heavy, labored breathing. And snow. Millions of snowflakes, each hitting the ground with a minuscule patter, landing in his hair, dotting his nose. Cleansing. It felt so good to choose, to take this moment to himself.

Then he stood and headed toward shore. There was one last thing to do. He'd made his final choice.

All five of Lila's dogs ran in an anxious, yellow circle. They surrounded Hester. The biggest one whined. "Shh," she whispered, glad for the warmth of their breath.

She crossed to the rusty green Chevy parked by the barn and opened the door. "In," she whispered. One by one, the dogs leaped into the cab till the air hung with the scent of wet fur. She searched under the seat and in the glove compartment for keys, without luck. "Stay," she whispered, and then left the dogs panting in unison, and edged toward the house. The door swung open to the warm kitchen. A fire burned in the woodstove and a nearly dry kettle whistled on a burner. Hester closed the door behind her with a gentle click. She turned off the gas beneath the kettle. In the silence, she could feel the taxidermied eyes of the deer heads staring at her. She whispered Kate's name into the quiet.

On the counter sat a bowl of cold tomato soup and a half-eaten grilled cheese sandwich, which Hester ate without a thought. She turned the faucet on and stuck her mouth into the stream of cool water. She took a knife from a butcher block and searched for a phone, only to find where the landline had been ripped from the wall.

She listened. To the silence. To the moans of the old house.

She held the knife in front of her and crept down a narrow hallway lined with photos and bookshelves. She jumped when her oversize sneaker caught the leg of a wooden chair and sent it skidding across the floor. She half expected a cat to leap from a closet. Ahead of her, light emanated from around a doorway, and from behind it, she could hear the rhythmic thumping of wood against wood.

She turned the knob. The door squeaked open.

Lila sat in the middle of the room struggling to break the duct tape holding her to a chair. When she saw Hester, her eyes widened and she shook her head frantically. "Where is he?" Hester whispered as she cut one of Lila's hands free. "Is Kate with him?"

Lila ripped the tape from her own mouth and gasped for breath. Her gaze jumped to the doorway at Hester's back. Hester spun around.

Sam held Kate against his hip. "I thought you were Gabe. He always had a thing for my sister."

Hester held the knife in front of her. She backed up to the fireplace and took a log from the woodpile. "Put her down," she said. "And don't come near me."

"Are you serious?" Sam said. "I couldn't come a step closer. You smell like piss. I'm surprised my sister hasn't passed out from the stench. What happened to you anyway? You look like a pre-teen refugee from a Disney cruise."

"Are you okay, sweetie?" Hester asked Kate.

"Is she okay?" Sam said. "What's Daddy making for dinner later?"

"Pizza!" Kate said.

He stepped from the doorway. Hester jabbed the knife toward him. "The cops are on the way," she said.

Sam hesitated and then shook his head. "There's no phone, sweetie," he said. "You must have noticed I pulled it out of the wall." He held up a cell phone, and then dropped it to the floor and crushed it with his boot. "That was my sister's. Anyway, the police are busy with a little double murder across town. It'll keep them occupied all night."

Sam took another step into the room and let his arm swing by his side. The hatchet in his hand made the chef's knife look about as useful as a pair of tweezers.

"Gabe will be here soon himself," Hester said. "He let me go."

"I knew he liked you, but didn't know he liked you *that* much. He's never let one go before."

"I guess I'm lucky," Hester said, glancing around the small room. There was a door at the other end.

Sam followed her gaze. "Don't even think about it," he said. "Women Gabe likes tend to wind up dead." He swung the hatchet over his head and swept a vase off a shelf. Lila screamed, and Kate started to cry as the pottery crashed to the floor.

Hester held out her hands. "Give her to me," she said. "Now!"

Kate wriggled in Sam's arm till he had no choice but to put the girl down. She ran across the floor and clung to Hester's leg. It took every ounce of Hester's resolve to stay focused on Sam.

"We're leaving now," she said. "You, do whatever you want. But we're leaving."

Hester took a step backward. Sam mirrored her. "Here's the problem," he said. "Even if the local police aren't on their way, there's a manhunt going on now. It's all over the news, and even the feds are involved, because Gabe crossed state lines and went through tolls with his Goddamned E-ZPass. They're looking for you and him. Probably me too."

"Listen, Sam," Lila said, struggling to pull the tape from around her bound hand, "I haven't ever talked to the cops, even when I found out you'd moved to San Francisco. Not once during all these years did I speak to anyone except her, even when they found that body in the woods, and I knew it had something to do with you."

Lila worked her hand free from the tape. She leaned forward to free her feet, and Sam took a step toward her. "Don't move," he said.

Lila sat up. Slowly. More slowly than Hester could have.

"Leave," Lila said. "I've kept your secrets all these years. I've always protected you. I bet she will too. All she wants is to get the kid out of here."

"The kid," Sam said with a raise of one eyebrow. "She's a cutie. Maybe I want her to come with me."

"Fuck you," Hester said.

"Language," Sam said. "Think about it, a single father with a kid like that . . ." He clucked his tongue. "I'll be the most popular man in town, no matter where I wind up."

"Come one step closer to us," Hester said, "and I'll kill you."

"How?" Sam asked.

He took another step into the room. Lila flinched. He swung the hatchet so that the blade sank into the doorframe, and then he turned without a word and walked away.

Hester stared after him. She put a hand to the wall. A shiver began at the base of her spine and ran up through her chest, and then she crouched down and hugged Kate and wanted to check every single inch of her to make sure he hadn't hurt her in any way. "Where's your rifle?" she asked Lila. "Where's Clovis?"

"Cut the tape," Lila said.

"Where is the fucking gun?" Hester said.

"In the kitchen," Lila whispered. "I'll get it. Go out the back. The keys to the truck are hanging on the wall by the barn door." She flinched. *Watch out!*

Hester spun to see Sam charging them. He wrenched the hatchet from the wall as Hester held Kate to her chest, rolled onto her back, and shoved Lila to the floor. Sam swung the hatchet, sinking the blade into Lila's arm. She cried out as blood spurted across the floor. Sam stepped over her. Hester rolled to the side and shoved Kate away. She raised the log as the blade nearly split it in half. She twisted at the log, and Sam fell on top of her. They rolled into a shelf and books cascaded around them. Sam's face was so close to hers she could smell his breath. Shouting, Sam called Hester a cunt and a bitch and a whore, and told her that she'd never, ever see the light of day again. They slid through Lila's blood. Hester grabbed the hatchet handle. Sam was strong. And angry. And she was losing her grip.

But she kneed him in the groin.

And she rammed her fist into his throat.

Fight!

She yanked the log and the hatchet away. She scrambled across the floor and drove the hatchet into the wall so that the log split off it. Lila crawled from the room, leaving a trail of blood behind her. Sam was doubled over in pain, and there was nothing in the world that Hester wanted more than for him to charge so that she could cleave his skull right in half. "Come on!" she shouted. "I dare you."

He charged.

She raised the hatchet over her head with both hands. He slammed his shoulder into her chest and the wind swept from her lungs. She crashed into the wall. The hatchet spun across the floor. She yanked the door open. She lifted Kate onto her hip. Sam clutched at her leg, and one of the sneakers slipped from her foot. She kicked again and dashed down a dark hallway toward the scent of hay and manure. She reached the barn door and wrenched it open.

Sam tackled her.

She shoved Kate forward. "Run!" she shouted, but Kate wouldn't move.

Hester clawed at what she could. Sam screamed as she dug her finger into his eye socket.

Her head snapped. His fist crushed the bones in her jaw. She spat out a tooth. He rammed a shoulder into her gut, and they sprawled across the hay-strewn barn floor.

He had her by the hair. She twisted around and kicked, but his knee was in her chest. He reared up, the hatchet in both hands.

"Sam."

Sam froze. Hester felt the weight lift from her chest.

Gabe stood in the doorway, the rifle to his shoulder, pointed at Hester. Kate cowered against the barn wall, her hands covering her face. "Go outside," Hester pleaded with her. "Go find the dogs."

Kate shook her head and sobbed.

"You made it," Sam said.

Even from across the room, Hester could see the tears streaming down Gabe's face. "Please," she said to him.

"Shut your mouth," Sam said, glaring at her. His eye was bloody from where Hester had gouged it. He turned his attention back to Gabe. "We'll leave. Together. Like we always do."

"Where?" Hester said. "Where will you go this time? How will it be any different? Listen to me, Gabe. This will never end. Not today. Not ever."

Sam ignored her. "Your choice, Gabe," he said. "Anywhere you want to go."

Gabe swung the rifle toward Sam. "What about her?" he said. "What about them?"

"You're at the stern," Sam said. "You can

finish this. You're in control."

"He's right," Hester said. "Listen to him. Get in your car and drive away. You still have time. You're more than this."

Gabe moved the barrel again. Aiming it at Hester. She fought the urge to close her eyes, to give in, and matched his stare. This couldn't be the last image Kate had of her. "Remember what I told you," she said, "at the dog park. In the cabin. I meant it then. And I mean it now. Don't prove me wrong."

Gabe pulled the trigger. The barrel of the rifle recoiled, and the blast reverberated through the barn. Hester wondered if it would be the last sound she'd ever hear.

And then Sam's eyes grew wide as he reached toward Gabe in surprise. Sam's face turned white, and an ink stain of blood spread across his shirt. Then, with a groan, he slumped forward on top of Hester. Blood spurted across her pajamas, and she gasped for breath as she fought her way out from beneath him.

Gabe stood in the doorway. The rifle's muzzle smoked. Hester scrambled across the floor to put herself between Gabe and Kate, but he dropped the rifle and slid to the floor, staring at Sam the whole time.

And then she crawled to Kate and held her like she'd never, ever let her go again.

CHAPTER 29

It took more than a half hour for the ambulance and police to arrive. Hester didn't move except to shiver uncontrollably and cling to Kate. She knew she was in shock. She knew she should go inside and sit by the fire, that she should check on Lila, but she couldn't look away from where Sam lay in the hay, his blank eyes staring right at her, even as the yard outside filled with flashing lights, even after a standoff where Gabe emerged from the barn and lay on the ground with his face in the snow so that a deputy could handcuff him. A kind-looking EMT wheeled in a gurney. "Come on, sweetie," he said. "We'll get you to the hospital."

"Shouldn't you take care of Lila?" Hester asked, her words slurred. It hurt to speak. She touched her jaw and could feel the swelling.

"There's someone with her," the EMT

said, as he checked her pulse and tried to slip an oxygen mask over her face.

"No, no," she said, batting his hand away. Another EMT tried to take Kate from her, and Hester shook her head again. "No!" she said.

"It's okay. We're checking her out. She'll be right next to you."

"I need a phone," Hester said.

The EMT dug one from his pocket and gave it to her. Hester shivered so much as they lifted her onto the soft gurney that she could barely punch in Morgan's number. When he answered, she hated herself a little bit because she started to sob and she couldn't manage to form a word. She handed the phone to the EMT so that he could tell Morgan everything was okay.

"Exposure," the EMT said. "Dehydration. Cuts and bruises. A broken jaw. We'll check them out at the hospital."

"No," Hester said. "I want to go home."

"Maybe tomorrow," the EMT said. "Let us take care of you now."

He gave the phone to Hester as she heard Morgan saying her name. "It's me," she said.

"I'll be there in two hours," Morgan said. "Even less, because my foot will be all the way to the floor." And then he talked softly, gently, and kept talking while Hester heard him hurrying around the apartment with the phone tucked under his chin. She heard him whistle to Waffles, and then thump down the stairs to the truck. "I'll stay on the phone the whole way," he said. "It'll be like I'm there with you."

The EMTs lifted Hester into the ambulance and then lay Kate down beside her. The girl nestled into the crook of Hester's arm. They lifted Lila in on a second gurney, and then they drove out of the driveway with the sirens blaring. "They're driving like it's an emergency," Hester mumbled into the phone. Her eyes began to feel heavy.

"You'll be fine," Morgan said.

"Why Aunt Hester cry?" Kate asked.

Hester touched the girl's face and smiled. "Because I'm happy," she said. "And because I missed you."

She listened to Morgan's voice as he told her about the press that had hounded him for the past twenty-four hours, about the visits from the police and the long interrogations. "Prachi and Jane were here the whole time," he said. "Prachi read them the riot act, but I guess the non-husband is the first person they suspect. A Detective White came around too. She's the one who sent the police to the house there."

And when he stopped talking, Hester listened to him breathe. She closed her eyes and felt like she might sleep for a week.

"Daphne sent a text earlier," Morgan said. "She heard the story on the news."

"Did she say where she went? Or what she's been doing?"

"No. I didn't ask either."

"Is she coming home?"

"She asked if she should," Morgan said. "What should I write?"

Hester looked out the back of the ambulance, at the snowy road unfurling behind them. She thought about Gabe. Of being unwanted. Kate closed her eyes, and her breathing grew steady. She stroked the girl's curly hair. Kate would be wanted, no matter what the cost.

"Tell Daphne to come home whenever she wants to," Hester said. "But that we'll be fine till then."

Hester submitted to the humilities of the courthouse security, signing in and emptying her pockets, walking through the scanner, hoping the whole time to avoid a patdown. Camera shutters clacked as she picked up her bag. Gaze forward, she told herself. Don't engage. God, had she zipped her fly? Maybe she should have worn something less casual than jeans?

She took the arching staircase instead of the elevator to the second floor and looked out over Boston Harbor through the floor-to-ceiling windows. She nodded to Detective White, who stood by the courtroom door texting someone. And then she waited on a hard plastic chair. No one had told her how much waiting there would be in court.

She hadn't seen Gabe since the short hearing in March, when he'd plead guilty to all of the federal charges against him — murder, kidnapping, crossing state lines in the act of a felony, etc. — and (thankfully) denied the press the long trial they'd predicted. He'd offered up detailed accounts of each of the six murders, while family members, who'd traveled in from as far away as San Francisco, wept.

Today, once the proceedings got underway, Hester took a seat at the back of the room, where she felt strangers staring at her and did her best to keep her expression neutral. In the two months since she'd left the hospital, she'd learned that a smile could be interpreted in many ways. Detective White took the seat beside hers. "Almost done," she said.

"I can only hope," Hester said. "Are you back to work?"

Angela nodded. "You?"

"Not quite," Hester said.

The judge entered. He conferred with the bailiff, and a moment later Gabe shuffled in wearing his orange jumpsuit and chains, escorted by two uniformed officers. His hair had been cut short, and he'd lost the beard. He looked as though he'd shed thirty pounds, and Hester was struck again by how young he was. He joined the court-appointed lawyer at one of the tables. The courtroom artist started in on his first sketch. Later, the sketches would show up on the local news, and in them Gabe's eyes would flash with evil, his chin would point, his teeth would glint in a barely perceptible smirk.

The press had had their fun with the story. Hester had managed to go from action hero to accomplice to victim in a matter of about ten days. She'd read countless stories with an unfounded subtext of sexual assault. Plenty of speculation, no matter what she said in interviews, had gone into what actually happened in the cabin on the lake. Now, *Lifetime* was interested in making a movie of the week about the whole ordeal. A staff writer had even called the other day. She didn't understand why Hester and Morgan had a dog door inside the house and had finally said that they'd changed it to a laundry chute in the script anyway. "A laundry chute," Hester had said. "Imagine dropping a child down a laundry chute!"

The judge read the charges against Gabe and asked if he'd like to make a statement before sentencing. Gabe stood with his lawyer. He shuffled from side to side. He opened his mouth as if to say something.

"Mr. DiPursio," the judge said, "please, let's be mindful of the court's time."

Gabe turned. Hester knew she should feel

angry or victimized or thrilled, or that she should at least play the part to satisfy this whole spectacle. She knew she should have been one of those reading a victim statement, one that would somehow make it onto YouTube, one that would empower with its eloquence. But she simply felt sad. She stood almost without thinking and shrugged away the voice that told her to be still. She took a step forward and nearly said Gabe's name. She still had trouble sleeping and still had panic attacks when Kate was out of her sight or when she heard a trunk slam, but she also knew that Gabe could have killed her at any time, that Sam had sent him to her house to do just that, but that he'd let her go, and that he'd taken her for a reason. She knew that she was the one person on earth who'd shown up for him at any of the hearings — certainly Lila was nowhere to be seen — and that she was the only person to offer him any comfort.

"I'm very sorry," Gabe said from the front of the room. He didn't look at anyone but her when he said it.

"Anything else?" the judge asked, and Gabe shook his head and listened as the judge told him he spoke for the victims when he handed down a sentence of six consecutive life sentences without the possibility of parole.

It was the best-case scenario, right?

It was what Hester should have hoped for. It's what she'd pleaded for in her op-ed against capital punishment that had run in the *Globe,* when she'd learned there could be power in playing a victim.

Afterward, as the lawyers gathered their briefs and legal pads and the other observers filed out of the narrow seats, Hester sat still. A woman paused on her way out to say she thought Hester was an inspiration.

"Thank you," Hester said.

She'd gotten used to having strangers stop her on the street, for good or for bad.

It was time to move on, and yet she still edged up the aisle to where the court artist dabbed the finishing touches on his latest sketch. It featured Gabe gazing lovingly toward the back of the court.

"Do you have one of me?" Hester asked, and the artist had the decency to blush as he flipped to the previous page. It was a good drawing, one that would run on the local news later that night with a caption that read, *Victim shows conflicted emotions.* And like all the drawings of Hester that had appeared on the news, she looked tiny and weak, almost forlorn.

"Can I buy it from you?" she asked.

"I can't," the artist said.

"I'll give you twenty bucks." And when he shook his head and put the pad away, she offered a thousand. Surely there had to be something physical to remember this whole thing by, something to press between the pages of a book. Something besides a pinkie left permanently numb from frostbite.

Outside the courthouse, Hester breathed in fresh air. It was filled with the sweet, piney scent of mulch. Today, on the last day of April, the sun shone. Beds of daffodils and a line of budding pink dogwoods announced that spring, after a few false starts, was finally, truly here. Detective White met her by the door. "Need me to walk with you?" she asked.

"Thanks," Hester said. "But I think I have this."

A handful of photographers lurked, and a single reporter asked her for a comment, but as she left the detective and marched past them with a practiced step, it was as though she could feel the story finally flittering away. Something more exciting would happen soon enough to make Hester Thursby another sordid footnote in local history. She thought about Gabe, who'd be shackled in a van headed toward the rest of his life by now.

She followed the path along the water to where Jamie waited on a park bench. The dogs — Waffles and Butch — ran in a circle on the grass with Kate at the very center. Kate broke away to run to Hester, and Hester crouched to hug her. "We playing tag!" Kate said.

"Who's winning?"

"Me!"

Hester watched the girl run to the dogs. Kate had survived everything unscathed. Once in a while now she mentioned "the bad man" but nothing else, and Hester and Morgan had vowed never to speak of what had happened in front of her.

"You survived," Jamie said, choosing the words as carefully as usual.

It had taken him a month to get out of the hospital after the shooting, a month in which Hester had visited him nearly every day. He was still recovering, and he had a new scar on his chest to join the one he'd received in combat. Hester had gone to pick him up at the hospital, and then brought him to the house, where he moved into Daphne's empty first-floor apartment. "It's better this way," she'd said when he'd tried to protest. "It's better than being alone."

Now, she rested her head on his shoulder

and let him put his big arm around her. "It wasn't that bad," she said.

Morgan could have come to the hearing too, but Hester had told him to go to work instead. He'd been supportive. Really, he had. So supportive that he'd taken a sledge-hammer to the wall between their apartments where the dog door used to be. "You should have a second egress," he'd said as he'd sat on his closet floor and sucked in air. Hester wondered whether he believed any of the stories the press had hinted at, lurid stories of sex and conspiracy. She still worried that that belief might fester into something bigger and dangerous and much more difficult to destroy, but she'd deal with that if and when it came.

"Why do I feel so bad right now?" she asked Jamie. "I should hate Gabe."

"We should hate a lot of people," Jamie said.

"Who do you hate?"

Jamie thought about it for a moment. As far as Hester was concerned, he had plenty of people to choose from. The police. The Afghanis. Gabe and Sam. Even Hester, in a way. "No one," he said, finally.

"You're a better person than me."

"That ain't true."

Kate broke away from the dogs and ran

over to them. Hester lifted the girl onto the bench beside her as her phone beeped. It was a text from Wendy Richards, asking about the hearing. Wendy had come to visit Hester in the hospital, distraught over "Aaron's" death, and the two women had somehow struck up a friendship. Her generosity had come in handy, especially during the worst of the media coverage, and Hester had found herself not only grateful, but liking the woman too.

Now, she tapped a message into her phone, and then read it off to Jamie. *"All okay."*

"All okay," Jamie said.

"All okay," Kate said.

Hester pulled Kate onto her lap and then lifted her into the air, toward a sky the color of delphiniums. It was hard to leave her, hard to trust that nothing terrible would happen the moment the girl was out of her sight. But it was even more important that Hester find a way to do just that, to trust again. She took a deep breath. "Can you do me a favor?" she asked Jamie. "Could you watch Kate for the day? There's something I need to do."

The chain blocking the driveway was gone, and the overgrown path behind it cleared. A sign hanging on the trunk of a tree said that the property had sold. Hester turned off the main street and drove into the woods. The birches were budding and the snow replaced by patches of fiddleheads poking through the fragrant forest floor. As she crested the hill and rode down toward the lakeshore, she barely recognized Little Comfort. She recognized even less of it as she pulled in beside the footprint of the old cabin, a shallow stone foundation and a pile of pine boards were all that remained of the little house. She was surprised by how little connection she felt to the place as she climbed out of the truck, but, really, the winter, the cold, that smell of smoke she thought would never wash off her skin, the terror, it wasn't this. It wasn't this day. It was far off, a distant nightmare that would somehow, someday, fade away.

By the shoreline, she looked out over the water. "Ice out" had happened on the lake two weeks ago; still, she closed her eyes and could imagine that gray sheet stretching to the horizon. For a moment, she could feel the cold seeping to her bones. She opened her eyes and took in the still, blue water, the chartreuse of the budding trees, the calls of the songbirds, the hope of spring. She felt warm sun on her face and believed she could remember this day, these images, instead. Eventually, at least.

Behind her, a twig snapped. "You didn't bring the kid with you?" she heard Lila say.

"No," Hester said. "I learned my lesson. She won't come to work with me anymore. You never know who the dangerous ones are, do you?"

"Sometimes it's obvious."

Lila sat on an outcropping of stone. Her left arm where her hand had been amputated was tucked into her coat sleeve.

"How have you been?" Hester asked.

"You mean this?" Lila asked, holding up her arm. "It's taking some time to get used to, I won't lie. I have a prosthetic, but sometimes it's easier to go bare. How about you?"

Hester shrugged. Her scars were invisible. "Kate started using pronouns."

Lila laughed.

"I kept wondering when it would happen, and then it did and I wasn't expecting it. There are only so many firsts, and they're exciting. But why didn't someone warn me about the lasts? Why didn't someone tell me how much these changes would hurt?" Hester finally looked away from the water to where the woman sat beside her. "I was surprised you didn't come to court today."

"I followed it online. I didn't have the heart to show up in person. Or the courage."

"It's over now. Or at least mostly."

"As over as it will ever be. Is that why you wanted to meet here today?"

"In a way. I guess I wanted to see Little Comfort one last time. In its glory. I wanted to wash away the winter."

"You picked a good day, though summer is even better. When the loons are out. When it's warm enough to swim."

Hester brushed dried lichen and pine needles from her jeans. She crouched at the shore and swept her hand through gin-clear water, and then let the droplets trail onto her tongue. It was still too cold to swim, but even as she thought that she found herself stripping off her clothes and tossing them to the forest floor. She stepped into the water, and then dove forward, the shock of the cold pressing on her chest and forcing the air from her lungs, but, as she surfaced, she felt cleansed. She dove again, into the silence, into another world, and pulled herself forward as long as she could, till her lungs felt as though they'd burst. She surfaced and looked up to the sky.

Back on shore, she shivered as she dried off with a t-shirt and then struggled into her clothes.

"You're crazy," Lila said with a smile. "It's already starting to feel different to me. The sale closed last week. We shouldn't even be here. I'll miss this place. So much."

Hester dug her keys from her pocket. It was time to go. "Will you?" she asked.

"Of course. I grew up here."

"Where will you go?"

"I don't know. Someplace else. North Carolina, maybe. Or Seattle." Lila bit her lower lip to squelch a smile. "It hasn't sunk in yet, but I can do anything. Anything I want."

"How much did you get for it in the sale?" Hester asked, though she already knew. Property sales were public record. Lila had sold for over two million dollars. Undeveloped lots on the lake rarely came up for sale, and the investment banker from Boston who'd bought it had already filed the paperwork to replace the cabin with a mansion.

Wills were public record too.

"I looked up your parents' will," Hester said. "I should have done that when I first met you. They left the property to you and Sam in trust. Both of you had to sign off to sell."

"I told you that when I first met you," Lila said.

"I thought that too, but then I went through my notes to see what you'd actually said. You told me to tell Sam that you planned to sell the property. But you couldn't do that without his consent. And he couldn't give his consent without coming out of hiding. You also didn't tell me that you'd petitioned the probate court to have the terms of the will changed and had been denied. You didn't tell me a lot of things, but mostly I think you knew he was dangerous and you hoped that he'd come looking for you when he found out you'd hired me."

"You think I planned all of this?" Lila held up the stump of her left arm.

"I don't know," Hester said. She backed up till she was at the truck's door. "All I know is that you said you'd kept his secrets. You said that to him while I was right there. And this worked out for you, and you're glad your brother's gone. And I helped make it happen."

"You can't prove anything."

"I know. And know that I know. Of all the awful people I met during this whole thing, I wonder if you might have been the worst. A little generosity, and you could have saved Gabe from all of this. One bit of grace. Enjoy the money. You earned it. Maybe we both did."

Hester stepped onto the running board and into the truck, and then started the engine. In the rearview mirror, she saw Lila's stony face, an expression that confirmed Hester had gotten it all, or at least most of it, right. Any other secrets, Lila could keep for herself.

Hester turned the corner. Little Comfort disappeared behind the budding trees. She revved the engine, barreling out of the woods and onto the road. She thought about Morgan and Jamie and Waffles. Even Daphne. She imagined Kate's laugh, her perfect little peals of delight. Her pronouns.

It was time to go home.

ABOUT THE AUTHOR

Edwin Hill has written for the *LA Review of Books, The Life Sentence, Publishers Weekly,* and *Ellery Queen Mystery Magazine.* He is the vice president and editorial director for Bedford/St. Martin's, a division of Macmillan. He received a bachelor's degree from Wesleyan University and an MFA from Emerson College. He lives in Boston with his partner, Michael, and their dog, Edith Ann.

The employees of Thorndike Press hope you have enjoyed this Large Print book. All our Thorndike, Wheeler, and Kennebec Large Print titles are designed for easy reading, and all our books are made to last. Other Thorndike Press Large Print books are available at your library, through selected bookstores, or directly from us.

For information about titles, please call:
(800) 223-1244

or visit our website at:
gale.com/thorndike

To share your comments, please write:
Publisher
Thorndike Press
10 Water St., Suite 310
Waterville, ME 04901